IRAQ'S
RETRIBUTION

R.W.KAY

Matador
9 Priory Business Park,
Wistow Road, Kibworth Beauchamp,
Leicestershire. LE8 0RX
Tel: (+44) 116 279 2299
Fax: (+44) 116 279 2277
Email: books@troubador.co.uk
Web: www.troubador.co.uk/matador

ISBN 978-1783063-017

British Library Cataloguing in Publication Data.
A catalogue record for this book is available from the British Library.

Typeset in 12pt Minion Pro by Troubador Publishing Ltd, Leicester, UK
Printed and bound in the UK by TJ International, Padstow, Cornwall

Matador is an imprint of Troubador Publishing Ltd

MIX
Paper from
responsible sources
FSC
www.fsc.org   FSC® C013056

T H A N K S

Finally, I must express my gratitude to friends who have helped with early drafts and encouraged me throughout the last six or seven years: Bob Fisher, Tim Gresty, John Knewstubb, Alan Powell, Ange and Mick Salt, Mo Trustham and especially Jean Barlow and Paul Watson.

AUTHOR'S NOTE

Iraq's Retribution is the final book in a trilogy of stories. The first novel, *A Nastia Game,* was initially published in 2009 and reprinted in 2013 by Troubador Publishing. The second book, *Bin Laden's Nemesis,* was published in 2012 (Troubador Publishing).

The heroine in *A Nastia Game* is Kathab al Jised, known as Kate. She is the Head of research, development and storage of Iraq's chemical and biological weapons programme during the Iran-Iraq war of 1981 to 1988. She meets and falls in love with James, an RAF software engineer, who has been seconded to help International Computers Limited sell a computer war game to Iraq. Soon after returning to England, James is apparently killed in Northern Ireland by the IRA. Kate, now heartbroken, begins feeding MI6 with Iraq's plans for the war and hiding supplies of biological weapons supplied from America. Brought to England for her safety during *Operation Desert Storm,* the liberation of Kuwait, she discovers by accident that James is alive and has been given a new identity for his protection.

In *Bin Laden's Nemesis,* the hero is Juan Quayle, a gifted linguist, who is recruited by Britain's Security Services to infiltrate al-Qaeda. Having successfully gained their trust, he teaches at a madrassa situated in the Caucuses for fifteen months learning much about their organisation and aims. The madrassa is overrun by Armenian troops when war breaks out with Azerbaijan in 1992. During the ensuing chaos, Quayle escapes and returns to the UK. After debriefing MI6, he retires to the Isle of Man, marries and begins a family, but the tentacles of al-

Qaeda catch up and destroy his wife and children. Vowing revenge, a plan to assassinate Osama bin Laden is meticulously woven.

In the final work, *Iraq's Retribution*, Kate and Juan meet up for an apocalyptic conclusion. Throughout the three stories of the Iraq Trilogy the heroine has been Kate. She has variously been described as looking like Ava Gardner or Queen Soraya.

When I began putting my ideas together for the first book, I needed an Iraqi heroine and came across Rihab Taha on Google. She had been in charge of research and development of Iraq's biological and chemical weapons programme during the Iraq-Iran war. Previously, she had completed a PhD in plant toxins at the University of East Anglia where her supervisor had been Dr Ian Gibson. Gibson subsequently became a Member of Parliament for Norwich North. In 2006, when researching details for *A Nastia Game's* plot, I found an article in *The Times Online* that described how Rihab Taha had been held by the Americans in Abu Graib gaol for two and a half years after the 2003 invasion of Iraq. The article claimed that Dr Gibson had been asked by the British Secret Intelligence Services to go to a 'Middle Eastern country' to confirm Taha's true identity. This he did, and Taha was subsequently set free.

The article speculated that Taha had worked for the British as a double agent during the 1980-1988 war. This became the background to *A Nastia Game*.

Rihab Taha has neither been seen, nor heard of, since her release.

I leave the reader to decide whether Rihab Taha bore a passing resemblance to two of the world's most beautiful women. On the left, Ava Gardner is about thirty, while on the right Queen Soraya is twenty-one. In the centre, Rihab Taha is forty-three and had just been released from Abu Graib.

I have tried to write the three stories in such a manner that they can be read independently; this necessitates some duplication by way of explanation from time to time. For those reading the books in order of publication, this should serve as useful revision. For those who choose not to read the earlier stories, you will, hopefully, wish to do so after enjoying *Iraq's Retribution*.

PROLOGUE

Friday, 21st December 2001

The red phone rang.

Who wants me on the scrambler? thought Mike Schriver, Head of the CIA section at the US Embassy in Paris. The conversation about to take place between the embassy and the United States over a secure line allowed classified material to be discussed.

'Mike, it's George here.'

Mike recognised his boss's voice immediately and the caller didn't have to give his surname. George Tenet, the Director of the Central Intelligence Agency since 1997 and based in Langley, Virginia, was a man with a fearful reputation. He had replaced a string of directors who had been unable to satisfy the needs of previous presidents and was already on the way to becoming the longest serving Director of the CIA since Allen Dulles. Although appointed by President Clinton, Tenet ran a tight ship that suited President George W Bush's managerial style.

'Hello, sir. What can I do for you?'

'It's rather long-winded, I'm afraid, but I'll try and keep it brief. Essentially, six weeks ago I authorised the assassination of someone who, potentially, could be very damaging to the reputation of the United States when we undertake *Operation Iraqi Freedom*.'

'A terrorist?'

'No, not exactly. She was the former Director of MI6.'

'Good grief, not Barbara Renton?'

'Yes, did you know her?'

'I met her once or twice – a fine figure of a woman. Very capable, too.'

'The President was led to believe from Tony Blair that she might make trouble by letting the world's press know that bin Laden is already dead, that Saddam Hussein had nothing to do with 9/11, and the weapons of mass destruction that are in Iraq have been so well hidden that they can never be found. In other words, there would be no earthly reason for invading Iraq.'

'But if she's dead, what's your problem?'

'I have a gut feeling that she escaped and almost certainly killed our men.'

'You said men – plural.'

'Yes, I sent two agents, Jim Dealey and Rocky Lopez, to the South of France where she lived. They have disappeared. I want you to go down there and find out what happened. I didn't inform you of the operation at the time because there was nothing required from your resources and I had to keep it as secret as possible under strict orders of the President.'

'I assume both Dealey and Lopez spoke fluent French?'

'Yes, they had both worked undercover in Quebec, keeping an eye on the FLQ, the Quebec Liberation Front.'

'Then they would have stuck out like sore thumbs.'

'Why?'

'Regional accents are very strong in the South of France; Canadian-French would be a dead giveaway. Whereabouts did they go?'

'Renton lived in a Department called the Aude.'

'Ah, near the Pyrenees. Even I, with ten years of living in France, would have a job disguising my Parisian accent to the local tongue. Where, exactly, did she live?'

'We only know it was in a village called Belveze.'

'OK, I'll get on to it at once, but it may take several weeks as the French like to take a fortnight off for Christmas and the New Year. The Aude's Department's offices are in Carcassonne and I'll have to go there to get Renton's address. Leave it with me and I'll contact you as soon as I've found out what happened. OK?'

* * *

Tuesday, 8th January 2002

'Hello, Mike. What have you got for me?'

'Nothing.'

'Nothing?'

'I've just returned from spending a couple of days in the Aude. Belveze is a nice little village with a population of, maybe at the most, 1,000. It's the sort of place where everyone knows everyone else. I found Renton's bungalow easily. It was boarded up; shutters on front and back doors as well as all the windows. I asked a neighbour had they seen her lately; I was claiming to be an old friend. She replied that Madame Renton had left months ago and had not returned. She didn't know when she would be back. I asked did she live alone; she replied, *"Oui"*. I went to the one and only bar that doubles up as a restaurant. They said she used to eat there sometimes, but hadn't been seen for ages. It's as if she's vanished.'

'The problem, Mike, is that Dealey and Lopez have vanished too – at the same time. Either they were successful and for some reason have not returned or, more likely, Renton escaped after getting rid of Dealey and Lopez.'

'I told you she was a gifted operator. She spent most of her career in the Caucuses: Georgia, Azerbaijan, and Armenia. If she could survive out there undercover, then it wouldn't surprise me that your two agents failed.'

'Her last job in MI6 was masterminding the assassination of bin Laden using anthrax. The Brits believe the mission was achieved successfully.'

'Yeah, I'd heard that rumour, but it is only a rumour without a body.'

'The trouble is, Mike, I have a gut feeling she may have some positive evidence and is still alive to use it against us when we go into Iraq. God knows what I'm going to tell President Bush.'

CHAPTER 1

Monday, 2nd April 2001

'Ladies and gentlemen, can I have your attention.'

He waited for the buzz of conversations between small groups in his audience to die away; although a few rudely ignored him and continued to carry on gossiping. After a few moments and satisfied he could talk louder than the dissenters, he began.

'My name is John Ward and as you know I was appointed Chief Executive of our hospital a month ago. I have used my time so far to meet as many of you as I possibly can. One thing has become obvious. In a hospital the size of Leicester General Infirmary, communications are difficult. Several of you have made the point forcibly and have said they are non-existent. I want to rectify that. From today, I will be holding a meeting on the first Monday of every month. I know you are all busy, but I expect you to attend.'

There were some murmurs of discontent.

He continued. 'The idea of the meetings is to give you the opportunity to have your pennies-worth. From now on there should be no one grumbling they are kept in the dark. As heads of departments you will be able to summarise your achievements of the previous month. I don't want a formal presentation; just stand up and in a couple of minutes draw our attention to anything unusual. Our gatherings will kick off with coffee and biscuits at nine o'clock and the meetings will begin at nine-thirty prompt. I would hope the meetings won't last any longer than an hour. If there are good reasons for your absence then I expect your deputy to attend…'

He finished his introduction by inviting, 'Any questions?'

There were some mumbles from the more dissatisfied, dyed-in-the-wool staff. The Consultant Geriatrician stood up. 'I would like to know why we haven't sufficient car parking spaces?' he asked. 'Your predecessor bought the field next to the current car park and promised to extend it three years ago.'

'Thank you for that question. It illustrates the point I made earlier about communications. The cost of a new car park for one hundred cars is £200,000.'

'I don't believe it,' replied the questioner.

'By the time the site is cleared, the drains put in, one foot of hard-core compacted, covered with tarmac and the lines painted, it is £2,000 per car. If you all feel that sort of money is better spent on the car park than on the four new beds for the Intensive Care Unit, then I am willing to alter the current year's plans.'

There was a deathly silence. For the first time that morning, John knew he had their total attention. He decided to attack. 'I have already approached several third party companies to see if they would be interested in building the car park and allowing them to recoup their costs by charging, say, £2 per car per day. So far, I have not had a positive response.'

He felt the highly qualified medical specialists were altering their perception of him. They probably had seen him as someone with five 'O' levels but he was as well qualified as them. A first degree in Economics and a PhD in monetary control systems from Keele University had set him up to become one of the youngest directors at Unilever before he had taken a sabbatical and an MBA at Bath University.

'Shall we meet on Monday, 7th May? Thank you for attending.'

The inaugural meeting of consultants and senior nursing staff broke up with a hum. He overheard a few agree that 'things were looking-up.'

During April, the usual jokes began to circulate about the monthly *prayer meetings*. The new Chief Executive was dubbed *Ayatollah Ward*; even the Asian members of staff, and there were many, both doctors and nurses, thought this nickname was funny. However, at the second meeting, John's reputation improved when he announced that a contractor had agreed to build the new car park providing he could charge £3 per car per day for five years. Thereafter, the park would belong to the hospital. As the first stirrings of dissent, after the initial gasps, began, John moved quickly adding that staff could use the facility for £20 per month. From their reaction, John knew they were on his side.

At the end of his report, he asked, 'Is there anything of unusual interest that you wish to report?'

Judy Wade, the consultant paediatrician, raised her hand and stood. 'About three weeks ago, a boy was born to a Bangladeshi family, the Farooqs, who was a pure hexadactyl. He had six fingers on both hands and six toes on both feet. What makes this unusual is that another boy was born with an identical condition about a year ago to a Pakistani family, the Rahmans. The odds of this happening are billions to one against. I have done a literature search and whereas children are occasionally born with an extra finger or toe, these two cases appear to be unique. There is nothing wrong with the child; indeed he seems perfectly healthy apart from his extra digits.'

John Ward looked around the room to see if anyone wished to comment.

Stuart MacKinnon, the registrar pathologist, soon to be promoted to consultant, stood and said, 'I would like to ask Judy a question. Do you know what happened to the Pakistani boy born last year? Was a surgical procedure implemented to remove the unwanted digits?'

'I'm afraid I don't know because the family moved away. I can try to find out, if you like?'

'It's just that there must be a link,' replied Stuart. 'Perhaps there may be an epidemiological explanation.'

'Can I suggest you put your heads together on this one,' said John. 'If you come up with something interesting, I'm sure the rest of us would be interested.' Others in the audience agreed and the meeting broke up a few minutes later.

* * *

3

Stuart had seen Judy around the hospital from time to time but had never been formally introduced. The path labs, on the edge of the site, were relatively isolated from the main part of the hospital; parking had never been a problem for Stuart, unlike for other staff. When he had first seen Judy, he had immediately thought how striking she was: tall, short fair hair and with an Amazonian build, she commanded attention. Her face had a natural, jolly smile; her eyes glinted, hinting life was fun.

A handsome woman; she could probably wallop me at tennis, he'd thought.

When she entered a room, heads would turn and appreciate her erect posture and smart attire.

They had agreed to meet, a week after the prayers session, in the staff canteen for lunch. Having arrived first, Stuart stood when she entered. Her permanent smile was more of a beam; her eyes sparkled, radiating light. She walked to their table. Somewhat formally, they shook hands.

'What can I get you,' he asked.

'Just a coffee would be fine. I only have an apple for lunch. I prefer to eat in the evening.'

He immediately felt embarrassed, having already chosen a steak and ale pie with chips. She looked at his full plate and, grinning to the point of laughter, she continued, 'Don't mind me. I live alone and enjoy cooking for myself.'

'I'm single too. Unfortunately, my skills in the kitchen are minimal. At home, I rely on ready-made meals. They're not always the healthiest.'

She grinned as she eyed him up and down. 'You look fit enough.'

'Jogging and occasional games of squash keep the flab at bay.'

'I found out what happened to the Rahman child. His family moved to Lincoln, my home town. The father opened a classy Indian restaurant near the cathedral. My opposite number in the Lincoln General Hospital had assessed the boy to be sufficiently fit to have an operation, but he died suddenly.'

'What from?'

'A full post-mortem revealed nothing.'

'That's bizarre. There must be a reason for an otherwise fit baby to die suddenly.'

'I believe the local pathologist called in Professor Hawke from University College Hospital, London...'

'He's the country's top paedo-pathologist; it's where I trained. I knew him quite well,' interrupted Stuart.

'And he could find nothing wrong either, other than the extra digits.'

'Is the Bangladeshi family related in any way to the Rahman family?'

'I don't see how they can be.'

'Is there any way we could find out?'

'We would have to get social services involved. It could be tricky justifying sticking our noses into families that are already traumatised.'

'It's just so unusual, Judy. These two incidences have occurred on your patch. I think you are justified in taking it further by looking into the backgrounds of the two families. I suspect the parents have both been exposed to some unusual external source of contamination, either here in Leicester or, perhaps, on the subcontinent. Did both fathers work at Bhopal, for example? The answer has to have an epidemiological basis.'

'OK, I'll get on to it and keep you in the picture. Oh, and there's one other thing.'

'What?'

'The Rahman boy died after six months and six days.'

'So?'

'The number 666 is the number of the devil.'

Stuart laughed. 'You're not superstitious, surely?'

She shrugged her shoulders and allowed Stuart to finish his lunch whilst they chatted about life as single professionals in Leicester. She mentioned she played badminton competitively in the local league. It allowed Stuart to tell her that he used to play for his university at Edinburgh. Consequently, they arranged to meet the following evening for a game at the nearby sports centre.

* * *

Under Any Other Business at the next prayers meeting, John Ward asked Judy if there was any news on the hexadactyl Bangladeshi child.

She explained she had interviewed the Farooq family and was going to see the Rahmans the following weekend in Lincoln. She added that she was hoping to find out whether there was some link between the families and would report her findings at the next meeting.

The following week the phone rang in the path lab. Stuart's assistant answered, and he called to Stuart. 'Dr Wade on the phone, boss.'

'Yes, Judy?'

'Can we meet sometime? I can't find a link between the Rahmans and the Farooqs.'

Stuart had joined Judy's badminton club and had already found himself in the club's first team, partnered by Judy. They were hitting it off well together, but their friendship was on a purely platonic, intellectual level. Stuart, however, had begun to realise they may have a future together. Her vivacious, almost mischievous, personality was infectious. She cheered him up if he was on one of his regular downers.

'I've never asked, but do you like Indian food?' he asked.

Without waiting for an answer, he added, 'There's a good restaurant near the university on the Fosse Road called *The Indian Spice*.'

'I know it,' she replied, sounding enthusiastic. 'Shall we say eight o'clock?'

'Fine. I'll book it.'

Judy walked tall. Her clothes always looked as if they had been made especially for her. When she entered the restaurant that evening, the other diners noticed her entrance. Stuart, waiting for her, noticed admiring glances from the male clientele.

They ordered'

While waiting for their starter, she began, 'It's not what we expected. There's no obvious link at all.'

'There has to be.'

'The only thing in common is that both the fathers worked briefly in Iraq as labourers.'

'When?'

'For about six months around 1982.'

'That would have been during the war with Iran. Did you ask them what they did?'

'They worked mostly on building sites, doing odd jobs.'

'Judy, my stepmother is an Iraqi. She told me about some of the chemical weapons they used during the Iraq–Iran war: nerve agents such as sarin and VX. I wonder if both fathers could have been exposed to something.'

Stuart knew his stepmother had been in charge of Iraq's research and development of biological and chemical weapons for twelve years. He was beginning to think it might be worthwhile asking her if she could come up with some ideas to explain the two boys' abnormalities.

* * *

Two days later, they met at the badminton club.

'Last night I had a long chat with my stepmother, Kate,' began Stuart. 'I asked her about how immigrant casual labourers were used during their war with Iran. Most of Iraq's young men were conscripted into the Army; so the authorities were lax about allowing men from the subcontinent into the country to do building jobs. They would gather in groups at certain street corners in Baghdad at six o'clock in the morning. Gang masters would come along and offer them a day's work. They were paid in cash and no records were kept.'

'They worked clearing up bomb sites, that sort of thing?' asked Judy.

'Yes, but they would hardly have come across something that subsequently altered their sperm to create birth defects. I asked Kate whether that was possible.'

'What did she say?'

'She wasn't prepared to tell me much over the phone. Her words were, "This is something I can only tell you face-to-face". I pressed her but to no avail. I'm due to take a week's holiday and said I'd go up and see them the week after next.'

'Where do they live?'

'In the West Highlands of Scotland, a village called Badachro.'

'I am ashamed to admit it, but I've never been to Scotland.'

'Then you must come. They have a guest bedroom. You'll love up there, as long as you like sailing and hill walking.'

'Sounds fantastic.'

'It is. Except at this time of the year, there are millions of midges.'

CHAPTER 2

Sunday, 24th June 2001

Stuart had discussed with Judy various options to travel to Badachro from Leicester.

'I would love to see something of Scotland,' she had replied.

They decided to leave Leicester after a leisurely breakfast and took their time driving up the M6 and M74. They stopped at the beautiful town of Moffat in the borders. They had booked separate rooms in the *Balmoral Hotel*. The receptionist gave them a quizzical look when handing them their keys, but said nothing.

The following morning they took a walk around the town and Judy bought herself a matching tartan jacket and skirt. Traffic was light as they negotiated the Edinburgh bypass, crossed the Forth Road Bridge and enjoyed the scenery of the A9. After stopping to refuel and have a sandwich at Dalwhinnie, they left the A9 for Spean Bridge, drove down Glen Shiel and stopped to admire Eilean Donan Castle, Scotland's most photographed site.

At Loch Carron they stopped for a cup of tea, sitting outside a café, bathing in the warm sun. The slight sea-breeze was sufficient to keep the midges away.

'On days like this, there is nowhere in the world so pleasant,' remarked Stuart. 'When you see Dad's place, you will see why he and Kate are so blissfully happy up here. He met her when he was in the Royal Air Force.'

'But he would have been married to your mother then, surely?'

'Mum and I first met Kate when my father brought her home to our house near Weston-super-Mare for a weekend. Dad and Kate were working together at Reading developing a computer war game for the Iraqi Air Force. Dad had designed the original game to train officers at the RAF Staff College at Bracknell. He had been appointed MoD's Project Officer and was helping ICL modify the game to meet Iraq's requirements. Then, when my father was in Baghdad training the Iraqis to use the game, Mum was killed in a car accident.'

'I'm sorry. I didn't know. I shouldn't have asked.'

'It's OK. He came back straightaway. Soon afterwards, he left the RAF and we came up here to live. I was only eight or nine at the time and went to the local school in Gairloch. We lived on our own for almost ten years. I was at Edinburgh University when Kate somehow found us. She had escaped from Iraq and was working in London for the government as an interpreter. They got together and I encouraged him to marry her. She's been good for the old man. He was getting into a rut before she showed up. She keeps him on his toes. You'll like her.'

'What does she do?'

'She has a PhD from Cambridge in botany and works two days a week at Inverewe Gardens doing some sort of research; I'm not sure what exactly. She'll be able to show us around the gardens. They are internationally famous. What she doesn't know about plants isn't worth knowing.'

They arrived at Badachro that evening soon after six o'clock.

'We've booked a table at the *Badachro Inn* for eight o'clock,' said Robbie, Stuart's father, after he and Kate had greeted them warmly.

'I've given Judy the guest bedroom and you, Stuart, have got your old room. I didn't know what you would want…' Kate's voice tailed away, somewhat embarrassed.

'That's OK,' Judy replied quickly with a smile, remembering the receptionist having the same problem the previous evening.

Refreshed after a shower and a drink, the four wandered down the garden, onto the shore and along the beach to the inn, accompanied by Kate's dog, Cal – a strong, large, male border collie. Conversation over dinner was largely about Stuart's progress at the hospital and Judy telling them about her family background. The daughter of a bank manager, her parents lived in a small village called Boothby Graffoe, near Lincoln. She had a younger sister and both had attended the local girls' grammar school in nearby Sleaford. By 10.30 pm, the two days of driving had begun to catch up with the two Leicester doctors.

'Tomorrow I'd like to discuss Iraq with you,' Stuart said to Kate as they wandered home.

'About how we used casual workers?'

'Yes, it's what I mentioned on the phone.'

* * *

The following morning, under a blue sky, the four sat in the garden having breakfast. Stuart explained why he wanted to discuss Iraq.

'Judy has come across two birth defects in Leicester that are so rare we believe there has to be a common link between the parents. However, one family is Pakistani and the other Bangladeshi. The only connection is both fathers briefly worked in Iraq during the war with Iran. We are wondering if they could have come across a substance, either chemical or biological, that may have affected their sperm.'

'Labourers came from the subcontinent all the time, stayed a few months, earned as much as they could have achieved in several years at home and left. No records were ever kept. Most worked on building sites, reconstructing buildings that had been bombed by the Farsis. My department used them to bury unwanted biological and chemical weapons supplied to us by the Americans.'

'So, there are no records of who the itinerant workers were?'

'No. We picked them up early, around six o'clock in the morning, from the corner of Kifah Street and Thawra Street, near the bus terminus. We usually chose four or five men. They sat in the back of the pickup with the weapons to be buried. I would drive ahead in a government car, sometimes with a chauffeur, and a sergeant would follow driving the truck.'

'What sort of quantities are we talking about?'

'Typically, three or four five-gallon containers, sometimes more.'

'What sort of biological weapons were they?'

'It varied but mostly anthrax, botulinium toxins and clostridium perfringens.'

'How carefully were they packed?'

'They usually arrived in thick glass vats. We would wrap them in something like expanded polystyrene before sealing them in stainless steel drums and burying them.'

'Was there ever anything unusual? A one-off, perhaps?'

'On one occasion they sent us a small two-litre bottle inside a lead lined box. It was labelled VX-R. I remember it because there was no explanation of what the R meant. Because of the lead protection, I guessed R stood for radioactive, but that didn't make any sense.'

'Quantities of VX were quite common then?'

'Yes. It's a nasty chemical weapon that affects the nervous system causing loss of muscle control, paralysis and invariably death. We always buried the canisters at least two metres deep.'

'So, how did you decide where to bury them?'

'I would lead the truck to the burial spot. Most of the sites I chose were in the Western or Al-Hijarah Deserts. On some occasions I headed north from Baghdad. Having pre-planned the location, I would check my latitude and longitude calculations when I arrived. I used the chess position method your father taught me to encrypt the records so only I could ever find the location. The team would then bury the canisters under the Sergeant's supervision while I waited in the car. The Sergeant would pay the labourers cash when they got back to central Baghdad. All the biologicals the Americans gave us were buried. Now they are hidden, they can never be found.'

'They were always in glass vats, inside stainless steel containers?'

'Yes.'

'Were the steel drums sealed permanently?'

'No. They had screw tops.'

'So it would be possible for the workers to unscrew the barrels and look inside?'

'Yes, I guess so.'

'The day you buried the VX-R, did you leave it inside the lead container?'

'Yes, I never opened the box. It easily fitted into one of our steel drums.'

Stuart nodded, as he stared blankly at the sky, listening to the gentle rustle of the trees in the light breeze. Nothing was said for some time before Judy asked, 'What are you thinking?'

Stuart didn't reply, but asked Kate, 'Would the lead box have been valuable?'

'Yes, of course. During the war all metals, particularly heavy ones, commanded quite a price on the black market.'

'Would it have been possible on the trip to the burial place for the labourers to have opened the steel barrel, peered inside, seen the lead box, taken it out, removed the contents and returned them into the canister, hiding the lead in the back of the truck?'

'I guess so. There would have been no reason for the Sergeant to check the back of the truck as he would have known how many barrels were to be buried and assumed they had not been interfered with.'

Stuart looked at Judy. 'I suspect that the two fathers of our hexadactyl boys were exposed to the VX-R for a few minutes while they stole the lead. It could have been sufficient to somehow alter their sperm cells.'

'It's a bit of a dubious explanation. Surely, if the radioactivity would have done any harm, then it would have made them sterile?' replied Judy.

The two doctors looked at Kate for an answer. 'I can't help, I'm afraid. I've no idea what we were supposed to do with the VX-R.'

'Well, how would VX have normally been used?' asked Stuart.

'Sprayed on the enemy from the Hughes helicopters, but we never used it. Mustard Gas and sarin were used extensively against the Iranians during their final push for Basra in the winter of 1987. Without the American helicopters Basra would have fallen and with it, Iraq.'

There was silence for what seemed several minutes.

Finally, Judy posed the question, 'What do we do now?'

'There's not much you can do,' Robbie remarked. 'After all, you can hardly go out to Iraq to find the missing VX-R, if we don't know where it is.'

'I was thinking more along the lines of going back to Lincoln and talking again to Mr Rahman, the Pakistani who fathered the first child. He moved his family there shortly after the boy was born. It would be interesting to discover if he remembers the incident and removing the lead box,' commented Judy.

'And then what?' asked Robbie. His body language was telling the two doctors that their mission to get to the bottom of the matter was not to his liking. 'Even if your theory is right about the father's exposure to VX-R, Iraq is a no-go area and neither of you can speak Arabic.'

'No, but I can,' smiled Kate.

'Kate, that's madness. Saddam tried to assassinate you. You would be arrested the minute you set foot in the country.'

'But I now have a British passport and a new name. No one would ever know.'

'Kate, that's rubbish and you know it. I won't let you go.'

Stuart had never seen his father so upset with Kate before. He quickly intervened. 'Look, Dad, let's take this one step at a time. I'll go to Lincoln with Judy. She knows the Rahmans and we'll take it from there. UNICEF always wants volunteer doctors to undertake one-year appointments. I could always go to Iraq under their auspices. I'd be safe that way. What do you think, Kate?'

Kate looked dubious. 'I'm not sure. The country is beginning to disintegrate; the no-fly zones are crippling the economy and the sanctions are decimating the population.'

Robbie didn't hide his horror; he asked his son aggressively, 'Have you any idea what life is like in Iraq?'

Stuart shrugged his shoulders.

'No, but Kate has. Tens of thousands, if not hundreds of thousands, of Iraqis are dying of malaria, cholera, whooping cough and God knows what. If the Mukhabaret, Iraq's Secret Service, were to find out who you were, then you would disappear quicker than I could say Jack Robinson.'

Kate agreed. 'Your father is right, Stuart. It's too dangerous to go out there. Even with some sort of UN protection, your safety couldn't be guaranteed.'

* * *

Stuart and Judy spent a further four days with Robbie and Kate. The weather was glorious, as it frequently is in mid-June in the North-West of Scotland. They sailed, fished and walked. Frequently, Kate and Judy would take Cal for a hike to Port Henderson, several miles away. As the two women began to get to know each other, a close friendship built up. They discovered they had both studied at Newnham College, Cambridge.

'I was there for four years between 1974 and 1978. Was Dame Felicity still the principal when you were there?' asked Kate.

'No,' laughed Judy. 'When you were there, I was still at primary school. Prof Patricia Hodgson was principal – a real battleaxe!'

'I suppose being a postgraduate student, things weren't too strict. I had several boyfriends and soon learnt how to sneak them back to my room. Have you known Stuart long?'

'No, not really. We seem to have hit it off quite well. He's joined my local badminton and tennis club. People keep looking at us as if something is happening, but we have both been around the block several times and I suspect neither of us wants to spoil anything by rushing.'

Kate smiled at her, thinking, *I'd like you as my daughter-in-law.*

* * *

On one of the days, they decided to visit Ullapool. On the way they stopped at Inverewe Gardens so that Kate could show Judy her research facilities and explain that her current task was trying to inhibit the growth of rhododendrons.

'They grow like mad in a wet climate like ours, becoming invasive and destroying native species. About five years ago, in Snowdonia National Park, conservationists discovered a house in a thicket they were flailing. The house had been forgotten and, over fifty or sixty years, it had disappeared in the bushes. Herbicides and rhodie-bashing are a crude form of control. I'm developing a chemical that when injected into a plant, whatever its size, small or large, stops its growth. When I worked in Iraq, one of my teams developed something we called enditon. It slowed peoples' nerve signals down. They would stop eating and drinking, they would become lethargic and weak as their breathing became heavy and, finally, stop. Enditon effectively accelerated old age. What I'm developing here has a similar base.'

'Fascinating; I can see such a substance having commercial possibilities.'

'It's not dissimilar to what I was doing at Cambridge for my PhD where I worked on toxins to counter leaf blight and rust on maize. I've always loved plants as opposed to animals. I think humans are the worst animals of all; I much prefer sheep,' she laughed. 'Perhaps that's why I love living up here; there are not many people, but plenty of sheep.'

'I think I know where you are coming from,' agreed Judy.

Continuing to Ullapool, they stopped to look at Gruinard Island, the scene of the anthrax experiment in 1942 when a flock of sheep was slaughtered in the name of biological warfare research. Judy had not heard of *Operation Vegetarian* – a plan to drop anthrax pellets over northern Germany in order to kill sheep and cattle and thereby starve the Germans into surrender.

'Thank God it never happened,' Kate explained. 'It might have got out of control and wiped out Europe entirely.'

'It's hard to believe anyone could even have conceived of the idea,' said Judy.

'Yes, as a doctor you'll know that inhaled anthrax spores are deadly. There wouldn't have been sufficient antibiotics to prevent the spread of the disease. The Americans gave us several thousand gallons of the stuff in the 1980s to use against the Iranians. Fortunately, it's now all hidden in the desert and no one will ever find it.'

'You falsified the records that well?'

'Yes, thanks initially to Robbie's idea of using a chess position. Later on, I just randomised the coordinates and buried them anywhere.'

'And when *Desert Storm* started, you were liberated to the UK?'

'Yes, that's when Saddam found out about the falsification of the records. He sent an assassin after me.'

'What happened?'

Kate sighed, 'Let's just say he wasn't successful?' She had decided not to tell Judy how she had killed the assassin and how Robbie and Stuart had disposed of his body.

Judy instinctively felt it was not the time to ask any more questions.

* * *

On their final evening together, the idea of further investigating the mystery of the hexadactyl children again became the main topic of conversation.

'I don't think there's much you can do about it even if you find the two fathers were working in Kate's teams,' said Robbie.

'I suppose not,' replied Stuart, 'except I was wondering if we could get any information about VX-R from the Americans. They have a very liberal Freedom of Information Act.'

'That could be dodgy. After all, I've always suspected the Americans were behind your mother's accident and have never trusted them since.'

Judy sat up. She looked at Stuart. 'You never told me your mother's accident could have been deliberate.'

Stuart looked at his father to explain.

Robbie looked at Judy. 'It's a long story, but when Stuart was only seven or eight, his mother's car went off the road near where we lived, down a cliff and into the sea. Stuart's sister was drowned and his mum died of her injuries. The police investigated and suspected that her tyres had been cleverly punctured to cause the accident. No one was ever found culpable and the evidence was largely unsubstantiated. At the time, I was working in Baghdad pioneering a war game that included much secret information in its data files. The software was protected using a unique method that required the users to know a particular chess position. The Americans were known to be interested in the protection method and I believe they engineered Emma's accident to frighten me into giving the secret to them. Her death was probably not what they wanted.'

'I'm sorry, I had no idea.'

'It's OK; it was a long time ago. But the point I'm making is that I wouldn't trust the Americans any further than I can spit. If you were to make a request to find out about VX-R, it could open Pandora's Box, including dragging Kate into the equation. If you're really determined to take it further, then I suppose I could discuss the matter with Peter Stacey.'

'Who's he?' asked Stuart.

It was Kate who answered. 'He was the Head of MI6 when I came to Britain from Iraq eleven years ago. He'll be long retired by now.'

'Yes, but I'll bet he still has contacts,' replied Robbie, looking at his wife.

'Do you know how to get in touch with him?' asked Stuart.

Kate replied, 'In those days, he had a house in Twickenham. I stayed there when I first arrived in the UK. I know he had a place in Wiltshire where he kept horses. His wife was a keen equestrian.'

'When we get back to Leicester, we'll check out the two families first and if, as we suspect, they were exposed to something in Iraq, then I'll let you know and perhaps you can trace Peter Stacey. Is that OK?' asked Stuart.

Robbie nodded in a less than enthusiastic manner.

CHAPTER 3

Saturday, 14th July 2001

Three weeks later, Judy took Stuart to stay with her parents for the weekend. On Saturday evening they went for a meal in Mr Rahman's restaurant, *The Saffron*, in the high town of Lincoln, near the cathedral.

Reluctant at first to admit the theft of the lead, he remembered being with a Bangladeshi and two fellow Pakistanis. He could not remember their names but admitted they each received fifty dinars in exchange for the box.

A similar story had been obtained from the head of the Farooq family a week earlier. A literature search by Judy had revealed no other children being born with similar defects, although in the subcontinent such births tended to be hidden and swept under the carpet. 'We will have to assume the other two Pakistanis have never parented a child,' remarked Judy as she discussed her findings with Stuart.

'I've been thinking about that,' replied Stuart. 'If the VX-R was strong enough to affect the workers, then it must have affected the Sergeant with Kate and, possibly, Kate too?'

'So there are possibly three more men out there with genetically modified sperm.'

'Yes, although Kate is never going to have children anyway and the exposure doesn't seem to have harmed her. Unfortunately, as you've said, neither Farooq nor Rahman will consent to giving you a sperm sample, so we're stymied there. I'll ring my father to see if he can find out more about VX-R from Peter Stacey.'

'Can you contact Peter Stacey?' he asked his father on the phone. 'We've checked-out the two fathers of the hexadactyl children and are certain both were in Kate's working party when the VX-R was buried.'

'I've done some delving already,' Robbie replied, 'and Peter Stacey has definitely retired. He was knighted in one of the Queen's Birthday Honours' Lists about five years ago.'

'So we're dealing with a knight of the realm?'

'His wife was called Jennie and it may be possible I can find their address from the electoral register. Kate thinks Jennie competed in horse eventing. That might help too. If that fails, then I have a contact, an old pal of mine from Air Force days, who lives in Wiltshire.'

Two days later, Robbie rang Stuart. 'I've had no luck tracing Peter Stacey. He's not in the phone book nor can I get anywhere with Wiltshire's electoral role. This evening I'm going to try contacting Tony Woods who used to work with me when I was at Bracknell Staff College. I know his address, as his eldest son's engagement was announced in *The Telegraph* last year, and I made a note of their address at the time. Kate has wanted to see the Eden Project for some time. I think it's about time we went. I'll tell him we're passing his place on the way to Cornwall and ask whether we can look him up.'

That evening, Robbie rang his ex-colleague. 'Tony? It's a voice from the past here, James Douglas.' There was a moment's silence before Robbie added, 'You remember; I was the systems analyst at Bracknell in 1974.'

'James!' The reaction at the other end was as if the listener couldn't believe his ears. 'Good God, I thought you were dead – shot in Northern Ireland.'

'It's a long story and I'm quite happy to fill you in with some of the details. I was wondering if I could pop-in and see you. My wife and I are visiting the Eden Project next week whilst having a holiday in Cornwall. I thought we could drop-by for a cuppa, perhaps.'

'Of course. Christine would be delighted to see you again. We were sorry to hear about Emma's accident. It happened when I was away with the squadron on an exercise in America. Soon after that, your death was announced in *The Times*. What's your second wife's name? What day were you thinking of coming?'

'Kate and I have been married for about ten years and we live in the North-West of Scotland. Would next Thursday, about mid-afternoon, be convenient?'

'OK, we look forward to seeing you. If you like, you can stay the night with us. It'll be good to catch up on old times. Computers have come a long way since we wrote those programs at Bracknell in BASIC.'

'That would be marvellous. I have much to tell you.'

* * *

As Robbie had expected, Christine and Tony greeted them warmly. It took well over an hour for the two families to catch up with the news. Tony had retired from the RAF as an Air Vice-Marshal and was now busy in local politics as Chairman of the Parish Council. Christine was busy with the local primary school, where she was a governor, and the village church. Kate had explained her Iraqi background without giving away too much detail, but included how she had initially met Robbie at Reading when working with the ICL team upgrading Nastia Game for use by the Iraq Staff College in Baghdad.

'I remember Nastia Game vividly,' Tony had remarked. 'Playing it manually was a real chore. It was so administratively intensive with everything having to be checked and rechecked before allowing a game move to take place. I had left Bracknell before you managed to automate it successfully.'

'We played it on the computer in November 1976 and Iraq bought the software through MoD Sales the following summer. ICL were quick to see its potential for selling their hardware and considerably enhanced it to meet Iraq's requirements. I was out in Baghdad helping to get the game up and running when Emma was killed in a car accident. I came back straightaway. After the funeral Stuart, my son, and I lived with the pongos at Fort Halstead. I was helping them develop a satellite tracking system. However, my heart wasn't in it and I asked to leave the RAF early. My so-called demise by the IRA was engineered. It allowed us to change our surnames to MacKinnon. You'll have noticed Kate calls me Robbie. It seems to match MacKinnon better. Stuart and I moved to a remote village in the Highlands. I took a part-time job teaching maths. Stuart eventually went to Edinburgh University and became a doctor. He's now the registrar pathologist at a hospital in Leicester and is one of the reasons we wanted to see you.'

'Oh?'

'Stuart has come across two Asian families who have had boys born that were pure hexadactyls; the babies had six fingers and six toes. The chance of one being born that way is millions to one against. Two in two years is theoretically impossible.'

'So how can I help?'

'Stuart has done some follow-up on the families who are not related in any way. The only common link is that the two fathers worked for several months in Iraq during the Iran war. He believes both were briefly exposed to a substance called VX-R.'

'I've heard of VX – it's a nasty nerve agent, if I remember rightly.'

'Perhaps Kate should take over from here.' Up to this point, she had said little and given nothing away about her past.

Tony looked at her to continue.

'I formerly worked as the Head of Biological and Chemical Weapons Research for the Iraq Government,' she began.

'Good grief,' interjected Tony immediately.

'No, it's not as bad as you may think,' responded Robbie at once.

Kate paused before continuing, 'I worked with MI6 to bury safely the worst of the biological weapons that the Americans were giving us regularly. It is the reason how I came to be rescued during the First Gulf War and brought back to Britain. The Allies were worried that I may be tortured to reveal where the weapons were buried.'

'But it was well known that you were using vast amounts of chemicals against the Iranians and even your own people, the Kurds.'

'Chemicals – yes, biologicals – no. Whenever we received agents such as anthrax, botulinium toxins and so on, I would get a party of itinerant workers to take them to a location in the desert and have them buried. The records of their location were doctored in such a way that only I knew where they really were. One of the substances that we received was labelled VX-R. We now suspect the R stood for radioactive. Stuart believes the two fathers, one a Pakistani and the other a Bangladeshi, who couldn't possibly have known each other, received a dose of radiation that somehow affected their sperm cells.'

Tony looked at Robbie. 'I'm still not sure what I can do to help.'

'We were hoping you might be able to help us contact Peter Stacey. He was the agent who initially recruited Kate in Baghdad. He became Head of MI6 and we thought he might be able to find out something about VX-R and whether it has other effects besides producing birth defects.'

'That's easy. I know him quite well.'

'Really? How?'

'He lives on the far side of the village. His wife runs a small stable and our daughter used to keep her pony there. I'll give him a ring and see if he can come over if you like?'

Half an hour later, Peter was hugging Kate as a long-lost friend. 'We have Kate to thank for saving the Middle East,' he said to Tony. 'Had the biological weapons supplied to Iraq by the Americans been used, God knows what the outcome may have been.'

'So Robbie has been telling me,' Tony replied. 'I hadn't realised you once served in Baghdad, Peter.'

'It was a long time ago and Kate was our best source of information for over ten years.' Peter turned to look at Kate again. Smiling, he said, 'You look terrific. Scotland is clearly suiting you.'

'I've gone paler,' she replied laughing. 'It's the only place where you can get a negative suntan. It took a while to get used to the wet winters and I have a part-time job at Inverewe Gardens. Have you ever been?'

'No, but I've heard of them. What do you do there?'

'I'm Head of their small research team.'

'Nothing dangerous, I hope?' joked Peter.

She laughed again. 'No, mostly making new species of miniature rhododendrons.'

That evening, the three couples adjourned to the village pub, *The Bluebell*, and in a quiet corner Robbie explained his son's suspicions about VX-R.

'I am not sure I can help,' Peter explained, 'but my successor Barbara Renton may be able to make a few enquiries. The problem is that although the Americans are officially our allies, we don't always share information of the type you are asking about. We knew, for example, thanks to Kate, that during the Iraq–Iran war the Americans were giving all sorts of chemical and biological weapons to Iraq but they denied it at the time. It's only recently, since The Riegle Report became public knowledge, that there has been a tacit acknowledgement of their folly. It's possible that our friends up the road may know something.'

'Up the road?' asked Robbie.

'Porton Down.'

'Of course, but we're not going to get very far with them.'

'No, but Barbara might. She is our best bet. I'll try and contact her tomorrow.'

* * *

Five weeks had passed since Peter had promised James and Kate to contact his successor at MI6. Although he had rung her the following day, as promised, he had heard nothing. Then one Friday evening, Peter's phone rang. It was Barbara. She had some news.

'Peter? It's Barbara. You stirred up a hornet's nest with that question about VX-R. Can you come up to town next week so that we can talk about it?'

'How about Tuesday, 4th of September?'

'Fine. Say eleven o'clock?'

Peter was puzzled as to why she had wanted him to appear personally in London and why it had taken her so long to come back to him.

However, he assumed that she had other more pressing matters and that the telephone line was not the correct medium with which to discuss something as secret as VX-R.

He arrived at Vauxhall Cross promptly and was ushered by a porter to the top floor. The Head of MI6's secretary rose from her chair, smiled, walked to the door behind her desk and knocked. Peter looked around his old office, little had changed, memories of his time in post flooded back.

Barbara emerged smiling and greeted him warmly. 'Come in, there's someone wanting to meet you again,' she said. They passed her secretary and went through into the inner office. He wondered about the significance of the use of the word *again*.

A portly man, in his late fifties or early sixties, dressed in a navy blue, lightweight suit with a suitably matching shirt and tie, rose to face Peter. His face looked vaguely familiar. He appeared to be sweating slightly and yet the room was not hot. 'Do you remember Brigadier Richardson?' asked Barbara as she held her hand out towards him.

Peter was unsure for an instant; then the penny dropped. 'Of course, Major Richardson. You were the Air Attaché in Baghdad.'

'Temporary assistant attaché to be correct; it's a long time ago Peter. Much water has passed under the bridge since then.'

'Quite a bit of it murky too,' replied Peter coldly.

Sensing a possible degree of friction, Barbara quickly intervened. 'Keith is now the Commanding Officer at Fort Detrick, Maryland. He's flown over to discuss VX-R with you.'

'I'm not sure I follow,' said Peter.

Again Barbara felt she should take the lead. 'Shall we sit down?' She pressed a bell and her secretary brought in a tray of coffee. 'When you asked me to try and find out something about VX-R, I initially contacted Dr Mike Cochrane.'

'Head of Porton Down?' asked Peter for confirmation.

'Yes. He'd heard of it; more a rumour actually. He visits Fort Detrick from time to time and told me that Keith would be the best person to talk to. I did just that and hence this meeting.'

CHAPTER 4

Tuesday, 4th September 2001

'Peter, can I start by asking what you know about VX-R?' asked the Brigadier.

'Not a lot. I know you supplied several litres of the stuff to Iraq during the Iraq–Iran war along with thousands of gallons of other biological agents.'

'You've read The Riegle Report, then?'

'Of course.'

'Then you know that President Reagan's deputy at the time was George Bush Senior and they were both determined Khomeini would not win the war. There were many of us in the Pentagon at the time who disagreed with what went on from 1981 to 1989, especially the supply of what is now commonly known as weapons of mass destruction. But how did you get to know about VX-R, it wasn't mentioned in The Riegle Report?'

'Do you remember James Douglas?'

'Yes, I do. He was the guy who wrote the war game software that the Iraqis used to plan the invasion of Iran. I met him when he was installing the system in Baghdad in 1978. He was something of a software genius, but wasn't he killed in Northern Ireland?'

'Officially, yes; unofficially, no. We gave him a new identity and he now lives the quiet life. He has a son, however, who is a pathologist in a hospital where two boys have been born pure hexadactyls.'

'Hexa… what?'

'They were born with six fingers on both hands and six toes on both feet. The statistical chances of that happening are trillions to one against. So, he and the consultant paediatrician did some investigating. They found out that both the fathers of the two boys, one a Bangladeshi and the other a Pakistani, were briefly itinerant workers at the same time in Iraq during the war with Iran. We believe they were exposed to VX-R when helping to bury it in the desert.'

'But it was supplied in a lead box. There shouldn't have been any danger.'

'Except these guys decided to take it out of the lead container to make a shekel or two by selling the lead. They buried it in what one of them described as a glass jar.'

'Shite! Was the VX-R buried with anything else?'

'I don't know. Why?'

'I suspect that if it was, it's possible the other substances could have become contaminated. The VX-R consignment, according to our records, included anthrax and tabun, another nerve agent that affects the lungs and kills within minutes.'

'I'm not following. Is there something about VX-R you're not telling us?'

'It's about the most toxic substance known to man. We gave up researching its properties years ago. Essentially, our scientists believe VX-R emits gamma rays that are infected, that's the best word I can think to describe it, with the nerve agent VX. In other words, it provides us with the potential to make a raygun that could shoot a nerve agent. We are not sure of its potential range, but it could be up to one hundred yards. It would pierce anything, except lead, within that range.'

'What the hell were you doing giving it to Iraq?'

'As I said, not all of us were in favour of what was going on. At the time, someone must have thought the Iraqis might do our dirty work for us by testing it under battlefield conditions. It was madness, as the Iraqis weren't even told how to use it. Thank God for that woman of theirs, what was her name, who buried it along with the other biological weapons?'

'You mean Kathab al Jised?'

'Yes, that's her; Dr Germ your newspapers dubbed her.'

'I suppose you know she worked for us?'

'No, I didn't.'

He's lying, thought Peter.

'What you're saying is that the VX-R might have radiated the other biological weapons that were buried in the same pit and corrupted them in such a way that they may also be capable of emitting poisonous rays?'

'I don't know. I'm only guessing as research stopped soon after we gave Iraq two litres of the stuff. By then scientists were realising that unless VX-R was kept within lead containers, then we had invented the contents of Pandora's Box. At Fort Detrick, well away from anything else on the base, there is a pillar nicknamed, incorrectly, *The Anthrax Tower.* It's made of reinforced concrete and stands about fifteen feet tall. When I took command of the fort, my predecessor told me that underneath there is a lead-lined pit that contains the remains of the VX-R experiments – notes, materials and equipment used, everything.'

'Then the devil's handiwork could be brewing somewhere in a desert in Iraq?'

'Yes, possibly. My worry, Peter, is that if it had been buried with gallons of anthrax spores and then, if the site was ever disturbed, and the spores released...'

Brigadier Richardson stopped, unable to imagine the consequences.

Peter speculated. 'Normal preventative measures against the anthrax would be useless?'

The Brigadier nodded, still speechless at the thought of what some of his colleagues had done fifteen, or so, years previously.

'I wonder if Stephen King could come up with a solution?' asked Peter, cynically.

Keith apologised. 'Yes, it is all rather science fiction. Presumably, it was al Jised who told you it could only have been the VX-R that would affect the two fathers in this way? Is she still working for you then?'

'No, not as such. We brought her back to Britain when things began to get nasty during *Operation Desert Storm.* We thought she would be safer with us as Saddam would have had no scruples torturing her to find where she had buried the biological weapons.'

'If we knew where al Jised had hidden the weapons, then maybe we could seal it off like the Soviets did with Chernobyl,' suggested the American General.

'Pour thousands of tons of concrete on top of the site?' asked Peter.

'It's an idea.'

'I very much doubt if she kept the records of where she buried the weapons. She coded the records using a chess position. Without the position, the files are impossible to decipher.'

'That sounds similar to the system used to protect the war game software?'

'Yes, it was.'

Peter decided not to amplify further. He had experienced problems with the Americans when he was Director of MI6. He wasn't going to reveal that Kathab had married James Douglas and they were living in the North-West of Scotland under their assumed name of MacKinnon. If Richardson hadn't known James Douglas was still alive, he was either a liar or was not up to speed with the file on Iraq's use of WMDs during the Iran war. Peter also knew that the Americans, thanks to General Schwarzkopf, had helped prevent the Iraqis using biological weapons during *Desert Storm*. He'd given too much away by telling Richardson that Robbie's son was a pathologist.

He must know about the chess method of concealing their whereabouts and that Kathab al Jised was working for us. 'You'll appreciate that al Jised's new identity is protected. I suspect even Barbara doesn't know it, nor where she lives.'

He looked at her for confirmation.

Barbara nodded. 'This was all before my time,' she said.

Peter continued, 'I know how to contact her. I will ask her to see if there is any way she may be able to remember where that particular consignment was buried. Failing that, then we're probably buggered as the two Asians won't know. Incidentally, do you know the date the VX-R was delivered to Iraq?'

'Our records show it was sent in January 1982.'

'Early in the war, then?'

'Yes.'

Barbara, who until now had been largely silent, suggested that when Peter had something to report they could arrange another meeting at her office.

The American Brigadier agreed, adding that he could always get back to London from Maryland at twenty-four hours' notice.

Barbara showed both men to the foyer. She shook hands with each. As she held Peter's hand, she gave it two quick, discreet squeezes. It was a well-rehearsed signal among MI6 operatives that spelt *don't go away.* She watched them leave in different directions and returned to her office, knowing her predecessor would return shortly.

'Ruth,' she said to her secretary, 'I want you to go down to the archives in the basement and get some files. I think I have some homework to do. Start with the annual reports from the Baghdad Station between 1978 and 2001.'

'Very good, Mrs Renton.'

* * *

Peter walked away from their meeting wondering why Barbara had signalled she wanted a private meeting. Richardson had gone but he needed to reassure himself that he wasn't being followed by any American operatives from Grosvenor Square. He turned into a side street and waited. No one came, it was safe to return.

'Peter, we've some catching-up to do. I wanted you to know that I am taking early retirement. I haven't officially done anything yet, but I am becoming increasingly frustrated with the lack of resources. Since you left, al-Qaeda has continued to expand exponentially, as Quayle said it would, and its threat to the West increases daily. We now have an international committee that meets regularly to pool data. The best source of information these days is the Indian NSG who have managed to infiltrate undercover agents into both al-Qaeda and the Pakistani ISI.'

'I understand your frustration, Barbara. Clearly things financially have not improved from my day. You will be missed.'

'Talking of Juan Quayle, do you remember him?'

'Yes, of course. He retired to the Isle of Man.'

'His family were murdered by al-Qaeda and he returned to us. For the past five years or so, he has been working as *The Daily Telegraph's* Middle East correspondent in Lebanon with the cover name of John Pearson. You may have read some of the articles that he has written, mostly anti-Israeli. Our plan was that he might inveigle al-Qaeda's trust to such an extent that he would get an interview with bin Laden. Then he would assassinate him.'

'But, surely, that would be tantamount to committing suicide?'

'Probably, we can't be sure. We have taken precautions, but it might boil down to Lady Luck.'

'And this is what you wanted to tell me?'

'I thought you should know that last week he and his local Lebanese helper received the long-awaited invite and depart for Pakistan tomorrow. They will travel to the north-west of the country and be chaperoned from Peshawar to meet bin Laden. Although Quayle doesn't know it, his minder is a Mossad agent who has done sterling work over the last five years getting Quayle interviews with all sorts of pro-Palestinian groups. He has also been keeping us informed of what has been going on; direct contact between Quayle and ourselves would have been too dangerous.'

'I've read some of Pearson's articles and often wondered why they were so anti-Israel. It never occurred to me that the whole business was a long-term put-up job. But wasn't he shot at one stage by the Israelis?'

'Yes. That was engineered too, although Quayle didn't know it. It was part of the plan to persuade al-Qaeda that his rhetoric was genuine. It worked too. Soon afterwards, he was invited to interview bin Laden.'

'How is he going to get close enough to kill bin Laden without being searched for a weapon?'

'He is going to use anthrax spores that will be released during the interview from the heels of his shoes.'

'Then Quayle will die too?'

'He has been inoculated and will be carrying antibiotics to take as soon as possible afterwards.'

'That will still only give him a fifty-fifty chance of survival.'

'Yes, we know, and that's if he's lucky. It's what he wanted.'

'So do you still want me to make contact with al Jised to see if she can remember where the VX-R was hidden?'

'Yes. I never knew her. She will trust you.'

'It's not going to be that simple. She's now married to Robbie MacKinnon. He was formerly James Douglas, the software specialist I mentioned earlier to Richardson. Douglas's first wife was murdered by the CIA, although we never proved it. Neither of them will be disposed to helping the Yanks extricate themselves from their own bloody mess.'

* * *

'Simon Rosenberg on the phone for you Mrs Renton.'

'Fine, put him on Ruth.'

The Head of Mossad Europe had helped Barbara set up Juan Quayle's gofer five years previously. It was Simon who regularly reported back to the Head of MI6 on the progress of the operation to assassinate bin Laden, even though he was not privy to all the details of the method to be used to kill the undisputed leader of al-Qaeda.

'Barbara, this morning they left Peshawar to meet bin Laden. They expect the journey may take three or four days to get to the rendezvous. Perhaps now you can let me in on the method to be used to carry out the act.'

'Quayle's shoes are specially made with hollow heels and soles, like Nike Air trainers. They contain anthrax spores under pressure that can be released. The plan is to release the spores during the interview. Bin Laden should die no more than three days later.'

'But Quayle will die too and, if our man is also in the room, him as well.'

'Yes, I'm afraid so.'

'You never told me this when I agreed to help you set this up.'

'I think you'll find I did. We both agreed it was a risk worth taking.'

'I thought at the time they might get shot. Dying by anthrax poisoning is a terrible way to go.'

'The only consolation is that it will be equally horrible for bin Laden. Their deaths may well save the lives of thousands, or even millions, of innocent people.'

Somewhat shaken by the news, Simon mumbled something inaudible and replaced his receiver.

Barbara looked at her desk calendar. It was Tuesday 4th September 2001. *Tomorrow I have to meet Jack Straw, the Foreign Secretary, and discuss my resignation with him.*

* * *

Sir Peter Stacey returned home that evening realising that he would have to make the long, two-day journey to the Scottish Highlands. Whether Kate would, or could, help with the identification of the site was doubtful. It certainly wasn't the sort of topic that could be satisfactorily resolved over the phone.

Although their number was ex-directory, he had little difficulty finding it. 'I want to come up and discuss something that cannot be said over the phone,' he said to Robbie. 'Will you be around this weekend?'

'Of course, will you stay with us? We have a guest room.'

'That would be nice. I will aim to arrive late on Friday afternoon.'

CHAPTER 5

Wednesday, 5th September 2001

'Sir, Mrs Renton has arrived.'

'Show her in, Judy. Oh, and Judy…'

'Yes, sir?'

'Can you make us some coffee?'

'Of course.'

The Foreign Secretary's PA went back to her outer office where the Head of MI6 was waiting. 'You can go in now Mrs Renton.'

'Barbara! I was surprised when I received your letter. Is it something I have done?'

'Of course not, sir. I have been thinking of taking early retirement for some time. The imminent Afghan invasion has raised the stakes in my battle with The Treasury to get money for more staff with Arabic qualifications. You can only hit your head against a brick wall so often. It's not only the New Labour administration that is reluctant to spend money on intelligence. The previous government was no better. The threat from al-Qaeda has been around for ten years and I have become tired of working in the dark with too few staff.'

'Barbara, please take a seat. Let me assure you I have to battle with The Treasury over everything, even paperclips. It was the same when I was in The Home Office. All I can say is that the PM has pledged President Bush our fullest support in Afghanistan. I'm not happy about it either. I worry it could become another Vietnam. However, it may work to our advantage. Gordon Brown will have no option but to find extra funds for our department, as well as the MoD. The Cabinet will back me and agree to increased recruitment for your department. Providing, of course, the graduates come from a mixed background and are not exclusively Oxbridge!'

The latter comment was made with a grin; a sly dig at MI6 and, possibly, Barbara's Oxford education.

'That idea is, if I may say so Minister, fallacious. Less than half of my staff are from Oxford or Cambridge. We even have Leeds graduates, like yourself.'

'Touché, Barbara! Touché.'

'However, if there is to be an expansion of our service, then I feel this is the right time to be going. A new broom and all that...'

'So, I can't persuade you to stay?'

'No, I have a small property in the Languedoc where I intend to spend my retirement.'

'Whereabouts?'

'In a village called Belveze, near Limoux.'

'It must be near Carcassonne?'

'Yes, not far.'

'A lovely part of the World. I don't want you to go, Barbara, but I wish you every happiness for the future.'

'Thank you, Minister.'

'Please, call me Jack. There are two subjects, however, I must discuss with you. The first is who do I recommend to the PM as your successor?'

'Historically, the Head has usually been someone with Soviet experience. I was, as you know, a specialist on the Caucasus States – Georgia, Armenia, Chechnya, Turkey and Azerbaijan –a mixed bag. However, I think you should appoint our current Head of the Middle East desk, Phil Jay, to be the next Head of MI6.'

'Fine, I will recommend him. The second thing may take longer. I would like you to fill me in on all you know about al-Qaeda. I have always read the minutes of your meetings with the international committee but why haven't the Americans joined? Aren't they taking al-Qaeda seriously?'

'No, but they should do. My predecessor, Peter Stacey, sent a warning memo to the CIA nine years ago, June 1992 to be precise, when Robert Gates was their Head. At that time, we had managed to get an agent called Quayle inside al-Qaeda the previous year. He worked undercover in one of their madrassas before returning to us. The trouble with the Americans is they won't listen. The Atlantic and the Pacific isolate them and they feel impregnable. I clearly remember Quayle debriefing Peter Stacey and warning us that al-Qaeda were planning to train suicide pilots to hijack aircraft and smash them into the Empire State Building. I have a feeling he may soon be proved right.'

'What happened to Quayle?'

'He retired to the Isle of Man, married and had a family. Three years later his farmhouse was attacked by an al-Qaeda arsonist. All his family were burnt to death. He was lucky to escape and he returned to work for us.'

'Was the assassin ever caught?'

'No. He was a professional hit man. Quayle returned to us vowing to eliminate bin Laden, al-Qaeda's leader. We gave Quayle a new identity; his operational name was Pearson. We even changed his appearance so no one would recognize him. For the past five years he has worked in Lebanon as *The Daily Telegraph's* Foreign Correspondent, writing predominantly anti-Israeli articles. We hoped his pro-Palestinian stance would merit him being invited to interview bin Laden so that he could assassinate him.'

'What happened?'

'He's in Pakistan now. It took five years to gain the trust of the terrorists, much longer than we expected. All foreign correspondents in the Middle East have a local man on the ground. Pearson's success was largely due to my arranging with Mossad for his gofer to be one of their agents. Pearson, however, never knew his helper was keeping tabs on him. Pearson has successfully interviewed leaders of Hamas, Fatah and Hezbollah. Ironically, all the contacts made for him were by an undercover Mossad operative.'

'Can we trust Mossad?'

'Yes; I believe Israel has more to fear from al-Qaeda than us. Pearson's assistant was tipped off a week or two ago that if they made their way to Peshawar, then someone on the staff of the *Salt Valley Sun*, the local newspaper, would guide them into the hornet's nest to meet bin Laden.'

'So we can only wait to see if the operation will be a success?'

'Yes.'

'How does Pearson hope to assassinate bin Laden?'

'Our best scientists at Porton Down came up with a scheme to release anthrax spores into the room during the interview.'

'Wouldn't that kill Pearson too?'

'Yes, but we have taken some precautions. He has been inoculated and will be carrying antibiotics in his wash bag.'

'Would that be sufficient to keep him alive?'

Barbara shrugged her shoulders and nodded. She hoped it would, but secretly had her doubts.

'How long does anthrax take to kill?'

'Without immunisation – two or three days. On the first day, those exposed to the spores would show the symptoms of a cold: a runny nose, a cough. On the second, their lungs would be full of discharging fluids. By then it would be too late to save them. Antibiotics have to be given within the first twelve hours, or else...'

'So, you think Pearson will kill bin Laden but could die himself?'

'Yes, I fear so.'

'What sort of information about al-Qaeda did he bring back in 1992?'

'Quayle was initially recruited by MI5 to ascertain whether there was a link between al-Qaeda and the IRA. The Provisionals were selling as much of their stock as they could prior to their arms being decommissioned by General Chastelain as part of the peace process.'

'I didn't know that. Was there a link?'

'Yes. He found out how the arms were being transferred at sea and, by chance, intercepted the infamous Gadhafi atomic bomb.'

'I didn't know there had been a Libyan atomic weapon.'

'Gadhafi had sold the IRA a crude nuclear device back in the mid-80s. The IRA ran scared, thank God, and never used it. Al-Qaeda was prepared to buy it and paid one million US dollars for it. It was transferred from an Irish fishing boat to a so-called Spanish boat in the Isle of Man. Quayle gained the trust of the al-Qaeda crew who were shipping it back to Ceuta. He travelled with them in a motor launch they had acquired in Southern Ireland. The RAF followed them and John Major, rightly, decided to sink the launch in the Bay of Biscay using Nimrod torpedoes. The bomb lies in 20,000 feet of water in the Atlantic.'

'What was al-Qaeda planning to do with it?'

'We never knew, but I would speculate: dismantle it, ship it to New York and reactivate it.'

'So Quayle survived the sinking?'

'Yes, and two of the crew; one of whom we believe was bin Laden himself.'

'My God! We had him in our grasp?'

'Yes, but we didn't know it. Don't forget, those were early days. We knew very little about al-Qaeda. That's why Quayle was so valuable as a source of intelligence.'

'Presumably, the Irish arms transfers stopped?'

'Yes. The Royal Navy stepped up patrols and worked closely with the Irish Navy. When Quayle returned, he told us there were hard line communists in the Russian Army involved with supplying the terrorists. Douglas Hurd visited Russia soon afterwards and informed Yeltsin. It took a little time, but Yeltsin eventually cleared them out. We believe al-Qaeda now buy their equipment from rogue states such as Iran, North Korea and on the black market in places such as Turkmenistan.'

'With money from Iraq?'

'No, we think not. Saddam Hussein is financially, as well as morally, bankrupt. Since the Kuwait affair and the imposition of the no-fly zones, he has been strapped for cash. He may have been sympathetic to al-Qaeda in the early years but for some reason he fell out with bin Laden who now relies on dissident Saudi princes, Yemeni businessmen and his own family fortune.'

'But the PM is under the impression that Saddam has restarted a nuclear programme by getting uranium from Niger and is secretly developing, what he calls, weapons of mass destruction.'

'With respect, Minister, that's a load of bollocks. Saddam's nuclear programme ended with the destruction of his Osirak plant by the Israelis in 1981. His American sourced biological weapons remain hidden and can't be found.'

'That's not what the PM's been told by President Bush.'

'I firmly believe the Americans are looking for an excuse to invade Iraq to get cheap oil.'

'Are you saying that the Americans have had a hidden agenda of their own?'

'I think they are making a case to invade Iraq by claiming Saddam is manufacturing WMDs. There are still some powerful Texan oil magnates who lost a lot of money when the Ba'ath Party nationalised the Iraq Petroleum Company in 1972. The IPC, you will remember, was largely owned by Esso. It's true, however, that Saddam has WMDs. Have you ever read The Riegle Report?'

'No. Should I?'

'Donald Riegle is a Senator for Michigan. When American soldiers began returning from *Operation Desert Storm* in 1991 complaining of Gulf War Syndrome, he took up their cause to get compensation. His investigations took several years, as much of the information was classified secret. What he found was frightening. His report claims that Gulf War Syndrome does exist and is not a figment of soldiers' imagination. It is the direct result of exposure to chemical weapons in Kuwait. However, the report went further. Riegle discovered that the source of the Iraqi WMDs was America itself. His report lists sixty-five shipments to Iraq of substances such as anthrax, West Nile Fever Virus, botulinium toxins, clostridium perfrigens and so on between late-1981 and November 1988. The invoices are all attached to his report. During that time, Bush's father was either Vice-president or President. He effectively approved their export to Iraq thinking they would use them against Iran in the eight-year war.'

'But they did use them against Iran.'

'The chemical weapons – yes, but the biological ones – no.'

'I don't see much difference,' said the Foreign Secretary.

'Largely control. Biologicals can spread on their own accord. Having said that, chemicals can get into water supplies, such as Agent Orange in Vietnam and cause terrible birth defects.'

'Then why are the UN Weapons Inspectors wasting their time searching for something that doesn't exist?'

'I didn't say they don't exist. It's just that they can never be found. Shall I explain?'

The Foreign Secretary filled their coffee cups and nodded.

'When *Desert Storm* began, we rescued an Iraqi double agent who was in charge of their chemical and biological weapons research, development and storage programme. She had been keeping us in the picture of what was going on in Iraq for about ten years. She frequently attended Saddam's Revolutionary Council meetings. She had persuaded the council that the safest way of storing the biological weapons they were acquiring from the Americans such as anthrax, and so on, was to bury them in the desert inside thick glass vats within sealed stainless steel containers. She doctored the records of their location by using an infallible method that relied on knowing a secret chess position. Only she could decode the records. We brought her back to Britain fearing the Iraqis would torture her to find out where the weapons were located. You may remember some of our soldiers subsequently suffered Gulf War Syndrome as well as the Americans. If Saddam did manage to spray our troops with chemicals, it would explain GWS. However, if he had used biologicals, then the whole of the Middle East could have been wiped-out.'

'So, Saddam has WMDs but doesn't know where they are. Why doesn't he say so?'

'He's too embarrassed and would prefer to play along with the pretence that he has power.'

'But by doing so, he's leaving himself open to being invaded by the Americans.'

'He knows the Weapons Inspectors will never find the weapons and is hoping that the UN will not, therefore, sanction an invasion as it would be illegal.'

Jack Straw sat quietly, nodding to himself. He was in a deep, pensive train of thought; weighing up pros and cons. He never said anything for many minutes. Then he asked, 'What other information did Quayle come back with that I should know about?'

'He gave us details on how they organise their madrassas. They have primary and secondary schools like us. Indoctrination and learning English is undertaken first, then students study subjects such as physics and chemistry to gain Western qualifications. They infiltrate Europe and the US for further education to become professional pilots, doctors, and so on.'

'Doctors?'

'Yes. From now on it's possible that we may have to accept that outbreaks of influenza and similar diseases have been engineered.'

'My God.'

'The madrassas are not only in Afghanistan either. Quayle mentioned they exist in Somalia, Yemen, the Sudan and Pakistan.'

'But not Iraq?'

'No.'

'Are you one hundred per cent certain that Saddam Hussein and Iraq pose no threat whatsoever to the West?'

'Yes. When I showed The Riegle Report to your predecessor, Robin Cook, several years ago, he didn't believe me either.'

'But he believes you now?'

'Yes, I think so.'

Jack Straw sat motionless; his face expressionless. In a world of his own, his head nodded slowly up and down. 'That figures,' he mumbled to himself.

'Pardon?' asked Barbara.

Jack looked up. 'Oh, nothing.'

* * *

Two days had passed since his meeting with Barbara and Peter Stacey in London when Brigadier Richardson entered the office of, arguably, the second most powerful man in the United States.

'Sit down Keith. How did you get on with the Limeys?' George Tenet,

Director of the CIA, pointed to a lounge chair in front of a low coffee table at the side of his large office.

'Well, sir, you were right; they know about VX-R.'

'Shite!'

'Apparently two Asian boys have been born pure hexadactyls.'

'Hexa … what?'

'I didn't know either. They have six fingers and toes instead of five on all their limbs. Statistically, it's impossible.'

'What's this got to do with VX-R?'

'Two doctors, one a pathologist and the other a paediatrician, at the hospital where the boys were born within a year of each other did some investigating: talking to the parents, that sort of thing. They discovered that the two fathers had been itinerant workers in Iraq at the same time during the Iraq–Iran war. The two doctors interviewed the fathers who admitted burying drums in the desert under the supervision of some Iraqi troops: a female officer and a sergeant. Whilst not being watched, they removed the contents of a lead box to see what was inside. They buried the glass demijohn and sneaked the lead back to Baghdad in the back of their truck to sell it for a few dinars.'

'So the VX-R was buried in the sand next to other substances without lead protection?'

'I'm afraid so.'

'How do the Brits know about VX-R? The whole thing could be a pure coincidence.'

'I've given that some thought. All Iraq's biological weapons were buried by their then Director of CB weapons research, Dr Kathab al Jised. I met her briefly when I was in Baghdad in 1978. She worked for the Brits as a double agent and was brought back to the UK when *Desert Storm* blew up. The interesting thing is that the pathologist is the son of the RAF software engineer, James Douglas, who designed the war game used by Iraq to test their plans to invade Iran. I also met him in Baghdad. I guess the pathologist told his father about the Iraq connection who then must have contacted Peter Stacey. He in turn made base with al Jised and she told him the only substance that could have caused the birth defects was VX-R.'

'I knew Stacey when he was Renton's predecessor.'

'In the VX-R consignment, the other biologicals were tabun and anthrax spores. I've asked our scientists back at Detrick had they any idea whether the VX-R could contaminate them or not. They just shrugged their shoulders; all the notes and equipment used in the VX-R experiments have been destroyed.'

'Do we know where al Jised buried the weapons?'

'No, but we know how the records were doctored to prevent them being found. A chess position was used to encrypt the latitude and longitude positions.'

'Without the chess position it's impossible to decipher them?'

'Yes. Sir Peter Stacey has promised to see al Jised. Her identity has been changed but he knows where she lives.'

'Stacey was a good egg. I'm sure he'll help us locate the stuff if he possibly can.'

'There's just one snag to that, sir.'

'Go on.'

'At that time the Brits were using the chess position to protect their software, your predecessor was Stansfield Turner. He was determined to discover how it worked.'

'Get to the point, man.'

'It was Douglas who designed the chess method. In order to encourage him to tell us the secret, we organised for his wife to have a car accident. Unfortunately, it went horribly wrong and she was killed along with their baby daughter.'

'Good God. Who knows about this?'

'Very few, but I have a gut feeling that Douglas always suspected we were at the bottom of the plot. It surely can't be a coincidence that Douglas used chess positions to protect software and al Jised used chess positions to protect the location of biological weapons in the deserts of Iraq.'

'What are you saying, man?'

'It's possible that Douglas and al Jised are close; even, possibly, living together. If so, they are not going to cooperate.'

'Keith, we've got to get that container of VX-R back. The President doesn't know about it, but when he does, he'll insist its return is top priority. He's already thinking of invading Iraq to get rid of Saddam Hussein and destroy their link with al-Qaeda. He sees cheap oil at the end of the rainbow.'

'Let's hope it doesn't come to that. Aren't the UN Weapons Inspectors trying to find the missing WMDs?'

'Yes, but they're not having any luck. The Iraqis deny they've got the stuff even though we gave it to them. From what you've just told me, they don't know where the weapons are either. The chess method explains it all.'

'Then we've got to hope Stacey comes up with where the VX-R is hidden.'

'If he doesn't, then we may have to undertake another operation; this time to frighten al Jised.'

'Unfortunately, we don't know where she lives. She'll have changed her name. She could be anywhere in Britain, or even abroad. Not even Barbara Renton knows. However, there may be a way of finding out…'

'Barbara and I have a good relationship. She's even confided that she is thinking of taking early retirement, but she wouldn't help on this one. How do you think we can find al Jised?'

'Douglas' son is the pathologist at the hospital where these two boys were born. If we put a tail on him, then he could lead us to his father and, probably, al Jised.'

'Fine, but how do we find him?'

'I was thinking one of your team in London might do some delving.'

'I'll put them on to it at once.'

CHAPTER 6

Thursday, 6th September 2001

Two days after meeting Richardson, Peter Stacey found himself heading to Badachro for the first time. He broke his journey and stayed with an old friend in Peebles, a small, picturesque town near Edinburgh. At the suggestion of his pal, he left early the following morning to avoid traffic on the Edinburgh Bypass. He crossed the Forth Road Bridge and sped up the A9. Less traffic meant the driving was not as tiring as the day before and, with beautiful scenery, much more pleasant. Beyond Inverness, he stopped to gaze at Loch Maree, said by the cognoscenti to be Scotland's most beautiful loch. Soon afterwards, he pulled off the main road and onto the single track road for Badachro.

Since first meeting James and Kate at the Wood's house seven weeks earlier, memories of how he had met them in Baghdad had been regularly floating around in the back of his mind. Kate had been the best agent he had ever recruited to MI6. Single-handed, she had saved the Middle East from a disaster that could have made the Black Death of the Middle Ages look like a mild outbreak of flu. Two thousand gallons of anthrax and 5,000 gallons of botulinium toxins, according to The Riegle Report, had been exported to Iraq. The possible repercussions, had they been released, made him shudder.

He remembered Wing Commander Gerry Platini, the Air Attaché in Baghdad, and how an Iraqi assassin had murdered Mrs Platini to get Kate's address. He had been embarrassed to discover years later that MI5 had neither made any real attempt to find Mrs Platini's assassin nor protect Kate. The assassin had disappeared; the only clue was that his hire car had vanished too. He thought he knew how, but he kept it to himself. If Kate and James had successfully killed the assassin and hidden the evidence, then that was not his problem.

He had always believed the Americans had planned the accident that killed James' first wife, Emma, on the tollroad at Weston-super-Mare. He knew James suspected the CIA too; consequently, both he and Kate had good reasons for not trusting the Americans. Persuading Kate to help locate the VX-R for the Americans was not going to be easy.

After all, why should Kate help? he thought. *We let her down, needlessly putting her life in danger. She seems happy living with James in the remoteness of the Highlands.* As his car stopped to allow someone to pass in the opposite direction, he noticed a large stag grazing in the heather a mere twenty yards away and thought, *With scenery like this, I can't blame her.*

He entered Badachro and remembered Admiral Johnson, the former Head of the Military Intelligence Committee, telling him about the wonderful, sheltered bay.

'Idyllic for a yachtie,' had been his words.

Armed with only the name of their house, he followed the instructions James had given him: *through the village, first right, you'll find Glenfinnan on the right.* He parked, entered through a wooden gate and walked down a sloping path of some thirty yards through a garden packed with a variety of bushes and trees. He knocked on the door of the bungalow. A dog barked; it was scraping on the other side of the door.

'Cal, sit down.' Kate had opened the door and commanded the border collie to behave. 'I'm sorry about that,' she said smiling. 'Cal's excited at seeing a stranger.' She opened her arms and they hugged.

She's fifty-one and doesn't look much different from when I met her at the Platini's house twenty-three years ago. She still smells as delectable too. What was the name of that perfume she uses? I've forgotten. I bought some for Jenny, but it didn't work for some reason.

'Welcome to Badachro,' she grinned. 'You must be exhausted.'

'Yes, it's further than I thought.'

'Would you like a cup of tea, or something stronger?'

'Tea would be marvellous.'

Kate showed Peter to his bedroom. 'Unpack your things and then come into the lounge and make yourself comfortable while I put the kettle on,' she said. 'Robbie is down the bottom of the garden working on the boat. I'll give him a shout.'

She smiled and left him to unpack.

The sun was still high in the sky when the three sat in the conservatory to take tea. 'The weather is looking good for the weekend, I thought you might like to come fishing with me tomorrow,' said Robbie.

'I haven't brought any suitable clothing, I'm afraid,' replied Peter.

'No problem, you can have a spare set of mine.'

Whilst Kate poured the tea, Peter remarked, 'When you've heard why I've come, you may not want me to stay too long.'

'Well, we guessed it would be something to do with VX-R.'

'Yes. Do you remember the acting American Air Attaché in Baghdad, Major Richardson?'

Robbie sniggered. 'I'll never forget him – an overweight, arrogant bastard. He was drunk at the 4th July bash at the British Embassy.'

'He's now a Brigadier and is the CO at Fort Detrick, the US's centre for research into biological weapons.'

'Good God. I wouldn't trust him with a fly spray. Why do you mention him?'

'I met him a couple of weeks ago at the headquarters of MI6. You'll remember, when we last met, I promised I would make some enquiries about VX-R. I contacted my successor, Barbara Renton, and she contacted her opposite number in the CIA. The outcome was Richardson being sent over the pond to see us. He's still fat by the way and sweats as much as ever. The Americans are scared shitless that the VX-R may not be contained in a lead chamber.'

'Why?'

'Richardson described VX-R as the most toxic nerve agent of all time. It emits gamma rays that are infected with VX. In other words, it works like a raygun shooting invisible deadly particles that can pass through just about anything except lead, possibly up to a range of one hundred yards, or more. They stopped researching the substance soon after sending a small amount to Iraq. Their worry is that if the VX-R was buried close to other biological agents, such as anthrax, then they too might become radioactive.'

'It seems a bit farfetched; after all, the two men who were exposed to VX-R never died. Whatever happened only appears to have affected their sperm,' remarked Kate.

'I agree it's strange, but it's the reason I'm here. Richardson wants to know if you can remember where you buried the VX-R.'

'I've no idea. I probably buried sixty or more consignments over a five-year period and, as you know, I doctored the records so that they could never be found. Does he know when the consignment was delivered to Iraq?'

'He said it was January 1982.'

'In that case it was early days of the war and would have been hidden using the chess position Robbie taught me in the sands at Ur.' She looked fondly at her husband and smiled. 'Remember that weekend?'

'Yes, vividly.' A glazed look came over his face as his eyes lit up.

Twenty-three years hasn't apparently dampened their ardour, thought Peter.

'I can still remember that chess position. I used it about ten times before buying a beginner's chess book to change the position to avoid too much repetition. What's the half-life of VX-R supposed to be?'

'Richardson told me it was about fifty years.'

Kate nodded, as if she was doing some sums.

Peter continued, 'So if we had the file with the records of the burial sites, you could decipher the latitude and longitude to get the exact position? Did you always have the same NCO in charge of the workers? Perhaps he may remember where you were that day.'

'Sergeant Ibn Zakreem was our admin wallah where I worked. I used him for most of the war but when Karbala-5 began, it was everyman to the decks. He went to defend Basra and I never saw him again.'

'Karbala-5 was early 1987 when the Iranians almost captured Basra?'

'Yes, they came within four miles of the town. Had it fallen, then

48

Iraq was finished. We lost 30,000 men defending it over the three months of the battle.'

'American Hughes helicopters and chemical weapons saved the day?'

'Mostly, although Saddam always claimed it was his fish lake.'

'Ah, the twenty-three mile long lake made by flooding the marshes and filled with electrodes.'

'Yes,' replied Kate. Then, after a pause, added, 'The records are, or were, kept safely in the Ministry of Defence – main building.'

'The one near Maidan Square?' asked Peter.

'Yes, in block number four, the one nearest the Abbasi Palace.'

'Would you be prepared to give me the chess position you used?'

'Not if you're going to give it to the Yanks, most definitely not. Sorry, but they created this problem; they can get themselves out of it. And anyway, how are they going to get the records? Break into the MoD building or invade Iraq?'

'Don't joke about it, many a true word...'

* * *

'I went through various past medical journals looking to see if there was an article on hexadactyl children.'

'And?'

'I found something in The British Journal of Pathology. It's a quarterly.'

'And?'

'I hit lucky. There was an article by the consultant pathologist at the Lincoln General Hospital, Dr Vincent Edwards. He had performed a post-mortem on a boy who had died mysteriously in Lincoln, but had been born in Leicester six months previously. The parents had moved in the meanwhile. There was no apparent reason for his death. Apart from the child being a pure hexadactyl, there was nothing wrong with him.'

'So?'

'So, I went to Lincoln and made a few discreet enquiries.'

'And?'

'I found that Dr Edwards had retired to a village near the Lincolnshire coast, a place called Burgh le Marsh. I went to see him, posing as an insurance investigator acting on behalf of the family. He told me he undertook the original examination but couldn't find anything wrong with the boy.'

'The post-mortem revealed nothing suspicious, such as the presence of a nerve agent like VX?'

'No. I then asked him, "What were the odds of a second boy being born a pure hexadactyl?"'

'What did he say?'

'His exact words were, "Less than zero – impossible, completely impossible". He was most emphatic. I told him another boy had been born with the same defects in Leicester. He wouldn't believe me. I said, "Check if you like."'

'And, did he?'

'He said he would ring the consultant paediatrician at Leicester who he knew well because of the first boy having been born there. When the call was answered, presumably by hospital reception, I heard him ask for Dr Judy Wade. Then the shit hit the fan. On the other end of the line, she wanted to know who I was and why I was making enquiries. Dr Edwards told her that I was an insurance assessor and was acting on behalf of one of the families. My cover didn't appear to wash with her, so I made a hasty getaway. However, I am certain Leicester is the right hospital and the current consultant pathologist there is a Dr Stuart MacKinnon – I checked that out. It's him you're after; I'm sure of it. Unfortunately, he will probably have been warned by the paediatrician that someone is making enquiries and may now be *en garde*.'

'You've done well, Jim. I'll pass that on to Langley and they can decide what to do next.'

* * *

'Dr Wade on the phone for you, Stuart.' There was a smile on the lab assistant's face as he held the phone for his boss to take the call. *I wonder how long it will be before he admits their relationship is getting serious.*

'Yes, Judy?'

'I've just had a call from the former pathologist at Lincoln General, Vincent Edwards. He's now retired. He conducted the post-mortem on the Rahman child and I got to know him quite well at the time as he wanted to know if there had been any birth complications before he conducted the PM.'

'So?'

'Well, someone has just been to see Dr Edwards and been asking questions about the hexadactyl babies. Posing as an insurance assessor on behalf of one of the families, he told Vincent there had been a second pure hexadactyl born here in Leicester. How he knew that, I don't know.'

'It's hardly top secret, Judy. It must be all around the hospital by now.'

'No. We warned everyone in the paediatric department to keep the birth quiet to respect the Farooq family's wishes. They're so ashamed that they haven't even told the grandparents.'

'These things have a habit of getting out. After all, everyone who has been coming to Ayatollah Ward's monthly prayer meetings knows.'

There was a pause as Judy thought through the implications of the secret becoming public knowledge as a result of her bringing the topic up in the first place. She consoled herself that had she not raised the topic at the second monthly meeting, she may never have got to know Stuart.

'Dr Edwards knew a second identical birth was statistically impossible. So he rang me to see if it was true. I thought you ought to know.'

'Perhaps it was a journalist trying to get a scoop?'

The only people who know outside the hospital environs are your parents and the former Head of MI6, the man you told me about. Apparently, as soon as this fellow realised I was demanding why he wanted to know, he made his excuses and left in a hurry. Vincent Edwards also mentioned that he thought the imposter had a transatlantic accent. I think you'd better mention this to your father.'

'I'll ring him straightaway. Are we still on for an Indian this evening?'

'Yes, I'll see you there at eight o'clock.'

* * *

'That's interesting Stuart. I think Judy is right to be concerned. When did this happen, by the way?'

'This afternoon, around three o'clock – an hour ago. '

'You won't believe this, but Peter Stacey is here now. He arrived this afternoon and we've just been discussing whether Kate might be able to remember where she buried the VX-R. I don't think there's any cause for alarm, but I'll talk it through with him at once and I'll get back to you if there's a problem.'

'I'm meeting Judy for an Indian tonight. If I'm out, leave a message.'

'You two seem to be getting on well?'

'I just enjoy her company, Dad.'

'I've heard that one before!'

* * *

Robbie repeated the story to the former Head of MI6.

'I think Judy was right and I am concerned too. I let it slip in conversation with Brigadier Richardson that Stuart was a pathologist when talking about the hexadactyl children. But I didn't say where. So I can only conclude that the Americans have been doing some digging, hit lucky and someone from the CIA posed as the insurance agent.'

'The question is: why?'

'They're hoping Stuart will lead them to Kate. I suggest that you tell Stuart to only communicate with you by good old-fashioned post in case they bug his phone.'

'Do you think there is a threat, then?'

'Yes. Now they know Stuart is your son, they'll soon find out he went to Edinburgh University for his medical degree. Then, it won't take them long to find your address. You and he must be wary at all times. I'm seeing Barbara Renton on Tuesday and Richardson will be there. However, I think I'd better talk to her at once. I have her private number, do you mind if I use your phone?'

CHAPTER 7

Friday, 7th September 2001

'I know we're meeting on Tuesday, Barbara, but I thought this couldn't wait. I hope you don't mind my ringing you this late on a Friday afternoon?'

'No, of course not Peter. What's the problem?'

'The Americans have been doing some digging and found out that Mrs MacKinnon's stepson is the pathologist at Leicester where the hexadactyl children were born. Are you now up to speed on Kate's background?'

'Yes, after we met, I read the files from the period you were in Baghdad up to the time she came to us and worked at Theobalds Road as an interpreter.'

'Then you know she found out where James Douglas was living, went to see him, survived an assassination attempt on her life and they have been happily married as Mr and Mrs MacKinnon for ten years. I believe the Americans are trying to discover where Kate lives in order to pressure her to reveal the location of the VX-R.'

'How will they link the stepson to her address?'

'Via the computers of the Royal College of Pathologists members' list and Edinburgh University's file of graduates. I believe the easiest way of protecting her is to remove his name from both sets of records. MI5 should be able to do it quite easily.'

'I'll talk to Sir Martin Harryman, Sir Charles Gray's successor, at once.'

On the following Tuesday, Peter Stacey arrived promptly for his meeting with Brigadier Richardson at Barbara Renton's office at Vauxhall Cross. Richardson had arrived before him. Aware that the Americans were trying to locate Kate through Stuart, and conscious of their connivance in the death of Robbie's first wife, he had decided to protect Kate as much as possible. He would deny that she remembered the chess position used to hide the VX-R.

'I went to see Kathab al Jised last week. She doesn't remember the consignment of VX-R. She tells me she used dozens of different chess positions to hide the CB weapons and there is no way they can ever be found except by digging up the entire country.'

'Do you believe her?' asked Richardson.

'I've no reason not to. Why?'

'I've been led to believe that in *Desert Storm* the Iraqis had begun to excavate for the weapons in a logical way; apparently making giant chess moves in the desert.'

'They knew the records had some connection with a chess position, but were indecipherable. They made a lucky guess on one occasion; since when they've found nothing, as I'm sure you well know from your satellite photographs.'

Judging from his manner, Peter began to realise that Richardson wasn't convinced about his pretence of Kate's innocence. Eventually, frustrated by Richardson persisting to quiz him, Peter decided the best form of defence was attack.

'Look, Keith, we know one of your men from the embassy has been digging and discovered the hexadactyl children were both born in Leicester. We're not fools. Barbara and I realise the CIA want to locate al Jised in order to find out where she buried the VX-R. You and I know the background to this case. We both know The Riegle Report divulged the scale of biological weapons your country supplied to Iraq during the war with Iran. Had the biological weapons been used, there would be no one left alive today in the Middle East. Moreover, although I can't prove it, I believe the CIA, possibly in league with Mossad, planned the accident at Weston-super-Mare that led to Mrs Douglas's death and that of her baby.' He paused to take a deep breath. 'What I'm saying is this. If there is any attempt to find and question Kathab al Jised, who has been given a new identity under our protection scheme, then the shit will hit the fan.' He looked to Barbara for support.

She responded immediately and assertively. 'Yes, tell Langley to forget trying any funny business; we take the protection of our RAPS people very seriously indeed.'

The Brigadier looked sheepishly at the floor. He knew what RAPS was all about; the CIA and the FBI had their own DPS, Disengaged Protection System, and sighed. 'I have no control over what the CIA do, but I will pass on your message.'

About an hour had passed since the meeting began when there was a knock on the door. Ruth, Barbara's secretary entered, apologised for interrupting and said, 'You'd better come and look at this.'

'What?' asked Barbara, somewhat annoyed at being disturbed.

'Please, come and look – all of you.'

The three went into the outer office where a wall-mounted TV was showing the Twin Towers being hit by hijacked aircraft. They stood frozen to the spot, totally dumbfounded.

It was Brigadier Richardson who eventually reacted, 'Good God!' He then froze again.

Barbara asked Ruth, 'What is going on?'

'They've done it this time,' she replied.

'Who have?' asked Peter.

'They've not said. Except to say there have been at least five simultaneous hijackings.'

Richardson went white as snow. 'It's al-Qaeda, the damned bastards,' he mumbled and, without asking, found a chair, sat down, mesmerised by the news unfolding on the screen. He was sweating profusely. Barbara and Peter stood staring at the television, unable to move, not believing what they were seeing. Perhaps as much as half an hour had passed before any of them moved. The American, still pale as a sheet, stood, and shaking uncontrollably, said in an almost inaudible voice, 'I think I had better get back to the embassy.'

'Yes, of course. I am terribly sorry at what has happened,' said Barbara as she ushered him to the door, into the corridor and to the lift.

Peter remained in Ruth's office. 'It sounds awfully callous of me, I know,' he said to Ruth, 'but do you think you could rustle up some coffee for Barbara and I?'

When Barbara returned, they went back to her office.

Alone and with the coffee that Ruth had supplied in quick time, they sat together in her easy chairs. 'I spoke to Martin Harryman at MI5 after you rang on Friday afternoon. Yesterday morning one of his men, accompanied by a Special Branch officer from The Met, persuaded the Royal College of Pathologists to remove Stuart MacKinnon's name from their computer records. At the same time, an officer from The Lothian and Borders Police had his name and details removed from Edinburgh University's files. Finally, an officer from the Leicestershire force checked with the chief administrator at Stuart's hospital. He has his salary paid into the local branch of Lloyds, who have his address as a house in Tudor Road, Leicester. There are no remaining electronic links between Stuart and his stepmother as far as I can see. Apart from torturing him, I don't see what the Americans can do.'

'I have warned Robbie and Kate MacKinnon of the potential danger to Stuart,' replied Peter.

'The World Trade Centre attack this morning will slow them down and divert their priorities. Do you think the threat to young MacKinnon is so real that we need to protect him physically?' asked Barbara.

'I wouldn't have thought so. Perhaps you could get the Leicestershire force to see the chief administrator again and get him to agree to report immediately if MacKinnon doesn't show up for work. The police could then whip around to his house to see if he's OK. If he's missing, then we know what we have to do. His father's house in Wester Ross is isolated, accessible only by a single track lane or from the sea. My guess is that if the CIA decided to visit them, then because it is so far away from anywhere, we would have time to get someone there first.'

By 5.00 pm GMT the phones were red-hot between Downing Street and Air Force One, President Bush's office in the sky. Elsewhere, chaired by Vice-president Dick Cheney, the hawkish Washington clique in The White House was already plotting retribution for the destruction of the Twin Towers and the attack on the Pentagon. The plan to invade Afghanistan had been scheduled for a few months later. It would be brought forward to 7th October. Now right-wingers were openly demanding that the President should give the go-ahead to simultaneously invade Iraq. President Bush, having initially been flown to Nebraska for safety reasons, was flying back to his seat of government. He was confused with the alarming amount of contradictory data that was arriving at the bank of computer terminals in his aircraft.

Tony Blair, his best buddy and most trusted ally, was receiving calls every few minutes. George W Bush secretly wanted his advice on the best way forward.

'Donald Rumsfeld wants me to bomb Baghdad tonight,' he told Tony. 'What do you think?'

'Three things, George. MI6 assure me that Saddam Hussein has no longer any links to al-Qaeda or bin Laden. Secondly, MI6 have been plotting bin Laden's demise for years and, believe me, he may already be dead. Thirdly, Saddam poses no threat whatsoever as he can't access the WMDs given to him during Reagan's tenure.'

'Are you telling me bin Laden has been successfully assassinated?'

'I can't be one hundred per cent certain, but we should know by this time next week.'

'And you're saying Saddam has no WMDs either?'

'No. What we are certain about is that he can't access them because they were hidden in such a way that they can't be found. The records of where they are buried are indecipherable.'

'Ah, rubbish, Tony. I know that bastard Saddam has the weapons. My father gave them to him when he was Vice to Reagan, thousands of gallons of anthrax, sarin, VX, the lot.'

'Yes, we know. We have the details on our files and I've read The Riegle Report. But Saddam never used the biological agents, George.'

'And that proves he must still have them and is planning to give them to bin Laden to destroy our cities.'

'George, you know I'll always support you. However, if you are going to go into Iraq as well as Afghanistan, then I'm going to have to keep it secret for as long as possible. I've several pacifists in my Cabinet. If they get wind of this, they could make trouble.'

'Sack them.'

'I've already slipped some of them sideways. It's not going to be easy for me, George. The other problem is going to be one of legality. I'll need to take advice from Goldsmith.'

'Who the hell is Goldsmith?'

'My Attorney General. I suspect he'll tell me that Resolution 678 is not sufficient and we'll need a clear mandate from the UN if we're to invade Iraq to implement a regime change.'

'Look Tony, do what I do with the awkward buggers.'

'What's that?'

'Work around them. Get to know who is with you. Invite them to your private office. Sit them down, give them a drink and make decisions out of Cabinet. I do it all the time; life is a whole lot easier.'

'You're suggesting I run a sofa government and keep your invasion plans off the Cabinet Agenda?'

'Exactly! My chiefs are planning to invade Baghdad in March '03. Meanwhile, we'll soften the place up a bit with the odd cruise missile. By then we'll have cleaned up Afghanistan. Resolution 678 is good enough for me.'

'I might have a problem with Barbara Renton. She's the Head of MI6 and is retiring at the end of the month. I don't see how we can gag her when she finds out we are going to war in Iraq to remove a threat that doesn't exist.'

'Look, Tony. I'm not going to be mucked about on this one. As far as I'm concerned, Iraq has WMDs that could be launched at a moment's notice and bin Laden is al-Qaeda's chief. That's good enough for me.

You leave her to me. What's her name again?' He picked up a pen to scribble the name.

'Your Head of the CIA, Tenet, will know her – Barbara Renton. She is going to retire to somewhere near Carcassonne.'

'Never heard of it. We'll find her and get her to change her mind.'

'That would be a big help, George.'

* * *

Later that night, George Tenet, the Director of the Central Intelligence Agency since 1997, was at the emergency meetings in the White House.

During a coffee break, President Bush took him to one side. 'With all this going on George, before I forget, I've a job for you that has to be kept strictly under wraps.'

'What is it, Mr President?'

'Now we've all agreed the Pentagon is to begin planning the invasion of Iraq, there may be a problem with the Brits helping us.'

'Why is that?'

'Their Head of MI6 is taking retirement and believes Saddam does not pose a threat.'

'Yes, I know. She told me she is retiring at the end of the month.'

'Prime Minister Blair thinks she could create trouble by going public with the fact that there is no evidence to link Saddam to either al-Qaeda or bin Laden. She's told Blair that Saddam doesn't even know where his own WMDs are.' He laughed, thinking this was funny. 'What a tosser,' he added as an afterthought.

'She is right. All the biological weapons we exported to Iraq were buried in their deserts and the records doctored in such a way they can never be found. We gave Iraq anything from thousands of gallons of anthrax to just two litres of VX-R.'

'VX-R? What the hell is that? And why such a small amount?'

'It is a top secret variant of the nerve agent VX. At the time it had recently been invented and we thought we could get Saddam to test it for us.'

'What does it do?'

'We don't know.'

'George, stop pissing me about.'

'Seriously, our scientists were too scared to try it out in case it went badly wrong.'

'OK. I'll rephrase, what was it supposed to do?'

'The R stands for radioactive. Doctors at Berkeley were experimenting with Thorium-90 trying to find ways Beta particles could be used to treat eye cancers. During further experiments, minute amounts of the protein drug Botox were infused with Californium-98 to investigate whether the drug could be absorbed through the skin rather than injected. The US Army Medical Command Centre at Fort Detrick picked up on the experiment and went further with various nerve agents. The results with VX were like something from a Stephen King novel.'

'Go on.'

'The scientists think VX-R emits gamma rays that are infected with VX. They can be fired like a ray.'

'We have a raygun? Why didn't I know about this? I'm the Commander-in-Chief.'

'The experiments were stopped because we couldn't be sure of their outcome. We have the potential of a gun that fires a nerve agent that will penetrate the body. The problem is storage. To confine the VX-R, it has to be kept in a lead jacket.'

'So why did we give two litres to Saddam?'

'We encouraged him to give it a try. If he killed his own troops, we would learn from the process. After all, we had hundreds of advisers out there watching and training the Iraqis.'

'And did he use it?'

'No. His Head of Research and Development persuaded him all biological weapons were too dangerous and she stored them at secret sites in the deserts.'

'Then we have to retrieve it, George.'

'Not that easy, boss. Iraq is about half the size of Texas. Imagine trying to find a two-litre bottle hidden somewhere in your home state.'

'I understand she was a British agent and they whisked her away to safety.'

'Correct, sir. Saddam Hussein can't find where his former Head of CB Research put the weapons. She doctored the records so well that they can't be found and will remain hidden for ever.'

'I believe that's a load of bollocks. Saddam's a canny bastard and is playing us and the UN Inspectors along.'

'If you say so, sir.'

'MI6 think bin Laden is dead. You're going to tell me you think so too.'

'Ah, the anthrax assassination. Whether it will be a success, or not, I can't say. It has been meticulously planned by MI6. The jury is still out.'

'The former Head of MI6, a Barbara someone…'

'Barbara Renton, sir – a fine figure of a woman.'

'She is retiring to the South of France. She knows too much and could pose a threat to our plans. I want you to change her mind.'

'I would advise against that, Mr President.'

'George, do you enjoy your job?'

'Yes, sir.'

'Then if you still want to be in it next year, send two of your best men to France. And secondly, find out where the Brits are keeping this bloody Iraqi woman and get from her how she cooked the records. I want that raygun back whatever the cost.'

CHAPTER 8

Wednesday, 12th September 2001

The following day there was nothing else in the newspapers, or on the television, other than the attack on the World Trade Centre. Stuart had arrived at work as usual, having travelled from his small Victorian house to the hospital by bus. Everyone was talking animatedly about the hijackings and postulating who had the resources and audacity to carry out the attacks.

His assistant had made them both their customary cup of instant coffee and they were robing-up for a post-mortem on a family – father, mother and two children, killed in an apparent arson attack on their home – when the phone rang.

'It's Dr Wade, boss.'

'Hello Judy, what do you think…'

However, he didn't have the opportunity to finish. It was Judy who sounded excited.

'Guess what, Stuart? I was called in at four o'clock this morning. The Farooqs brought their little boy into casualty. The A and E registrar on duty couldn't find anything wrong and, as he knew about the hexadactyl business, he thought I should come in at once. The boy was hyperventilating; there was nothing we could do to slow him down. He died at 8.36 am, exactly six months, and six days after being born.'

'My God, that's uncanny, but it must be a coincidence surely?'

'Stuart, it's more than uncanny. It has to be related to Mr Farooq's exposure to VX-R when he was in Iraq. We've got to get to the bottom of this.'

'I agree, but I'm not sure what we can do. Kate is the only person who knows where this stuff is.'

'Yes, but I'm concerned. When can you do the autopsy?'

'Not until next week, I'm afraid. The police are on my back over the four arson victims killed at Braunstone on Monday night. It will keep us busy until Friday. I am already wondering, however, if I should get my old Prof to come and help with the Farooq child.'

'Prof Hawke?'

'Yes. Alternatively, you could ask that retired pathologist from the Lincoln City Hospital who did the PM on the Rahman child to assist. What was his name? Vincent somebody?'

'Vincent Edwards; it was him who wrote the article in the Journal of Pathology. I am sure he would be interested in seeing the Farooq boy. If you are happy, I'll give him a ring to see if he can come down here on Monday. Would that be OK?'

'I don't see why not.'

* * *

Although America was in crisis from the attacks of the previous day with all civilian aircraft grounded, Wall Street trading suspended, and the military on A1 Alert, there were pockets of government that were frantically busy; none more so than the CIA. President Bush's ultimatum to Director George Tenet that the Iraq VX-R had to be retrieved at whatever cost was just one of dozens of priority tasks. The responsibility for locating al Jised had landed on the desk of Lee Hefferman, nominally Head of Personnel in the US Embassy at Grosvenor Square in London, but in reality the leader of some ten CIA agents permanently based in Britain – all with bogus job titles. He had called them together. Brigadier Keith Richardson, who was temporarily stranded in the UK as a result of the ban on transatlantic flights, attended.

'Ladies and gentlemen, I know how you must be feeling after what happened yesterday but our work goes on. Indeed, it is more important than ever. Yesterday, our Director was asked personally by the President to undertake a vital mission that has a bearing on what occurred. We are lucky to have with us today Brigadier Keith Richardson who is the Commanding Officer at Fort Detrick, our main centre for research into chemical and biological weapons. In a few moments I will ask Keith to explain the background to the task we have been given as he knows its history better than anyone else. However, before that, I can tell you that our Commander-in-Chief has authorised that *Operation Enduring Freedom*, the liberation of Afghanistan, will begin on 7th October. Along with support from the Brits, the aim will be to destroy the camps used by al-Qaeda to train the terrorists that hijacked the aircraft yesterday. Furthermore, when the Afghan business has been put straight, Iraq will be next. What Keith is about to tell you is related to the future overthrow of Saddam Hussein's regime.' He stopped, turned and gestured, 'Keith?'

'Thank you, Lee. Firstly, let me say that the task you have been given will not be easy. Indeed, it may be nigh impossible. It will take enormous amounts of tact and diplomacy as I shall explain. What we essentially have to do is discover the exact location of two litres of a substance called VX-R that was hidden somewhere in Iraq eighteen years ago. How many of you have read The Riegle Report?'

He looked around the room. Most hands had gone up.

'Then you know that from as early as 1981, we were legally exporting to Iraq various substance that would aid their research into chemical and biological weapons. Whether this was right, is not for us to decide. However, from the beginning, the Head of Iraq's CB weapons research was a woman called Kathab al Jised. I met her briefly when I was temporary Air Attaché in Baghdad in 1978. We didn't know it at the time, but she was working for the Brits; feeding them with snippets about the Iran war as well as burying the most toxic of the CB materials we were supplying. She kept records of where the substances were being buried, but was cleverly coding the latitude and longitudes using a chess position. Without the chess position, it is impossible to decipher the location of the weapons. When *Desert Storm*, the liberation of Kuwait, began, she was brought back to Britain so that she could not give away the secret locations of the CB weapons. They have remained undiscovered to this very day.'

He paused to see if everyone was paying attention. Satisfied, he continued.

'Our scientists at Fort Detrick believe the most dangerous biological weapon ever invented was something called VX-R. I don't need to tell you that VX is a nasty nerve agent that can kill within minutes. VX-R was a radioactive variant that transmitted rays of VX. However, it was never tested properly and some idiot had the bright idea of giving it to the Iraqis to test it for us. For seventeen years no one knew what had happened to it, but last year a boy was born in Leicester who was a pure hexadactyl. In other words, he had six fingers and six toes. Then, earlier this year, another boy was born with the same defects, also in Leicester. And guess what? The fathers, not related in any way, had both worked in Iraq during the war and been in the same gang that buried the VX-R. Al Jised is the only person who has any idea where the VX-R is buried. She was given a new identity by the Brits using a scheme they call, appropriately, RAPS – Retired Agent's Protection System. Consequently, we don't know her whereabouts which are kept Top Secret by MI6. However, there is evidence to suggest she has a stepson who is the pathologist at the Leicester General Hospital. I gather one of you has done some detective work and discovered his name, but before I hand over to him to tell you what he has found out, a word of warning. The British Secret Services know we have done some rooting and we have been warned off trying to uncover al Jised's location. We are going to have to tread carefully despite the President's wish to get the VX-R back. If we upset the apple cart, then they may withdraw from being our allies in Afghanistan and, possibly, Iraq.'

He turned to Lee. 'Thank you, Lee.'

Lee Hefferman stood up, thanked Keith, and asked Jim Preston to summarise what he had discovered from his trip to Burgh le Marsh.

'...so there we are. MacKinnon is al Jised's stepson, he is single, has his own small house near the centre of Leicester, appears to have a relationship with the hospital's paediatrician, Dr Judy Wade, and keeps himself fit. He seems to be our best bet as a potential conduit to finding out where al Jised lives.'

'Our next step is to do some delving,' said Lee. 'We might be able to find more about MacKinnon from the files held by The Royal College of Pathologists and Edinburgh University.'

'Why Edinburgh?' asked someone on the front row.

'In the list of appointments in the hospital, he is given as being an MD and ChB (Edinburgh) and an MRCPath. There is a further clue there. Some eighty per cent of students at Edinburgh University are Scottish. It's reasonable to assume al Jised and her husband live somewhere north of the border. So, we are going to tackle this on two fronts. I want two of you to go to Leicester, find yourselves an apartment somewhere near MacKinnon and begin 24/7 monitoring. I will relieve you weekly. Meanwhile, Ruth…' he paused to look at his best software wizzo, who responded with an embarrassed smile, '…will check out computer files: banks, local councils in Scotland, phone books and so on. Any questions?'

'There's another line of enquiry you may wish to follow.' It was Brigadier Richardson who had spoken.

'Oh?' asked Lee.

'Al Jised and the RAF Officer who designed the war game used by the Iraqis to plan their invasion of Iran were close and I wouldn't be surprised if they are living together. I also met him when I was in Baghdad. His original surname was Douglas and he lived near Weston-super-Mare with his first wife. She died in a car accident. It might be worth doing some genealogical research into their backgrounds as it could provide a clue as to where Douglas went to live when he left the Air Force.'

'Excellent! We'll follow that one up. Thank you. I suggest we meet in two weeks' time when we'll pool our information.'

* * *

On the following Monday, 17th September, Stuart met Vincent Edwards, the former consultant pathologist from Lincoln's City Hospital; he had driven from Burgh le Marsh to Lincoln and joined the A46 to Leicester – a journey of less than two hours . They greeted each other as any pair of consultants would; their mutual respect being underpinned by each other's achievements.

'Congratulations Stuart on your recent appointment as a consultant. I must say I was surprised when Judy confirmed there was a second hexadactyl boy born in Leicester. It must be trillions to one against such an occurrence.'

'I agree, but the other unlikely thing is that both boys died exactly the same age – almost to the very hour.'

'Have you done a preliminary?'

'No. I thought I'd wait until you arrived.'

At the hospital, Stuart introduced Vincent to Judy. They had talked many times over the phone about the Rahman boy, but never met. 'This is Dr Judy Wade, the consultant paediatrician who I gather you've spoken to many times. She would like to attend the PM, if that's alright with you?'

'Of course. Is there anything you want to tell me before we begin?' he asked Judy after they had exchanged affable greetings.

Judy looked at Stuart. 'Did you tell Vincent that we may have found a common link?'

'I didn't bring the topic up as much is pure speculation. However, now that Judy has mentioned it, this might be the time.' The retired pathologist listened intently to the theory of the fathers' exposure to a nerve agent in Iraq. Stuart was careful not to be too specific.

'So, you believe the fathers' sperms were somehow affected by exposure to a nerve agent and this has resulted in the boys being born as hexadactyls?'

'Yes,' replied Stuart, 'but I can't see how being a hexadactyl should cause both healthy boys to die suddenly.'

'No, nor can I. My hunch is I must have been looking the wrong way when I did the first PM on the Rahman child. Now we know about a possible nerve agent, however, I think we should concentrate on this boy's nervous system.' He looked at Judy, 'It could be a messy PM; we're going to have to remove the brain.'

'I'll be all right,' she replied, smiling and thinking, *Perhaps the old boy thinks I might be squeamish.*

After the usual scrubbing down, the post-mortem began.

They began with the lobotomy. The more experienced pathologist then turned his attention to the child's neck, tongue and throat.

He stopped after some time and turned to Judy. 'How well did you know this boy?'

'The delivery was perfectly normal. The notes from the Health Visitor taken at one and three months describe how he was developing satisfactorily, although not putting on much weight and somewhat reluctant to take food. Her reports also mention he was a quiet child, but seemed happy.'

'Did she say whether the boy slept a lot or appeared tired?'

'I have the notes here. Let me look.'

Dr Edwards continued with his investigation while Judy fumbled in the file.

'The Health Visitor says that he was always asleep when she went to see him and had to wake him to do the obligatory tests.'

'Does she report on his eye co-ordination; following an object moved in front of his face?'

'Poor responses, it says here.'

Vincent grunted, nodded and carried on. He had begun to dissect the child's lungs.

Half an hour had passed and he had said nothing. Stuart had largely watched, admiring his colleague's use of his instruments.

'You mentioned eating and swallowing food.'

Again, Judy flicked through the notes. 'Poor to eat; minor consequential loss of weight.'

He removed his face mask. 'MG.'

'MG?' asked Stuart, in disbelief.

'Myasthenia Gravis,' announced Judy. 'Surely not?'

'Is that possible?' asked Stuart. 'I thought it was an old persons' disease.'

'Not necessarily, look at the symptoms: poor eye co-ordination, excessive sleeping, quiet behaviour and poor to swallow. The signals from his brain are not getting to his muscles. Then there's this...' He pointed to a minute tumour on the hypothalamus that was so small it needed the magnifying glass to see it. It was little bigger than a full stop on a page of print.

'If you hadn't told me about the father's exposure to a nerve agent, then I would have missed seeing that. I suspect the Rahman boy died of MG too. I admit I never thought of dissecting the hypothalamus. This boy's muscles have been getting proportionately weaker from the day he was born, despite his body trying to recover by saving energy whenever possible.'

All three were dumbfounded to think that a six-month-old child had died of MG. 'I am sure it is a medical first,' said Vincent. 'Do you want me to write up our findings for the journal, or will you?'

'To be honest, I'd prefer not to have the PM written up at all.'

'Oh, why not?'

'The existence of nerve agents in Iraq is a highly classified military secret. Our knowing about it is purely accidental. You'll have to trust me when I tell you that there are only a handful of us who know about it in the UK. Bearing in mind what happened last week, making it public knowledge could prove to be embarrassing for someone we know.'

'OK, Stuart, we'll leave it at that.'

CHAPTER 9

Wednesday, 10th October 2001

'Believe it or not, it is four weeks since the attack on the Twin Towers and we had our inaugural meeting to determine where Kathab al Jised, or Mrs MacKinnon, lives. I will ask you in turn to tell us what you have found out. It is only three days since *Operation Enduring Freedom* began. However, I have been assured by Langley that it is going well and the Pentagon is forecasting the Taliban in Afghanistan will be a spent force within six months. Now, let's start with you, Bill.'

'Well, sir, you gave me the task to investigate the genealogy of James Douglas and his first wife, Emma Knight. You will remember that Brigadier Richardson had suggested this may be a possible clue as to where Douglas went to live after his identity had been changed by MI6. I went to Weston-super-Mare and found their old address in a village called Kewstoke. I spoke with the Douglas's next door neighbour, Mrs Norris. She remembers them well and the unfortunate car accident. She told me that immediately after his wife's funeral, Douglas took his son and in-laws to Scotland...'

'Ah, that makes sense,' interrupted Lee Hefferman. 'MacKinnon is a Scottish name.'

'It's more than that, sir. It's a Highland name, specifically from around the Isle of Skye.' Bill paused before continuing, 'I split my search in two. Firstly, the Douglas line. James Douglas was born and educated in the Isle of Man. I had to fly there to get his birth certificate as the island is not in the UK. His parents are dead; he was the only child. I managed to track down two cousins. They hadn't heard from him for years; not since his death was announced when he was supposedly shot by the IRA in Northern Ireland. They assumed he had been buried in Ireland. They weren't aware his wife had predeceased him. To be honest, they didn't seem to care. They were one hundred per cent certain he wasn't living on the island. "If he had come back from the dead", one of them said, "everyone over here would know about it."'

He paused to see if there were any questions. There being none, he continued, 'I found getting the background on Douglas's wife easier. Her birth certificate showed that Emma Knight's father was a Londoner who had been in the RAF during World War Two. She had been brought up mostly in Tottenham. From her parent's marriage certificate, I discovered her mother was a Miss Pat MacKinnon. She had been born in Tain, a town in the North-East of Scotland. I got a copy of her birth certificate. It tells us her father was a lighthouse keeper. I went to Tain, but could find no one who could remember the family. Lighthouse keepers were notoriously peripatetic. I went to the nearest lighthouse at Tarbat Ness and found that her father had been the head keeper there from 1915 to 1921. Presumably after that, he went elsewhere.'

'That's excellent, Bill. It ties in with what Gina discovered.' Lee looked at Gina Seaton to continue.

She stood up. 'I found that there are 2,115 MacKinnon households in Britain. Of these, 748 are in England, fifty-three in Wales, and forty-two in Northern Ireland. That leaves 1,272 in Scotland. The vast majority are in the central belt – Glasgow to Edinburgh – with 453 families living in Fyfe and all points north. There are pockets of concentration, most notably in Inverness, Perth, Fort William and the Isle of Skye.' She stopped, nodded to Lee and sat down.

Hefferman rose from his chair. 'We are monitoring Stuart MacKinnon and his girlfriend Judy Wade. We have planted two devices in each of their homes.' He didn't mention that the doctors would be unaware that their beds had been bugged. *After all, that's where most secrets are often revealed.* 'We have attached tracker devices to their cars. We have rented a first-floor flat diagonally opposite MacKinnon's house in Tudor Road. It is our listening post and we are recording all movements. So far, nothing of interest has been revealed. There is no doubt that both are suspicious and on their guard. If Dr MacKinnon is contacting his father, then it can only be by post. Sooner or later, however, they will slip up and we'll be ready for them.'

The meeting became a free ranging discussion on what to do next. In the end, it was decided that three agents would go to Perth, Fort William and the Isle of Skye to begin to make checks on the MacKinnon families living there.

* * *

That evening, the two doctors were travelling back from a badminton match against Coalville. Having won all three of their games, the couple were in an upbeat mood.

'I have been looking at the weather forecast for the weekend; it looks as if it's going to be dry and sunny. I don't suppose you'd like to come away with me? I'd like to show you where I went to school in Kewstoke and where Mum, Dad, Jennifer and I lived. I'd like to visit my mother and sister's grave.'

He momentarily took his eyes from the road, hopefully to steal a positive look on her face.

She turned her head, smiling quizzically. 'What's brought this on?' she asked.

'I've been thinking about it for some time. I know you've met Kate and Dad but I think you should know a little about my early days. Don't get me wrong, I'll book separate rooms in the hotel.'

'Why?'

'Why what?'

She asked. 'Why separate rooms? Her face was covered with a mischievous grin.

Stuart felt embarrassed and felt his heart beating rapidly; his hands on the steering wheel began to sweat, yet felt cold. He glanced at her again; she was still beaming.

'Well, if you are sure that would be alright…'

'Of course it will be alright,' she replied, putting her right hand on his left thigh and squeezing it firmly.

That night Stuart never went home. His first liaison with Judy was a success, despite his nerves. Neither knew, however, that their every move was being overheard.

* * *

Both doctors finished at lunchtime on Friday and eagerly threw their holdalls into the back of Stuart's car. He had planned the scenic route to the West Country – the *Fosse Way*. Following them from a safe distance, so as not to be seen, was an inconspicuous, silver-grey, family saloon.

Stuart had originally planned to stay in a small hotel in the village at Sand Bay but having broken the ice, he had decided they should stay at the plush *Grand Atlantic Hotel* on Weston's sea front. That evening at dinner, with a bottle of Moet almost finished and a second on order, he asked Judy the most difficult question any man ever asks.

She instantly said, 'Yes'.

'Tomorrow I will buy you the engagement ring of your choice. There is an excellent jeweller on The Parade and if you can't see what you want, we can always go to Bristol.'

The following morning, the couple walked into the town centre. They found the ring: an eighteen carat gold, solitaire diamond mounted on a platinum shank. Hand in hand, they wandered back to their car. Stuart bought a large bouquet of yellow roses as they passed a flower shop. 'Mum's favourite,' he explained.

They drove to Kewstoke along the tollroad where Stuart's mother and sister were killed. He stopped and showed Judy the dangerous right-hand bend where his mother's Fiat had left the road. 'This is the first time I've come back here to look,' he said. She put her arm around him, buried her head in his shoulder and hugged him. He felt reassured that he had a companion with whom he could share everything. Judy would be his best friend for life. They stood looking over the cliff at the sea some thirty feet below. It was grey, the waves crashed noisily against the rocks. It looked cold; it was cold. The woods behind them were silent; no birds sang, there was no rustling in the trees. After a few minutes, they re-entered the car and drove to the car park at Sand Bay.

They walked up the lane that they had just descended, not noticing a silver-grey saloon coming down the hill. At the top of the rise, they entered the churchyard. Behind the church and with a view north toward Sand Point, was a well-defined rectangle with a concrete border. Filled with white stone chippings, the marble headstone read:

Emma Patricia Douglas
Born 3 October 1940
Died 17 July 1978
Aged 37 years

Also

Jennifer Helen Douglas
Daughter of the above,
Born 13 December 1976
Died 17 July 1978
Aged 19 months

May they rest in peace

Stuart stood, head bowed, hands together, tears flowing over his cheeks as he placed the bouquet on the marble chippings. After many minutes, he turned and whispered, 'I'm sorry,' as he wiped his eyes. Judy said nothing. She was weeping with him.

They left the cemetery. At the top of Crookes Lane he pointed to his old primary school and then, 'That's where we lived,' he said pointing to the second of two dormer bungalows. In the driveway of the first was an elderly woman emptying her shopping from the boot of her car. Stuart crossed the road, stood by her gate and asked, 'Mrs Norris?'

She swung around, a puzzle on her face. 'Yes,' she replied.

'It's me – Stuart Douglas – I used to live next door.'

Astonishment appeared on her face, as she screwed her eyes to focus for a closer look at the young man standing in front of her.

'Stuart?' She approached him and examined his face. 'You've changed; you've grown up.'

'Well Mrs Norris, it was twenty-three years ago since we left, but you look just the same.'

She blushed, 'Oh no, dearie me, no. I was a lot slimmer then.'

Stuart introduced Judy. 'This is my fiancé,' he said proudly.

'Would you like a cup of tea?' she asked. 'Stephen would like to meet you.'

'Stephen is Mrs Norris's son,' explained Stuart. 'He used to teach me to play soccer on the field next to the house.' He pointed to the village playing field.

In the cosy lounge, there was animated conversation about events in the village that had occurred in the intervening twenty-odd years. After Mrs Norris had asked after Stuart's father and had been told he lived in Scotland, Stuart added, 'He married Kate. You may remember her, she stayed with us for a weekend and came from Iraq…'

'A pretty girl,' remarked Mrs Norris. 'She came for your mother's funeral but was too late. You had gone away with your grandparents and James. Funnily enough…' She paused for a moment. The topic had obviously triggered a recall button somewhere in her brain. 'Someone came here last week asking about you and your family.'

'Really? Who?'

'He didn't say, but I could tell he was an American, I'd swear to it.'

The two doctors looked at each other. Their faces told the other what they were both thinking.

It was Judy who asked, 'He didn't pose as an insurance investigator, did he?'

'Now I come to think of it, I believe he did.'

Soon afterwards, the pair made their excuses and left.

They'd continued down Crookes Lane and had gone a hundred yards towards the shore before Stuart began, 'I think I'd better ring Dad right away, don't you?'

'Yes, but not on your mobile. Use a public call box.'

'There's one at the bottom of the lane outside the post office.'

* * *

He picked up the phone and gave his name: 'Lee Hefferman.'

'Sir, it's Bill. I'm ringing from Kewstoke, near Weston-super-Mare, on my cellphone. We followed MacKinnon and his girlfriend. I thought you'd want to know they're booked into *The Grand Atlantic Hotel* in Weston for two nights sharing a double room. They got engaged this morning. I watched them buy a ring, which she was wearing when they left the shop. However, the bad news is they've just left MacKinnon's old next door neighbour's house and have made straight for a public phone box. I suspect they are letting his father know that we've been making enquiries about his whereabouts.'

'OK, Bill. Keep on their heels for the rest of the weekend.'

* * *

'Dad, I'm ringing from a public phone box at the bottom of Crookes Lane in Kewstoke.'

'What on earth are you doing there?'

'Judy and I got engaged this morning.'

'Congratulations, that's wonderful news. Kate and I thought she was a super girl. She'll make you a wonderful wife.'

'I thought I'd bring her down here to see where we used to live. I've just left Mrs Norris's house. She and Stephen ask to be remembered to you by the way. However, there has been someone down here asking questions about us. It sounds as if he was the same person who was digging around at Lincoln and found the pathologist, Dr Edwards, who did the first post-mortem on the Rahman child. Mrs Norris was certain he was American.'

'There's not much Mrs Norris could have told him.'

'She told him that we went away after Mum's funeral to Scotland. It's a big clue as to where to start searching for you and Kate.'

'Fine. I'll get in touch with Sir Peter Stacey and let him know what is going on. Don't worry, everything will be alright. Give our love to Judy and enjoy the rest of your weekend.'

* * *

'Peter? It's Robbie MacKinnon. I'm sorry to be ringing you on a Saturday morning but it looks as if the CIA is on our heels...'

'Listen, Robbie, Barbara and I covered your tracks pretty well and apart from knowing you are using the cover name of MacKinnon and that most people with that surname live in Scotland, I'm not sure how they can find your location. Barbara retired at the end of last month and about the last thing she did was put your protection posture up to *Amber*. Her successor is Phil Jay. I know him well; he used to work for me. I will have a word with him. I have his private number. If there's a problem, I'll get back at once.'

* * *

'Phil, its Peter Stacey. I'm sorry to be ringing you on a Saturday, but you did say...'

'That's OK, I'm only washing the car. What's the problem?'

'It's this business with the VX-R. It's making me feel as if I've never been away from the job. Did Barbara fully brief you about what's going on before she retired?'

'Yes, I think I'm up to speed. As far as al Jised is concerned, we're on *Amber Alert,* one up on the normal RAPS posture. Has there been a development?'

'It looks as if the Americans have ignored our warning to back off and are actively trying to locate al Jised, or as she is now, Kate MacKinnon. They recently have been asking questions in Weston-super-Mare.'

'Well, Barbara put all those computer precautions into place. Now they've made this move, then I guess we'll have to go to the next stage of protection – *Red Alert*.'

'What are you thinking of doing?'

'I'll get one of my wizzos to make some checks to see exactly how the Americans are getting their info.'

'Then?'

'Well, if you or I were handling this operation, we'd have bugged young MacKinnon's house and put a tracker on his car. I'll bet that's what the Yanks have done. It will take us less than a day to prove I'm right. I'll instigate the higher alert state immediately. I'll send someone up to Leicester first thing tomorrow morning and let you know what's happening.'

* * *

'You were right, Peter. Stuart MacKinnon's house had two listening devices: one in the lounge and one under his bed. Believe it or not, they had put a twenty-four-hour watch on his house from a flat across the road. Until he returns from Weston, however, we won't be able to check out his car. Today being Sunday, everywhere was quiet and has made it easier to enter his house and his girlfriend's apartment.'

'Did the Americans see you making the checks?'

'No, they knew he was away in Weston too and were probably having a lie-in. We entered his house from the rear yard. His girlfriend's flat was similarly tapped, as well as her car. We've removed all the devices and tomorrow I will ask Lee… what's his name?'

'Hefferman?'

'Yes, Hefferman, to come and see me. I'm not having them interfering with our former staff. I will show him the listening devices we've collected and tell him that our alert states have been raised from *Amber* to *Red* as a result of his actions. He'll know what that means. He'll have to remove his operatives from their flat in Tudor Road or risk my raising the matter to ambassadorial level. Then he would be facing the possibility of his staff being expelled.'

'He won't like that. I'll contact Robbie MacKinnon and let him know what you have done.'

CHAPTER 10

TOP SECRET
NOTES TAKEN AT A SPECIAL MEETING OF THE COMMAND
REVOLUTIONARY COUNCIL – WEDNESDAY, 17 OCT 01.
PRESENT:

Chairman – Saddam Hussein, President of Iraq
Secretary – Sahib al-Majid, Head of Civil Service
Members – Tariq Aziz, Foreign Minister
Izzat Ibrahim, Vice-president of Iraq
Hashim Ahmed, Minister of Defence
Ali Hassan al-Tikriti, Chief of General Staff
Mohammed Denmadi al- Najaf, Chief of Military Procurement
Aflaq Kifal al-Kammuna, Minister of Finance
Archivist – Fatima Shada al-Samarra, Note Taker for Secretary

ITEM – OUTCOME OF al-QAEDA ATTACK ON WORLD TRADE CENTRE AND INVASION OF AFGHANISTAN

The Chairman outlined the reason for the meeting. He invited the Foreign Minister to explain what was rapidly becoming common knowledge in the UN Headquarters at New York. He added that as usual the Secretary would include reported speech in the notes where he felt it appropriate. Saddam Hussein was a great believer in being able to tie down exactly who said what at his meetings.

Tariq Aziz reported that it was strongly rumoured that President Bush had made up his mind that Iraq was responsible for the attack on the Twin Towers. He had illegally invaded Afghanistan ten days previously and was now planning to invade Iraq.

The Chairman asked, 'How soon will he be ready?'

The Foreign Minister replied that he thought it would be at least a year before the US could strike because so many of their forces were committed to the war in Afghanistan. 'The Yankees arrogantly believe they can defeat the Taliban in six months, I will bet they can't do it in six years.' Everyone around the table nodded approvingly and laughed; none louder than Saddam.

The Chairman asked the Minister of Defence and his Chief of General Staff for their views.

Ali Hassan spoke first. 'If we are to deter the Americans, then we must threaten the Americans with the biological weapons they supplied us with during the war with Iran.'

'Unfortunately, as you know, we don't know where they are. That tart al Jised hid them under our noses. We've been through this before,' replied the Chairman.

'I sent one of our best assassins after her, but he never came back,' groaned Ali Hassan.

'So, it's reasonable to assume she is still alive and living somewhere in Britain,' said Tariq Aziz in a soft but authoritative voice. Despite being the sole Christian in the Council and, therefore, from a minority of less than five per cent of the Iraqi population, Saddam invariably tended to defer to Tariq's wisdom and judgement. Whereas most of Saddam's closest advisers were from his own al-Tikriti tribe and had been chosen to fill the higher ranks in his government because he felt he could trust them, Tariq had risen to the number-two spot through being a clever politician. He had a much superior grasp of international affairs and was diplomatically savvy.

'The bitch got away with it scot-free,' growled Ali. 'Our man found her, we know that much.'

It was widely believed that Ali, Saddam's first cousin, had tried several times to discredit Tariq, but on each occasion had been foiled by Saddam's intervention. There was, consequently, considerable friction between the two men.

'How do you know that?' Tariq's question was asked in a manner that could be construed as being condescending.

'He used exiton as a truth drug on the wife of the former British Air Attaché in Baghdad, Wing Commander Platini. Mrs Platini told him where al Jised was living but she died as a result of overdosing the drug. Our man returned to London and lay low for three weeks to let the police inquiry die down. He then went after al Jised but never returned. Even his hire car disappeared. Unfortunately, our man never told anyone her address for security reasons,' grumbled Ali.

'The need-to-know principle; he was quite right,' smiled Tariq.

'If you think so.'

There was a pregnant pause. The Chairman said nothing; he was enjoying the confrontation and was wondering what might happen next.

'So if your assassin could find where she lived, could we do it again?' asked Tariq.

'We would have to hope Platini himself knew the address,' replied Hassan sarcastically, before adding, 'and this time we will torture her properly before killing her.'

'I don't think that would get us very far, do you?' asked Tariq. He looked at his leader and without waiting for a nod to continue, proceeded, 'Rather, I was thinking along the lines of persuading her to tell us where some of the burial sites are.'

'And how do you think we could do that?' spat the Head of the Army.

'We explain the very existence of Iraq is dependent on her. We appeal to her sense of nationalism. If I remember rightly, her husband was Brigadier Amer Rashid?'

'So?' asked Ali Hassan.

'I knew him quite well. He was vehemently anti-American. We'll have to hope some of it rubbed-off onto his wife.'

The Chairman had listened to the conversation long enough. 'So, what are you proposing, Tariq?'

'We send two men to find and then interrogate Platini. When they have the address, they dispose of him in such a way his body will never be found. They leave no traces of their presence at his home.'

'Then?'

'I will slip into Britain and try and persuade al Jised to give us the chess position.'

'It wouldn't work,' interrupted Sahib al-Majid. Everyone turned to stare at the man who was generally considered by the upper echelons of Iraq society, outside Saddam's clique, to be the most intelligent member of the CRC.

The committee then turned to Saddam to see his reaction. He looked blank, somewhat taken aback that his Foreign Minister's idea had been dismissed so summarily.

'What do you mean?' Saddam asked the Head of the Civil Service.

'As soon as the authorities in Britain realise something has happened to Platini, they will put two and two together. They will quickly realise what is going on. Al Jised will be given twenty-four hour protection.'

'Well, have you got a better idea?' asked Tariq Aziz, somewhat miffed that his plan had a fatal flaw.

Al-Majid looked to Saddam for his approval. 'If I may suggest, sir?'

'Yes, go on. I am interested in what you are proposing,' replied the Chairman, waving his hand for Sahib to proceed.

'Firstly, I don't think there is a need to rush. I suggest our best detective, Chief Superintendent Rajem Sakeem, be sent to England incognito to find Platini and then do a recce; get to know his habits and find out what the security precautions are at his home. As you rightly pointed out, if Mrs Platini knew al Jised's address, then almost certainly, so does Platini. Somewhere in that house there will an address book with al Jised's name in it. I bet he even sends her a Christmas card each year.' He paused to look at Tariq and smiled. It was a sly dig at the infidel's religion. It didn't go unnoticed by most of the Council members. 'Sakeem will find the address by breaking into Platini's house when he's gone to work without him knowing.'

'And if he can't find her address?' asked Saddam.

'Then, plan B.'

'Which is?' asked the Foreign Minister, feeling somewhat resentful that Sahib's plan was clearly superior to his.

'We resort to using exiton after first administering ketamine.'

'Why do that?' asked Ali, excited that, at last, chemicals were to be used.

'We enter his house when we know he is asleep and carefully inject him with ketamine. Then when he wakes up in the morning, he will believe he has been dreaming. He will never know he has told us al Jised's address.'

'Assuming this all goes to plan, who goes to see her?' asked Saddam.

'Mr Aziz, of course. She knows him from when she used to attend our meetings. She will realise that, if he has taken the trouble to find her and travelled to Britain incognito, she will have to take him seriously.'

'And if she doesn't help us, what then?'

'I will hint that the next time our assassin will be successful,' remarked Tariq Aziz with a smile on his face; indicating that he, somewhat reluctantly, approved Sahib's superior plan.

The meeting then adjourned, there being no *Any Other Business*.

* * *

'So that's the plan, Sakeem. What do you think? Can you do it?'

'It's a great honour to be asked, sir. I think my English will be good enough too. However, I would like Ali Jegauck to come with me.'

'Who's he?'

'The best burglar in Baghdad.'

'You're joking?'

'No, sir. If Platini's house has an alarm system that I am unfamiliar with, I will need him.'

'You want me to have him released from jail?'

'He's not in jail.'

'Why not?'

'Because he is the best. We've never caught him. We know he is at the bottom of most of the grander house break-ins, but he never leaves evidence.'

'Do you know how to contact him?'

'Yes. His English is quite good too.'

'A bonus, then. Go for it. I will instruct Sahib al-Majid's staff to prepare the necessary papers. You will fly to Amsterdam via Moscow, pick up Dutch passports and a Dutch registered car and enter England via Rotterdam and Hull.'

'How long have I got?'

'Take your time. Spy out the land carefully and only when you are certain, make your move.'

* * *

Three weeks later, the Chief Superintendent was back in Tariq Aziz's office.

'Is this what you wanted?' he asked with a smile. He handed the Foreign Minister a note. Aziz read it: Glenfinnan, Badachro, Wester Ross, Scotland.

'Is that all?'

'That is al Jised's address,' he replied. 'Exactly as it is written in Platini's book. That's what you asked me to get.'

'I'm sorry, but I thought there would be more details; perhaps a phone number?'

'That was all there was in Platini's address book.'

'How did you get it so easily?'

'Platini still lives in the house where that fool Arif Rashid, sent by Ali Hassan, killed his wife. He retired from the RAF some years ago but now works part-time teaching English to overseas students. We watched him go off to work. Jegauck disabled his alarm system in minutes, picked the lock even quicker and we walked in. I went directly to his writing desk in his study and found his address book straightaway. We were in and out in less than ten minutes. Jegauck said it was the easiest 250,000 dinars he's ever earned.'

'How much?!'

'If you want the best, then you have to pay for it.'

'OK, I'll authorise it. You had no trouble getting into England?'

'None whatever. The Dutch passports worked a treat.'

* * *

After several weeks of correspondence, initially at diplomatic level, Tariq Aziz had arranged to have a telephone conversation with his opposite British counterpart, Jack Straw.

'Tariq, how can I be of help at this difficult time?'

'As you know Mr Straw, the Americans are becoming very hostile towards my country, accusing us of plotting the attack on The World Trade Centre and harbouring madrassas where the terrorists are being trained by al-Qaeda. It's a pack of lies, of course. They're looking for an excuse to invade us after they have dealt with the Taliban in Afghanistan.'

'Why would they want to do that?' Jack knew Tariq was telling the truth; his former Head of MI6, Barbara Renton, had fully briefed him on the matter before she had taken early retirement a month previously.

'I think you know – a three-letter word with two vowels.'

'I have little influence on American foreign policy, Tariq. All I can do is to express my feelings in Cabinet.'

'Yes, I realise that Jack. However, I think you may be getting the wrong end of the stick for my call. What I want is a personal favour.'

'Go on.'

'If the Americans invade us next year, then it is highly unlikely my wife and I will ever get the chance to visit Britain again. As you know, we are Christians and I would consider it a great favour if you would allow us to make a private visit to see Canterbury, Salisbury, Lincoln, and York. My wife also wants to see Princes Street in Edinburgh and, being interested in military history, I would love to see Scapa Flow.'

'That would take at least two weeks.'

'Yes, I realise that. I would want no help from your government and would travel incognito, if that's alright?'

'I don't see a problem. I will arrange for you to have a two-week visa. How do you propose to arrive?'

'I was thinking of flying to Heathrow from Amman.'

'OK, Tariq, I'll get the necessary paperwork underway.'

'That's good of you, Jack. However, if you don't want any adverse publicity, then you had better have the visas made out in our former names – Mikhail Yuhanna and my wife as Roya Rihab al Yuhanna. I will have passports made with those names at this end.'

* * *

The private phone rang in the office of the Head of MI6, Phil Jay.

'Phil, it's Jack Straw here.'

'Yes, sir, what can I do for you?'

'Just to let you know that I've given Tariq Aziz permission for him and his wife to make a private visit to Britain next month. They will be travelling incognito, visiting various Christian sites – cathedrals, that sort of thing. Both being Christians, they want to see how we celebrate the period leading up to Christmas. I want you to keep a discreet eye on them while they're here. I don't want them to be interfered with by either Mossad or our transatlantic friends. They will arrive on a BA flight from Amman on Saturday, 8th December, and will be hiring a car for two weeks.'

'Understood, sir. We'll track his car and each evening, wherever they stop, we'll check all is OK.'

'Thanks Phil. Let me know if there is a problem.'

CHAPTER 11

Friday, 23rd November 2001

A *Catalan* is a coded letter that has been addressed to *The Catalan Dept* at Vauxhall House, the HQ of MI6. There is no such department but rather it is a signal to the central registry, where all correspondence is received. The registry staff know the package must be treated as top secret and be taken to the Director's secretary immediately. The scheme had been in existence since the formation of MI6. Its function is to protect agents whose cover has been compromised. The codename's origin has been lost in the mists of time. Invariably, the system leads to agents being given a different identity to protect them when they settle in a new, secret location. The *Catalan* arrangement was used to protect Kathab al Jised when she was rescued from Iraq during *Desert Storm*. She was given the name Kate Jackson, before her marriage to Robbie MacKinnon.

The *Catalan* letter, having landed on his desk, Phil Jay knew what he had to do: a trip to the bowels of the building, where the most delicate secret files were kept in a vault, known as Section Sixteen. Even he had to sign a log book before entering and opening the letter. He then had to link the first line of the letter, in this case: *When shall we three meet again, in thunder, lightning, or in rain* to an index. That led him to a complete list of MI6 agents and their details. He was somewhat surprised when he saw the name related to the Macbeth quotation was BARBARA RENTON.

That can't be right, he thought. *There's no need for her to be on the protected list. What the hell is going on?*

The contents of the letter had then to be decrypted manually using the quotation as the key. It took Phil almost an hour; he was out of practice and hadn't done it for several years. He read the letter:

> I know the use of *Catalan* is highly irregular, but I have recently had to take extreme action to protect myself from what I believe was an attempted assassination by CIA thugs. I now wish to implement the *Catalan* system and take on the identity that has been held in reserve on my personal file. You will also find on file the dates and location for a liaison meeting.

He signed for her personal file and returned to his office. Sure enough, there were the details: her precautionary new identity and a location for a meeting: *Café du Chateau*, Vizille, 1100 hours, fourth Tuesday of each month. He looked at his desk calendar. He thought, *That's next week. I can't make it - a meeting of the Joint Chiefs. There's no way I can make Barbara wait a month. I wonder if Peter, my predecessor, can go.*

'Peter, it's Phil. I thought you ought to know, this morning we received a *Catalan.*'

'Who is the letter from?' asked Sir Peter.

'It's from Barbara. That's why I'm ringing you. She sounds desperate and wants a meeting next week. Can you come up to town and see me as soon as possible?'

Peter Stacey glanced at his watch. 'I could catch the 1305 train from Swindon and be with you by three o'clock.'

'Excellent. I'll make sure we are expecting you in reception.'

* * *

'I wouldn't have bothered you if it hadn't been Barbara,' Phil explained. 'But it looks as if she has been targeted by the CIA.' He handed his predecessor the decoded letter.

Peter read it carefully, 'I know Barbara well. We both do. And we

90

both know she wouldn't have sent this if she wasn't sure of her facts. The question that worries me is why would the CIA want to kill her?'

'I've been thinking of that too. I've been wondering if it has something to do with Quayle's assassination of bin Laden.'

'The anthrax attack? Do we have any idea if Quayle survived?'

'No, there has been no news other than confirmation by local Pakistani officials in the NW Province that there was a bad outbreak of anthrax centred near a town called Gilgit. It occurred a week after Quayle and his minder left Peshawar.'

'But bin Laden's demise would hardly justify attacking Barbara.'

'Other than one of the excuses the Americans will be using to invade Iraq next year will be to smoke out bin Laden. They may be worried that Barbara would spill the beans and tell the world that he was already dead.'

'So, you want me to travel to Vizille next week and meet her?'

'Can you go? We'll pay your expenses, of course.'

* * *

The *Café du Chateau* lies across the square from the Vizille Chateau, the site in 1788 where the French Revolution was triggered. Peter had flown to Lyon, hired a car and overnighted in nearby Uriage les Bains, a lovely spa village less than ten miles from Vizille. In the warm winter sunshine he was able to sit outside with a coffee and croissant reading the continental edition of *The Daily Telegraph*.

'Where's Phil?' He looked up and there she was, as chic as ever. *Smarter than the smartest French woman,* he thought.

He stood up and they hugged. After the usual pleasantries, Peter began, 'Now what is all this about?'

'You know I bought a house in a quiet village in the Aude, near Carcassonne?'

He nodded, remembering she had bought it many years previously.

'I had been away for several days visiting a friend in Collioure. When I returned, I needed to get a few things in our local *8 à huit*: milk, bread and so on. Over the years I had got to know the proprietor very well. He said, "Two Americans have been asking questions, wanting to know where you live." I asked when and he told me they were staying up the road in the next village, Alaigne. The only place they could be staying there is owned by an Englishman from the Wirral. His wife and he run a small bar, restaurant and hotel with perhaps three or four bedrooms. I often go up there for lunch. I rang him. I told him not to mention it to the Americans and asked him, "What are they like?"'

'And?'

'He told me he didn't like them. "They are big-headed, brash and rude. They both think they can speak French; their vocabulary is good, but their accents are terrible," he said. "They both carry revolvers in sling holsters," he added.

'I asked him how he knew and he told me he hadn't done a short service commission in the Cheshire Regiment for nothing. I knew then they had come to get me. However, I didn't work in our service for thirty years without learning something.'

'Go on.'

'The best way to solve a problem is to ensure you don't have one.'

'Yes, I remember you always believed in forewarned is forearmed.'

'Several years ago, I had a specialist firm of security builders come down from Paris. They put a plated door on the front of the house and an identical door on the inside of the entrance corridor. Both were keyless and operated by a zapper. They effectively made a cell when closed together. They also installed a two-way comms system. I then put a grill in the ceiling between the two doors. About the last thing I did before retiring was to persuade Dr Mike Cochrane at Porton Down to let me have a one-litre cylinder of cyanide gas. I told him it was to poison a hornet's nest. He didn't believe me, but he didn't argue.'

'I think I know what is going to happen next.'

'They came the following morning. Through the intercom I asked them what they wanted. They had the nerve to call me Barbara and said they had been sent by George Tenet to ask me a few questions. I opened the outer door with the zapper and closed it behind them, trapping them between the two doors. I released the gas. They were dead within minutes.'

'And you hid their bodies.'

'That was the hardest bit, putting them into my car. They are in a shallow grave up in the hills beyond La Bezole. No one will ever find them, except perhaps the foxes.'

'When was all this?'

'A few weeks ago. I have now left Belveze permanently and am living in Juan Quayle's apartment in Antibes. If I know my former neighbours in Belveze, they won't notice I am not around for a month or two yet. Meanwhile, I want you to get me the new identity as detailed in my file, with the appropriate documents for myself as Mme Richet and, in case he ever turns up, M Richet for Quayle.'

'Do you think he survived the bin Laden attack?'

'I honestly don't know. However, if he did then he will turn up in Antibes. I helped him buy a property there when he left the Isle of Man after the murder of his family. We agreed then that we would use it as a bolt-hole if we were ever in trouble.'

'OK Barbara, I'll make sure you have all the necessary documents within a few weeks.'

* * *

'I'd like to come and see you immediately, Mr Straw.'

'Why, what's the problem, Phil?'

'It's not the sort of thing we can discuss over the phone.'

'In that case, how about a working lunch in an hour's time? My diary is full until tomorrow. I'll get some sandwiches in.'

* * *

'There are three things, Jack. Firstly, the Americans have made an attempt to assassinate my predecessor, Barbara Renton.'

'What? When?'

'A couple of weeks ago...' The Head of MI6 related the story Barbara had told Peter Stacey. The Foreign Secretary sat transfixed hardly able to believe his ears. 'Consequently, we are implementing RAPS, the Retired Agents Protection Scheme, codenamed *Catalan*. We are giving Barbara a completely new identity. All future contact with her will have to go through Section Sixteen; her pension from now on will be paid into a numbered Swiss Bank Account and so on.'

'I remember her sitting where you are now; she told me how much she was looking forward to retiring near Carcassonne. Thank God she survived the attack. But why would the Americans do it? What threat did she pose?'

'I have discussed this with Peter Stacey and we believe it is tied up with the impending invasion of Iraq next year.'

'I am not so sure it will be next year, Phil. Things are beginning to go awry in Afghanistan. The PM thinks the Americans have bitten off more than they can chew. It may be 2003 before they are ready for Saddam.'

'Well, whenever it is, we believe Barbara was the sort of person who would use her contacts to let it be known that bin Laden is already dead and Saddam had nothing to do with 9/11 nor has he any WMDs.'

'The PM is committed to going along with President Bush and already his press secretary is drafting a case to put to Parliament to support the invasion.'

'But that's preposterous. Is my department not going to be consulted and asked to provide intelligence?'

'I don't know, Phil. I'm only the Foreign Secretary. What goes on in the Cabinet Office is outside my control. So,' he paused to fill his tea cup, 'will Barbara be totally safe with her new ID?'

'I hope so, Minister. As far as I know, we've never lost any previous RAPS. This brings me to the second topic, an agent of ours from Iraq formerly known as Kathab al Jised.'

'Ah, Dr Germ?'

'She has been under RAPS for ten years without any problems but recently the CIA have been trying to discover her whereabouts.'

'Why?'

'Again, Peter and I have a hunch that it may be something to do with the preparations for invading Iraq. Al Jised's stepson is a pathologist at the Leicester Royal Infirmary, called Stuart MacKinnon. There have been two children born at the hospital in the past fifteen months who are pure hexadactyls.'

'What is unusual about a child having six fingers?'

'The odd thing is that these two boys had six fingers on both hands and six toes on both feet. The theoretical chances of it happening are millions to one against. MacKinnon did some digging and discovered that both fathers had been in Iraq at the same time. Both, apparently, had been exposed to a substance called VX-R. It was one of the WMDs given to Iraq by the Americans but, strangely, is not mentioned in The Riegle Report. However, al Jised remembered receiving it as they were only given a small quantity – a mere two litres. She buried it along with all the other biological junk that they were given.'

'So how long has this VX-R been buried?'

'About eighteen years.'

'So what are you trying to say?'

'In trying to find out what VX-R was supposed to do, MacKinnon got his father to ask Peter Stacey if he knew anything about it. Peter had never heard of it and approached Barbara. She, in turn, asked the CIA what they knew. Almost immediately, they sent the Director of their research centre at Fort Detrick, Brigadier Richardson, to see us. He wanted to know how we knew anything about it. There was clearly a panic on. He admitted that the VX-R was given to Iraq to trial. The Americans thought it was a radioactive nerve agent that would work like a death ray and stopped all research on the substance. However, it appears all it does is affect male sperm.'

'Why wasn't it protected by a lead liner?'

'Originally it was, but the two Asians pinched the lead to make a shekel or two and, being exposed to the rays, their sperm was somehow damaged. Usually I believe such exposure would cause infertility. What is even stranger, however, is that both boys died after six months and six weeks.'

'A coincidence surely?'

'Yes, sir, but it is a hell of a one.'

'You've been reading too much Stephen King, Phil. How have the Americans been trying to discover al Jised's whereabouts?'

'Through MacKinnon. They have planted listening devices in his house and his girlfriend's apartment. They put a tracker on his car and kept watch on his home from across the street. It is totally unacceptable behaviour and I have told Lee Hefferman that it must stop. All their bugs have been removed and we believe al Jised's location is still secret. I have made it clear that any further intrusion into either Dr MacKinnon's private affairs or his girlfriend's will be taken up at ambassadorial level. I hope you support my stance.'

'Of course, you were quite right. There was a third thing you wanted to bring up?'

'We will keep an eye on Tariq Aziz as you requested. We will track his hire car and every evening make sure he is safe in his chosen hotel.'

'Excellent. Thanks for letting me know.'

CHAPTER 12

Friday, 7th December 2001

Each day at Britain's major international airports such as Heathrow, Gatwick, Stansted and Manchester, the local Special Branch police check with the car hire companies about their bookings for the following day. Anyone who has a serious criminal record on Interpol files, or is suspected of undesirable political activities has their car fitted with a tracking device. It was, therefore, somewhat different when Sergeant Hobbs approached the receptionist at the Avis desk at Heathrow. 'Hello, Pat, I gather you have a Mr Yuhanna hiring a car tomorrow?'

She checked her list and nodded affirmatively.

'What car is he having?'

'A Vauxhall Astra, registration number TB51NHX. It's already valeted and parked in lot G120.'

She knew Brian Hobbs well, as he was one of several Special Branch officers permanently based at Heathrow. She had worked at the Avis desk for many years and had always found him to be one of the more approachable of the local police. However, this was the first time he had given away the name of someone to be tracked. Usually, the process was conducted more secretively. The officer would glance down the list, take a few notes and disappear. She never asked, but guessed the police had a method of attaching a device without the need for the car keys, *perhaps behind a hub cap*. On this occasion he asked for the keys. She handed them to him with a puzzled expression.

'Don't worry, Pat, I'm not going to steal it. I'll bring the keys back in five minutes.'

Mr Yuhanna must be a VIP, she thought.

* * *

Married Iraqi couples flying into Amman airport from Baghdad are an everyday occurrence. However, Iraqi couples who transfer to a British Airways flight to London with prepared visas are a different matter.

The Israeli secret service, Mossad, has a worldwide network of sayanims. Essentially amateur and part-time, they act as the eyes and ears for the professional Israeli agents. An attendant, and sometime baggage handler, at one of the check-in desks, Araf Ahmad, real name Ariel Finklestein, had worked at the airport for five years. He regularly reported anything he considered unusual to his Mossad handler. That day something struck him as odd; he could have sworn he recognised a passenger from the Baghdad flight. Although sporting a shaved beard and having frameless spectacles, he thought the traveller to London looked remarkably like Tariq Aziz. By the time the BA flight was passing through Italian airspace, Mossad HQ in Tel Aviv had been alerted. A signal to the Head of Mossad in Britain, Simon Rosenberg, was sufficient for him to send an agent, with a hidden camera, to Heathrow to meet the incoming flight.

Mr and Mrs Mikhail Yuhanna picked up their hire car keys from the Avis desk and without any hitches found their Astra in the lot G120. Unknown to them, they were being photographed, complete with their car and its registration number.

The Mossad agent caught the Piccadilly Line train and returned to central London. An hour later, Simon Rosenberg was briefing the Israeli Ambassador that Tariq Aziz and his wife were incognito in the UK. Furious, he picked up his phone and called the Foreign Office, requesting to see Jack Straw as soon as possible.

Meanwhile, Tariq Aziz had driven onto the M25, but almost immediately turned west onto the M3. Near Fleet, he turned off into the service area. 'I'm sorry about this, dear,' he whispered into his wife's ear over the music being played on Classic FM, 'but I have arranged to exchange cars for the duration of our vacation. The British police will have fitted a tracker on this one.'

With the benefit of a pre-arranged signal, two strangers shook hands. 'You know what to do for the next ten days,' Tariq said. 'This is your schedule.' He handed the agent a list of places he was to visit. The bearded man, approximately the same age and build as Tariq, wearing identical glasses, looked at his itinerary: Salisbury, Hereford, St David's at Lampeter, Chester, Lichfield, Lincoln, Norwich, and Canterbury. He was to visit all the major cathedrals in southern Britain.

'You and your partner are to act as tourists. Pay all your bills with this credit card. Should you get asked to show passports, use these.' The receiver glanced at the names and smiled. *Aziz has thought of everything.*

'We will meet here in twelve days' time. Any questions?'

'No, sir.'

* * *

Having been away from London visiting his constituency in Blackburn over the weekend, it was Monday afternoon before Jack Straw could receive the Israeli Ambassador.

'Scholmo, you know as well as I do that if a foreign dignitary comes to Britain as a private citizen with a legal visa, then there is nothing wrong with that. I hear what you say about Iraq still being officially at war with you, but they are hardly a threat to your security. I will record your concern, but am not prepared to give details of his proposed itinerary nor his date of departure. Rest assured, we are keeping a discrete watch on his whereabouts and I warn you not to try and interfere with him in any way. Is that clear?'

'Yes, Minister.' *I wonder if the CIA is aware Aziz is in the UK*, he thought.

* * *

'Lee? It's Simon Rosenberg here. How are you?'

'Fine, Simon. To what do I owe the pleasure?'

'I thought you may be interested to know that Tariq Aziz and his wife entered the country last Saturday on a private visit with the approval of the British Government.'

'You're joking?'

'No, I'm not. Our ambassador saw Jack Straw an hour ago to make a formal protest, but was told in no uncertain terms that it was none of his business.'

'I suppose that if he's here on a limited visa, then there's nothing we can do about it. However, it would be nice to know why he's here. What else do you know?'

'Only that he has an Avis hire car, a grey Vauxhall Astra, registration number TB51NHX.'

'By now, he could be anywhere.'

'I agree, but Aziz must know of your government's intentions to invade Iraq as soon as you have tied up Afghanistan. There has to be a connection, surely?'

'Simon, the preparations that are in hand to invade Iraq must be the world's worst kept secret. I am wondering if this is purely a private visit to see sights that he will never get the chance to see again once the war starts.'

'Aziz's wife is a devout Chaldean Catholic. I can understand her wanting to see Rome, but not Canterbury.'

'Simon, you may have just hit the nail on the head. I'll bet a pound to a penny that they are visiting Christian sights. I am short of men on the ground at the moment. I have been warned off from an operation we were conducting that, ironically, had something to do with Iraq. I daren't upset the apple cart with MI6 but, perhaps, you could use your sayanim network to advantage – get them to watch sights such as Canterbury and York.'

'If we spot him, what good will that do?'

'Let us know at once, it may give us a clue as to what his ulterior motive is for the visit.'

* * *

A week after arriving at Heathrow, Mr and Mrs Yuhanna had seen the great cathedrals of Canterbury, Lincoln, York, and Durham. Sporadic sayanim reports of their being sighted were received, but their accuracy was in doubt when, on the same day, Mr and Mrs Aziz were seen visiting both Chester Cathedral and Lincoln Cathedral at the same time. They had arrived at Edinburgh, shopped in Princes Street and visited the Palace of Holyrood.

'I had planned, dear, to take you to the Orkney Islands tomorrow but have changed my mind; there is some private business I must attend to. I will probably be away for two days; I hope you don't mind? From the tourism brochures I see there is much of interest to see around Edinburgh. I have arranged for you to have a private guide to show you around Melrose Abbey and Rosslyn Chapel tomorrow, and then St Andrews the following day. I will leave early tomorrow morning but should be back the following afternoon. I will ring you tomorrow evening to let you know I'm all right.'

On Monday, 16th December, he left at 7 am and drove north on the A9. He was bypassing Inverness as local traffic was building-up around lunchtime. At a roadside caravan café, he stopped and had a cup of steaming coffee with a bacon sandwich, liberally doused with brown sauce. *Delicious,* he thought. *I am glad I'm not a Muslim and can eat such wonderful, tasty food.*

With the winter sun low in the sky, he was able to marvel at the grandeur of the scenery as he passed Loch Maree. It was almost two o'clock as he entered Badachro. He drove slowly through the village searching for a house called *Glenfinnan,* but couldn't find it. Realising he was about to exit from the village, he stopped to check his map. He turned the car around and retraced his route. He saw a sign pointing to the *Badachro Inn* on the left. He diverted and parked outside. He entered and ordered a large coffee. A helpful barmaid told him he had missed the single track lane on the right-hand side that led to *Glenfinnan.* From the inn's conservatory, she pointed across the bay.

'That's it over there.' She directed his gaze to a small bungalow in the trees.

A few minutes later, he was knocking on a door and heard a dog bark. *Thank God, they're in,* he thought. *If they'd been out, heaven knows what I would have done. This place is miles from anywhere.*

Kate answered the door whilst holding an excited collie back from jumping up on Tariq. She clearly didn't recognise him. His beard, now with a month of growth, hid his otherwise distinguishing features. He bent down and offered the dog the open palm of his right hand. After smelling the remaining odour of the bacon sandwich, the dog proceeded to lick it enthusiastically. Tariq rose to look Kate in the eye. *It is eleven years since I last saw her but she doesn't look a day older.*

Speaking in Arabic, he said, 'Kathab, you don't look any different since I last saw you at the Command Revolutionary Council meeting on 1st December 1990 when you asked Saddam why he wanted to target Israel with Scuds.'

Her face dropped; she screwed her eyes to see through his beard. Then she went pale as she realised who he was. 'Tariq Aziz.' She spluttered his name. Then, 'What the hell are you doing here? How did you find me?'

There was fear in her eyes.

He smiled. In his soft, Assyrian accent, he replied, 'Don't worry. I am alone and will not harm you.' He spread his arms out wide and still smiling said, 'You can search me if you like.'

She remained frozen to the spot. Dumbfounded for several moments, she eventually called back through the kitchen, 'Robbie, come quickly.'

A man appeared behind her and Tariq took this to be James Douglas, the former RAF officer who had helped the ICL team install the war game software used to plan the invasion of Iran in 1978.

'Hello,' Tariq said in English. 'I know this is a shock but my name is Tariq Aziz and I have come to see Kathab. I come in peace and intend no harm to you or your family. I am on my own and have driven up from Edinburgh this morning to see you.'

'I don't trust him, Robbie. There's a catch somewhere.'

'I give you my word; no harm will come from my visit. All I ask is that you hear me out.'

It was Robbie, standing to one side, who said, 'Then you'd better come in.'

Tariq passed through the kitchen and entered the lounge. At the far end, a panoramic window allowed a magnificent view across the bay. He could see the inn from where he had been given instructions by the barmaid. Beyond, in the far distance, the hills were covered in a sprinkling of snow.

Kate had slowly begun to relax. She asked Tariq if he would like a coffee. As she returned to the kitchen, Robbie stood and held out his hand. 'We never met when I was in Iraq. My name is Robbie MacKinnon.'

Tariq smiled. 'Yes, over there we still remember you as James Douglas. I am, as you know, Tariq Aziz, Deputy Prime Minister of Iraq. Coming here alone is highly irregular as I am sure you will appreciate. However, I have a legitimate visitor's visa from your government. My wife and I are Christians and have been visiting the wonderful cathedrals of England for the past week. I have left her in Edinburgh for a couple of days while I come to see Kathab. I am hoping she can help us.'

'Us?'

'Iraq. The Americans are planning to invade next year after they have eliminated the Taliban in Afghanistan. They are claiming we planned the 9/11 attacks and are harbouring and helping to train al-Qaeda terrorists. Neither accusation is true.'

'I am unsure what Kate can do about it.'

'Can do about what?' asked Kate as she entered the room with a tray of coffee.

Tariq began to explain what the problem was and how, if the Americans were to invade and overthrow Saddam's regime, total chaos would ensue.

'It's all very well for Bush to go on about democracy but there isn't a single State in the Middle East, except possibly Israel, where it works; and there it only applies to the Israelis, not the indigenous Palestinians. Syria, Egypt, Libya, Kuwait, Lebanon and Saudi Arabia are all kept under control by strong leadership. We are no different. If the Kurds and southern Shias had their say, then the country would collapse. I am not trying to make out we are perfect. Far from it, but in Iraq women can work and earn the same salaries as men, they don't have to wear the veil, they can inherit their late husband's estate, and there is no compulsory divorce. We have free hospitals and primary schools. All this could change unless we can persuade the Americans that it is too dangerous to invade.'

'So to ask the question again, what can I do about it?'

'You are the only person who can decipher the records that show where you hid the chemical and biological weapons that the Americans gave us during the Iran war. We would ask you to consider the outcome of an invasion: tens of thousands of innocent Iraqis killed, maybe hundreds of thousands, and pit that against the threat we could make if we had some of those weapons that you buried. We are not wanting details of all the sites, just one or two so that we can use them to defend ourselves.'

'You do realise that controlling biological weapons is virtually impossible?' asked Kate.

'Yes, it's far from ideal, but the choice is either to continue Saddam's rule or face the hell of a government run by a corrupt DAWA Shia clique, most of whom are currently sheltering in the West or Iran.'

Kate looked at her husband. 'I don't know, what do you think?'

Robbie looked at his wife. 'A week ago, I would have said forget it. Now I'm not so sure.'

He turned to Tariq to explain, 'The Americans have been hounding my son and his fiancée, bugging their apartments and putting trackers on their cars.'

'What for?'

'We believe they are trying to find Kate for the same reason as you. They know your country has still got the biological weapons they gave you between 1981 and 1988. They either want to destroy them before next year's invasion or at the beginning of it. They realise the only way they can ever find them is by getting Kate to reveal their location.'

'My God, I'm sorry. I had no idea. Presumably, they haven't been able to find you?'

'No, and I doubt if they ever will unless they are extremely lucky. Do you think they know you are in the country?'

'Not as far as I'm aware. I'm sure I wasn't followed.'

There was silence in the room as the three looked at each other. Kate glared at Tariq, her eyes alight with fire, her face passive with determination and concentration as she thought through the consequences of his proposal.

'If I was to help you, there would have to be stringent conditions.'

Both men stared at Kate.

CHAPTER 13

Monday, 17th December 2001

'For a start, there's my security. What's to stop you killing me after I've shown you where the sites are?'

'You have my word...'

'Sorry,' interrupted Robbie. 'No offence, but that is hardly a guarantee when you still have hotheads around like Chemical Ali. Besides,' he turned to look at his wife, 'there's no way you are going.'

Kate frowned. 'Why not? I'm the only one who can decipher the records.'

'We're not going to discuss this. You've forgotten it was me who taught you how to use the chess method. I insist I go. Furthermore, there would have to be a quid pro quo.'

'A what?' asked Tariq.

'An exchange. I meet you in, say, Paris. And someone precious to Saddam comes back with Kate to Scotland.'

'Such as?' asked Kate, puzzled.

'I don't know... say Mrs Hussein and their youngest daughter... and it won't do to try any trickery. We have both seen Mrs Hussein when we were in Samarra and would recognise a doppelganger.'

'I'm unsure whether Saddam would agree.'

'Then, it's no deal,' added Kate, 'and there's another thing.'

'Oh, what?'

'Robbie will take you to an early site where, if I remember, there were several gallons of anthrax spores, a lot of tabun, and a small bottle of something labelled VX-R. He will bring back the VX-R.'

'What is VX-R?' asked Tariq.

'It's a defoliant, rather like Agent Orange in the Vietnam War, but it's radioactive and emits rays that destroy a plant's photosynthesis. I have been carrying out research at the gardens at Inverewe where I work and would like to understand more about it. It would be of no use to you.'

My God, what the hell is she talking about? thought Robbie, trying not to look surprised.

'I can't see a problem with that,' replied the Deputy Prime Minister.

'There's another thing,' added Robbie.

'Go on.'

'When I'm out there showing you where the weapons are located, I insist I am accompanied by someone I know and can trust.'

'Who?'

'Azi Tumbrah.'

'Lieutenant General Azi Tumbrah?'

'Yes, I assume he's still alive.'

'Of course, he's our number two in the Air Force. How do you know him?'

'Kate and I worked closely with him, firstly at Reading when we were enhancing Nastia Game, and secondly when I helped implement the war game at Al-Rashid in 1978.'

'Fine, I'm sure that will be OK too.'

'Then, it only remains to arrange a date to make the exchange in Paris,' said Kate.

'I'll have to clear it with Saddam, of course, but I think he will agree to your demands. We have a couple of agents who live in London and work undercover for us. If I give you one of their mobile telephone numbers, you could ring them early in the New Year. By then we should be able to offer you alternative dates. Incidentally, what will you do with Saddam's wife when she is with you?'

'I'll be polite and show her the respect she would expect from being the President's wife. Now, are you planning to drive all the way back to Edinburgh this evening in the dark? You are welcome to stay here if you wish and leave in the morning. Perhaps, we can catch up on what has been happening at home since I left.'

'In that case, I insist I take you both for a meal to the inn down the road. It looked a most agreeable place when I dropped in earlier.'

The evening passed pleasantly as the two Iraqis put the world to rights. However, as all three began to relax, Kate couldn't resist asking the question that had been nagging her since Tariq's unexpected arrival. 'How did you find me?'

'Needs must when the devil drives. I knew of the attempt by Ali Hassan's hit man and how he used exiton to extract your address from Mrs Platini. I am sincerely sorry that he administered too much of the truth serum and she died. But I thank God you survived Arif Rashid's attack. You'll be delighted to know, your escape still rankles Ali, by the way.' He paused to watch a satisfied smile appear on Kate's face. 'I realised that the best chance of finding you lay with Group Captain Platini having your location in his address book. I sent our best policeman to England. He watched the Group Captain's movements for several days. Having established a pattern, he was able to enter his house without leaving a trace when Platini left for work. He found the book and came back to Baghdad with your address.'

'That makes sense,' remarked Robbie. 'We still get a Christmas card from Gerry every year.'

Tariq smiled inwardly, remembering the dig made at him by Sahib al-Majid during the Command Revolutionary Council meeting.

'Who else knows of our address?' demanded Kate.

'I can assure you, no one else. Now, can I ask you a question?'

'Go on,' replied Kate.

'What happened to Arif and his car?'

'He had an accident when his car went over a cliff.'

Tariq chuckled, nodded his head and said quietly, 'Excellent.'

Conversation moved on, but Robbie was left wondering why Kate wanted the VX-R. He knew her well enough to wait until the morning when Tariq would have left. Even then he had doubts as to whether he would get to the bottom of her plans.

At one point, Osama bin Laden's name was mentioned. 'Why did he fall out with Saddam?' asked Robbie.

'Saddam, believe it or not, never trusted him. Saddam's long-term ambition is, and always has been, to be the leader of the Arab world. He saw harbouring bin Laden as contrary to his plans. Besides, bin Laden was always demanding funds and as you know, ever since the Kuwait affair, we have been strapped for cash. Anyway, bin Laden was assassinated three months ago by the British Secret Service.'

Robbie and Kate stared at each other in surprise. 'We didn't know that,' Robbie exclaimed. 'There's been no mention of it in the press.'

'It's in America's interests to keep it quiet. Bin Laden is one of the excuses they're going to use to invade us, after all.'

Flesh was then put on the plans to exchange the Husseins – Amsterdam rather than Paris and Kate drew a sketch of the container she wanted to transport the VX-R back to the UK.

* * *

The following morning, after Tariq had left, Robbie broached the subject that had been eating him all night. 'Why do you want me to bring back the VX-R?' he asked.

'It is because of your son that we are in this mess,' she replied sharply.

'That's a bit unfair.'

'Yes,' she said slowly regretting her cutting reply, 'I suppose it is. However, I thought he may be able to do some experimental work at his hospital laboratory to find out what exactly is causing hexadactylism.'

'Is that the real reason? Your excuse that it is a plant defoliant was very clever.'

She smiled coyly, but didn't reply.

'I've been thinking overnight that we'd better tell Peter Stacey that Tariq has paid us a visit, don't you?' asked Robbie.

'Yes, I suppose you're right, but don't mention the VX-R,' insisted Kate.

Robbie had enough faith in his wife to know there was method in her madness. He would push her no further.

He picked up the phone and dialled the number that he had used so often recently. 'Peter? It's Robbie. I thought you ought to know that we've had a visit from Tariq Aziz, no less.'

There was an incredulous gasp. 'What? You are joking?'

'No, he stayed with us for the night and left about an hour ago to return to Edinburgh.'

'What did he want?'

Robbie related the events of the previous afternoon and evening, omitting reference to the VX-R but explaining how he would be going to Baghdad in exchange for Saddam's wife and daughter.

'Now hang on a minute, Robbie. This is daft. Letting Saddam have some of the CB weapons that Kate hid all those years ago would be to undo all her good work.'

'We lay awake all night thinking about it, Peter. We are not planning to give away the locations of all the sites, two at the most. The weapons they acquire as a consequence should be sufficient, hopefully, to deter the American invasion.'

'Nothing will deter Bush, Robbie; you know that. He's crazy and sees himself on a mission to bring democracy to the Middle East.'

'There was one other gem Tariq dropped into the conversation.'

'Oh, what was that?'

'He claimed MI6 murdered Osama bin Laden.'

'He said that?'

'Yes; is it true?'

'You know I can't answer that, but let's just say there has been a rumour to that effect. But until a body is produced, there can be no proof.'

* * *

'I believe you wanted to see me privately, Tariq. What news do you have from your trip to Scotland?'

'Apart from it being cold, wet, and windy?'

Saddam stared blankly. An impatient man at the best of times, Tariq thought he had better continue quickly and answer his question.

'I joke, Mr President. Al Jised has laid down certain conditions.'

'Cheeky cow! What does she want?'

'Firstly, a guarantee of safety; she will not come to Iraq herself. Instead her husband, the former Squadron Leader James Douglas, will come on her behalf. MI6 has given him a new identity, Robbie MacKinnon. I believe you once met him?'

'Did I?'

'At the refurbishment of the Caliph's Palace in Samarra in 1978.'

'God, was it that long ago?' He sank into a deep muse and looked depressed. 'So much has happened in the intervening twenty-three years,' he remarked quietly, as if talking to himself.

'MacKinnon knows the chess position that was used for the early shipments. He will lead us to just two sites where the key will unlock the location. As a quid pro quo for his safe return, you are to send your wife and youngest daughter, Hala, to stay with al Jised, now Mrs MacKinnon.'

Saddam's eyes narrowed. Although used to his erratic swings of moods, Tariq could sense foreboding creeping up his spine. Saddam was all powerful in Iraq and ruled with a steel fist. Tariq knew his position as Foreign Secretary was secure; no one else possessed his exceptional diplomatic skills and had his contacts outside Iraq. However, he could see his President was not pleased at being dictated to by a former traitor and he remained frozen while Saddam chewed over the ultimatum that had been given to him.

'Where is the exchange to take place?'

'Initially MacKinnon suggested Paris, but I have suggested Amsterdam as flights through Moscow would be easier and safer.'

'What else does the bitch want?'

'At one of the sites we will excavate, there will be a two-litre bottle, marked VX-R. She wants her husband to bring it back with him. However, we are to provide a lead lined box for him to get it past customs when he returns to Britain via Rotterdam and Hull by car. Apparently it is radioactive. She has even given me a sketch of the box she wants with its dimensions.'

'What does she want this VX-R for? I am not happy about it. I don't mind getting rid of my wife for a few weeks, even if I have to buy her some new clothes.' He laughed at his own joke. Even Tariq could see the funny side and smiled appropriately. 'Surely VX is a nerve agent; we may need it ourselves.'

'I asked her why she wanted it. She tells me it's a defoliant; a bit like Agent Orange was in Vietnam. The VX-R radiates rays that kill plants by stopping their chlorophyll from converting sunlight into energy. The process of photosynthesis is halted and the plants die. In Scotland, al Jised works at a nearby garden, of international repute, called Inverewe. She wants to analyse the substance as part of her research.'

'So we may be glad to get shot of it?'

'Yes, I would have thought so.'

'And when am I to get rid of my wife?'

'I have suggested when the weather gets better; perhaps, the beginning of April.'

'Fine, although I am not happy about letting Hala go.'

'The trip could be good for her education,' said Tariq hopefully.

'I suppose it can't do her any harm. How do you propose they slip into Britain unnoticed?'

'As I've said, they will fly to Amsterdam via Moscow; they will then travel via Brussels to London on the Eurostar. Al Jised has agreed to draw up an agenda for them to see the sights in London before taking them to Scotland. I have agreed we will pay for their expenses, if that's OK?'

'Fine, get on with the arrangements. But make sure we have men in place following them the whole time. I don't trust al Jised; she duped us before. It mustn't happen again. Anything else I should know?'

'MacKinnon wants Lieutenant General Tumbrah to accompany him at all times.'

'Why?'

'He thinks he can trust him.'

Saddam smiled, 'I suppose it's one way of guaranteeing keeping Ali Hassan off his back.'

* * *

It was Christmas Eve, a Monday, and the weather was cold but the sky – a pale blue. The sea reflected the overhead brilliance as a blanket of azure silk. The winter sun sparkled on the crests of the choppy waves beginning to be whipped up by a storm far out to sea. It had been almost two months since the Americans' attempt to assassinate Barbara that had forced her to depart Belveze.

She was slowly settling into Antibes. The Cote d'Azur was much more cosmopolitan, the pace of life more hectic. Barbara felt lonely in Juan's apartment in Rue Albert 1st. She would frequently wander to the gardens at the bottom of the rue, meander west along the bay towards the Cap d'Antibes and find somewhere for lunch. But eating alone, even in a delightful setting, was no fun. Melancholia would set in; the short-term despondency was alleviated by drinking too much – an aperitif, a full bottle of wine and a cognac – but it made matters worse when the effects had worn off.

Peter Stacey had been good to his word. The documents had arrived showing her to be Mme Barbara Richet, wife of Juan Richet. She had all the necessary certificates to satisfy French bureaucracy: national identity cards, driving licences, birth certificates, a marriage certificate, even death certificates of Juan's and her own imaginary parents. The necessary paraphernalia for modern life would pass any inspection by officials, but the documentation's arrival had disturbed her. It was against her effervescent personality to be depressed for long and the papers had made her think about Juan.

Was he alive? What happened after he released the anthrax spores? If he died, where would his body be?

She remembered all those years ago when he had proposed to her and she had rejected him. 'Go and find a younger woman and raise a family,' she had said. She had hurt him. She had pretended that she had spurned his offer as some sort of self-sacrifice; an altruistic, idealistic principle just because she was ten years older. She now realised she was wrong. She had been totally selfish, wanting to continue her free-living

113

lifestyle where she had complete control over the men in her life. She could change them whenever she wished. Her melancholy worsened as she thought how she had encouraged Juan to become the Middle East journalist writing anti-Israeli articles to gain favour with al Qaeda; how she had planted a Mossad agent to watch him and how she had engineered him being shot at Bil'sallin Farm.

Tomorrow would be Christmas Day and she would be alone. She sank to the depths of despair and thought about whether it would be feasible to travel to Pakistan to find Juan.

Pull yourself together, Barbara. Go and do your shopping. Visit the hairdresser. Get off your ass and do something.

CHAPTER 14

Thursday, 10th January 2002

'I've brought you all together so that you are up to speed with the latest developments regarding the hunt to find the former Iraqi research scientist, Kathab al Jised,' announced Lee Hefferman to his team.

'Several things have occurred since last October when I was called to see the Head of MI6, Phil Jay, and was told to call off the search. I agreed in order to prevent Jay raising the matter to ambassadorial level. The consequences of that could have led to some of us being expelled from Britain. As you know, I then put everything on the back burner. Nevertheless, the President's order for us to retrieve the VX-R from Iraq remains extant and al Jised is the only person who knows where it is. It was unfortunate that things turned out the way they did. Had al Jised's stepson, the pathologist MacKinnon, not visited his former next door neighbour in Weston-super-Mare and discovered we had been making enquiries, then everything may have worked out successfully. Sadly MI6 was alerted to our intentions and blew our operation. However, George Tenet has confirmed that, although we must keep the Brits on our side, we must keep looking for al Jised. We must, therefore, play our cards closer to our chests. Also, just so as you know, our efforts in the Isle of Skye, Fort William and Perth to discover a likely MacKinnon family came to nothing except to eliminate several hundred possibilities. Again, we were unlucky; one of the families we approached happened to be a senior police officer who contacted New Scotland Yard Special Branch to find out what was going on.'

He paused and took a sip of water. 'Now, on what appears to be a separate tack, but is related. When President Bush was discussing with Prime Minister Blair the consequences of 9/11, the name of Barbara Renton cropped up. She was the Head of MI6 who took early retirement at the end of September. She had convinced Blair that Osama bin Laden was dead, that Saddam was not responsible for the 9/11 attacks and that he has no idea where his weapons of mass destruction are because al Jised made such a good job of hiding them. I'm sure you see where this is leading.'

He paused. 'The case we will be presenting to the United Nations Security Council for the liberation of Iraq is based exactly on those three assertions: to capture bin Laden, destroy al-Qaeda's training camps and make the world safer by neutralising the WMDs. The President is worried that Renton cannot be allowed to spill the beans to the international press before we invade Iraq. On President Bush's instructions, Director Tenet implemented an operation to remove Renton last November and sent two french-speaking agents to the South of France to find her. They never came back and have not been heard from since. The Director is now convinced that Renton survived. She has disappeared and discreet enquiries by my opposite number in Paris have revealed nothing.'

He took another sip of water. 'Next is the mystery of Tariq Aziz's visit to this country last month. The question I had to ask myself was, "Why now?" We used our friends in Mossad to follow him. Unfortunately, we did not know his itinerary for the duration of his stay here. Sayanims picked up sightings of him at Chester, Lincoln and Canterbury Cathedrals. He and his wife are Chaldean Catholics so their trip may have been innocent; simply to visit religious sites, but I have my doubts. Could he have had an ulterior motive? If so, what? Any ideas?'

He looked at his audience.

'What if he somehow knew the whereabouts of al Jised?' It was Ruth who spoke. She was by far the most intelligent member of Lee's team.

'But how could he have known and, if he did, why visit her now?'

Ruth was looking him in the eye but her face was blank. Lee knew her brain was working overtime to find a plausible answer.

'The Iraqis know we are planning to invade next year. Up to recently we have not been a threat to them, hence the answer to "Why now?" Somehow they found her address and sent their most reasonable and personable ambassador to coax her into helping them retrieve their WMDs.'

'But would she help them? We believe the Iraqis tried to assassinate her at one time but failed. They're hardly going to be flavour of the month.'

'I don't suppose we are either,' added Ruth.

'Why's that?'

'You told us that we were responsible for her husband's first wife's death.'

'True...'

'I think we're missing a trick. There's something we've overlooked. The Iraqis found al Jised the first time when they tried to assassinate her. How? There must be a weak link in a chain between her and someone in the UK. When did they try to kill her? Can we do some background research? Someone in our organisation must know something? It was presumably sometime after *Desert Storm* in 1991.'

'That's eleven years ago. No one here was in London then,' replied Hefferman.

A joker at the back was heard to remark, 'I was still in sixth grade.'

'There maybe something in our archives downstairs, but I doubt it,' added Ruth.

Lee agreed. 'I'll make contact with Langley and find out who was here between 1991 and 1992.'

He took another sip of water.

'So, what other possibilities are left?' he continued. 'The two doctors have got engaged. They are both thirty-somethings; so the chances are they may get married sooner, rather than later. If they choose the bride's home village and a church wedding, then banns will have to be read. I want a volunteer to attend services at Boothby Graffoe Church on a regular basis. Alternatively, they could have a registry office wedding, probably in Leicester. Again, we will have to be vigilant. I want a volunteer to move to Leicester and get a job in the hospital as a porter. Porters in a hospital tend to be peripatetic. They work in a lot of departments and get to know many people at grass-roots level. If I know nurses, the hospital will be awash with the news of their engagement and rumours will soon spread as to when they will be getting married. It's ninety-nine per cent certain that al Jised will attend her stepson's wedding. Any questions?'

* * *

'Have you discussed the wedding with your parents?' asked Stuart.

'I know you're not too keen, but they would like us to be married in our village church. It's where my sister and I were baptised and confirmed.'

'That's OK. Have you told them that we don't want it to be too big?'

'You know Mum. It's a chance for her to show off a new dress to her friends. I can't see it being any less than forty or fifty guests. Will Robbie and Kate come?'

'Of course. They will want some of their friends to come too: Doc Macdonald and his wife, George Young and his wife… no more than ten, I would have thought.'

'So I can tell Dad that there may be up to sixty guests?'

'Yes, I would have thought so.'

'Who will be your best man?'

'I've been thinking of that. I guess my old school buddy, Jim Murray, would be the best. I was his best man when he got married to Fiona immediately after we graduated at Edinburgh. He's a GP in the Orkneys.'

'It's a long way for him to come.'

'It's the reason I don't see him very often!'

'Are we still looking at late March for the date?'

'The best day for guests would be a Saturday, so it's either the 23rd or the 30th I guess.'

'The 30th is Easter weekend; I can't see our vicar being able to do it then. Can you?'

'No I suppose not. Maybe the following weekend, April 6th, would be better; the weather could be warmer too.'

'That's about three months away, so I'll get Dad to book the date.'

* * *

The biannual meeting of the international working group on al-Qaeda was being hosted by the French. A quiet location was always chosen, usually a hotel where companies regularly held training courses. To the casual observer this get-together appeared no different; particularly as in the foyer the notice welcomed *'Le Côntrole Data Organisation de Paris'*.

Presumably yet another boring computer software company, thought the receptionist as she entered the title of the meeting on the daily-updated board.

The *Hôtel Mercure* in Blois was strategically placed overlooking the River Loire, a few minutes' walk from the town centre and only two hours from Paris.

The security services attendees were the Indian NSG represented by General Gobal Rao, the German MAD represented by General Gunter Werner and the Israeli Mossad represented by Simon Rosenberg. Phil Jay, as Head of MI6, was attending for the first time since taking over from Barbara Renton. The Chairman, Jean-Claude Chastain, Head of the French DGSE, in his opening remarks welcomed Phil and asked that the minutes record the committee's thanks to Barbara, wishing her happiness in her retirement.

Acknowledging the welcome, Phil noted their thanks but felt somewhat embarrassed as he knew that the others present knew nothing of the attempted assassination in Belveze.

The meetings' agendas always had the same structure: each delegate would give a report on developments over the past six months within their sphere of influence. Phil was to give the second report.

'Gentlemen,' he began, 'you will remember it is almost ten years since Barbara Renton's predecessor, Sir Peter Stacey, set up this committee as a consequence of one of our agents returning successfully from undercover work inside al-Qaeda. The same agent subsequently volunteered to mount an attempt to assassinate Osama bin Laden. Five years ago, after extensive training, he was sent to Lebanon posing as *The Daily Telegraph's* Middle East correspondent, using the name of John Pearson. Such journalists always need a local man on the ground to help them make contacts. Unknown to our man, Mrs Renton and Simon here,' he paused to nod at Simon, 'had agreed Pearson's local gofer should be a member of Mossad. With established and secure lines of communications, the aide, ostensibly his photographer, was able to keep both Simon and ourselves in the picture; if you'll excuse the pun.' He paused to see if there was a reaction to his flippant remark; there was none.

He continued, making a mental note not to stretch his audience's grasp of the English language. 'In late August, last year, Pearson and his helper were invited to interview bin Laden somewhere in North-West Pakistan. They were picked up from their hotel in Peshawar on Tuesday, 4th September. We have heard nothing from them since. However, we believe the attack was successful, but Pearson and his assistant perished in the operation.'

From their body language, it was clear that, apart from Simon, none of the others knew of the plan, although the Indian representative, whose face was always inscrutable, seemed less surprised than the others. It was the Chairman who asked, 'What makes you think they killed bin Laden when we all saw him bragging on al Jazeera TV after the Twin Towers attack?'

Phil looked at Simon. 'Shall I explain, or will you?'

Simon's gesture, showing the open palm of his hand, was a sufficient response.

'I'll answer your question Mr Chairman in three parts. First of all, the weapon used was anthrax. Our man's shoes had hollow heels and soles, like a famous brand of trainers. The space was filled with anthrax spores under pressure. Each shoe had a hidden button that when pressed would release the spores into the atmosphere during the interview with bin Laden.'

'But everyone in the room would die. It was a suicide mission?' asked Jean-Claude.

'Yes. Our man knew that.'

'But I didn't.' It was Simon Rosenberg who interrupted. 'I knew the operation was risky, of course, but I'm not sure I would have given the go-ahead had I known the choice of weapon.'

'If I can explain,' continued Phil apologetically. 'The idea was that both our men would receive a vaccination of Biothrax. However, they left Lebanon in such a hurry that this could not be arranged. There was a bad outbreak of anthrax in late September around Gilgit, in the Kashmiri district of North-East Pakistan. So severe was the problem that a specialist veterinary officer from our Ministry of Agriculture was invited by the Pakistan Government to assist and give advice. He helped the Pakistanis contain the spread of the outbreak and returned to the UK with a sample of the anthrax. Analysis showed it was Vollum 1-B, the most virulent of the eighty-nine strains of anthrax and identical to that used in the attack.'

'But that doesn't prove bin Laden died,' observed General Rao. 'And, incidentally, India does not recognise Pakistan's rights to North-West Kashmir.'

'I accept both of your points. However, until a body is produced, we will never know one hundred per cent if bin Laden is dead.' Phil paused and then moved on. 'The second part of my assertion is that bin Laden's TV appearance after 9/11 was pre-recorded. You will remember that bin Laden neither mentioned the Twin Towers falling, nor did he mention the numbers killed. He merely bragged about the attack and that he could outwit the Americans. Analysis suggests the tape may be one of several that had been produced in advance to be shown after future al-Qaeda attacks.

'You said there were three parts to your claim,' reminded the Chairman.

'On the 15th September, perhaps one week after Pearson interviewed bin Laden, an obituary appeared in the *Gilgit Gazette* for someone called Moab al Saidenn.

'We know this was one of several aliases used by bin Laden. It mentioned a sudden illness and that he died on 12th September. The timing would be right as the inhalation of anthrax spores takes three or four days to kill. Then last December, the reputable Egyptian daily, *Al Wafd*, also announced al Saidenn's death due to sudden serious breathing problems the previous September.'

He stopped and the Chairman asked the others if they had any questions. There were none.

He would have liked to announce that the Iraqis believed bin Laden was dead too, but this would have upset a tin of worms about Tariq Aziz's visit to the UK before Christmas. He didn't want to go there, so kept quiet and the next delegate, General Rao, began his report.

Unexpectedly, Rao confirmed the anthrax outbreak in northern Pakistan, but again referred to the area as 'the disputed province of Kashmir'. He confirmed the disease had been 'particularly virulent' but had not appreciated it could have been 'part of a scheme' to eliminate bin Laden. However, his plant inside the Pakistan ISI had heard rumours to the effect that 'bin Laden and half a dozen of his followers had perished'.

'We will never find his body,' he added, 'but I am leaning towards the same conclusion as my colleague from the United Kingdom.'

Something was telling Phil Jay that the General knew more than he was letting on and wondered if any of the others detected his duplicity.

CHAPTER 15

Friday, 11 January 2002

Kate used the mobile number given to her by Tariq to contact the Iraqi 'sleepers' and explain that 'due to unforeseen circumstances' the arrangements for Mrs Hussein to visit the UK in exchange for her husband to go to Iraq would either have to be brought forward to 18th March or else wait until May when the weather would be better.

After consultation in Baghdad, it was agreed that Monday, 13th May was acceptable and detailed arrangements would be drawn up. The exchange would occur at Schiphol Airport, Amsterdam. A certain *Mrs Sajida Talfah* and her daughter would fly in from Moscow, accompanied by a *Mr Azi Talfah*, alias Azi Tumbrah. Kate and Robbie would fly from Edinburgh. Kate would accompany Sajida and Hala to Rotterdam by train. They would sail overnight to Hull. There, a train would take them to York. Then they would catch the main East Coast Line to Edinburgh, pick up the car left at the airport and drive to the north-west highlands. Meanwhile Robbie and Azi would return to Baghdad via Moscow. A week later, on Monday 20th, the reverse would occur.

'I think that you should hire a car at Schiphol and, instead of bringing Saddam's wife back to Britain, you take them to Switzerland or southern Germany,' suggested Robbie.

'You're saying you don't trust them?' asked Kate.

'Something like that. If the Iraqis don't know where you are, then they can't do anything silly.'

Kate agreed, although she appeared more excited at making

preparations for Stuart's wedding. Robbie had bought a small sports car the previous year and saw the wedding as an opportunity to 'give it a spin'.

'After the wedding, let's go for a holiday in the MX-5,' he had remarked.

'Where to?'

'I thought the South of France; you will be able to stock up on your favourite perfume. Four or five days to get down there, a week there, and four or five days to get back will give us plenty of time for me to prepare to go to Baghdad.'

'A great idea,' she enthused.

* * *

'Ruth, I've a little job for you.'

'Go on,'

'Langley has done some digging and come up with some useful info. When al Jised was recruited to work for the Brits prior to the Iraq-Iran war, the British Air Attaché in Baghdad was someone called Wing Commander Platini. Langley believes al Jised was friendly with the Platinis and she may have kept in touch with them when she was brought back to the UK during *Desert Storm*. It's a long shot, but I'd like you to delve a bit further. Find out where Platini lives; go and see him. Find out if he is sympathetic to our plans for Iraq and whether he knows al Jised's address.'

A week later, Ruth reported back to her boss.

'Finding Platini was easy, he lives in a village just off the A1 near Grantham. He's retired from the RAF but works in the local college part-time. I did some delving; did you know his wife was murdered?'

'No, I didn't. How?'

'Eleven years ago, she was found tied up in a chair apparently having died from a heart attack. However, the pathologist at the inquest admitted to being puzzled because Mrs Platini was fit and healthy and he suspected an unknown drug had been administered to her.'

'Was anyone ever caught?'

'No and that's what makes it so intriguing. I can't find out anything about the investigation. It has all the hallmarks of a cover-up.'

'You mean the Security Services were somehow involved?'

'Yes, and it will mean Platini is not going to be cooperative. Pushing him may do more harm than good.'

'OK, in that case, we're going to have to hope al Jised turns up at her stepson's wedding.'

'Do we know any more about that yet?'

'Harry, who is under cover in Leicester, has found out that it's to be on Saturday, 6th April, near Lincoln. We'll be there waiting.'

* * *

The wedding was at two o'clock in Boothby Graffoe's village church. Robbie and Kate had left Badachro early the previous day and travelled as far south as Harrogate. Heading down the A1 the following morning, they bypassed Leeds and Kate was reminded of her visit to the Leeds General Infirmary in May 1991 to try and find her sister, Lina – a consultant neurologist.

Kate had been shocked to discover that Lina had married a psychiatrist and was living in New Zealand. Kate had visited her sister and husband once in the intervening years and began wondering how her sister would be coping as the recent mother of twin boys. The memories were made more poignant by knowing that she and Robbie would spend the night in Grantham, near Colsterworth. It was there that she had stayed two nights with Gerry and Sally Platini and where she had discovered that Robbie was living in Badachro.

A chance remark over dinner that I resembled Queen Soraya changed my life, she thought.

They had invited Gerry to the wedding but agreed they would not reveal that his house had been broken into by Tariq Aziz's policeman to get their address. Kate was looking forward to seeing him again after eleven years. However, she was unsure as to how she should broach the subject of Sally's murder. *It's because of me that she was killed. God, what will I say to him?* She fell quiet for the rest of the journey, getting more and more despondent as they neared Grantham.

Robbie had planned the journey to give them sufficient time that morning for him to show Kate the RAF College at Cranwell, where he had served as a junior officer and Stuart had spent the first three years of his life. The elegant splendour of the college and grounds deepened Kate's blues as it reminded her of the Military Staff College at Al-Rashid where Robbie had implemented the computer war game in 1978. It was whilst he was there that their friendship had become intimate. Fortunately, Robbie didn't appear to notice her low spirits.

Afterwards they drove to their overnight hotel, *The Angel*, in Grantham where they had arranged to book in early and change for the wedding. Kate had designed her own dress and had it made locally in Gairloch from a lightweight material. Predominantly of dark olive-green and tied at the waist with a broad purple belt, it exaggerated her fine figure. It was similar to the dress she had worn when Robbie had met her at the 4th July celebrations in Baghdad twenty-five years previously. Although now almost fifty-two years of age, she still had a firm, slim figure that caught admiring glances from both women and men.

In that dress, there will be no one at the reception looking better than you, thought Robbie as they climbed into their sports car to drive to Boothby Graffoe, some eighteen miles away.

The reception, after the service, was being held in a marquee in the grounds of Judy's parents' home, adjacent to the church. At the celebrations, Kate and Robbie met Judy's parents for the first time. The MacKinnons were standing in a group with Peter and Jennie Stacey, Dr Macdonald and Sandra, his wife, and Gerry Platini when Bernard and Laura Wade joined them.

'You couldn't have chosen a better day for the wedding,' remarked Robbie to his new in-laws. 'This rear lawn of yours has a wonderful setting, facing as it does the west and overlooking the Trent valley.'

'Yes, we found this house thirty-five years ago. Laura fell in love with it immediately. I had some doubts with it being next to the village churchyard, but we've never seen any ghosts wandering around.'

'The garden must extend to about an acre; a similar size to our patch in Scotland.'

'Yes, spot on. But, if you don't mind me saying so Robbie, I was expecting someone with a highland name like MacKinnon to have an appropriate accent. You're not from Scotland? You've got a slight Manx accent, if I'm not mistaken. '

Robbie laughed and, without thinking, admitted to having lived most of his formative years on the Isle of Man. 'I was educated there as a youngster when my father was a lighthouse keeper.' This was totally untrue, but he had told this tale so often that he had begun to believe it himself.

Bernard explained. 'I spent five or six years in Douglas before I met Jill. I worked for the Midland Bank in those days and was in a small team that set-up the offshore facility there. You've kept the trace of a Manx drawl.'

'You must be quite a phonologist, as I haven't lived there since going to university,' Robbie replied.

Laura chuckled and admitted that her husband had a keen ear. Recognising dialects was one of his hobbies.

This acted as a red rag to a bull.

It was Peter who challenged Bernard. 'I'll bet you can't guess my background.'

'I would say north Somerset, somewhere near Bath.'

'Incredible, spot on.'

It was Jennie's turn. 'Where am I from?' she asked.

'To give me a chance, just read this passage.' He pulled a small card from his inside pocket.

'This is the party trick,' laughed Laura.

Jennie, always conscious of her appearance, somewhat embarrassingly had to don her reading glasses if she was to accept the challenge. She need not have feared, however, as she instantly recognised the six lines as being from Prospero's final speech in The Tempest.

Now my charms are all overthrown,
And what strength I have's mine own,
Which is most faint: now 'tis true,
I must be here confined by you.
As you from crimes would pardoned be,
Let your indulgence set me free.

After reading the passage, she proudly declared, 'I learnt that speech at school; it's from The Tempest.'

'Quite right, Jennie, and spoken like an educated person from North Yorkshire.'

Her face dropped. She thought years of living abroad with Peter and mixing with the smart set in Wiltshire had forever drowned the clue to her northern roots. 'Harrogate, actually,' she admitted quietly.

'Dr Macdonald, you are clearly a pure bred highlander, but you, Kate, are not. I detect you have been taught BBC English as a second language and it has softened over many years to become similar to the doctor's.'

'Judy has already told you Kate was originally from Iraq,' interrupted Robbie.

Bernard giggled. 'Yes, I am showing off. Please forgive me.'

After a few moments of silence, as they supped their drinks, Bernard continued, 'I've always found accents interesting. Here in Lincolnshire, there is quite a difference between those living in East Lindsey and those living around here in Kesteven. The two boroughs are side by side and the locals may only be twenty or thirty miles apart, yet sound different.'

Peter added an observation. 'I have known Robbie for over twenty-three years and hadn't noticed his dialect before. But now you've mentioned it, I can hear a similar accent from another Manxman I know.'

Robbie looked at him and had to ask the obvious question. 'Oh, who's that? I might know him.'

'His name was Juan Quayle.'

'A good Manx name. You said "was". Is he dead?'

'I don't know what happened to him; it was many years ago when I knew him.' Peter was regretting bringing up Quayle's name.

Conversation moved on and Bernard, having been briefed on his in-laws background by Judy, as far as she knew it, picked up on Robbie's time in the RAF. 'Did you ever serve up the road at RAF Waddington?'

'No, but I was at Cranwell for three years on the staff as a junior officer. Stuart spent his early childhood there. My first wife and I had a house in Ruskington.'

Unsure whether he should ask further questions about Robbie's family and his first wife, Bernard moved on. 'I see you came down from Scotland in that little red Mazda MX-5. I have admired them for some time. Do you like it?'

'Kate and I are off to France in it tomorrow. We thought since we were so far south,' he paused to smile at his Gairloch friends, 'that we might as well make the most of it. Up at home, we have a 4x4 for most of our day-to-day needs. This trip will give her a good run.'

'Where are you going?'

'We will head for the Côte d'Azur, nowhere in particular.'

'Jill and I know a nice hotel in Antibes, we can recommend. It even has its own private beach.'

'Go on. I'd be interested because Kate wants to go to Antibes and get stocked up with Arpege.'

'Arpege?'

'Yes, it's her favourite perfume and is difficult to source in Britain. She came across it a long time ago when she was at a conference in Nice. Normally, we get it sent through the post.'

'The hotel is called *The Royal*. It's just around the corner from the bottom of Rue Albert 1st, heading towards Juan-les-Pins. You can't miss it. At this time of the year the weather will be lovely and it won't be too crowded, although the sea might still be a tad cold.'

'I know exactly where it is,' remarked Kate, 'but it could be a little expensive.'

As people began to circulate prior to the wedding feast, Kate was able to manoeuvre Gerry to one side. Alone, she tried to express her sorrow for Sally's death and admitted that 'if it hadn't been for me, it would never have happened.'

'Kate, it's almost eleven years ago. You mustn't blame yourself. Our children have given me wonderful support and I have my faith. There isn't a day goes by when I don't think about her. Sally was delighted when you looked us up and she often talked fondly about your trip to Nottingham together.' He stopped and paused, his eyes full of moisture, he looked away and sniffed. Clearly embarrassed, he apologised, 'I'm sorry.'

Kate put her arms around him and hugged him. 'Gerry, I loved Sally too. The assassin who did it perished in a most horrible manner. He now lies at the bottom of the Atlantic – a meal for the crabs.'

He nodded, wiped his eyes and blew his nose.

A waiter came from the marquee and announced the wedding lunch was served.

'Gerry,' suggested Kate, 'why don't we meet up this evening at that Chinese restaurant you took me to all those years ago?'

'*The Hop Sing*?'

'Yes.'

'OK, I'll book a table for nine o'clock.'

And with that they moved into the marquee, to sit at their pre-arranged positions.

* * *

'Boss? I'm ringing from Boothby Graffoe. I watched al Jised arrive with her husband. They're in church as we speak. MacKinnon has a red MX-5 and I've attached a couple of trackers to the underside. Do you want me to hang around or shall I return to London?'

'Just a minute, let me check they're transmitting correctly...'

A minute later, Lee Hefferman was able to give his agent the all-clear. 'Everything is fine, Harry. We've got his car on the scope and from now on wherever he goes we'll know. You can return... well done. Oh, by the way, what is its registration number?'

130

'TN 51 THB.'

'Thanks Harry. We'll get their address from the DVLC's computer.'

Lee went to his scrambler terminal that connected him directly to the ops centre at Langley, Virginia. He didn't expect his Director to be at work on a Saturday so he left a message marked 'Urgent for eyes only of DCIA-GJT'. He knew the message would be delivered directly to George J Tenet by courier within an hour of receipt:

Have located al Jised. Request instructions as to how to proceed. Hefferman.

As he left the embassy, he approached one of the Metropolitan Police Officers from the Diplomatic Protection Group standing on duty at the entrance. He showed the officer his diplomatic identity card. 'Is there any chance you could get me the details of the owner of a car that I accidentally scraped in the supermarket car park this morning? I would like to write and tell him I will pay for my carelessness.'

The officer examined the pass and replied, 'I don't see why not. Do you want me to do it straightaway, or can it wait? I'll be back here on duty on Monday.'

'Monday will be fine. Please leave a note in reception for my attention. Thank you.' He handed the PC a slip with the registration number and make of car.

The PC examined the note. 'Very good Mr Hefferman, it won't be a problem.'

* * *

It was unusual for Lee Hefferman to go to the office on Sundays. However, that morning he entered his operations centre after attending his local Baptist church. 'Is the MX-5 on the move yet?' he asked the VDU operator.

'The car left Grantham an hour ago and is heading south down the A1.'

'That's interesting. Perhaps we had the location of their home wrong;

131

we based our assumption on their son studying at Edinburgh. I was expecting them to be returning to Scotland.'

'At the moment, they are going around Biggleswade at a steady seventy.'

'Have we had a reply from Langley to my signal?'

'No, boss.'

'If one comes in today, give me a ring and I'll come straightaway.

'OK, sir.'

* * *

It was four o'clock that Sunday afternoon when the phone rang in Lee Hefferman's apartment in Queen's Street, Mayfair.

'Boss, it's the duty officer.'

'Has a reply come from Langley?'

'No, sir. I thought you ought to know right away. The MX-5 we are tracking is stationary on the quay at Dover, presumably waiting for the next sailing to France.'

'Shite! They're going on holiday. We'll lose them in France if we don't do something quickly. I'll come into the office immediately.'

A brisk ten-minute walk saw Hefferman back in the embassy in Grosvenor Square. A quick scan through his confidential work diary found the number he wanted: Mike Schriver's cellphone.

'Mike, it's Lee here. We have a problem.' He quickly explained the need to keep tabs on al Jised and her husband's car that was, by then, on the P&O 1615 hours sailing to Calais. He gave the frequency details of the tracker and was assured that the Paris Embassy would be able to follow the MX-5 wherever it went in France.

'Is this anything to do with that failed attempt to remove Barbara Renton last November?'

'No, why?'

'It's just that there's an Iraq connection. Is there something I should know about this that you're not telling me?'

'Honestly Mike, as far as I know, Renton neither met nor knew al

Jised. We want to persuade al Jised to tell us where she hid the WMDs before we go into Iraq next year. We want to get rid of Renton to prevent her from spilling the beans. It's probably two different sides of the same coin.'

'So, you're sure they're not going to meet up? If you want me to get two of my men to follow their car, I will?'

'I'm awaiting instructions from Langley, as we speak. As soon as I know how GJT wants to proceed, I'll be in touch.'

* * *

The Metropolitan Police have some 760 DPG officers in total. The busiest shift, but the most popular, is the daytime: 0700 to 1500 hours. Officers gather at their central HQ in Beak Street at 0600 hours to read *Daily Routine Orders* and be given any special instructions for the day. On Monday, 8th April, PC Grant was called to one side by the Duty Sergeant. 'There's a Special Branch Inspector wants to see you in my office – now!'

Grant's face registered surprise. *Is this what I've been waiting for? A move out of the DPG at last?* He moved across the briefing room with hopeful expectation of being transferred to Special Branch. At the Sergeant's office door, he knocked and entered.

A plain clothes officer asked, 'Grant?'

'Yes, sir.'

'Sit down.' Without further ado, he asked, 'You made a request for a DVLC check to be made on a car when you came off duty on Saturday. Why?'

'A Mr Hefferman from the US Embassy asked me to.'

'Why?'

'He said he'd knocked a car in a car park and wanted to write to the owner to recompense him.'

'Doesn't that seem odd?'

'It's nice that some people are honest enough to admit their liability.'

'Do you know who Hefferman is?'

133

'No, sir.'

'He's the embassy's head honcho in the CIA. He had an ulterior motive for wanting that car owner's address. It happens to be a CPV.'

'Christ!'

'Exactly, a Covertly Protected Vehicle. Now, here's what you're going to do…'

* * *

Hefferman, after receiving a note from the DPG officer that there must have been an error with the registration number of the car and knowing that his operative would not have made such a mistake, realised the car was a CPV. *The police will inform MI5 as routine. There could be ructions.* Realising he wasn't going to get al Jised's address that way, Lee rang his French colleague to explain he needed the MX-5 to be discreetly followed and the couple to be watched until surveillance experts arrived from the States the next day.

'Where are they now?' Lee asked.

'They overnighted in Leon in Northern France and are on the A26 heading south towards Dijon. I'll send a car east from Paris immediately, but I'd advise Langley that their men should fly into Geneva if they're to minimise the chase over the next few days.'

'Thanks Mike. I'll let them know at once.'

* * *

'Yes?'

'Inspector Dodson here, Special Branch.'

'What can I do for you, Inspector?'

'You will want to know that the Head of the CIA in the American Embassy, Lee Hefferman, tried to make an illegal inquiry as to the owner of one of your cars last Saturday.'

'Are we talking about TN 51 THB?'

'Yes, sir. How do you know?'

'The DVLC computer automatically warns us when that happens, but thank you for letting us know. We are following the matter up.'

CHAPTER 16

Tuesday, 9th April 2002

Kate and Robbie had driven sedately through France, stopping at family-run hotels listed in their *Logis de France* guidebook. They had arrived at Aix-les-Bains mid-afternoon and parked by the side of Lake Bourget, France's largest natural lake. One hundred yards behind them, an insignificant grey Renault Megane drew up. Agents Bill Reid and Rod Addison from the US Embassy in Paris had been following the M-X5 on their tracking device and, having finally caught up, made visual contact for the first time. The MacKinnons left their car and walked along the lakeside in the shade of the gardens, unaware they were being watched. When they turned inland towards the city centre, the two agents were sufficiently experienced not to follow. Instead they discreetly returned to the MX-5 to check the two bugs were securely attached. Having satisfied themselves, they sat under a tree with an ice cream and waited, admiring the view across the lake towards the Col du Chat.

'I have a feeling they will stop somewhere around here this evening,' remarked Bill casually.

'Will we follow them to their hotel?' asked Rod.

'No need; we'll satisfy ourselves they are overnighting and find somewhere here in Aix. Do you fancy a trip to the casino tonight?'

'If it's on expenses.'

* * *

The following day, Wednesday, 10th April, the happy couple left their hotel situated on the lakeside at Bourget-du-Lac and drove leisurely south via Chambery, Vizille and Gap on the N85, known as the *Route Napoleon*. Over a stop for lunch, Robbie suggested a detour. 'I think we should take a trip over the highest pass in Europe, the Col de la Bonnette.'

Unsure of the consequences, Kate agreed.

'There will be snow on the top of the pass,' Robbie enthused. 'The road is almost 9,000 feet.'

The diversion, although fascinating and allowing them to see marmots scurrying over the slopes of the hills in the warm sun, was slow. They stopped near the top of the col, but decided not to climb the peak, the *Cime de la Bonnette* at 9,383 feet, due to the preponderance of snow and the consequent drop in temperature. They descended south and found a small hotel for the night at Valberg.

On Thursday, they drove through the *Grande Canyon du Verdon*, stopping frequently to admire the view, and arrived in Antibes in the late afternoon. They had booked a reservation in *The Hotel Royal* before leaving Valberg and were delighted to find their bedroom on the third floor overlooking the sea. Before dinner, they were able to walk westerly along the promenade towards the Cap d'Antibes in the evening sun. They were enjoying the warmth of the evening mixed with the salty sea-air. They inspected the private beach opposite *The Royal* with its own restaurant facilities and sun-loungers. They were eagerly looking forward to spending many lazy hours there.

On Friday, however, the weather was dull and so they decided to head east to explore the old town. Kate acted as guide; she had visited the beautiful resort when attending a conference in Nice on behalf of the Iraq Government in the mid-seventies. She was surprised to see how little had changed.

They found the Picasso Museum, located in the Chateau Grimaldi, was open and decided to enter. Robbie admitted that he was somewhat sceptical about Picasso's work. 'I've always felt he was a con-artist,' he admitted. 'It isn't real art like Constable or, better still, Turner.'

They slowly meandered around the gallery. Kate noticed Robbie was spending longer examining the exhibits: pottery, sculptures as well as paintings. He had gone quiet too.

'Well, do you still think Picasso was a fraud?' asked Kate as they left.

'No, I've changed my mind. That was a real eye-opener. His blue period was particularly inspiring. From now on I'll look at his work in a new light.'

They wandered through the covered market, heaving with people. Robbie stared at sights unseen at home: the variety of olives – all shapes, sizes and colours; the numerous types of honey – those made from sunflowers as yellow as lemon curd; flowers that he hadn't a clue what they were; and fish – octopus, tuna, giant langoustines and ugly crabs. Kate was equally fascinated, but with the variety and style of the fabrics – yellows, blues and reds patterned in the Provence style.

It was 1.30 pm by the time they had absorbed the bustling atmosphere that was so uniquely French. They headed towards the bus station, found a busy fish restaurant bedecked in blue and white tablecloths, were shown to a suitable table, sat down and realised the clouds were dispersing; the weather was brightening up. The sun was highlighting the colours of the buildings around them, particularly those painted in warm, sienna pigments.

As they studied the menu, they realised the couple sitting at the table adjacent to them were speaking English. Although they were talking quietly, Robbie thought he could detect the man had a Manx accent. He looked carefully at the couple without staring, trying not to make it obvious that he was listening.

Robbie and Kate ordered their lunch.

However, as the minutes passed, Robbie became more and more convinced that the stranger was a Manxman whose partner was an attractive woman, perhaps in her late-fifties, *a bit older than Kate.* The woman seemed captivated by the story she was being told; smiling and nodding enthusiastically to encourage him to tell her the next episode.

Robbie remembered the wedding the previous week and how Judy's father had detected his own accent. Their dishes had arrived. He and Kate ate in silence. By the time they had finished their starters, the adjacent couple had finished their coffee and were waiting for their bill to arrive. Robbie, convinced he was right, decided to take a gamble.

He leaned towards the pair, smiled and said to the man, *'Kanys ta shiu?'*

A frown appeared on the man's face, as if annoyed Robbie had spoken to him.

'Pardon?' he asked.

Embarrassed, Robbie repeated the greeting; one of the few phrases he knew in the Manx language.

A half-smile replaced the frown. *'Braew, braew. As shiu?'* the stranger replied.

'I hope you don't think I was being rude, but I thought I detected a faint trace of a Manx accent and as I am from Douglas I thought I should introduce myself.'

'It's a small world. Are you on holiday?'

'Yes, we're staying at *The Royal*, and you?'

'We live here, but we must go. Maybe we'll see you around if you are here for a while.' Realising it was no use pretending to be French, and not wishing to appear to be rude, Juan thought he had better introduce himself using his undercover name. 'I'm John Pearson, by the way, and this is my wife, Barbara.'

Robbie and Kate stood and introduced themselves.

Kate then asked, 'Perhaps you might like to join us for dinner one evening?'

Barbara smiled and, without hesitation, replied, 'That would be nice; we occasionally go to *The Royal*. Would tomorrow evening at eight be OK?'

'Excellent. I'll make sure we have a table with a view,' replied Kate.

Both men were thinking, *How can women get on with each other so quickly?*

* * *

'Don't you think that was a bit risky?' asked Juan as he and Barbara wandered back through the narrow side streets, past the colourful, offbeat shops to their apartment.

'Why?'

'You know why. They could be anyone. Just because he knows a few Manx words doesn't mean he's Manx.'

'I was intrigued because I know who they are,' replied Barbara.

Juan momentarily stopped in his tracks and looked at his companion. 'You do?'

'Yes. I read her file last year before I retired. She's Kathab al Jised and is now called Kate MacKinnon. She was once described by the tabloid press as Dr Germ. She was an agent of ours during the Iraq-Iran war and the SAS brought her back to Britain for her protection at the beginning of *Desert Storm*. She's a fellow RAPS like us. He is too. He was formerly an RAF officer who was supposedly shot by the IRA, but in reality it was an elaborate deception to give him a new identity. His original name was James Douglas.'

'Good God. But you still haven't answered my question. Why agree to meet them for dinner? You know damn well we never eat at *The Royal*.'

'I want to find out what they are doing here. Is it pure coincidence or is there something going on that we should know about? I noticed you eyeing her up too. Don't get any ideas.'

'She's an attractive woman.'

'I repeat, don't get any ideas.'

* * *

'Kate, don't you think you were a little hasty inviting them to dinner tomorrow evening?'

'I was intrigued and want to find out if he's Juan Quayle.'

'Who?'

'Juan Quayle… you remember… the guy Peter Stacey mentioned at the wedding reception – the other Manxman he knew.'

'You think it could be? He said his name was John Pearson.'

She ignored him. 'It's turning out to be a lovely afternoon. Let's go down to the beach and test out the hotel's sun loungers.'

* * *

'Mike Schriver.'

'Boss, Bill Reid here.'

'Where are you Bill?'

'We're in Antibes. The MacKinnons are obviously going to stay at their hotel, *The Royal*, for some time. This morning they went to the Picasso Museum, then wandered through the market and had an al fresco lunch afterwards. But you'll never guess what.'

'What?'

'They sat next to Barbara Renton.'

'Are you sure?'

'Certain. You gave us a photo of her at the beginning of the year when you briefed us about the disappearance of our two agents that had been sent to smoke her out. Renton was with a man... he could be her boyfriend as they held hands when they left the restaurant... and they briefly chatted with the MacKinnons. I got the impression that the women might know each other. I have sent Rod to follow Renton. I assume I have done the right thing? Incidentally, when are the two operatives from Langley going to show up?'

'Their aircraft was delayed and because we knew then that the MacKinnons were heading to the Mediterranean, Langley has arranged for them to fly directly to Nice overnight. They should arrive first thing tomorrow morning. Where are you and Rod staying?'

'Around the corner from *The Royal*, a little two-star hotel called *Le Ponteil*.'

'I'll tell Langley and they will be with you by mid-morning.'

'OK.'

Mike Schriver knew the ropes. He went straight to his telecoms room and began typing a *flash top secret* message that was automatically coded before being sent to CIA HQ – *Director's eyes only*. In essence, the message simply conveyed the discovery of Barbara Renton's whereabouts. He knew the outcome. The two agents, probably female and personable, preparing to catch up with al Jised to persuade her to cooperate, would

141

be substituted by two hit men. *Renton's days are numbered,* he thought as he pressed the transmit button.

* * *

An hour later came the reply. The two original agents' flight to Nice had been cancelled. Instead, agents Carswell and Hollis were preparing to fly to the US Air Force base at Mildenhall in Suffolk. They would transfer to a Learjet C-21 with diplomatic clearance to fly to Nice airport. Bill Reid was to meet the US Chargé d'affaires, based in Marseilles, in the lobby of *The Negresco Hôtel.* Together they would drive in the diplomat's car with CD, corps diplomatique, registration plates to the airport and await the agents' arrival at the eastern, private terminal. Their expected time of their arrival would be 1830 hours. The four would return to *The Negresco,* from where Bill would then drive the two agents in his car to Antibes, a distance of some twelve miles. Meanwhile, his colleague was to maintain surveillance on Renton.

When he'd seen Carswell's name, someone walked on Mike's grave. He knew Carswell was the Department's top hit man and had a fearful reputation. Apparently he enjoyed planning his executions to the finest detail. Mike also knew the use of the Marseilles' Chargé d'affaires would guarantee immunity at the airport from the *douane* and police. After the 'executive action' – *I like the euphemism* thought Mike – Carswell and Hollis were to be taken back to *The Negresco,* transfer to the diplomatic car, proceed to the airport and fly back to Mildenhall.

Mike rang Bill Reid back. He was sitting with Rod sharing a beer in *Le Ponteil's* garden while waiting for dinner. After going through the details, Mike asked, 'Any questions?'

'Do you really want to know what I think?'

'Yes, of course I do.'

'Apart from leaving me to pick up the pieces, it won't work.'

'Why?'

'Langley has no idea what the traffic is like on the Promenade des Anglais at that time of the evening; or that there's nowhere to park near

The Negresco except in the hotel's underground car park. And access to that is only with the assistance of the concierge. You'll have to trust me to make some minor changes to the transport arrangements.'

'OK, Bill; I've known you long enough to accept you'll make the right decision. Get on with it.'

* * *

The following morning, Saturday, 13th April 2002, the sun shone in a clear blue sky. 'A day to rest and recuperate,' suggested Kate to Robbie. After a leisurely breakfast, they walked across the road to the hotel's private beach complete with its own refreshment facilities. They chose a pair of sun loungers from where they could plunge into the sea easily and have lunch supplied by the outdoor restaurant. The south-facing complex looked across Antibes public beach towards the Cap d'Antibes; the scent from the nearby pines was aromatic. Eric, the head waiter and supervisor, was always on hand to provide anything required.

'This is the most perfect setting I've ever come across,' said Robbie. 'I can see why Barbara and John, or Juan, if that is who you think he is, have chosen to live here.'

Moments later, he had fallen asleep.

CHAPTER 17

Realising the MacKinnons were settled for the day at the private beach, the two agents from the Paris Embassy took turns to keep a discrete watch on Barbara Renton's apartment. Barbara went shopping to the small supermarket at the top of Rue Albert 1st in the morning, buying essentials such as vegetables and some groceries. She was as chic as any Frenchwoman, clearly spoke French fluently and appeared to know some of the local women. Bill Reid smiled, however, when she picked up a copy of *The Daily Telegraph*.

A giveaway that you're not French, he thought. *You don't know we've found you.*

After lunch, Barbara and Juan left their apartment carrying leather holders. They walked to the bottom of the boulevard and met a gathering of about a dozen men and women of their own age. They spent the afternoon playing *petanque* socially on the shaded *boules* pitch with the gentle sea breeze rustling the pines. As he sat sipping a *pression* outside on the pavement of a roadside bar opposite the park, Bill couldn't help thinking, *What an idyllic setting for whiling away the time.*

About 200 yards away to the west, on the *Hôtel Royal's* beach complex, Kate and Robbie were leisurely finishing their *salad Nicoise* accompanied with a bottle of *Tavel* rosé and a bottle of *Badoit*. When they had finished and, being unused to sitting in such a strong sun for so long, Robbie suggested they should return to the hotel, change into something suitable and go for a stroll to explore more of Antibes.

After a quick shower, they headed towards the old town. Passing through the seaside gardens, they stopped to watch the *boule* players; quickly realising that John and Barbara were playing. They gave a friendly wave and Barbara responded with a hand signal and mouthed for them to wait for them to finish their game.

Minutes later, Barbara was excusing herself to her French friends and approached Kate. 'John and I need a break, this is thirsty work. How about having a beer with us across the road?' She nodded towards the bar where the CIA agent was innocently sipping his pression.

The four crossed the road and sat outside under a large sunshade a few tables away from the American. The noise from the traffic, while not busy, prevented everything they were saying from being overheard. Nevertheless, Bill picked up sufficient conversation to know that they were dining together that evening in the *Royal*.

In any operation, it is frequently one tiny snippet of intelligence that makes the difference between success and failure. Reid was sufficiently worldly-wise, *This is it! A plan of action instantly came to mind. He had an excuse to justify changing Langley's unworkable plan. Tonight will be the night,* he thought. He decided not to hang around. He called the waiter, paid *l'addition* and left.

* * *

The two American operatives booked out of *Le Ponteil* and stored their luggage in the boot of their car.

'It's going to happen tonight,' Bill told his colleague. 'As soon as it's over, we are heading back to Paris. You keep an eye on things in Antibes, while I go to Nice and meet Carswell and Hollis.'

He knew the traffic along the Promenade des Anglais would be busy. The roadworks near the racetrack at Cagnes-sur-Mer were causing chaos and he realised his best bet was to park the car before he reached the *Hippodrome de la Côte d'Azur*, then hail a cab that could use the fast bus lane to avoid most of the trouble. He parked prior to reaching the world-famous ziggurat apartments at the *Marina Baie des Anges* and found a taxi to take him towards Nice. It was almost 1800 hours when he reached *Le Negresco*. As he approached the hotel, the limousine with CD plates was parked conspicuously at the front on yellow lines. He noticed it had smoked glass windows so that no one could see the occupants. *Excellent,* he thought, *it will make the switch easier.*

A uniformed concierge, bedecked with more gold braid than a South American admiral, appeared from nowhere, opened the large swing doors at the top of the steps and welcomed him to the hotel. Bill walked into the lobby and instantly recognised the US diplomat, an assistant ambassador, whom he vaguely knew. 'I must apologise for my late arrival, but the traffic around Cagnes was so bad that I had to abandon my car on the far side of the racetrack and catch a taxi.'

The Chargé d'affaires begrudgingly nodded, displaying his displeasure which he compounded with a look at his wristwatch and mumbled something about 'having to get a move on.'

As they drove towards the airport in the CD limo, the ambassador asked, 'Can you tell me what's this all about?'

'Don't you know?'

'I wouldn't have asked if I knew. Langley hasn't told me anything.'

'Perhaps it's better not to know, sir,' replied Bill. 'If I tell you that we're picking up two hit men, then you can surmise the rest. As a result of overhearing something this afternoon, I can tell you that it should be all over by ten o'clock this evening. The two guys we're meeting will be able to leave immediately after they've taken their so-called executive action. What I would like you to do when we have picked them up in half an hour or so, is to take us to my car on the far side of the Loubet ziggurats and be there for our return around 10 pm. Whatever you do in the meantime is your affair, but for heaven's sake don't be late. You will then take them back to the airport and they can return to Mildenhall.'

The diplomat nodded but remained silent as he drove the one mile to the eastern entrance of the airport, then followed the signs for *aerogare diplomatique et privé*. A policeman checked their passes at the barrier to the complex. He told them where to park and as they left the car, they saw an unmarked Learjet being directed to a slot on the apron near the small, private terminal. Showing their credentials for the second time in as many minutes, the diplomat and Bill were allowed access to the small reception building. They saw a sign marked *Arrivée* and moved to the entrance. A few minutes passed before two tall, well-built men – one in his mid-forties, the other perhaps ten years younger – entered. They were dressed identically in dark grey suits and wore matching fedoras that covered much of their faces. Behind them came the two pilots, a Captain and a Lieutenant, both dressed in USAF flying overalls.

The Chargé d'affaires approached the dark suits and introduced himself.

Feeling something of a second-class citizen, Bill had to make himself known. 'I'm Bill Reid from the Paris Embassy.'

'Carswell,' is all the first man said. There were no smiles; his chiselled face was pot-marked; he needed a shave. Chained to his left wrist was an attaché case – *the diplomatic bag.* The second man nodded acknowledgment, smiled and looked as if he had made an effort to be presentable but remained silent.

He's presumably Hollis, thought Bill.

The two business men, after furtively looking around the deserted reception area, immediately began asking questions about the whereabouts of their quarry and if she was currently under observation. Bill briefly explained why he had altered the proposed course of action. Carswell listened, thought for a few moments and nodded agreement.

Then Bill asked, 'Before we leave here, can I have a quick word with the pilots?'

Another nod signified OK.

A man of few words, thought Bill.

Bill introduced himself to the aircrew. He told them that he believed their two passengers would be ready to fly back to England anytime between 2200 and 2215 hours. They should file their flight plan for a take-off accordingly. Meanwhile, he suggested they should wander across to Terminal One and find a suitable place for an evening meal. The two officers thanked him and said they would tell air traffic control that they wished to depart at 2215 hours.

Bill then returned to the waiting men. 'I had to park my car about four miles away on the Antibes side of the airport. We will travel there in the ambassador's car to make a switch. I will then fill you in on the details of the plan. OK?'

I don't want the Chargé d'affaires to know too much, thought Bill.

Minutes later, the four Americans were heading back towards Antibes. The Chargé d'affaires drove while the three CIA operatives sat in the rear. The going was pathetically slow negotiating the roadworks past Cagnes.

'God, the traffic's awful,' remarked Hollis.

'There are roadworks everywhere. It's only about twelve miles to Antibes but it's going to take us forty minutes to get there at this time of the evening,' replied Bill. 'Shortly the road splits. Hopefully most of this traffic will bear right onto the RN7. We will stick to the road known as *au bord de la mer.*'

'Then you'd better tell us everything you know about Renton,' whispered Carswell to ensure the diplomat couldn't overhear.

'She lives with a bloke, we don't know his name, in a penthouse near the bottom of a wide boulevard called Rue Albert 1st. We hit lucky two days ago when we saw her sitting having lunch in the open air talking to a couple we have been following through France.'

'This is the couple calling themselves MacKinnon?'

'Correct. Mrs MacKinnon was formerly an Iraqi-MI6 double agent. She hid biological weapons in Iraq and the plan was to see if she would reveal their locations.'

'Yes, we have been briefed about her. However, when you found Renton, the Director decided her elimination was more important. He believes al Jised can wait as the invasion of Iraq is at least eighteen months away.'

'In a few minutes, we will pass the ziggurat apartments at Loubet. You may have seen them when you were coming into land. There is then three miles of unlimited car parking on the beach side of the road where I left my vehicle earlier. We will change cars but we will have to be quick. Have you noticed that we're being followed?'

The two officers instinctively turned around but only saw a stream of cars following.

'It's the silver Peugeot 206 three cars behind us. It came out of the private airport complex shortly after us and is about as inconspicuous a car in France as you can get,' explained Bill.

He leaned over the empty front passenger seat to talk to the diplomat. 'That's my grey Renault Megane about one hundred yards ahead. I want you to swing suddenly across the road and park on this side of it. We will get out, keep low and get into my car – hidden from view by your limo. The gendarmerie following us will have passed before they realise what is happening. While they're thinking whether to park on the sea-side of the road as well, we will have swung back onto this side of the road in my car and then be behind them. There are traffic lights ahead where they either go ahead or turn right under the railway line. Whatever they do, we will do the opposite. Now, GO for it.'

The assistant ambassador did what he was told. He pulled the steering wheel hard left, swung the limousine across the road and narrowly missed an oncoming car that had to break, its horn hooting.

Bill watched the Peugeot 206 pass their position still heading west; the driver and his passenger both peering to see what was going on. 'NOW.' The three opened the back doors of the limo, scrambled the two yards to Bill's car, already opened with his zapper, and got inside. Reid's car had been backed into its slot. He started it up and signalled that he wished to cross the road and head towards Antibes. A considerate driver crawling towards Cagnes flashed for him to proceed; he crossed over and was now eight or ten cars behind the 206. In his rear-view mirror, he saw the CD registered car reversing on the beach's hard shoulder and integrating itself into the flow back towards Nice. *I hope to God he's here for ten o'clock,* thought Bill.

At the traffic lights, Bill saw the gendarmerie car turn right. It would pass immediately under the railway line that runs parallel to the RN7. He drove straight on, passing Fort Carre, drove through the old town and arrived at a crossroads with Rue Albert 1st. He turned onto the boulevard and stopped. 'If we get out here, I'll show you the geography.'

They walked a short distance towards the town centre. 'That's Renton's apartment block,' Bill said, pointing towards a five-story building with a plush, gilded-framed, glass door foyer entrance and a vehicle access ramp to its underground car park to one side.

'It looks expensive,' remarked Carswell.

'They're all expensive,' joked Bill. 'Nothing is cheap in Antibes. Renton and her boyfriend live in the penthouse on the top floor. Now let me show you the rest of the patch.'

They retraced their steps and walked towards the sea. As they turned right towards the Cap d'Antibes, Bill said, 'We know Renton is having dinner with the MacKinnons as we speak in *The Royal Hôtel*, two blocks further along. My plan is it will be dark when they go back to their apartment. That will be the time to do it.'

'Yes, but I am not happy with all these pavement cafes. There will be too many people around,' replied Carswell.

'My gut feeling is they will take a short cut through the back streets. It will halve their journey. Let me show you.'

Bill showed them the hotel and then the several shortcuts available to Renton and her partner. 'A ten-minute walk becomes a five-minute one.'

'I agree. Where is your colleague?' asked Hollis.

'I'm here.'

They swung around. Standing behind them was Rod. 'I followed Renton and her partner into the hotel. They met the MacKinnons in the bar, had a drink and went into the restaurant ten minutes ago.'

'Excellent,' remarked Carswell. 'I suggest we've time to snatch some *moules frites* and then prepare for them coming out.'

CHAPTER 18

Saturday, 13th April 2002

The four new friends made their choices for dinner while sitting in the cocktail lounge enjoying an aperitif, unaware they were being watched by the lone drinker at the end of the bar. The head waiter had taken their orders and they had chosen their wine.

'It was nice of you to invite John and me for dinner,' Barbara began.

'Have you lived here long?' enquired Kate.

'No, not really; since just before Christmas. I don't wish to be rude, but I think we should stop playing games, don't you?'

'What do you mean?' asked Robbie.

'You noticed John had a Manx accent because you are originally from the Isle of Man yourself. Your real name is James Douglas and you,' Barbara turned to Kate smiling, 'are Kathab al Jised from Iraq.'

Neither Robbie nor Kate had expected the bombshell. Their eyes widened with surprise.

After what seemed a long pause, Robbie asserted, 'Then you must be Juan Quayle, not John Pearson, and you know Peter Stacey.'

It was Juan's turn to be put on the back foot. 'How do you know Peter?'

'I first met him when I was in Baghdad in 1978.'

'Ah, when you implemented the war game with some staff from ICL. You had initially met Kate at Dataskil House in Reading?' interrupted Barbara.

'Yes. You seem to know a lot about us,' replied Robbie.

'I should do. Until six months ago, I was Peter's successor at MI6. I've read your files and know, for example, that the Americans have been pestering your son to find Kate's address. As everyone knows, they have an agenda to go into Iraq, supposedly to find the missing weapons of mass destruction, and are trying to find out where you hid them during the war with Iran.'

Robbie looked at Kate and Kate returned the look. Their eyes sent a message by telepathy: *Not a word about Tariq Aziz's visit.*

Barbara continued. 'We have much in common; more than you probably realise. However, before we begin to reminisce, there is one thing I want to clear up. How did you find us yesterday lunchtime?'

'It was pure chance. Last week my son Stuart got married. We invited Peter Stacey and his wife, Jenny, to the wedding in Lincolnshire. Our daughter-in-law's father, Bernard, turned out to be something of an expert phonologist and, although I haven't lived on the island for over thirty years, he recognised my Manx accent. Guessing where people come from turns out to be one of his party tricks. During the conversation, Peter accidentally let it out of the bag that he knew a Manxman called Juan Quayle. But that's all he said about you.'

'Then what happened?' asked Barbara.

'We had travelled down to the wedding from Scotland in our MX-5 and I'd said to Bernard that we were going to have a touring holiday in France after the wedding. We had planned to come to Antibes as Kate has been here before and gets her perfume sent to her regularly from the shop near the bus station. She thought she would stock up. Bernard recommended we stay here at *The Hôtel Royal*. Yesterday we spent the morning in the Picasso Museum, wandered through the market and found that lovely fish restaurant near the Post Office by accident. Choosing to sit next to your table was a pure fluke.'

'Getting back to things we have in common,' continued Barbara. 'Do you know that Juan was an assistant military attaché in Baghdad for eighteen months?'

'I didn't know that,' exclaimed Kate, keen to find out more of Juan's background. 'When were you there?'

'Oh, it was from late 1973 to the Spring of 1976. The guy who had been posted to go out there fell seriously ill and there was no time to train a replacement on the Arabic course. I was finishing Sandhurst and the Army Personnel Centre saw I could speak Arabic. My mother was Egyptian and I was sent out at short notice.'

'Is that where you met Peter Stacey?'

'No, the MI6 operative there in my time must have been Peter's predecessor. I can't remember his name.'

'What about Gerry Platini?'

'The Air Attaché?'

'Yes.'

'He arrived about six weeks before I left. I remember him.'

The conversation continued between Kate and Juan for several minutes as Juan reminisced about places he had visited in Iraq such as Babylon and Ctesiphon.

Barbara was looking at Robbie. After a pause in the conversation, she probed, 'Is there any way the Americans could have followed you here after the wedding?'

'I don't see how. We've been on the road for a week. Nothing has happened; we've not seen anybody.'

'Where is your car now?'

'Under your feet somewhere, in the hotel's underground car park. Why?'

'I am thinking whether it could have had a tracker stuck on it when you were at the wedding,' said a concerned-looking Barbara. She then asked Robbie, 'I assume your cars have always been registered as being covertly protected.'

Before he could answer, Kate interrupted and asked Barbara, 'What is that exactly?'

'Your registration plates can't be traced through the DVLA computer.'

'To answer your question, the answer is yes. If it will make you feel happier, we'll have a look under the car for any interference after dinner,' said Robbie.

Service in French restaurants can often be slow. However, the restaurant was not full and by a quarter to ten, they were finishing their desserts.

'Rather than having coffee here,' suggested Barbara, 'why not come back to our flat. It's only a five-minute walk. It will give you some fresh air before you retire for the night. What do you say?'

Kate looked at Robbie, who nodded approvingly. She answered, 'That would be lovely, but I will need to go up to our room and get a cardigan. It might be chilly when we come back.'

'In that case, Robbie can come with me now and we can get the coffee percolator going. Juan will wait while you go upstairs and we'll see you back at our place in a quarter of an hour.'

* * *

As they descended the steps of the hotel, Barbara and Robbie turned left and after a few yards they linked arms. 'We'll take the shortcut and turn down here into the Avenue de l'ilette,' she suggested.

Although still busy on the well-lit Boulevard Marshal Leclerc, with the cafes and bars bustling with revellers, the side avenue, by contrast, was dimly lit and quiet. Cars were parked on both sides of the narrow street. Despite the vehicles being half parked on the pavements, it was difficult for traffic to proceed in either direction. Barbara and Juan consequently strode down the middle of the avenue that was, effectively, little more than an alleyway. Only a solitary man wearing a Fedora was approaching them. Behind, a second man similarly dressed was, unbeknown to the couple, following them. As Barbara and Robbie neared the approaching man, he raised his hat, smiled, and fired twice with a silenced 9 mm pistol from almost point-blank range. Barbara and Robbie fell as one, each with a hole in their foreheads. Quickly the two men pushed and rolled the two bodies under two parked cars, their bodies coming to rest in the gutter. They then rapidly walked up the avenue.

The only words spoken were when the elder man asked, 'Did you remove the two trackers from the MX-5?'

'Yes.' He tapped his jacket pocket to indicate their location.

At the top of the avenue, they turned right into the Avenue Maiziere and in two minutes they had reached Rue Albert 1st. A minute later, they were at Bill Reid's car and reassembling the guns into the diplomatic bag. With the attaché case locked to his wrist, Carswell, with Hollis, got in the backseats of the Megane.

'Let's go.'

Bill glanced at Rod in the passenger seat and started the car up.

There was hardly any traffic along *au bord de la mer* and, within fifteen minutes, the two men had said their farewells and were in the diplomatic car heading for the airport. Bill breathed a sigh of relief, got out, opened the boot, took out a pair of Belgian car plates and for the fourth time since leaving Paris the previous week changed the car's registration.

'If we drive two hours on, two hours off, we'll be in Paris by lunchtime tomorrow,' said Bill. And with that, he turned the car around, headed back towards Antibes, turned right at the first set of traffic lights, headed up to the RN7 from where they would join the A7 and head west.

* * *

Kate came down the stairs from her room with a cardigan draped over her shoulders. 'I am sorry I was so long but I decided to change my shoes as well,' she smiled. Together they strolled along the Boulevard Marshal Leclerc, the bars and restaurants on their left, and the noise of the breaking waves of the Mediterranean on their right. When they reached Rue Albert 1st, they turned up the boulevard towards Juan's apartment. Ten minutes after leaving *The Hôtel Royal*, they entered the block of flats. They took the lift to the top floor. The door of the escalator opened onto a carpeted corridor that led to the luxury penthouse suite. Juan led the way to his apartment.

'That's funny, I would have thought Barbara would have left the door open,' he remarked as he inserted his key.

He pushed the door open and shouted, 'Barbara, we're here.'

There was no reply. The lights were out. He turned to Kate. 'That's strange, they are not here. There's something wrong.'

'Perhaps they stopped for a nightcap in one of the bars and we missed them,' suggested Kate.

'I doubt it, but we should retrace our steps.'

They went back to *The Royal* stopping to look in likely places, but found nothing.

'I think we should look up the side streets in case they took a shortcut,' suggested Juan.

They turned into the Avenue de l'ilette and were soon back at the apartment. Again they entered; again there was no one there.

'There's something radically wrong. I'm going to ring the police.'

'Will they do anything until twenty-four hours have elapsed?' asked Kate.

'They will when I tell them the former Head of MI6 has been abducted.'

'I'm not sure I would do that. They will probably think you're some sort of crackpot. I suggest we ring Peter Stacey and tell him what has happened.'

'Have you his number?'

'It's in Robbie's address book which I know is in our room at the hotel. He brought it with him so as to be able to send friends postcards.'

They ran back to *The Royal*, retrieved the book and were back in Juan's apartment in less than fifteen minutes.

It was nearly eleven o'clock, ten o'clock in England.

'Peter? It's Juan Quayle here, I'm sorry to be ringing on a Saturday evening. I'm ringing from Antibes in the South of France.' Without waiting for a reply, he continued, 'We have a major problem. Barbara has gone missing.' He quickly regaled the story of how Kate and Robbie had accidentally bumped into them the previous day and how they had dined together that evening. He stressed how he and Kate had searched in vain and that he was concerned something was drastically wrong.

'Have you rung the police?' asked Peter.

'No. They probably won't do anything for twenty-four hours.'

'True. Stay where you are.' He wrote down Juan's address and phone number. 'I'll contact Vauxhall Cross and get them to implement a *Flash* priority operation by the DCRI, the French Central Directorate of Interior Intelligence. However, it may be up to an hour before someone contacts you.'

'OK, we'll wait here.'

* * *

There then began a series of calls, each one necessitating the initial receiver to ring back to confirm authenticity.

Peter, having tried unsuccessfully to contact his successor, Phil Jay, rang the duty officer at MI6 HQ. *There's no time to be wasted trying to find him.*

The duty officer rang back to confirm the call was not from a crank although he had recognised Peter Stacey's voice, as he had worked in Peter's department ten years previously. Nevertheless, procedures in Top Secret Routine Orders were rigid for a good reason. *Belt and braces,* thought the duty officer as he checked Peter's contact telephone number in an annex.

The MI6 officer, having accepted Peter's request as genuine and thankful that he could speak decent French, rang the DCRI duty officer, Claude Bonneau, at Levallois-Perret, a suburb of North-West Paris.

Claude rang back on a scrambled line to Vauxhall Cross after initially checking the protocol of a *Flash Op Order Request* from the UK authorities. He wondered whether he should check with MI5, Britain's internal intelligence service, first.

He read the operational instructions carefully: *If the officer is satisfied the use of 'Flash' is correct, then he is to proceed with all haste to implement the request.*

Having listened to the problem, Claude realised the possible repercussions of doing nothing until the morning, especially as it would be a Sunday. He knew speed was of the essence. Therefore, instead of going through the Regional Centre in Marseilles, he bypassed one layer of bureaucracy and rang the DCRI duty officer in the Department of the Alpes-Maritimes.

Based in Nice, Michel Dufay was woken; he looked at his watch. It was almost midnight. He listened carefully to his superior. 'Get down there pronto with a police dog and a dozen men. Search the area thoroughly between *The Hôtel Royal* and Mme Richet's apartment. Do you know the area?'

'Yes, sir. Antibes is my favourite spot on the Côte d'Azur.'

'Report to Monsieur Juan Richet at this address,' he spelt out the details. 'Tell him what we are doing.'

'I'll be there in less than half an hour.'

'My orders tell me I have to raise this case as a priority class-one. That means I have to inform our Deputy Director immediately. He will almost certainly be coming down tomorrow to see what you have done. He'll expect a full brief when he arrives. Don't let the side down. This could be the biggest case you'll ever get to handle. It's not every day that a former Head of a national security service mysteriously disappears on your watch.'

* * *

'Yes?'

'Monsieur Richet?'

'I'm Michel Dufay from the Department of the Interior in Nice. Can you tell me what has happened?'

Juan rapidly explained the events of the evening and how Barbara had gone missing between *The Hôtel Royal* and their apartment in Rue Albert 1st.

'Your French is excellent, monsieur. Have you an item of Madame's clothing that the dog can use for her scent?'

'I used to teach French in England. Will a pair of her stockings do?'

'I would think that will be fine. Do you wish to accompany us during the search or would you prefer to stay here?'

'I'll stay here with Mr MacKinnon's wife, if you don't mind.'

The dog handler began in the dining room where the foursome had eaten a few hours previously. The hotel manager showed the handler where 'the elder lady' had sat. The dog appeared to sniff her chair for several moments, then her stockings – again. With that, he walked through the foyer to the steps of the hotel. After descending, the dog turned left strongly pulling on his leash. He had picked up a scent. Michel followed the handler, impressed how a dog's senses can be so more refined than a human's. The dog turned into the Avenue de l'ilette. Halfway down, it stopped and began barking at a white van. Michel's first reaction was to imagine that their quarry was inside the van. The gendarme dog-handler shone his torch under the van and soon disillusioned him. Underneath, stretched out in the gutter, was Mme Richet, *or whatever her name is,* thought Michel.

Seconds later, on the opposite side of the Avenue, underneath a 2CV, the dog-handler found Mr MacKinnon.

The street was cordoned off; a scene of crime officers and an ambulance were requested urgently. Michel drudged back to Juan's apartment to give the bad news.

CHAPTER 19

Sunday, 14th April 2002

Anyone who is suddenly told that their spouse has been shot in the forehead by what appears to be a professional hit man, their body dumped under a van parked in the street and left to rot would, quite understandably, break down when being told the news. So it was a somewhat tentative Michel Dufay who took the lift to the top floor penthouse in the Rue Albert 1st just after midnight. He pressed the doorbell anticipating having to cope with all sorts of outpourings of grief.

When Juan opened the door, he greeted Michel and asked him to enter the sitting room. However, the reactions of both Juan and Kate when given the news of their spouses' deaths surprised the DCRI officer. Neither showed any emotion whatsoever.

They knew they were dead! They did it, were his first thoughts. He was unaware that only six years previously Juan's entire family had been assassinated by an al-Qaeda executioner. He did not know that Kate's parents and her husband had died as a result of the Iran-Iraq war of the 1980s or that she'd witnessed prisoners in Abu Graib jail being murdered by exposure to gangrennex when their skin literally melted from their bodies. Both had been traumatised to the point where the value they put on life had become cynically distorted.

Consequently, Michel decided to follow the correct procedures. 'I hope you understand that I have to caution you. It will be necessary to eliminate you from our enquiries. We will have to search your apartment and Madame MacKinnon's hotel room. Also, we will require the clothes you were wearing this evening to test for powder residue and so on.'

'Yes, of course,' replied Juan. 'It is a pity, however, that in the meantime the assassin will be getting further away.'

'I can assure you that we will not rest until the crime has been solved. Your wife was an important woman and I am conscious there will be a political backlash over her murder.'

'The wheels of motion that have brought you here were initiated in London just over an hour ago by the former Head of MI6, my wife's predecessor. Do you mind if I ring him to let him know what has happened?'

'No, please go ahead.'

* * *

'Peter? I've bad news. Barbara and Robbie have been shot – single shots to the forehead, definitely an assassination. I am wondering if whoever did it thought Robbie was me.'

'Juan, I'm so sorry this has occurred. I had been keeping my fingers crossed, hoping for the best. But to be honest, I had a nasty feeling this might have happened. I have taken the liberty to book a flight to Nice first thing in the morning,' he paused to look at his watch. It was still Saturday in England, but only just: 2353 hours. 'I will arrive at Nice airport at eleven o'clock. I have been unable to contact Phil Jay, but tonight's duty officer used to work in my section and has cleared it with the French DCRI. I'll put Phil in the picture tomorrow. My presence will add a bit of gravitas. Indeed, the DCRI's number two, Edouard St-Julian, is flying down first thing from Paris, so the French are taking it seriously too. He will meet me at the airport. We should be with you before lunch. The presence of both of us will ensure the local police don't drag their heels.'

'That's good of you Peter. Is there anything you want me to do in the meantime?'

'No, I don't think so. How is Kate taking it all?'

161

'Very well, at the moment.'

'She's been married to Robbie for ten years. She's a very special person. Look after her.'

'She's concerned about telling Stuart that his father is dead. The problem is that he's on his honeymoon, but all she knows is that he's in Cephalonia.'

'I'll get someone from MI6 onto it right away. By the time I arrive, we'll have found out where he is staying. Juan, you know that this is either the work of al-Qaeda or...'

'Or the CIA and I know who I'm putting my money on. Al-Qaeda would have blown us up in the hotel.'

'You're probably right, but we must keep an open mind. I'll see you in the morning.'

* * *

Meanwhile the Avenue de l'ilette had been sealed off and was swarming with a scene of crime officers. The bodies had been removed to an ambulance after the necessary photographs and the local senior Antibes police detective had been called from his bed to take charge of the investigation.

'What is so bloody special about these two English tourists that I have to be called from my bed at this hour on a Sunday morning?' he had grumpily asked Michel Dufay, who he had never met before.

Members of the local *Police Nationale* tend to have a jaundiced view of the young high-flyers who work for the DCRI. With their plush offices based on the Avenue de Verdun overlooking the spectacular Promenade des Anglais, with no streetwise experience and only a university degree to their credit, policemen like Chief Inspector Anton Dubois, who had risen from the lowest ranks by hard work, had little time for them. *They have it easy.* It irritated him that they came in at the top to prestigious departments such as the DCRI. *After all, they were in the same business.* Whenever he brushed shoulders with them, they ruffled his feathers. Despite only having met Dufay for less than a minute, Inspector Dubois already perceived two problems. Firstly, Dufay looked young enough to be his son and yet he held an equivalent rank. Secondly, the DCRI operated on the principle that knowledge was power; *they never tell you anything but will expect me to sort out their bloody mess.*

However, Dufay's reply surprised him.

'This is a political assassination. The repercussions, if we get it wrong, will go all the way to the Élysée Palace. Our Deputy Director of Operations, Edouard St-Julian, is flying here first thing later this morning. I have to meet him and he'll want a full briefing.'

Chief Inspector Dubois noted the use of the word *we*.

'So I assume everything is to be kept hush-hush. Then who the hell are we dealing with? Algerians? Basques? Al-Qaeda? Who?' he asked.

To his amazement, Dufay didn't hesitate in replying. 'The CIA.'

'Have you sealed Nice Airport, the local railway stations and the A7 at the Antibes péage?'

'There's no need. The assassins have left already in a US Air Force jet.'

Dubois spluttered and coughed, then angrily asked, 'Then if you know who did it, what the hell do you want me for?'

'You've a damn sight more experience with murders than I have,' confessed Dufay, 'or more than anyone else on the Cote d'Azur for that matter. This is about finding evidence that will convict *les salauds.*'

Dubois had been around long enough to recognise bullshit, but was flattered even if it came from *un poupin*. 'You still haven't answered my question, what makes them special?'

'Up to about six months ago Mme Richet was the Head of MI6, Britain's Secret Intelligence Service.'

'Bloody hell; why would the CIA want to kill her?'

'They were worried that she might blow the whistle on America's proposed invasion of Iraq.'

Dubois, like so many senior policemen who have risen from the ranks, was primarily a law and order man. Usually anti-liberal and right-of-centre, they saw political correctness as a scourge on ordered society. President Chirac, for all his wheeling and dealing, had routed the socialists when coming to power. He had already made it clear that France would oppose the Iraq invasion at the UN Security Council. For the Chirac-man that he was, this explanation was good enough for Anton Dubois. *Mme Richet was one of us.*

'One final question. Why?'

'Why what?'

'Why here?' He waved his hand to indicate the street. 'Why now?'

'I'm not sure I follow you.'

'The first question I ask in any investigation is why now? Not how, not when, not who. You told me Mme Richet lived in Rue Albert 1st with her husband?'

'Yes.'

'Since she retired six months ago?'

'I believe so.'

'Then why has it taken the CIA six months to organise a simple hit on an unarmed woman?'

'You tell me.'

'Because they didn't know where she was. I assume her location would not be in the public domain and that she and her husband lived under an assumed name?'

'Yes, the name on their passports is Richet but my controller in Paris knows that her real name was Renton.'

'Which means that the man...' he paused to look at his notes, 'Monsieur MacKinnon, was an innocent bystander. Clearly, the couple with whom the Richets dined were followed to Antibes. How did they come here?'

'By car; it is in the underground car park of the hotel.'

* * *

Dubois' men set to work. Almost immediately, there was clear evidence that the MX-5 had, at some time, carried two trackers. They had been removed recently but the tell-tale signs of their location remained – clear spaces on the bodywork surrounded by the grime of travelling through

164

France. The butt of an extinguished cigarette was found near the car; *Careless,* thought Detective Constable Claude Gautin undertaking the garage search. He sniffed it, *Definitely neither Gitanes nor Gauloises,* and placed it carefully into an evidence bag.

He called for the dog handler. The dog, a spaniel called Jacques, was normally on duty at the airport where all baggage was sniffed as a matter of routine.

'I am sure one of the assassins was here under the car when he removed several trackers. Do you think your dog can pick up a scent?'

'Let's see, shall we?

The dog was given what appeared to be meaningless instructions. After smelling Claude – *Presumably to eliminate me from his enquiries,* he bizarrely thought to himself – Jacques proceeded to rummage under the MX-5. He came out, barked at his handler and wagged his tail. *Presumably he's saying, 'I have a lead.'*

'Come on,' said the handler. 'He's found something.'

They went up the car ramp to the boulevard. At one o'clock in the morning, the road was deserted. Instead of turning immediately left as the detective had expected, Jacques led them across the road diagonally to the right. In a small grassed area under a palm tree was a bench. The dog sat down and barked again.

Detective Gautin looked at the dog-handler, puzzled.

'Whoever took those tracking devices sat here. Jacques is telling me he has a strong scent.'

'From here, he could see everyone entering and leaving the hotel,' Claude replied. He looked around the bench and found what he was looking for. 'Another fag end; I'd swear it's the same brand as the other.'

Still wearing his latex gloves, the detective placed the remains of the cigarette in another polythene specimen bag. 'Possible DNA evidence,' he explained. 'Now, can we see where *le bougre* went next?'

The handler nodded to his four-legged friend and away Jacques went, tugging on his lead. They remained on the sea side of the boulevard as far as the Avenue de l'ilette. The dog stopped and looked at his master, who nodded approval for the dog to cross the road. They walked the fifty or so yards to the scene of the crime where Inspector Dubois was discussing something with Agent Dufay. Claude explained to his boss about the evidence he had gathered.

'Excellent. Now see if the dog can pick up where they went after the shooting.'

'They? You think there were two of them?' asked Detective Gautin.

'Neither was shot in the back. One must have been walking toward them and the other guy was following them from the hotel making sure they didn't turn and run. Furthermore, Agent Dufay, here, has been showing me some photos from the airport's CCTV. The pictures show two Americans arriving in a US Air Force plane six hours ago with a diplomatic bag. They were met by the US Chargé d'affaires from Marseilles. He drove them towards Antibes along the coast road. They were followed by the Gendarmerie but were given the slip by a well prepared car manoeuvre. My bet is those are the two bastards who did this.'

Claude looked at the DCRI officer and asked, 'Did they, at any time, touch anything as they came through the arrivals hall?'

'Why?' asked Dufay.

'Because if we could get a sample of their DNA at the airport, it might match the DNA on the two cigarette ends found at the underground car park and where one of them kept watch.'

Michel hastily glanced through the bundle of the still photos taken from the airport's CCTV. 'There,' he said and pointed at one of the Americans closing the door to the reception area. 'His hand is bare; he will have left fingerprints and DNA on the door handle. I'll get security on to it right away.' Seconds later he was issuing instructions to have the door isolated as potential evidence.

Accompanied by Dubois and Dufay, Detective Claude and the dog-handler followed Jacques to the end of the Avenue, they turned right and when they met Rue Albert 1st, they turned left. The trail, after about one hundred yards, crossed the road opposite the Russian Orthodox Church.

'The trail ends here,' explained the handler. 'They must have had a car parked for their getaway.'

Dubois looked around. There was no one in sight. 'Where's Boris?' he asked.

'Do you mean old Victor Polinov?' queried Claude.

'I've always called him Boris,' replied the brusque senior officer.

Victor Polinov was a Russian émigré, well known among the inhabitants of the boulevard as the resident tramp. He spent all his days sitting on the bench in front of the somewhat gloomy church acting as its unpaid caretaker and protector. Unknown to all but a few, he had a key that allowed him to sleep indoors at night – in lieu of wages.

'He'll be dossing inside the church,' explained Claude. 'He's its twenty-four hours a day caretaker. The priest believes it's the reason why they have never had a break-in.'

'I can't see him being much good if there was a burglar,' scoffed the Inspector.

'Apparently, old Victor was in General Zhukov's army that took Berlin. He's as tough as old nails.'

'Well, get him out and ask if he saw either the car parked here or the guys getting away.'

The seventy-seven-year-old may have been bedraggled, dirty and smelly but was no fool. 'Yes, there was a grey Renault Megane parked there for several hours until two Americans got in the back at about ten o'clock. There were two others in the front. They drove away.' He had spat as he said the word American.

'How do you know they were Americans?' asked the Inspector.

'By the suits they wore and their big trilby hats.'

It was Michel's turn to ask the $64,000 question and show him the photographs taken at the airport. 'Could these be the two men you saw?'

The old boy's eyesight was not as sharp as it would have been in 1945, but his reply was logical, 'The suits and hats are the same.'

This old guy could be an important witness, thought Michel, *but we're going to have to give him a bath before he goes anywhere near a judge.*

CHAPTER 20

Sunday, 14th April 2002

The Deputy Director of the DCRI arrived half an hour early from Paris in an executive jet; one of the fleet flown by the *Armée de l'Air* on behalf of the President of France, the higher ranking government ministers and very senior officials. However, a nervous Michel Dufay had arrived even earlier to meet his boss for the first time. After introducing himself, he accompanied him to a VIP lounge where the aroma of fresh coffee permeated. Laid out on a low table between two easy chairs was a breakfast of orange juice, yoghurts, croissants and coffee. Judging by the look on his face, St-Julian was pleased.

'Fill me in on all that has been achieved during the night,' he requested.

Michel briefed him methodically, concluding with the witness seeing the Americans getting into the car in Antibes and the possible DNA evidence that might link one of them to the hotel car park and the MX-5. 'The swabs taken at the airport and on the two cigarette ends are getting top priority, but we won't have the results until this evening,' he added.

'Without the DNA, the case against the so-called American diplomats is persuasive, but not totally conclusive. We now know the aircraft they used to leave here was diverted to the US air base at Geilenkirchen in Germany. By now the two assassins will be half across the Atlantic and there will be little we can do except make a protest at the highest diplomatic level. I think you and your team have done well. I will be meeting Sir Peter Stacey, the former Head of MI6, when he arrives here from London in about an hour's time. For how long have you booked this private lounge?'

'Until 1300 hours, sir.'

'Excellent, I'll wait here until Sir Peter arrives. Have you done anything about the press?'

'The newspapers? No, sir. I thought I'd better leave that to you, with it being so political. At the moment I don't think they know anything has happened.'

'They'll soon be swarming all over the place. I'll prepare a statement and get Sir Peter to approve it. Then the local police can release it. As you've been up all night, I suggest you get some rest. I expect Sir Peter will want to go to Antibes immediately. Who's in charge there?'

'The man on the ground is Chief Inspector Dubois, our best detective on the Côte d'Azur. Shall I contact him and tell him to be standing-by at *The Hôtel Royal* to give the statement to the press?'

'Yes, do that. We must show the British that we are on top of the case. If I need you, I have your number.'

Michel left the airport thinking to himself, *If I can get four hours shuteye, I'll be lucky. Poor old Dubois won't get any!*

* * *

Peter's flight was almost thirty minutes late. St-Julian, having examined the DCRI file on the former Head of MI6 from 1990 to 1993, and having made a mental note of his photograph, recognised the erect, mid-sixties stranger at once.

'Sir Peter Stacey?' he asked, as he met him in the Arrivals' Hall. 'I am Edouard St-Julian, Deputy Director of the DCRI. Welcome to France. I am sorry for the circumstances that have brought you here, but I am instructed by our Minister of Internal Security to give you all possible assistance. I was led to believe that Mme Renton was not only your successor but a friend?'

As they shook hands, Peter thought, *Thank heavens he speaks good*

English and seems happy to do so. Most of these upper-class Frenchmen insist on speaking their own lingo and I'll bet he knows my proficiency is poor. 'Thank you Edouard for meeting me and the speedy response your department has shown. As you know I retired some six or seven years ago, but Phil Jay, our current Director of MI6, could not be contacted last night and I thought I was the best person to come over, as I knew Robbie MacKinnon as well as Barbara. I actually was responsible for recruiting Mrs MacKinnon to the Service too. The cooperation shown by your staff in Paris to expedite this unfortunate matter promptly has been exceptional. I have no doubt your team on the ground here on the Cote d'Azur will have been equally efficient.' Peter was hoping that the compliments would guarantee a positive response. He added, 'You seem to be happy to talk in English?'

'Yes, of course. I saw on our files that your grasp of our beautiful language is classified as *'only average'*.'

They laughed together at the Frenchman's joke.

I'll get on with this fellow, thought Peter.

'Before we go to Antibes, I would like to fill you in on what we have found out so far. Let us go to the VIP lounge where we will not be disturbed.'

Over coffee, Edouard methodically briefed the former Chief of MI6 on the events of the previous evening. 'So you see, we have a prima facie case against the two US agents who were, no doubt, CIA. I expect the results of the DNA and fingerprint tests will, as you say in English, tie up the loose ends. Unfortunately, diplomatic immunity will prevent us ever getting the bastards back to prosecute in France.'

'You know the background reasons for Mrs Renton's assassination, do you?'

'No.'

'Did you know the CIA had tried to kill her before?'

'I never knew that, where?'

'She had retired to a small village in the Aude; a place called Belveze, near Limoux…' He explained how Barbara had foiled the plot on her life, moved to Antibes and how MI6 had given her a new identity: Mme Richet.

170

Having listened to the saga, Edouard apologised for his ignorance. 'The Belveze business was probably kept at the Departmental level of the gendarmerie because they were not privy to the fact that Mme Renton had ever been in MI6. She was probably seen as just another English widow who had retired to France. It sounds, however, as if she was a *femme formidable*.'

'She was an amazing woman in more ways than one. So, too, is Mrs MacKinnon, the woman widowed last night. She is an Iraqi by birth and was our best double agent in Baghdad during the Iraq-Iran war. We brought her back to Britain when she was about to have her cover blown during the liberation of Kuwait. She married Robbie MacKinnon whose first wife was also killed by the CIA, but, again, we could never prove it.'

'This all sounds very complicated.'

'It is and I'm not sure the CIA knows they have killed Mr MacKinnon. I suspect they think they've killed Barbara Renton's partner.'

'Monsieur Richet?'

'His real name is Juan Quayle. He recently returned from a mission to kill bin Laden in Pakistan.'

'Ah, the infamous anthrax assassination?'

'We thought Quayle had died; we always presumed the assassination could end up being a suicide mission. It's only very recently that we found out he had managed to get back safely to Antibes.'

'Are you saying he slipped into France without reporting back to MI6?'

'Yes.'

'Isn't that odd?'

'He'd bought the luxury apartment in Antibes five or six years ago when he and Mme Renton were having an affair. When he decided to slip quietly back into France, I don't expect he thought Barbara Renton would be there waiting for him, as he wouldn't have known about the Belveze business.'

'And we never knew either.'

Peter smiled. He could see where this was leading. 'True,' agreed Peter.

'That makes him an illegal immigrant.'

'Not really, he is a British citizen and probably used his British passport, showing him to be John Pearson, to enter France.'

'If I remember rightly, that's the name he used when he was the Middle East correspondent for *The Daily Telegraph* and wrote all those anti-Israeli articles. That would mean he's living here under false pretences.'

'I think you'll find his French passport, marriage certificate, driving licence and so on, in the name of Richet, are all genuine.'

'Genuine fakes, you mean.'

The two men chuckled at the chicanery. They both knew the score; there were several ex-French agents living in London with forged English passports to protect their identity.

Peter continued, 'I would like to see Mrs MacKinnon first of all, if I may. Her stepson was married last week. Indeed, I attended his wedding. She only knew they were having their honeymoon somewhere in Cephalonia. We have discovered their hotel and I know she wants to tell her stepson that his father has been killed.'

'A terrible thing to have to do. I will take you there at once. However, first of all just glance over this press release that I have drafted...'

Peter looked at the statement, smiled and handed it back. 'It's in French.'

Edouard grinned. 'It would be no good in English. I will translate: *Around 11 pm on Saturday, 13th April, an armed robbery took place in the Avenue de l'ilette in Antibes. Monsieur and Madame Richet, a retired Parisian couple who had recently moved to Antibes, were murdered during the attack. Police are asking witnesses to come forward and are seeking the whereabouts of a grey Renault Megane with an Ain Department (01) registration.*'

'Why describe MacKinnon and Barbara Renton as married and from Paris?'

'It will keep the public and press off our backs. Down here, everyone hates Parisians. No one will come forward and the major local newspaper *Nice-Matin* will barely give the affair a mention.'

'That's excellent. I know Phil Jay didn't want our embassy staff in Paris to get involved; he'll be delighted when I tell him what you have done.'

* * *

St-Julian stopped outside Juan's apartment and accompanied Peter to the door where a solitary gendarme stood guarding the entrance. St-Julian showed his credentials and gave a brief explanation for Peter's presence. After entering the marble-floored reception area, Peter took the lift to the top floor.

A second gendarme was on guard outside Juan's door. He saluted and stood to one side, clearly having been briefed from below by radio.

Peter knocked and Juan opened the door. Behind him stood Kate, as beautiful and regal as ever despite having stayed the night in Juan's flat. The three stood in a triangle hugging each other. All three were at a low ebb and nothing was said for several minutes.

'I'm not sure words can express my feelings for what has happened,' said Peter. He looked at Kate with a lump in his throat and emptiness in his stomach. Knowing that she felt even worse than him, he tried to cheer her up.

'I have a phone number of the hotel in Cephalonia where Stuart is staying.'

'I'm not sure I can tell him,' she whispered.

'I'll tell him, if you wish. He will remember me from the wedding.'

'No, it's something that is my responsibility.'

And that's something you've never fought shy of in the past, thought Peter as he remembered how she single-handedly prevented the Saddam regime from using biological weapons.

He handed her a slip of paper.

'What time is it in Cephalonia?' she asked.

'They're an hour ahead.'

She looked at Juan. 'Can I use your phone?'

'Of course. Take the one in my bedroom. You'll have some privacy there,' replied Juan.

She disappeared into the adjacent room and closed the door.

Peter looked at Juan. 'She's an amazing woman.'

'Have you known her for long?' asked Juan.

'Since 1978, when I recruited her to work for us in Baghdad. She was Iraq's Head of Research into biological weapons and kept us in the picture as to what was going on during the Iraq-Iran war.'

Juan nodded and was quiet for a few moments, then casually remarked, 'I think she was crying most of the night.'

'Hardly surprising; she'd been married to Robbie for ten years.'

'She'll probably be feeling like I was after my family were burned alive – suicidal.'

'It might sound heartless, even cruel, but she'll pull through. She's one of the strongest characters I've ever met. She once gave me a right bollocking that I'll never forget when I made a sarcastic remark about Iraq's chemical weapons.'

'She'll know all about anthrax, then?'

'Forgotten more than we'll ever know. Talking of which, that brings us to your attack on bin Laden?'

'What about it?'

'The Pakistan Government asked for a specialist from our Ministry of Agriculture, Fisheries and Food to go and give advice on a bad outbreak of anthrax south of Gilgit last September. He came back with a sample and Porton Down confirmed it was Vollum 1-B, the same strain that you used in the attack.'

'I wasn't exactly sure where I was at the time when I met bin Laden. The truck in which we travelled had blacked-out windows. I guessed we were heading north and wondered if we were in Afghanistan, as it was a three-day journey from Peshawar. But if we were near Gilgit, as you said, then our direction must have been more north-easterly. It explains a lot for what happened subsequently.'

'You said "we". Who was with you?'

'Mir from *The Salt Valley Star*, his armed escort who I nicknamed

No-Name, and Kazim, my photographer. We met bin Laden with his entourage at an isolated farmhouse. After the interview, he made me write up the article exactly the way as it was to be published. He insisted I make some minor alterations and then approved it, giving it to Mir. We then gathered together for photographs. I was able to release the anthrax spores and, after about fifteen or twenty minutes, the four of us departed to return to Peshawar. Two days later, Kazim and Mir had died. I assumed the anthrax must have killed bin Laden and his cronies as well.'

'We believe it did. There were two announcements to that effect. One was in the Gilgit newspaper soon after your attack and one in the Cairo daily, *Al Wafd,* a couple of months later. Since 9/11, the Americans have practically blown the Tora Bora Mountains to bits trying to find bin Laden, but haven't found him. Last month Donald Rumsfeld virtually admitted they are assuming he's dead. But why didn't you come back to Britain and let us know you were safe? We thought you had died in Pakistan.'

'I have only been back here since February. I needed to recuperate fully; it's taken a lot out of me. My plan was to make contact when I felt stronger, but you can imagine my surprise when I found Barbara here in Antibes. I'm glad she was, however, as she sped up my recovery considerably.'

'Did she tell you about the attempt to assassinate her in Belveze?'

'Yes. It's why she fled here. It didn't take the bastards long to find her the second time either.'

'We think they were following Kate and Robbie MacKinnon. They discovered Barbara by accident.'

'Ironic, really. Had I not retained my Manx accent, then the MacKinnons would never have introduced themselves. It was Robbie who asked me if my name was Juan Quayle.'

'I guess that's my fault for mentioning I knew you at his son's wedding.'

'It's not your fault that an innocent remark led to such tragic consequences. It's the CIA and that bloody maniac Bush who killed Barbara, not you. Believe me; I shall have my revenge … somehow.'

175

'You had grown fond of Barbara?'

'Yes; after Molly and the kids were killed by al-Qaeda she was genuinely sympathetic and helpful. I had become very depressed and had contemplated suicide. My attitude to the bin Laden assassination began with the idea that I didn't care whether I returned or not. However, I always felt better when in Barbara's company and I slowly realised there was a life after Molly's death. During the five years I was in Lebanon as *The Telegraph's* correspondent, I never saw Barbara, but I thought about her a lot. I'm not sure I wouldn't have survived the aftermath of the anthrax assassination if I hadn't wanted to see her again.'

'So, what happened in Pakistan?'

CHAPTER 21

Sunday, 14th April 2002

Before Juan could reply, however, Kate re-entered the room. The two men looked at her.

'Well?' asked Peter. 'How did he take the news?'

'Stuart has gone to Ithaca for the day with Judy. They won't be back to their hotel until this evening.' She wiped her eyes, clearly upset at not having been able to make contact with her stepson.

'In which case, there's little we can do,' said Peter. 'Did you ask the hotel to get him to ring here as soon as he arrives back?'

'Yes, the receptionist spoke excellent English. I told her it was most urgent.'

There was a pause as Peter seemed to be thinking. 'I am wondering if Edouard St-Julian can help. He's the Deputy Head of French Internal Intelligence and met me at Nice airport when I arrived.'

'What do you think he could do?' asked Kate.

'Well, Stuart will want to come here immediately and I am thinking that this afternoon the French could send an aeroplane to Cephalonia, wait for him to return, and then he could fly here at once.'

'Would they do that?' asked Kate; her face brightened as her hopes were raised.

'We can only ask. Shall we go round to *The Hôtel Royal* and find him?'

A few minutes later, Juan was showing Peter where the murders had occurred. Kate was still very much in a state of shock and said nothing as she looked vacantly at the empty street, cordoned off with police tapes. The consequences of losing her husband had not truly sunk in.

Peter, who had known her for over twenty years, remembered how stoic and cool under pressure she could be. *She survived the traumas in Iraq during the war; she'll come up trumps again,* he thought.

What he didn't know was what was going through her mind. After the Iranians had killed Amer, her first husband, she had thrown herself into her job determined that her contribution to the Iraqi war effort would lead to victory. Not for nothing had she been the first, and only, woman to be made a 'Hero of Iraq', the country's highest honour. Now the seed of bitter determination had been re-sown. *I lost count how many times Amer told me never to trust the damn Yankees. I've got to find a way to get even and I think I know how. However, now Robbie is dead, who can I get to help me?*

Much to the annoyance of the hotel manager, Chief Inspector Dubois had turned the hotel's conference hall into the police incident room. It was there that Peter was able to introduce Kate and Juan to Deputy Director St-Julian. He then acquainted *les trois Anglais* to Inspector Dubois as *'notre homme sur le terrain'*. He said it in a manner that implied admiration for the achievements of the Inspector's team during the night.

Peter explained the predicament of being unable to contact Stuart and that it was likely that he and his new wife would not now be able to arrive 'until sometime tomorrow.'

'I came here from Paris in one of the executive jets of the President's Flight,' volunteered St-Julian. 'If it is not required, then it could fly to Cephalonia with Mme MacKinnon and pick them up. They could return here later this evening; the flying time can't be more than two hours.'

'That's very good of you, could you do that?' asked Peter with a wry smile, unnoticed by the Frenchman.

'It will be necessary for one of my assistants to travel with Mme MacKinnon. I'll get young Michel Dufay to go. He will need briefing. Is that OK?'

Peter looked at Kate, who nodded back approvingly. An hour later, Kate, accompanied by the young intelligence officer from Nice, who had been rudely woken from his sleep, was flying over central Italy towards Cephalonia.

* * *

At the suggestion of Inspector Dubois, the four men agreed to take lunch at *The Hôtel Royal's* private beach club across the promenade from the hotel. Sitting in the shade, with a pleasant breeze blowing from the sea, they sipped their aperitifs whilst choosing from the *table d'hôte*.

'I would be intrigued to hear from the horse's mouth, as I believe you say in England, how you managed to kill bin Laden and escape back to France,' said the aristocratic Frenchman to Juan.

Juan looked at Peter, his face registering surprise and at the same time asking whether he should answer the question.

But Edouard was quick and continued before Peter had a chance to reply. 'I think we have a right to know how you managed to get into France with a fake passport.'

'You mean the one that shows me as John Pearson?' replied Juan.

'I suppose so; I know your real name is Juan Quayle and you are living in Antibes as Jean Richet. It's highly irregular to say the least.'

Before Juan could begin, however, Peter looked at Edouard. 'I assume Inspector Dubois is security cleared to the highest level and understands the implications?'

The two Frenchmen looked at each other and nodded affirmatively.

Juan then repeated what he had told Peter earlier about flying to Karachi, travelling upcountry to Peshawar, meeting Mir from *The Salt Valley Star* who then drove them, accompanied by a minder, to meet bin Laden somewhere to the north, a journey of three days.

'It was a Friday morning, the seventh of September, when I finally was able to interview him. I won't bother you with the details, but afterwards he made me write up the article for *The Daily Telegraph*, as he wanted to approve it. We then posed for photographs. It gave me the opportunity to release the anthrax. There were nine or ten of us in the room for about twenty minutes including my gofer, Kazim, who was the

179

photographer. Also, there was Mir and the minder, who I had nicknamed No-Name, as well as bin Laden's entourage. We left bin Laden at the farmhouse in mid-afternoon to return to Peshawar the way we had come.'

Juan paused to see if there were any questions.

He continued, 'That evening we camped early, as it was pouring with rain. Progress was slow over the mud tracks that pose as roads up there. On Saturday morning, we woke to find it was snowing – very hard. The Mitsubishi's windows kept steaming up, despite the heaters being full on, and making headway was slow. I had taken my antibiotics and didn't feel too bad, but I noticed the others had begun to sniff and wheeze. At some point, Mir got lost in the snow storm. We probably went miles out of our way. After several hours, he turned the truck around and tried to retrace our steps. We ploughed on but I now believe we were heading in the wrong direction – more south than south-west.'

'Why do you say that?' asked Peter.

'If you travel due-south from Gilgit, you are making a beeline for the Indian border. I suspect that by Saturday evening we had only made seventy or eighty miles from the farmhouse. On Sunday Mir and Kazim were sneezing, their eyes were constantly running and their coughs suggested their lungs were full of mucus. I asked Mir if we were on the same road that we had taken when going north, but he reacted angrily; I guess his fever made him irritable. We probably covered one hundred miles that day before stopping early to make camp. After our meal, however, both Kazim and Mir were sick. They went into severe bouts of rigor, then coughed up blood and died within minutes of each other.'

'What did you do?' asked Anton.

'No-Name put the bodies in the back of the truck. We agreed to leave for Peshawar at first light. We settled down in our one-man tents, but the next morning the bastard and the Mitsubishi had gone, leaving me with the two dead bodies. I took my antibiotics and buried them as best as I could. I began trekking south. I walked all morning on tracks that were slippery and muddy. Around midday, I came across the Mitsubishi in a ditch. No-Name was dead inside. The truck was largely burnt out. I salvaged what I could and pressed on. I estimated I was making no more than two or three miles per hour. Peshawar must have been still one hundred miles away. Unbeknown to me, of course, I was going in the wrong direction. As darkness drew in, I pitched my tent, climbed inside, took my last penicillin capsules and made a meal on the primus. Half an hour later, I was sick and went into uncontrollable rigor. I thought I was going to die like Mir and Kazim. I began hallucinating, remembering when I was a little boy. Then, I guess I passed out.'

During the telling of the tale, Juan's three colleagues had been slowly eating their lunch. They had to wait patiently for the next phase of his story and allow him to catch up.

'When I woke up, I was lying on a bed of hay covered by several layers of sheepskins. I was in a small barn with an open fire in the centre. I was to discover that, for over two weeks, I had been continually slipping in and out of consciousness as my fever raged. A woman about my age was sitting nearby. She turned out to be the shepherd's wife and I was able to converse with her in Urdu. She told me she had managed to get me to occasionally sip the liquid from a lamb broth made with barley and some vegetables; although I don't ever remember having any. The day after I came round, her husband appeared. Ajay spoke quite good English and told me he had found my tent, with me unconscious inside, while out rounding up his flock of bharals – a cross between a sheep and a goat. He had carried me back to his bothy where he and his wife live for the summer. During my period of unconsciousness, he had driven some of his flock to the market in Kupwara, about five days away. He explained that, without the bharals, the Indian border town was only a two-day walk.'

Juan finished his *moules* before continuing. 'I asked Ajay where we were. He told me we were about ten miles inside Pakistan, near the Line of Control. During the winter, he said, he and his wife live in Kupwara in the Indian Kashmir Valley, but in the summer they come up to their hill station in Pakistan with their flock. However, the Indians are building an electric fence to stop cross-border raids and this would be the last time he would be able to live the nomadic life.

'A few days passed and I had regained my strength. I felt fit enough to travel with them to Kupwara. Ajay's wife, Didda, made a form of yoghurt from goats' milk. I guess it acted as an antibiotic in my stomach. The winter was drawing in, yet as we descended down into the valley it got noticeably warmer. We had few problems crossing the Line of Control and I saw neither Indian nor Pakistani soldiers. Mind you, Ajay knew where they would be and how to avoid them. At times he would scout ahead and leave me with Didda; then when he returned, we would change direction. It took us two days to go little more than twenty miles. I stayed with them in Kupwara, a small village, for a couple of days. Then at Ajay's suggestion, I reported to the local police station. My problem was that I had entered India without a visa. I still had my British passport with the name of John Pearson that I had used to enter Pakistan and hoped that I could talk my way out of any administrative trouble. I was to discover how tied-up in bureaucracy India is. Duplicate and triplicate copies are not enough. Everything has to have ten copies – with no carbon paper either.'

'So, by now it must have been mid-October?' asked Peter.

'Yes, although I was surprised how mild it was in the valley. The village policeman turned out to be a Sikh from Amritsar and, presumably remembering the 1919 massacre, was, therefore, somewhat anti-British. He saw me as an illegal immigrant. "You are a spy," he declared. I was locked up and isolated for several days. Perhaps he thought this would break down my resistance. To be fair, however, I was well looked after; as long as you like curry – morning, noon and night.'

'So how did you get away?' asked Edouard.

'I kept telling him the same story that I wanted to speak to Lieutenant General Gobal Rao of the NSG. When I had first mentioned his name, PC Singh scoffed. "Oh no, oh no," he kept repeating. "Impossible, most irregular, highly unorthodox." They were his exact words, over and over again.

'After a week of this, an Inspector appeared. I was to discover he had come from the State capital of Srinagar. He listened, but he also insisted it was "impossible, most irregular, and highly unorthodox" to allow a prisoner, that's what he called me, to see a General. I asked him how could I know the name of the Head of the NSG, if I wasn't an important person myself. He looked askance, thought for a while and then asserted, "Because you are a spy."

'Another week passed and I was taken to Srinagar. By now it was November and I was hoping things would soon be sorted. For two weeks I kept insisting on seeing General Rao and, finally, a Colonel appeared. He told me he worked for General Rao in the NSG HQ in Delhi. "I need something to prove who you are," he said.

'"Tell General Rao I met Fatima in Riyadh," I replied. "Tell him to ask her where she took me the day I disappeared. When the General has the answer, I will tell him everything about why I am here."

'The mention of Fatima worked wonders. Three days later, I was flown to Delhi accompanied by the Colonel. I was accommodated in a hotel but under conditions of house arrest. I was allowed to wander outside but always with an armed guard. Christmas came and went. Then in late-January, I was taken to the Indian NSG HQ and met General Rao. He apologised for all the delay and secrecy, but stressed it was essential that I was checked out. Communication with Fatima, he explained, was tortuous and typical turnaround with her was a month or six weeks. "Now, where did she take you the day you left for Naxcivan?" he asked.

'I knew then that I was on firm ground as I had never mentioned Naxcivan to anyone. "She took me to the Al Masmak Castle, then to the TV tower where she allowed me to use my VISA card to pay for lunch," I replied.

'"Welcome," he greeted me. "Now tell me what you want me to do and how you come to be in India?"

'I told him my story about being *The Telegraph's* correspondent in Lebanon and the assassination of bin Laden. He told me Barbara had retired and at their recent meeting of the al-Qaeda group he had met Phil Jay. "Too slippery for my liking," he said.'

Peter smiled. The remark was lost on the other two.

'I decided to ask if he would allow me to leave India without informing London. He agreed to keep it under wraps and I flew first of all to Rome, then to Nice. I arrived in France in the middle of February.'

CHAPTER 22

Sunday, 14th April 2002

The pleasant lunch dragged on as the four men pondered the future of the Middle East in view of the war in Afghanistan and the pending invasion of Iraq. Their conclusion was that the West's insatiable appetite for oil was the root cause of the problem. It was almost five o'clock when St-Julian's mobile rang.

'The aircraft is expected to leave Cephalonia in half an hour, and will arrive at Nice airport at 1940 hours,' he said after listening and saying, '*Oui*,' several times. He looked at his watch. 'I expect you would like to meet them?' he asked Peter.

'I think we'd better get ourselves organised, don't you?' Peter replied. Turning to Inspector Dubois, he asked, 'Is there available accommodation in the hotel?'

'It seems quite quiet,' he replied.

'Then you and I, Edouard, had better book ourselves a room each and also get a double room for Stuart MacKinnon and his wife. I don't suppose Kate will be too keen to stay in the hotel, but there aren't many alternatives.'

'She spent last night in my spare room, but I suspect she'd prefer to have Stuart somewhere near her,' said Juan.

'Will you be OK in your apartment?' asked Peter.

'I'll be fine, but there's one thing I'd like to bring up,' said Juan.

'Fire away.'

'Last night at dinner we discussed whether the Americans had followed Kate and Robbie in their MX-5 from Stuart's wedding. It now seems they did; hence, how they found Barbara. The question is could they have checked the registration number plate with the DVLC computer and found out where the MacKinnons live? Barbara wasn't convinced the MX-5 was covertly protected, despite Robbie's assurance that it was.'

'It was; so that line of enquiry wouldn't have got them very far except to alert Scotland Yard and ourselves that the CIA was up to no good. I'll ring Phil Jay in a few minutes to tell him what has happened. I will be suggesting he puts a twenty-four hour police guard on their house in Scotland. In the longer term, however, Kate will almost certainly have to consider moving.'

* * *

After sorting out the hotel accommodation, Peter rang the Head of MI6.

'Phil? It's Peter here. I'm sorry to be ringing you on a Sunday, but I want to keep you in the picture, especially as I couldn't contact you when this all blew up yesterday.'

'That's OK; I got the message you left and knew you would do the right thing. I'm glad you rang as the French have at last discovered Barbara's problem in Belveze. On Thursday, I had a visit from Mike Watts, Head of Special Branch, with two of his senior officers. Apparently, the French police in Carcassonne raised a query with Scotland Yard about Barbara's disappearance in Belveze.'

'What did you tell them?'

'Not much. I told them to keep Barbara's true identity under wraps and let the French treat Barbara's disappearance as just another missing person. Now, what's happening down there?'

* * *

St-Julian drove Peter and Juan to meet the incoming Dassault Falcon 50 from Cephalonia. The VIP executive jet landed and taxied to the same private part of the airport that had been used by the American assassins a little over twenty-four hours previously.

Introductions were made and Peter noticed that Stuart's wife, Judy, seemed to be more composed than her husband.

'I have booked you into the hotel and your room is next to Kate's,' he said. 'I hope that will be acceptable.'

Stuart nodded but said nothing. Judy smiled appreciatively.

'I have a feeling that you may not be hungry, but I have also taken the liberty of booking the six of us to have dinner together. It will give Edouard and me a chance to fill you in on developments. Is that acceptable?'

Again Stuart, looking pale and ashen, nodded silently.

They drove back to Antibes in silence.

Over dinner Edouard described the achievements of the French detectives.

When he had finished giving the facts, Peter continued. 'I know what has happened has been a dreadful experience and I can't even come close to imaging how you must all feel. However, I believe the police have done as much as they can to investigate the murders. What Edouard didn't mention is that he has faxed a report to the Minister for Foreign Affairs, Dominique de Villepin, who will be calling the US Ambassador to the Quai d'Orsay tomorrow morning to register a protest and demand the return of the two assassins to face trial. Of course, the Americans will deny the accusations and claim diplomatic immunity. I have sent a report to Barbara's successor, Phil Jay, who will take up the matter with Jack Straw. Tonight I would like you to think things over so that tomorrow we can discuss where we go from here. Edouard assures me you do not need to rush things and if you feel you want more time than that... fine.' Sir Peter paused and waited.

There was silence for several minutes before Stuart spoke. 'Before dinner, Kate and I agreed that Robbie will have to be flown home. Apparently in his will he wanted a funeral service in Gairloch followed by a cremation. Until Kate told me, I never knew that he wanted his ashes to be scattered in the Isle of Man; he hadn't lived there since leaving school and I don't remember him ever talking about it.'

The others looked at Kate. She was taking the whole experience badly. Her eyes were still red, almost forty-eight hours after the event. When she spoke, she was barely audible. 'I was surprised too. I can't remember him mentioning the Isle of Man until we made our wills together some years ago; although I knew he had been born there.'

'As a fellow Manxman, I know how he felt. We all want to return to the land of our birth,' remarked Juan. 'The gem of God's earth,' he added after a slight pause.

Everyone looked at him puzzled.

Feeling embarrassed, Juan explained. 'The phrase is the second line of the Manx National Anthem. Did he specify where he wanted his ashes to be scattered?'

It wasn't exactly a tactful question, but after wiping her eyes, she eventually replied, 'Robbie was a keen golfer. For some reason or other, I believe he wanted them to be buried on the 17th tee at Castletown Golf Course.'

Juan smiled. 'The Gully hole; from there he'll see a lot of balls getting lost in the sea and hear some choice language.'

Somehow the remark insinuating that Robbie would be alive to enjoy watching golf lightened the gloom. Even Kate smiled and dried her face.

'The Department will arrange for an aircraft to fly Robbie's body to Inverness and then to be taken to Gairloch,' assured Peter.

He then turned to Juan. 'What about Barbara?'

'I guess her three children and ex-husband will have to be told,' replied Juan.

Peter frowned. 'What three children and ex-husband?'

'When I began dating her after I had returned from Moscow and we were preparing my report on al-Qaeda at Woodside, she told me she was married soon after her 18th birthday, had three children before she was twenty-two, left her husband as soon as the children had reached adulthood and joined the civil service to become a PA to a grade three.'

'At that time you thought she really was a PA typist with top security clearance?'

'Yes; I had no reason to disbelieve her story.'

'That's what made Barbara so good in the field. She could convince people by spinning a wonderful yarn. She wasn't exactly an inveterate liar, but she could be convincing. Look,' he paused for a few seconds, 'how long did you know Barbara?'

Juan appeared reluctant to answer the question He was clearly bewildered at discovering his partner for the past three months since returning from Pakistan might not have been all she seemed. 'Well,' he began. 'There were the three or four weeks at Woodside in Devon,' he paused. 'Then a couple of months, on and off, when I was preparing to go to Lebanon. Finally, we've been here posing in Antibes as man and wife since I returned from Pakistan – what, six months altogether?'

'You're not really married then?' asked Kate, intrigued by the unfolding story.

But before Juan could answer, Sir Peter continued, 'When Barbara survived the first attempt on her life in Belveze, she invoked something we call a *Catalan*.'

'A *Catalan*?' asked Stuart. 'What's that?'

'It's the codename for the system we have of changing someone's identity in order to protect them. Your father was James Douglas before he moved to Scotland and we gave him the new ID of Robbie MacKinnon. Yes?'

Stuart nodded, remembering the day his mother and sister had died in the car accident at Kewstoke, their funeral and the subsequent upheavals.

'Your father was given a new ID to protect both of you. We did the same for Barbara after the Americans tried to kill her in Belveze.'

He stopped and looked at Juan directly. 'Juan, do you really want to know the full story of Barbara's background?'

'Yes.'

'It could be upsetting.'

'I'd prefer to be told the truth.'

Sir Peter looked at Kate, Stuart and his wife, before returning his gaze to Juan. 'Perhaps you may want the others to leave.'

'I think in view of what has happened and that it might have been me who could have been shot, not Robbie, then Kate should know everything.'

'OK. Did it never occur to you that there was no way Barbara could have joined the Security Services around the age of forty, learnt to speak Georgian and Armenian and, finally, spend time in the Caucasus? She then ran the region's desk at Vauxhall Cross and made her way up the promotion ladder to become my successor?'

Juan's face looked blank. He was silent for some time as he realised the timescales were impossible. 'I guess when we initially began our relationship, I was mesmerised by her vivaciousness. I had never encountered a woman quite like her. At one time, I asked her to marry me. She turned me down, saying that her first marriage had been enough. I believed everything she told me. I can see now that her story didn't add up.'

'If it's any consolation, you weren't the first person she had charmed.'

'When I presented my al-Qaeda report to you and Sir Charles Gray, she sat next to you. I did wonder about her then. However, I never had the chance to press her for the truth. She had spurned my proposal, which upset me, and I didn't expect to see her again. When I returned to join MI6, she kept up the pretence. I should have asked her then about her background but she had cast her spell on me again. I was captivated by her wit and bubbly personality. I confess I didn't know she could speak Armenian and Georgian.'

'Let me tell you about her early years; it may help you to forgive her behaviour. She was born at the beginning of the Second World War. Her father, who was in the Desert Rats, was killed in North Africa. She was brought up by her mother and aunt in a small town in Northamptonshire. Her mother died of TB in 1952 when she was eleven. Her aunt looked after her and she won a scholarship to go to a good school nearby at Wellingborough. In the sixth form, she won a scholarship to go to Lady Margaret College, Oxford. Then, within months, her aunt died of cancer. She achieved a double first in history and philosophy. For her DPhil, she researched the history of Naxcivan and its complex relationship with Nagorno-Karabakh and Turkey. I believe her thesis is still considered to be the seminal work on the topic. She spent two years in what is today Azerbaijan. R W Southern, the professor of modern history at Oxford at the time, offered her a Fellowship at Bailliol, but she went back to Armenia and married a Captain in their army. He was killed in a skirmish with Azerbaijani troops six months later. She came back to Britain and joined MI6 in 1967. After attending the long Arabic course, she was attached to our embassy in Tbilisi. She had married the second secretary in the embassy within six months. He, too, died shortly afterwards of a heart attack. I think she began to think she was jinxed: her father, her mother, her aunt, then two husbands – all died relatively suddenly. She threw herself into her work and became the best specialist on the Caucuses we ever had. Linguistically, as I've said, she was fluent in Armenian and Georgian, and could get by in Russian, Turkish and Farsi, as well as Arabic. She came back to England the same week as I returned from Baghdad in 1978 and we became good friends. She seemed to go from one affair to another without ever getting too close to anyone. So,' he paused and looked at Juan, 'the fact that she insisted that we issued her with a marriage certificate and a passport for you as her husband was not by chance. I believe she wanted you to return from your bin Laden mission and for you to become man and wife. The earlier subterfuge was her attempt at protecting you.'

Juan's face was buried in his hands. He was clearly moved. His mind was racing. *After all we've been through, Barbara really loved me. For the second time, I have lost my wife at the hands of an executioner. Like with bin Laden, I will extract revenge; this time it will be Bush.*

'So, Barbara insisted our passports and other French documents were genuine?' asked Juan.

'Barbara insisted on the correct documentation,' confirmed Peter.

'Perhaps real is a better adjective than genuine,' smiled Edouard.

'Nonetheless, you will be entitled to a widower's pension. You are her sole relative; there never was an ex-husband or three children. You are the sole recipient of her estate. Did she tell you what she wanted in the event of her death?'

'No, but I know where she would like her remains to be scattered.'

'Where?'

'At the bottom of the Rue Albert 1st in the gardens, where she could watch the petanque.'

'She won't see anyone lose their balls there,' said Stuart dryly.

Everyone laughed.

CHAPTER 23

Monday, 15th April 2002

On Monday morning, Edouard St-Julian began pulling strings with the public services to proceed as rapidly as possible with the repatriation of Robbie's body to Scotland and Barbara's funeral arrangements.

We all react differently to the death of a loved one. For some the event is too traumatic; we go to pieces and need help and support. For others the senses become numb; we appear to feel nothing and neighbours think we are hard-bitten. For many it is a time to pull their socks up and get the necessary jobs done; there will be time to reflect later. Juan, since the death of his beloved Molly and family in the Isle of Man, had become something of a complex, opaque character. He had reacted then by getting organised and focusing his energies to extract revenge on al-Qaeda. That Monday he grasped the nettle and visited the *Mairie* to report the death of Mme Barbara Richet. He collected *l' acte de décès* – the death certificate. It triggered the thought, *How bizarre that Barbara Renton will never officially die.* Next, he contacted the Church of England vicar at the Holy Trinity Anglican Church in Nice. The rector, Father Robin Letts, agreed Barbara's funeral could be held in the Russian Orthodox Church on the Rue Albert 1st. It was, he agreed, by far the most convenient location as, afterwards, he would take the short service at the local crematorium in nearby Biot. The vicar explained Barbara's remains would be available for collection the following day, but, he added, to bury them in the gardens at the bottom of the Rue Albert 1st would require special permission. Juan discovered,

192

however, that Edouard's intervention would remove the mountain of bureaucracy.

By contrast, Stuart was still suffering from the loss of his father; Judy appeared the more phlegmatic of the pair. She accompanied Peter and Edouard to the airport to arrange the repatriation of Robbie's body back to Inverness. A Lear jet, usually used to return ill holidaymakers to their country of origin, would be available in two days' time, unfortunately the same day as Barbara's funeral.

Meanwhile, Kate and Stuart consoled each other of their loss by doing little – simply lying in the sun at *The Hôtel Royal's* private beach. Their low spirits did not help the time pass quickly. Peter was surprised by Kate's reaction as she had been so strong when he had handled her as an MI6 agent in Iraq; however, he admitted to himself, *It was well over twenty years ago.*

Judy, by contrast, was the antithesis of her husband and kept herself busy. She accompanied Peter and Edouard to the pathology laboratories in Nice to get the DNA results. The DNA was identical on both cigarette ends; the brand, *Hilton*, could only be bought in specialist shops in France, but was popular in the United States. The evidence on the airport door handle was, unfortunately, inconclusive. Nevertheless, as far as Edouard was concerned, it confirmed Inspector Dubois's suspicions: the younger of the Americans had been in *The Hôtel Royal's* car park.

Both Peter and Edouard immediately contacted their respective headquarters in London and Paris respectively; official reports would follow in writing. Both felt there was now sufficient evidence for French and British Governments to take the matter up at the highest level, but both men were sufficiently experienced, and cynical, to believe little would happen.

To avoid Tuesday becoming something of a drag, Edouard hired a minibus. He arranged for the six of them to make a trip to the hills behind the Côte d'Azur. 'It will take their minds off their recent tragedy,' he had explained to Peter.

He took them to Vence for morning coffee and a wander around the bric-a-brac market. Crossing the River Var, they lunched in the hilltop village of Aspremont before driving along the *Grande Corniche* to visit the Roman remains of the *Trophée des Alpes* at La Turbie. Edouard had admitted over lunch that he hadn't visited this part of France since being a teenager, but enthused over the Roman history of the *Via Julia Augusta* that connected Rome to Gaul. 'This trophy makes me feel humble,' he declared as he took his party around the grounds. From the terraces of the gardens they viewed the splendid panorama of the coast with Monaco 400 metres below their feet.

On Wednesday, Kate, Stuart and Judy left Antibes early to fly to Scotland with Robbie's coffin. A take-off time of 0900 hours would allow the crew to return to France that afternoon. The organisation of the French officials was impeccable. Stuart, by now with his grief under control, was conscious that they would have faced greater problems had it not been for the Deputy Director of the DCSI. He thanked him profusely. Before they left their hotel, Juan arrived to see them off and promised he would attend the funeral in Gairloch the following week.

Peter had agreed to drive the MX-5 back to Britain on Thursday, the day after attending Barbara's funeral. The service in the Russian Orthodox Church at eleven o'clock was minimalistic – at Juan's request. There were only a handful of attendees including Inspector Dubois and two of his team. At the crematorium in Biot, the rituals were completed in minutes and Juan agreed to collect Barbara's ashes the following morning. After a light lunch, Peter and Juan saw Edouard off from the airport to return to Paris; both agreed his presence had been invaluable. That evening the two men met for a drink at a bar at the bottom of the Rue Albert 1st, before wandering into the old town to dine.

'What are your plans for the future?' asked Peter.

'I've decided to go home to the Isle of Man,' replied Juan.

Peter showed some surprise.

Juan noticed his reaction and explained. 'Although I can speak French fluently, I know no one down here. I will always be seen as a foreigner by the locals. By returning to the island, I should be able to create a circle of friends, join a golf club; that sort of thing.'

'But in the Isle of Man they think Juan Quayle is dead, surely?'

'I realise that, so I was thinking I would return as John Pearson. I assume the ID documents given to me by MI6 all those years ago will stand scrutiny by the Manx authorities?'

'They'll do that all right, but what happens if you bump into someone who used to know you?'

Juan laughed. 'I'll have to dream up an excuse to explain what happened without breaking the Official Secrets Act.'

'Won't returning there remind you too much of Molly and your children?'

'I think of them every day, Peter. I have never stopped thinking of them. It's what kept me going during the bad times in Lebanon and fuelled my determination to carry out bin Laden's assassination. At least this way, I will be near their grave and be able to go to it whenever I want. Do you realise I've never even seen it?'

'I'm sorry, Juan. I didn't mean to be crass.'

'It's OK. I had to leave the burial details to George Costain, the local police inspector. He is one of the few people who knew I didn't die in the inferno at my farm. It's ironic really that I have your old colleague, Sir Charles Gray, to thank for all this. Without him coming to St Bees, I would never have met Molly, had children of my own, met Barbara or visited Pakistan. It's incredible that one small decision can make monumental life changes. I suppose he's retired now?'

'Yes, he retired around the same time as me. He went back to his beloved Marlborough where he became chairman of the school's governors.'

'He went to Marlborough School?'

'Yes. He had left there in the early forties to join Bletchley Park and worked in Hut Eight for a while with Turing then under Hugh Alexander. After the war, he went to Sidney Sussex College, Cambridge to read mathematics.'

Conversation never stopped as the two men reminisced about their time spent in Baghdad; Juan as the assistant military attaché and Peter, who had arrived a few months after Juan had left, as the local security officer. Both had visited Babylon, Samarra and Ctesiphon during their period in Iraq and both wondered how a country that had seen the birth of civilisation with the advent of writing, mathematics and architecture could have fallen so far.

'The problem began in 1920, after World War One,' said Peter, 'when Britain was given the mandate by The League of Nations and drew maps across the Middle East. We gave Iraq virtually no coastline and cooped up the Sunnis, Shias and Kurds into one pot. It was made worse by making Faisal king when he wasn't even an Iraqi and giving all the power to the minority Sunnis.'

'Yes, but the Sunnis were the educated elite. They had been groomed by the Sunni Ottomans for almost 400 years,' replied Juan.

They agreed that Saddam Hussein was no saint and only kept control of the disparate population by brute force. 'Nevertheless, he liberated women by employing them in government positions, introduced compulsory education to the age of twelve, and provided free hospitalisation to all its citizens,' said Peter.

'For which he won an award from UNESCO, I believe,' added Juan. 'And now they are suffering badly from the No-fly Zones and the imposition of sanctions.'

'You don't know the half of it,' replied Peter. 'Although medicines are not officially being denied to Iraq, an article in *The Guardian* last year claimed that over a thousand children are dying each month due to poor diet, a breakdown of sanitation and basic hospital facilities. Madeline Albright was interviewed on CBS TV and claimed the death of more than half a million children was "worth it." Can you believe it? Clinton has a lot to answer for.'

'And the Americans justify this to get Saddam to give up his weapons of mass destruction that, despite the place crawling with UN Weapons Inspectors, have never been found.'

'Quite, and for which we have Robbie and Kate to thank. There will be chaos if the Americans invade next year,' sighed Peter. The thought of the possible consequences dampened their spirits for the rest of the evening. As they said their farewells, they agreed to meet at Robbie's funeral in Gairloch the following week.

* * *

Peter left the next day for his three-day journey back to his home in Wiltshire. Juan returned to Biot for Barbara's remains. He discreetly scattered them in the gardens next to the boules pitch. He put the apartment on the market with a nearby *immobilier*. By not asking a silly price, the penthouse was sold within hours to the first viewer that evening. A completion date of 31st May was agreed. Juan then began planning how to get to Gairloch for Robbie's funeral and his move to the Isle of Man.

A day later, he flew to Liverpool direct with Easyjet, caught an evening flight to Ronaldsway Airport, hired a car and booked in for four nights in *The Sefton*.

Can it really be eleven years ago since I first stayed here? he thought as he registered into the hotel. *God, it's seven years ago since Molly and the kids were murdered; so much has happened in that time.*

His first task, the next morning, was to visit Molly's grave at Bride Parish Church. It was weird looking at his own name on the headstone, but there it was:

In memory of

Juan Hasani Quayle, age 44
Molly Anne Quayle, age 32
Peter Luke Kelly,   age 10
Mikey Robert Kelly, age 8
Sophie Grace Quayle, age 4
Heather Indira Quayle, age 1

who died together in the
tragedy at Ballajorra on
Wednesday 5th July 1995

May they rest in peace together

197

He looked at the state of the grave. Someone had been keeping it neat and tidy. There was a bouquet of flowers. *They've been placed here quite recently.* He wondered if it had been George who had been looking after it. He wandered down to his parents' grave. A different site revealed itself: weeds and an air of neglect. He tidied it as best as he could and vowed that in future he would look after it properly.

He spent three days looking around the island for a suitable property to buy that was convenient for shops, a golf course and a pub. He found a spacious, luxurious, three-bedroomed penthouse apartment with a private garage in Port St Mary. *The Point Hotel* had been converted into six luxury flats seven years previously with a penthouse on the top floor. With only one previous owner, it was in excellent condition and needed little updating. It gave Juan a panoramic 180° view south over the sea.

'On a clear day, you can see Snowdonia,' claimed the estate agent.

Yes, about twice a year if you're lucky, thought Juan.

Nonetheless, *The Old Vic* was only one hundred metres away; the golf course, with its own bar and restaurant, about the same distance and basic shops no more than a five-minute walk. The asking price was well inside his budget and he signed a contract for a completion date a few days after his Antibes' sale would be finished. He wondered if Sylvia was still the barwoman in *The Old Vic,* the pub where he had first met bin Laden and the crew of the *Dom Pedro.* He stuck his head through the door and looked into the saloon. It was empty; there was no one behind the counter, but the ambiance hadn't changed. *Still a spit and sawdust establishment,* thought Juan.

He flew to Glasgow the following afternoon and hired a car to drive up the west coast. He reached Glen Coe, checked into the *Ballachulish Hotel* and settled for the night. He arrived at Gairloch in plenty of time for the two o'clock service, having pre-booked into *The Old Inn* for his second night in Scotland. He had arranged to meet Peter who had driven from Wiltshire in the MX-5 and planned to return home by train. Over lunch, Peter explained that the shit had hit the fan over Barbara's assassination. His written report, submitted to Phil Jay, had been passed to Jack Straw verbatim with a veiled threat from the Head of MI6: *Deport the American diplomats undertaking surveillance activities from Grosvenor Square, or he could not be responsible if there wasn't a leak to the press.*

'God knows what will happen,' said Peter. 'I suspect it's already up at Prime Minister level.'

'Quite right too. Let's hope the French take a similar stand.'

'If I know them, Chirac will go the whole nine yards with Bush.'

The small church was packed for Robbie's funeral. *Unlike for Barbara,* thought Juan. Afterwards, the wake was a traditional highland affair with copious quantities of alcohol, mostly scotch, being consumed. To Juan's surprise, Kate, Stuart and Judy did not accompany the coffin to the crematorium. Only the vicar went to oversee a short service in Dingwall, an hour's drive away.

Stuart explained that this was common practice in the highlands whenever there was a cremation. 'The family are expected to host the wake and outdrink the guests.' He smiled to himself, adding, 'We will pick up the ashes tomorrow, then all we have to do is to arrange for myself and Kate to go to the Isle of Man next week. Judy has to return to work and will go back to Leicester in the car tomorrow.'

'I have just bought my own property on the island. If you like I will remain in Gairloch for a few days and travel with you. I'll be able to show you around.'

'We'll take you up on that.'

CHAPTER 24

Thursday, 25th April 2002

'I'm sorry that I have not been able to see you any earlier Jack but my schedule is exceptionally busy. When my PPS told me you wished to bring Phil with you, I guessed things must be serious.'

'I fully understand Prime Minister. You know Phil Jay, of course.'

'Yes, nice to see you again, Phil. How's your father?'

'As well as can be expected, Prime Minister.'

'Please pass on my regards to him.'

The three sat down around a circular coffee table; previously leather chairs had been arranged equidistant from each other. A white coated waiter approached and asked whether they would like their coffee 'with or without cream'. With their china cups filled, he left the room.

'If I may, Prime Minister, I'll let Phil explain,' began Jack Straw.

'You will remember, sir, that last October my predecessor, Barbara Renton, took early retirement.'

The PM nodded, indicating Phil to continue.

'She had bought a house near Carcassonne, but hadn't been there long, only a few weeks in fact, when the CIA sent two thugs after her. Their attempt to assassinate her failed. Barbara had prepared a trap and outwitted them; I suspect they died instead. We are unsure how the Americans found her address, as she had kept it under wraps.' He paused and thought he saw a flicker of guilt pass across the PM's face. *He knows about the Belveze affair!*

Phil continued. 'As a consequence of her narrow escape and fearful that they might try again, Barbara requested that we implement *a Catalan.'*

'*A Catalan?*' asked the PM.

'It's a codename for a system where we give someone a completely new identity for their personal protection. Every conceivable possibility is covered; the system has never failed – until now.'

'What do you mean?'

'Twelve days ago, a week last Saturday, Barbara was shot in the South of France, execution style – a single bullet to the head.'

'Good God.'

'The evidence points irrefutably to the CIA. A USAF plane landed at Nice airport in the early evening. Two hoods, one known to us as Carswell, were met by the US Chargé d'affaires based in the South of France. Because of their diplomatic clearance, no checks on their hand luggage could be made. They then cleverly evaded being followed by the gendarmerie. Several hours later, they returned to the airport. There is considerable evidence they were in the street at the time when and where Mrs Renton was shot. The question is, Prime Minister, what are we going to do about it?'

'Jack?'

'Firstly, Prime Minister, I believe you must take this up with President Bush and insist the two assassins are returned to France to face trial.'

'You know they won't do that.'

'Yes, but President Bush must be made to know how strong we feel about it. Secondly, what Phil hasn't told you is that Grosvenor Square's spooks put a tail on two of our former agents who were also covered by our protection scheme. They were followed to Antibes, where Mrs Renton was shot.'

'I don't follow you.'

'The two agents were known as Mr and Mrs MacKinnon. She was the Iraqi double agent who hid the biological weapons in Iraq in such a way that they could never be found during their war with Iran.'

'I remember you telling me about her. The popular press at the time called her Dr Germ. She used some sort of chess code.'

'Grosvenor Square has been trying to trace Mrs MacKinnon ever since the Pentagon began planning the invasion of Iraq. They tried to persuade a Metropolitan Police Officer to give them details of the MacKinnon's car. We warned them off, but it appears they ignored us.'

'Jack, as you well know, the planned invasion of Iraq is only a rumour. We don't know for certain; and anyway, why would the Americans want to find Mrs MacKinnon?'

'Prime Minister, you know the forthcoming invasion is about as certain as the sun rising in the east tomorrow morning. They want Mrs MacKinnon to reveal the method she used to hide the biological weapons. By following the MacKinnons to the South of France, after their son's wedding, the Americans hit lucky and spotted Barbara Renton. They rapidly put a plan into action to kill her. I want your backing to expel the entire diplomatic intelligence team from Grosvenor Square.'

'How many are there?'

'At least eight, maybe ten.'

'Bush won't like it.'

'I'm not happy either, but the alternative is to do nothing and let them piss all over us. If the press got hold of the assassination and we were seen to be weak, then...' Jack Straw left the sentence hanging.

The PM said nothing as he thought through the consequences.

Phil, sensing it was the right moment, added, 'At the moment, the Antibes execution has been kept from the press. When Barbara was killed, they also shot Mr MacKinnon.'

The PM's eyes widened as he stared at Phil. 'Why kill him?'

'He was the former RAF officer who designed the war game that was used by Iraq to plan their invasion of Iran. He also created the clever software protection system that is now used to secure many of MoD's secret files. We believe the CIA killed his first wife and daughter to put pressure on him to reveal the method's secrets; now they have killed him too. On this occasion, however, it was probably an accident; he just happened to be in the wrong place at the wrong time.'

'This is getting out of hand. Go ahead. Call in the US Ambassador and give him forty-eight hours to repatriate his intelligence staff. I'll ring

Bush this afternoon, but before I do that, you'd better fill me in with all the details...'

* * *

'George, are you sitting comfortably?'

'Hi, Tony. What's up?'

'About now, your ambassador here in London is being given forty-eight hours to expel your team of intelligence officers.'

'What? You can't do that!'

'We can, and we must. There is too much circumstantial evidence that shows your boys have not been playing by the rules. They've murdered the former Head of MI6, Barbara Renton, and a retired RAF officer, MacKinnon, who happened to be with her at the time. Your guys in London were warned off from trying to locate Mrs MacKinnon ages ago, but took no notice. I'm sorry George, but it has gone too far. Using diplomatic immunity is one thing, but utilising it to kill a former senior servant of the Crown is something altogether different.'

There was silence on the phone.

Thinking they may have been cut off, the PM asked, 'George, are you there?'

'Yeah, I hear yer. I'm thinking; that's all.'

'George, so far there has been nothing in the papers about this. We want to keep it that way, but I must be seen by my Cabinet to be doing something. My ambassador in Washington has requested to see Colin Powell tomorrow to deliver the strongest possible protest. He will ask for the perpetrators to be returned to France to face trial.'

'You know that's impossible, Tony.'

'Yes, I know, but the French will be doing likewise. I'm sorry, George; all I can suggest is that in five or six months' time, you ask to reintroduce your intelligence officers to London. I will ensure the request is handled sympathetically.'

* * *

The following day, when the London team were preparing to fly back across the Atlantic, the shit was hitting the fan in Langley, Virginia. Colin Powell, George Tenet, and General Richard B Myers, the Chairman of the Joint Chiefs of Staff, accompanied only by their private, personal secretaries, were in conference. The twin protests from the British and French Governments had ignited a powder keg. Colin Powell was furious with the CIA Director that he had not been informed of the plot to kill Mrs Renton.

'How the hell did you think you could get away with it? You must have known her personally; that compounds the crime, as far as I'm concerned.'

'The order to eliminate Mrs Renton came from the President on the evening of 9/11. We sent two agents to her village in the South of France, but they disappeared. The cunning fox must have outwitted them somehow. When we found she was in Antibes, we had no option but to finish the job. There wasn't any time to tell you, or the President. If I had let her escape, I would have been seen to be incompetent. And yes, I did know her. She was an exceptional Director in every way. However, if she had gone to the press about the fallacious justification for our invasion of Iraq, then the world would crucify us.'

'What are you saying, George?'

'I don't wish to be disloyal, but you know as well as I do that for ten years UN Weapons Inspectors have been crawling all over Iraq looking for WMDs and haven't found anything.'

'That's because their records were cleverly doctored.'

'Quite – by the former Iraqi double agent who now calls herself Mrs MacKinnon.'

The Secretary of State nodded, apparently accepting the Director of the CIA's assertion. 'When I was overseeing *Desert Storm*, I remember General Schwarzkopf telling me how the Iraqis were using some goddamn chess method for hiding their biological weapons. I learnt then that the CIA was trying to fathom how the technique worked and by error they killed the wife of the guy who had designed it. Now a similar error has killed the guy himself. What a cock-up.'

There was a brief pause in the heated conversation and General Myers tried to change the subject. 'Look, we can't cry over spilled milk. Our plans for the liberation of Iraq are at an advanced stage. Are we going to let this setback stop us?'

'No,' replied Colin Powell, 'carry on. This mustn't get in the way. I intend to let the protests from the Brits and the French fall on death ears. However, George, I can understand why you would like to find Mrs MacKinnon and get her to reveal how she hid the WMDs. How many men have you got left in Grosvenor Square?'

'Two: Lee Hefferman, nominally Head of Visa Applications, and Ruth Danski, theoretically Head of the typing pool, who just happens to be one of our very best software gurus.'

'Then I suggest they carry on looking for Mrs MacKinnon, but stress the delicacy of their task.'

* * *

The scrambler rang twice. Lee Hefferman was hosting a small buffet for his departing troops in one of the embassy's reception rooms when a worried member from the HR department entered.

'Excuse me, sir, but your Director is on the scrambler.'

Caught with a champagne flute in his hand and about to deliver a farewell speech, he asked, 'Who?'

The clerical assistant stretched towards her boss and whispered in his ear. 'George Tenet.'

Lee rushed out of the room, announcing. 'I'll be back in a minute.'

'Yes, sir, Lee here. How can I help?'

'I know it's nine o'clock over there, but I have just come out of a meeting with Colin Powell. Operation Iraqi Freedom is going ahead and the Secretary of State agrees we should continue to try to find where Iraq's WMDs were hidden.'

'Sir, it's because of tailing Kate MacKinnon that we are in this bloody mess. The Brits will close this place down if we get caught again.'

'We know the risks, but there is only you and Ruth Danski left who have any chance of finding where the missing VX-R was hidden. The Brits won't be expecting you to continue the search. When Carswell killed Renton, he also shot Robbie MacKinnon. There must have been a funeral. Check to see if there have been any obituaries in local newspapers; ask Ruth if she has any ideas. There must be a lead somewhere, surely?'

'I'll do my best, sir, and get back to you.'

God, he's mad. Has he no idea what ill feeling has been created by this business?

Lee returned to the party, saw Ruth and whispered, 'When this is all over, I'd like a word before you disappear.'

* * *

'What is it, boss?'

'HQ wants us to discreetly continue to search for Mrs MacKinnon's whereabouts.'

'Don't they know what damage this business has caused?'

'George Tenet told me to ask you whether you have any ideas.'

'I have been thinking whether we missed a trick.'

'And?'

'What do you need to get to university?'

'Go on.'

'Qualifications: *O* levels and *A* levels, or their Scottish equivalent.'

So?'

'We search through academic results for the year that Stuart MacKinnon went up to Edinburgh University; either electronically through the exam boards' computers or local newspapers that always print the local schools' results.'

'Brilliant, Ruth. What would we do without you?'

'A pay rise would be nice!'

CHAPTER 25

Four days after the funeral, Juan accompanied Kate and Stuart to the Isle of Man. Having arrived at Ronaldsway Airport in the late afternoon, they picked up a hire car and booked into *The Sefton*. That evening Juan persuaded them to try 'an excellent Indian restaurant not far from here.' They walked along the seafront to the bottom of Broadway and five minutes later were being ushered into *The Taj Mahal* by a tall Asian wearing a Kashmiri jacket.

Juan recognised him instantly as the same proprietor that had greeted him and Molly when they dined there for his forty-third birthday, eight years previously. Memories flooded back, crashing on his consciousness like waves on a beach. It had been the night they made love on their way home in the back of the car on the Sulby side of Snaefell Mountain and where Heather had been conceived. *I wonder if he'll recognise me. It should be OK; I've changed a lot.*

Before leaving Scotland, the three had agreed that Robbie's ashes should be scattered the following morning and thereby allow Stuart to fly back to East Midlands Airport, near Leicester, where Judy would meet him in the late afternoon. Kate wanted to see something of Robbie's island: where he was born, the schools he had attended and his parents' grave. She would stay for a further two days. She was looking forward to being shown around by Juan and, over their curries, reminisced how when Robbie had visited her parents at Samarra in 1978, her younger sisters had been mystified by the whole concept of an island.

'I remember them asking Robbie how big the sea was. They didn't believe him when he had described how its colour could change with the weather in a few hours and how it could be calm one minute and have gigantic waves the next. I suspect he embellished his description for their benefit.'

'No, he probably was nearer to the truth than you think. If it is fine tomorrow, then from Castletown Golf Course you may be able to see the Welsh Mountains seventy-five miles away; on the other hand, if the mist comes in, you won't even be able to see the sea seventy-five yards away.'

Stuart and Kate discussed their future with Juan over their meal. 'We have agreed it is impractical for Kate to look after *Glenfinnan's* one-acre garden on her own. Also, it is very isolated, especially in the winter. We have put the house on the market and have had an offer already,' he said.

Kate continued, 'I am thinking of moving somewhere nearer to Stuart and Judy. What do you think?'

'I think it's a good idea,' replied Juan. 'As we get older we need to find somewhere that is convenient for shops, restaurants and so on. Badachro is, what, seven miles from the nearest shop?'

'Are you calling me old?' laughed Kate.

'No. Please don't take me the wrong way. I only meant to say we have to be practical about these things. I believe I've found an ideal spot near the local golf course, the shops and a pub. If you like, I will show it to you tomorrow after we have dropped Stuart off at the airport.'

Juan paid the bill with his credit card in the name of John Pearson – the identity he would use for the rest of his life. Juan didn't notice the waiter looking carefully at his face, nor at the back of his left hand, while he entered his pin number. Afterwards in the kitchen, Gopal approached Ajit. 'Well, what do you think? Did you look at him? Is he Major Quayle?' he asked his friend.

'I couldn't see much resemblance; and besides Quayle was killed in the fire at the farm. We know that for a fact; it was in all the newspapers.'

'Look, I'm just going outside for a minute or two. I won't be long.'

'Where are you going?'

But Gopal had already left, leaving Ajit alone except for their locally recruited kitchen hand.

Gopal stood on the pavement and looked to his left. Near the bottom of Broadway on the opposite side of the road, he saw three people turning right towards the centre of Douglas. He quickly followed them. Under the Villa Marina Arcade, he saw them fifty yards ahead. He slowed to their ambling pace, keeping his distance, watching while they chattered socially. They passed The Gaiety Theatre and entered *The Sefton*. He ran to the hotel's entrance and through the revolving doors saw them enter the lift. *They are staying here,* he thought. He turned and a few minutes later, he was back at *The Taj Mahal*.

In the kitchen, he explained to his partner, 'I had a good look at him when he was paying the bill. I think it is Quayle. He's changed a bit. He even speaks differently, but there was something about him. That faint mark on his left hand where a scar had healed, for example. The way he carried himself – I'd swear it was Major Quayle. Did you notice the woman he was with? She could be from the Middle East: Jordanian or Syrian. I think we should report it.'

'If you do, then you may regret it. Remember what happened the last time. The police were crawling over us for weeks afterwards. We were lucky they didn't realise there was a gap in our alibis after we left Tynwald Fair.'

'What do you mean?'

'It took us over an hour from leaving the fair to collect Mwt at the farm and for us to get back to Douglas. From St Johns to Douglas is only fifteen minutes. You and I have a cushy number here; we've had a good life. Are you going to risk it for an organisation that is floundering now that Osama is dead?'

'We vowed on the Koran to fight for al-Qaeda. Are you going to go back on your oath?'

'Look, we did our bit when we helped Mwt al-Swd destroy a mother and four innocent children. I think you should forget it and let sleeping dogs lie.'

'I'll think about it.'

* * *

The following day, they had dressed in appropriate clothes for tramping over a golf course. Juan drove Kate and Stuart to Derbyhaven and took the track that leads to the lighthouse at the end of the Langness peninsula. Near the old rifle butts, he parked the car and they walked across the course to the seventeenth tee. They agreed the back tee, *the tiger tee*, so called as the tee box was painted with yellow and black stripes, was the most suitable site to scatter the ashes.

'I can see Dad laughing as the balls go into the gulley,' said Stuart. 'What is the carry to the fairway?'

'It must be nearly 200 yards,' replied Juan.

Meanwhile, Kate was admiring the view: along the coast north-east towards Douglas, north to the hills of South Barrule and west towards Port St Mary. 'It is a beautiful place,' she said. 'I can see why Robbie wanted to rest here.'

They stood silently for some minutes after scattering the ashes, each with their own thoughts. They then retraced their steps to the car and, as there was sufficient time for lunch, Juan took them to *The Colby Glen;* the first place where he had taken Molly eleven years previously. The pub hadn't changed and the food was as good as ever. Bizarrely, a thought crossed his mind as he looked at Kate. *I wonder if this could be the beginning of a lifelong friendship with this beautiful woman. Who was that American actress she looks like?* His mind went into a trance trying to remember a long-lost name. He had noticed how attractive Kate was when he had first seen her at lunch in Antibes. Barbara had noticed the way he was looking at her and had warned him off. He smiled to himself as he remembered the scowl Barbara had given him when mildly rebuking him. He knew then that nothing could happen. But now things were different. Barbara and Robbie were dead. *The field is wide open. I must let her make the first move. Just watch out if she drops any hints,* he told himself.

They dropped Stuart off at the airport and waited for his plane to be called. When satisfied there was no delay, Juan looked at Kate and asked, 'What now?'

'I don't know. You're the guide. You tell me,' she smiled.

'You told me Robbie was from Douglas, perhaps we could visit his former haunts tomorrow. I mentioned last night that you might like to see where I have decided to buy an apartment in Port St Mary.'

'Yes, I'd love to see it.'

They drove from Castletown along the coast road. As they descended Fishers Hill, the sun shone on the sparkling bay in front of them. The azure blue of the sea, with Port St Mary nestling under the green hills behind, was a view to behold.

'Gosh, it's beautiful here,' remarked Kate for the nth time.

'You're seeing it on a good day. A storm in January can be something altogether different.'

They drove into Port St Mary, down the High Street to the bottom of Queen's Road and parked facing the sea. They got out and Juan pointed to an apartment block behind them.

'There,' he said. 'What do you think?'

'Wow, what a position – thirty yards from the sea.'

'I have bought the penthouse on the top. From there you can see Wales on a good day.' *I am beginning to sound like an estate agent.*

'The view must be spectacular,' she said. 'I am envious.'

'Let's go for a stroll,' he suggested. *I am glad she likes it. Maybe she will come and stay sometime.*

They walked along Clifton Road. On their left – the sea; on their right -- a row of nicely kept bungalows. As the cul-de-sac began to turn inland, Juan saw a *For Sale* sign. However, Kate had seen it too. It was a dormer bungalow that appeared to have a rear garden that backed directly on to the golf course. The road beyond petered out to a gravel path.

'Where does the path lead to?' she asked.

'I think it goes up to Glen Chass... up there.' He pointed to a hill, perhaps a mile distant. 'There is a path that goes all the way around the coast to The Sound.'

'The Sound?'

'It's the most southerly tip of the island. It would be a good place to take Cal for walks.' He was encouraging her to return and stay with him.

She seemed to ignore his suggestion and, instead, walked towards the bungalow. Standing by the gate to the driveway, she asked, 'Can we go and have a look?'

'Why? Do you think you could be interested?'

'I could be,' she replied. 'We've sold *Glenfinnan* at Badachro and, as you said, it's too isolated for me on my own. I have discussed the finances of the sale with Stuart and we have come to a mutual agreement.'

'My only concern is that you won't know anyone here on the island.'

'I'll know you,' she replied, smiling.

'OK. Let's go and see what it's like.' *It would be nice having her living around the corner. Just steady down, Juan. Don't get silly ideas.*

'We'll have to go into Port Erin to the estate agent first and get the details.' Juan noted the selling agent was the same as the one he had used for his apartment. 'With luck, we may be able to see it quickly.'

The agent recognised Juan and was enthusiastic. He eagerly persuaded the owner to receive Mrs MacKinnon in thirty minutes. 'She has no property to sell and will not require a mortgage,' he enthused to the sellers. 'It could be a quick sale.'

He turned to Kate. 'The vendors are a Mr and Mrs Skelly. The property is in excellent order.'

And so it proved. The garden was pristine; the kitchen's fully fitted units were barely three years old. Although only having two bedrooms, both had an en suite bathroom. The lounge to the front had limited sea views. Kate had made her mind up; she wanted it.

'It's ideal for me,' enthused Kate when she had been shown round by Mrs Skelly.

'I don't want to put a dampener on it, but can you afford it? It's not cheap,' asked Juan.

'Definitely,' replied Kate. 'It's perfect.'

'Well, I'm only going to be a five-minute walk away if you ever need someone to change a fuse.'

They returned to Port Erin. A draft agreement was signed. Kate would pay the full 10% deposit within seven days. The estate agent arranged for a local solicitor to handle the sale. A tentative completion date in mid-June was agreed.

Afterwards, they strolled up Port Erin promenade to Bradda Glen. At the café, they sat and had late afternoon tea in the warm sun. 'You know,' she said, 'I could never have dreamt all those years ago when Robbie came to Samarra and regaled us about the Isle of Man that one day I would end up living here.'

'It's a long way from Iraq. When I was a schoolboy in Ramsey, I would never have thought of seeing Baghdad either. My mother taught me Arabic and it was pure chance that someone fell ill, so I was the only person who could fill the post in the British Embassy.'

'Did you enjoy your time there?'

'Yes, I made the most of the opportunities to visit the ancient sights such as Ctesiphon and Babylon.'

'Did you get to my home town of Samarra?'

'Yes, I shall remember the Al-Askariyah mosque for as long as I live; as beautiful as the Taj Mahal.'

'You know the Americans are planning to invade Iraq next year?'

'Yes, it's the world's worst kept secret. If I could do something to stop them, I would.'

'Perhaps you can.'

'I don't see how. After the CIA killed Barbara I vowed I would get revenge, but I feel impotent. There's no way I am ever going to be able to get near Bush and do a Lee Harvey Oswald.'

'I also have vowed to get revenge for Robbie's death, but unlike you I have the power to extract it. However, I need help.'

'How can I help?'

'It is a long story. I will discuss it over dinner this evening if you wish, but there is a proviso. I want your assurance that what I tell you this evening goes no further.'

'You have my word.'

That evening, they chose a quiet corner table in the hotel's restaurant. Kate described how she and Robbie had been visited by Tariq Aziz and their agreement to uncover to the Iraqis two sites of buried biological weapons. In exchange, she explained, the idea had been for Robbie to bring back the two litres of VX-R to Britain.

'But what good would it be?' asked Juan. 'Two litres wouldn't kill that many people.'

'It has the potential to do untold damage. I explained to Tariq that it was a type of radioactive defoliant; he believed me. My plan is simple. I take it to the States and attend baseball games, rugby games, boxing matches, tennis tournaments, and cinemas; anywhere where there are large numbers of young males. Their sperm will be affected and in years to come thousands of children will be born hexadactyls and die six months later. I have calculated that in three months of travelling around the States, the VX-R could afflict a quarter of a million men in the right age group. Imagine what that would do to their arrogant, pretentious, self-righteousness?'

'It's a brilliant idea but I see several snags.'

'Go on.'

'Can you trust Tariq Aziz to keep his word?'

'He agreed I would closely chaperone Saddam's wife and favourite daughter while Robbie was in Iraq. He knows my background in chemical and biological weapons and that I engineered President Bakr's death. I trust Tariq and believe Saddam won't take any risks with his youngest daughter. They are expecting me to return to Scotland with them, but I was thinking of hiring a car and taking them to Paris instead. In that way, any plans they may make to tail me would fail.'

'How were you planning to get the VX-R back, if it's radioactive?'

'Robbie was to return to Europe with the VX-R in two lead foil containers that I have designed. We would come back to the UK by either train or boat.'

'How long would all this take?'

'In Iraq? Five days max; if you agree to take Robbie's place, you would be back in no time. Will you do it?'

'Do you need to ask? The biggest headache would then be to get the stuff into the US.'

'I have some ideas for that too...'

* * *

Taj Mahal, Broadway, Douglas, Isle of Man
Fri 26 Apr 2002

Yesterday a man came into our restaurant called John Pearson. He reminded me of Major Quayle who was supposedly killed with his family at their farm seven years ago when Mwt al-Swd plotted their assassination. Pearson was accompanied by a middle-eastern looking woman. I thought you may be interested in this development.

The handwritten note was copied three times and posted to three different addresses in Bradford, Birmingham and East London. Gopal knew he would not get a reply for at least a month. He thought no more about it.

CHAPTER 26

Tuesday, 30th April 2002

Juan took Kate to see where Robbie had grown up in a terraced house in West Douglas, to his schools and to his parents' grave in the nearby village of Onchan. Over lunch at *The Liverpool Arms,* they continued to discuss the problems of getting the two litres of VX-R into the United States. Kate was happy that her plan was firming up and, as Juan could speak Arabic, felt things shouldn't go wrong when he would be in Iraq. But there was one snag in her plan...

'Can you play chess?' she asked.

'Not really. I know the moves; that's about all,' he replied. 'Why?'

'I initially used a system of coding the locations of the biological weapons using a chess position that Robbie had taught me.' She stopped. Momentarily, her mind flashed back to the sands of Ur where she and Robbie had spent a frenzied, full-blooded weekend together.

Juan waited for her to continue.

She blinked and shook her head. 'Sorry, I was somewhere else. You are going to have to learn a chess game up to a certain position. Then I will have to explain how to decipher the records with the knowledge of the position.'

'It sounds complicated.'

'It isn't really. Perhaps we'd better go into Douglas and buy a cheap chess set so that I can show you the moves. By writing the moves down and going over and over the game, you'll soon remember the position used.'

216

The afternoon was spent in *The Sefton's* residents' lounge as Kate showed the game Robbie had taught her twenty-four years previously. She was surprised that she could still easily remember the game. It brought back many memories: attending Iraq's Command Revolutionary Council meetings with Saddam as Chairman; persuading Chemical Ali, his cousin, that biological weapons must be stored well away from population centres; and Arif Rashid, the Azerbaijani, who had travelled to Scotland to get the position before attempting to assassinate her. After half a dozen plays of the game, Juan was getting the hang of what the next move would be. Kate then explained how she coded the records.

'I would superimpose this position, using an imaginary board with one kilometre squares, over the map of the area where I had chosen to bury the biological weapons. I would then choose a square with a piece on it; say this one at *b2*.'

'The black bishop.'

'Yes,' smiled Kate. 'Then I would record that square's latitude and longitude as where the weapons were buried.'

'But, surely, they would go to that square and find the weapons?' asked Juan.

'They would, but find nothing. Here's the clever bit. I would actually bury the biological weapons at that square,' she said pointing to *g7*. 'It's over five kilometres away.'

He looked puzzled. 'Why?' he asked.

'Because that is where that black bishop had been before its move to *b2*. The actual burial is always at the square previously occupied by the piece you have chosen. As you are the only person who knows that position, the system is infallible as there are more positions on a chess board than there are atoms in the universe. Not even the world's most powerful computer could guess that position.'

'An incredible idea; it's so simple,' remarked Juan. 'But how do I know you have chosen the square *b2*?'

'You're catching on quick – full marks. You'll notice that when you examine the records there are random full-stops in the description of what has been buried. The first dot after a letter will tell you the piece's

217

file, in this case *b,* and the first dot after a number, in this case *2,* will give you its rank.'

After a further half-hour of going over the method of concealment, Kate sensed Juan had maxed out. They stopped for afternoon tea and conversation drifted to arranging their future meeting in Amsterdam.

'When I meet Saddam's wife and daughter at Schiphol, you'll return to Baghdad with an old friend of mine, Azi Tumbrah. He will chaperone you in Iraq. He attended the RAF's Staff Course at Bracknell in 1977 and was responsible for our Air Force buying the war game. You could argue the game is what has got us into this mess, but that's another story. Robbie and Azi eventually got on well together and he will look after you. As I've explained, as far as the Iraqis are concerned, they think I am returning with the Husseins to Britain. However, I will drive them to Paris via Bruges. I will not tell Mrs Hussein until you and Azi have gone into the departure lounge and I have confiscated their mobile phones. You are not to tell Azi of this change; otherwise he may get a message to someone. This will guarantee we are not followed by anyone from the Mukhabaret, as if they are watching us incognito at the airport, they will not be expecting the three of us to depart in a hire car.'

'The Mukhabaret is the Iraqi Secret Service?'

'Yes, you can normally spot them a mile off; most of them look like Saddam.'

'But won't they have a car at Schiphol too?'

'Yes, but the public car parks are at least a quarter of a mile away from the Avis car park. They will never know in which direction I left.'

'Why will I be flying to Baghdad via Moscow?'

'The US and the UK are still implementing the no-fly zones and trying to curtail international flights. The safest route in and out of Baghdad is through Moscow; although more and more international carriers, who believe the no-fly zones are illegal, have recently begun to ignore the US and UK. Air France, Air India and Pakistan International Airlines have lately resumed flights to and through Baghdad.'

'You seem to have thought of everything.'

'I have been planning this ever since Tariq Aziz visited Robbie and me two months ago. Now, about our travel arrangements…'

Juan stopped her. 'Can I suggest we both fly into Amsterdam on Saturday 12th? We could spend Sunday together and go through everything with a fine-tooth comb. We could then meet Azi with Mrs Hussein at Schiphol on Monday afternoon.'

'That's OK by me. When I get home tomorrow, I'll contact Saddam's undercover agent in London and tell him you are going to Baghdad instead of Robbie. I will insist that there is to be no reception for Sajida and Hala at the airport; everything is to be kept low-key.'

'But you think there will be someone from the Mukhabaret planted there to follow you?'

'Almost certainly; that's why I will change the plans at the last minute.'

'How old is Hala?'

'She's now twenty-one.'

'Will you be able to control the pair of them on your own in Paris?'

'I think they will have been instructed on the importance of finding the locations of the buried weapons. They won't have their mobile phones and I shall be watching them like a hawk. And, anyway, four days in Paris will probably become a glorified shopping expedition for the two of them. My hardest task will be getting them out of the department stores, such as *Galeries Lafayette,* and persuading them to visit *The Louvre.* Azi will bring Sajida and Hala through Dutch immigration, hand them over to me and then will return with you to the departure lounge for the flight to Moscow. When you come back, they think it will work in reverse. However, it will not. Instead of returning via Moscow on the 0830 hours Aeroflot flight, you and Azi will catch the 0810 hours Air India flight to Geneva where I'll meet you with the Husseins. I have checked the flight times; everything links up fine with our flight from Charles de Gaulle to Geneva. You mustn't tell Azi about the switch, however, until the last minute.'

'When I am in Iraq, how will I be able to keep contact with you?'

'I'm afraid mobile phones between Iraq and Europe are unreliable. But don't worry; my sister, Hind, lives in Egypt with her husband. We will use her as an intermediary. Landlines from Iraq to Egypt are fairly good. Ring her each evening between six and seven o'clock. I will ring her an hour or two later to see if everything is OK. If things go tits up, I have several plans.'

'Are you going to tell me what they are?'

'As part of my research into restricting the growth of rhododendrons at Inverewe, I have been able to redevelop enditon.'

'Enditon?'

'It's a compound we made when I was Head of chemical and biological weapons research at Al Muthanna. It slowly breaks down the nerve signals from the brain to the essential organs. If taken orally – it's colourless and odourless – the body begins to slow down and death comes painlessly within a week. It leaves no trace; autopsies find nothing. It's as if the person wanted to die. I'll take some with me to Paris.'

She took out of her handbag what appeared to be two ballpoint pens.

'If I get really desperate, I have these.'

'What are they?'

'They are not what they seem. They are the last of my gangrennex sprays. The droplets are one hundred times stronger than a wasp's sting. Imagine being stung by a thousand wasps simultaneously. Within two seconds, the skin begins to melt and the nervous system stops. It was the most horrible substance my research teams created at Al Muthanna. If you are obstructed from returning to Geneva, this could be the fate awaiting Sajida Talfah and her daughter. I have lived with these spray-guns in my handbag ever since I left Iraq in 1991. I had to use one when Saddam sent his assassin after me. It saved my life, but I have lived in fear of a second assassin for the last eleven years. It's not easy living on the edge of a precipice the whole time. I can't say I've ever got used to it.'

Although unaware of the effects of gangrennex, Juan shuddered at the thought of skin melting on a live body. 'I'm sorry; I didn't know the Mukhabaret had come after you.'

She shrugged. 'After booking in on the Air India flight, you must immediately ring Hind and tell her the switch has been successful. She will ring me in Paris and I will then fly with the Husseins from Paris to meet you in Geneva.'

'So how will we get back to the UK from Geneva?'

'We will drive back to Paris that afternoon. Stay one night near the *Gare du Nord* and catch the Eurostar on Saturday morning.'

That evening the receptionist at *The Sefton* booked two single rooms for Juan and Kate at *The Grand Hotel* in central Amsterdam and an Avis hire car for five days, to be picked up at Schiphol airport.

The following morning, Kate flew back to Glasgow. After seeing her off, Juan drove the six miles to Port Erin. There, he arranged to rent an apartment in the *Cherry Orchard Aparthotel* for two months. It would become his base from where he would make preparations to move into his penthouse. He then flew to Liverpool for his connection to Nice.

* * *

Ask any restaurateur, 'What is your busiest evening?' and they will always reply, 'Saturday.' Consequently, they will attempt to pack in two sittings to maximise their profit at the risk of alienating some of their clientele.

On Saturday, 11th May, *The Taj Mahal* was full of first sitting guests when a handsome dark-eyed stranger, aged about thirty-five, wearing a smart, grey business suit, entered the restaurant alone. Gopal approached him and asked, 'Have you a reservation?'

The young man, whose colouring suggested he hailed from the sub-continent, and, who Gopal thought could be Anglo-Indian, smiled.

'No,' he answered, 'I have come from London to speak to Gopal about this note that was sent to our leader two weeks ago.' He produced the note which Gopal recognised instantly.

'As you can see, we are very busy. Can it wait until tomorrow?'

'No,' replied the stranger in an authoritative manner. From his confident, polished demeanour and bearing, Gopal realised *This guy must be a permanent member of The London Set-up*: a hard core of militant Islamists, no more than a dozen or so, who ferment unrest with sympathisers and organise young British Muslims to travel to madrassas for training. Gopal had never met any of their members before; a shiver travelled down his spine. *By Allah, what have I done?*

'Please come through to the back,' said Gopal gesturing for the stranger to go through into the kitchen.

They passed through the hectic kitchen into the backyard and Gopal began, 'I can't tell you anymore than I put in my note.'

'Nothing? Didn't they teach you anything at Miranshah?'

Gopal knew at once that the stranger was a genuine member from *The London Set-up*. Only they would know where he and Ajit had trained together in a camp to the west of Miranshah in the North-West frontier of Pakistan.

'I followed Pearson to *The Sefton*; he was staying there.'

'Is he still there?' grunted the stranger, who to Gopal seemed to be growing taller with every question.

'No. I went back on the Wednesday and asked the receptionist if Mr Pearson was still there. I used as an excuse the fact that an umbrella had been left in the restaurant and no one had come to claim it.'

'What did she say?'

'She asked how I knew Mr Pearson had stayed there. I told her that we had spoken socially that evening as I served him and his two friends. This seemed to satisfy her. She told me Pearson had left and took the register out from under the counter. She turned back a few pages, read the entries and swung the book around for me to have a look. She laughed as she said, "It's a long way to send a lost brolly if it isn't his." I looked at his address. It was *Carlton 15, Rue Albert 1ˢᵗ, Antibes, France.*'

'He lives in the South of France!' exclaimed the operative.

'It looks like it.'

'We have a cell in Marseille. I'll have to get on to them as soon as possible. I only arrived on the island two hours ago. Where is the best place to stay?'

'Where Pearson stayed, *The Sefton.*'

'OK. I'll go and book in there for the night and catch the first plane back to London in the morning.'

'Why? What's the rush?'

He pulled a photograph out from his inner breast pocket and showed it to Gopal. 'Is this Pearson standing next to Osama?'

222

'Yes, that's him all right. But how did he get to meet Osama?'

'Pearson is the bastard who tried to kill Osama with anthrax near Gilgit.'

'We were led to believe Osama is dead.'

'That's what we want people to believe. The Americans think they killed him in the caves of Tora Bora but he is alive; though not well. He has to have dialysis twice weekly, although I understand someone has volunteered to donate their kidneys. After recuperation and rest, he should be more active.'

'This is great news. But how did he survive the attack?'

'Pearson, who we believe worked for MI6, did not know Osama was on a heavy dose of strong antibiotics for a urine infection. His medicine saved him, but not the others who were in the room with him when the anthrax was released.'

'So, Pearson must have had antibiotics too?'

'Yes. We found the bodies of Pearson's gofer and our two colleagues who had taken Pearson to see our leader, but we never found Pearson… until now. You have done well. I must fax this photo to *The Marseille Set-up* as soon as possible for them to plan Pearson's assassination.'

And without further ado, he turned, strode out through the kitchen and left.

* * *

On Sunday, 12th May, Juan flew to Schiphol from Nice and met Kate at *The Grand Hotel.* Although dressed casually, she looked a million dollars: her fine figure showed no sign of aging flabbiness and her face showed few wrinkles. Her eyes sparkled and flashed excitement for the anticipated adventure that lay ahead of them.

As they walked along the banks of the canals, basking in the afternoon sunshine, Kate recounted how she had known Saddam Hussein's wife's niece, Roya Talfah. They had been contemporary students at Baghdad University. She told Juan how Talfah had used her privileged position, as a member of the al-Tikriti clan, to bully other students in the Air Corps and how she had been forced to endure Roya's company when she had travelled to England to attend Robbie's wife's funeral.

'Roya was the spitting image of Saddam's wife, Sajida Talfah. I am not looking forward to meeting her as it will bring back some unhappy memories,' said Kate, shivering visibly as she thought about her past experiences with Roya.

'Do you want to tell me about it?' asked Juan as sympathetically as he could.

'Roya was butch; she kept fit and was very strong. She had unusual sexual habits. I was to discover she was a hermaphrodite when she raped me.'

Juan stopped dead in his tracks. His face had dropped, his eyes widened, his mouth opened but no words came out.

'It was twenty-four years ago and I haven't thought about it for ages, but I guess it never goes away. I shudder to think how I will feel when I see Sajida.'

Juan offered his hand and she took hold of it. It seemed the most natural thing to do and Juan said nothing. It was a moment when silence is golden. They took a few further steps before Juan whispered, as if he wanted no one to hear, 'I'm sorry.'

Kate, still holding Juan's hand, pulled herself to her full height. 'I was to get my own back later.' A faint smile had appeared on her beautiful face; her eyes were focused thousands of miles away.

Juan knew not to interrupt her momentary trance and they continued to walk holding hands in silence.

They crossed a bridge over a canal. In front of them lay a *salon de thé*. 'Would you like some tea?' ventured Juan.

'That would be lovely,' she replied, as her mind came back to earth. They sat outside the cafe at a pavement table and ordered tea and some pastries.

'In those days, I was in charge of research into chemical and biological weapons. One of my teams had developed something called exciton that stopped the body's defensive mechanism from overexerting itself. I tricked Roya to its exposure and she died in a swimming pool of a heart attack.'

'You killed her?'

'Yes. She raped me. She got what she deserved.'

Juan nodded thoughtfully. *I must make sure I don't cross this woman and yet, she is so beautiful. She keeps reminding me of someone I've seen in the movies, but who?*

There followed a period of silence during which the waiter brought their tea.

'Would you like me to pour?' she asked. 'It's tradition in Iraq for the woman to always pour.' Her mind was flashing back to October 1982 when in the presence of Saddam Hussein, she had poured the tea for President Bakr and added enditon to his cup. *God, all I've ever done is murder people. Will Allah ever forgive me?*

Seeing her in an apparent trance and trying to take Kate's mind off Roya, Juan asked innocently, 'How did you meet Robbie?'

'We met at ICL Reading when I was attached to help design the war game that we had bought from the Ministry of Defence. I was at the time a Lieutenant in the Iraq Air Force Reserve and I had just completed my PhD at Cambridge University. ICL were improving the simulations for us while they were installing the computer mainframes in Baghdad. Robbie had written the original programs and was the MoD's project officer. One weekend, he took me to meet his family in Weston-super-Mare. When he came to Baghdad to train our officers in how to use the game, I took him to meet my family in Samarra. He had to return prematurely from Baghdad when his wife and daughter were killed in a car accident. I went to England for the funeral with Talfah, on the pretext of getting the chess key to allow us to make changes to the game's data files. Unfortunately, we were too late and I missed meeting Robbie as he had taken Stuart to Scotland.'

'So, what happened next?'

'The war with Iran began and President Reagan began supplying us with chemical and biological materials for weapons. I was made responsible for their safe storage and decided the biological materials such as anthrax, West Nile Virus and so on, should be hidden where they could never be found. I kept in touch with Peter Stacey who was MI6's man in Iraq. I gave him and his successors snippets of information from time to time.'

'Yes, Peter told me you had been the reason why biological weapons were never deployed in the war.'

'As you know, in order to pay off Iraq's huge debts from the war with Iran, Saddam invaded Kuwait to prevent them underselling his oil. When *Desert Storm* began, Peter arranged my escape to Britain and I acquired a new identity. By sheer luck I met Robbie and we married.'

'So you've had plenty of time to acclimatise to your new name. Twelve years ago I was Juan Quayle, a somewhat frustrated schoolteacher in Cumbria. Then I was persuaded to join MI5 to try to infiltrate al-Qaeda; I became Alan Quine. Then in Morocco, al-Qaeda gave me a Libyan passport with the name Khalil el Majid. When I returned to Britain after almost eighteen months, I married Molly using my real name of Quayle and we began a family. When they were murdered by al-Qaeda, I vowed revenge and took on yet another persona; this is how I came to be John Pearson. I've lived with his name for seven years, but there are times when I get confused as to who I really am.'

'Then you could say we're a pair of has-beens!'

They both laughed.

After dinner that evening, Juan showed Kate that he could set-up the chess position and convinced her that he was confident he could pull off her plan to get the VX-R.

CHAPTER 27

Monday, 13th May 2002

It took just over two hours for Kamal al Yousa to travel from Marseille to Antibes along the A8. He found the *Carlton* apartments, parked his car nearby and entered the plush foyer.

'Can I help you?' asked the concierge.

'I have come to see Monsieur Pearson,' replied the al-Qaeda assassin.

'Who?' queried the concierge.

'Monsieur Pearson.'

'There's no one here with that name.'

The operative carefully withdrew from his inner breast pocket the fax he had received from London. He folded it in two to hide one of the faces in the photograph, originally taken near Gilgit eight months previously. He showed Pearson's face to the caretaker.

'Ah! That's Monsieur Richet. His wife was shot in the street last month in an apparent robbery; a terrible business. It's the reason he sold up and has left. There's already a new occupier in the top floor flat – Monsieur Gautier.'

'Did Monsieur Richet leave a forwarding address? I'd like to write to him.'

From under the counter, the elderly man retrieved a notebook. He opened it at a fresh page, put his reading glasses on the tip of his nose and read slowly, 'Care of the *Sefton Hotel*, Douglas, Isle of Man.'

Unaware that someone from *The London Set-up* had discovered the location of Pearson from the *Sefton*, al Yousa thanked the concierge and returned to Marseille pleased with having done an easy day's work.

A quick fax to let them know what I have found out and then a spot of lunch before I go fishing, he thought as he wrote:

From Marseille 02:
To London 04

Pearson (he called himself Richet *here) no longer lives in Antibes. His apartment has been sold. His forwarding address for correspondence is: c/o The Sefton Hotel, Douglas, Isle of Man.*

* * *

Hisham Chundri looked at the text. *What the hell is going on? We're going round in circles.* He remembered what Gopal had told him; Pearson reminded him of Quayle.

But Mwt al-Swd was successful. The national papers said the entire family was killed in the fire. It was even mentioned on TV. I don't particularly want to go back to the Isle of Man unless it's absolutely necessary.

He decided he must show the fax to his number one, gave him a call and arranged to meet him in *The Maple Leaf,* a pub near Covent Garden that is heaving during the lunch hour, but is usually quiet in the evenings. They agreed to meet at seven o'clock.

Ashraf Khalif read the text. 'When you told me its contents, I began thinking. We know Pearson was an MI6 agent planted in Lebanon to write anti-Israeli articles for *The Daily Telegraph.* We think his gofer who accompanied him to Gilgit to interview Osama could have been a member of Mossad; although we can't be certain of that. We know Quayle infiltrated our organisation, working for the British SIS, when he taught in our Naxcivan madrassa. The conundrum is whether Quayle survived the inferno at his farm and MI6 used his apparent disappearance as a cover to create Pearson. The attempt to kill Osama with anthrax was no ordinary assassination. It was highly planned and must have taken considerable resources. Quayle's disguise as Pearson fooled Osama but I'm afraid his eyesight is not what it was. Releasing the anthrax from the heels of his shoes was tricky and amounted to a possible suicide mission. Not many men would take such a risk or have the incentive to do it.'

'I didn't know that. What do you mean by releasing anthrax from his shoes?'

'Pearson's shoes had hollow heels pumped full of anthrax. When we found the burnt-out Mitsubishi truck in the Kashmir, there was a pair of discarded shoes. We believe Pearson improvised and made himself something more comfortable from the foam padding of one of the vehicle's seats before he carried on walking south. We think he managed to cross into India and make his getaway from there.'

'I can see the link between Quayle and Pearson is strong. It also explains how Pearson has turned up on the Isle of Man. After I called you to meet me here, I rang Kamal in Marseille.'

'Go on.'

'The concierge in Antibes told Kamal that Pearson was using the name Richet. Only an organisation like MI6 could so easily have provided him with a new identity. One other thing he learned. Richet's wife had been murdered; apparently she was shot in the street. The concierge believed it was the reason Richet left Antibes so quickly.'

Ashraf looked thoughtful, nodded his head and said nothing for several moments. 'I am certain that Quayle and Pearson are one and the same man. We're going to have to go back to the Isle of Man and make sure this time the job is done properly. Get our two men there to begin digging. Find out where Quayle, or Pearson, or whatever name he is now using, lives.'

* * *

The plane from Moscow arrived on time. Azi came through to the arrivals area with Saddam's wife and daughter. Everything seemed casual and friendly. Kate and Azi hugged briefly before Sajida and Hala were introduced to Kate. She then introduced Juan to the three Iraqis in Arabic as John Pearson. Juan responded in Arabic, surprising them with the use of their native tongue.

Sajida asked, 'How come you can speak our language?'

'My mother was Egyptian,' replied Juan. 'However, I am a little rusty.'

'It's a shame we haven't time to catch up with our lives since we last met,' said Azi to Kate. 'I was sorry to hear James had been killed; I'd been looking forward to meeting him again after all these years. It's hard to believe it is twenty-four years since we all worked together at Reading.' Juan noted Azi had used Robbie's previous name.

'John will tell you what happened on the return flight,' replied Kate, 'and how we came to meet.'

Meanwhile, the two ladies were checking that all their baggage had arrived. *It seems excessive for five days,* thought Kate. They said their farewells, then Juan and Azi went through to the departure lounge to await the return Aeroflot flight to Moscow.

* * *

'I don't know how much you have been told,' began Kate, 'but I am sure you realise it is essential to Iraq that John uncovers the location of the biological weapons and returns safely to the West. Your husband has agreed that you and Hala should be under my protection for the duration. I am sure you agree that we should make this experience as pleasant as possible, but you will understand that I will be on my guard. If I have any suspicion that the Mukhabaret are tailing us, then I will not hesitate to warn them off and you will bear the consequences.'

Sajida said nothing; Hala looked at her mother.

Kate thought she had got the message across but decided to lay the warning on thick. 'If you are wondering what I am capable of, remember it was me who poisoned President Bakr and provided the means to assassinate Ayatollah Khomeini. Your cousin-in-law, Ali Hassan, sent an executioner after me; he died horribly. I possess several concealed weapons and won't hesitate to use them. Now, give me your mobile phones.'

It was Hala who spoke. 'Dad stressed to us the importance of getting the hidden weapons to use against the Americans. I can assure you we simply wish to enjoy the next five days as much as possible. Life in Iraq has been miserable since the imposition of UN sanctions; children are dying everywhere because we have no chlorine to purify water.'

'Then you will be delighted to learn that, instead of travelling back to Britain, I have organised four days in Paris.'

Both their eyes lit up. They looked at each other smiling broadly. 'That's marvellous,' said Sajida. 'I've always wanted to go there. I've heard Paris in the spring is beautiful.'

'I hope you've brought your credit cards,' laughed Kate. 'The apartment stores are second to none.'

As they left the terminal building, Kate explained she had hired a car for the duration and had booked them into a hotel that evening in Bruges. 'It's a beautiful old town and is known as the Venice of Western Europe. We can look around tomorrow morning before continuing to Paris.' She examined her watch; it was three o'clock. 'It will take us about three and a half hours to get to Bruges; we'll be able to shower before dinner.'

'Excellent,' replied Hala. 'I'm looking forward to this already. You've no idea what it's like at home these days. Perhaps I can get my bridal gown in Paris?'

She looked at her mother for approval.

'Hala is getting married in a few months to Brigadier General Kamal Sultan al-Tikriti. It will be a big wedding. A gown from Paris would be the epitome of sophistication.'

'That's your mother's approval, then,' exclaimed Kate to Hala.

* * *

Sitting in business class, the three and a half hour flight to Moscow passed quickly as Juan explained how James had been given a new identity after the death of his first wife and daughter. As Robbie MacKinnon, he had settled in the Highlands of North-West Scotland. After leaving Iraq during *Desert Storm*, Kate had met Robbie by accident and they had been married for eleven years. He went on to describe how he had met Kate and Robbie in Antibes. He explained the murder of his partner, Barbara, and Robbie as a street robbery that went wrong. Juan avoided mentioning the CIA involvement, his own spurious past and the fact that he had once been a junior military attaché in Baghdad.

As Juan passed through passport control, he had a moment of worry as he remembered his interrogation in the Lubyanka ten years previously. He need not have fretted as Azi waived their diplomatic passes and their documents were not inspected. They spent a quiet night in an airport hotel before the following morning's flight to Iraq.

At Baghdad airport, a black Mercedes with a chauffeur was waiting to take them into the city. Baghdad had changed from when he had left in 1976. It was much busier: the traffic was more hectic. Ugly, soviet-style apartment blocks had sprung up everywhere like weeds. 'The no-fly zones and the sanctions have been a disaster for us,' said Azi. 'There is supposed to be an exchange of oil for medicines, the so-called oil for food programme, but the Americans are making a fortune out of the exchange rates. It's extortion that would even embarrass Al Capone. When I was in Reading in 1978, we were exchanging one Iraqi dinar for three US dollars. Today, I need 9,000 dinars to get one dollar. Children are dying at the rate of 500 per day with typhoid, diphtheria, malaria and so on because we can't get chemicals to purify our water supplies. The UN humanitarian co-ordinators are resigning in droves as they are so embarrassed by what is happening. Boutros-Ghali was vetoed out of doing a second term as the UN Secretary General by the damn Yankees because he spoke up and didn't approve of what was happening here. And recently, Madeleine Albright went on TV saying, "The death of half a million Iraqi children is worth it." It is essential we do all we can to make the Yanks think twice before they invade us.'

'I'm not sure a hundred gallons of Sarin, or whatever, will stop them.'

'True, but we have to try. The UN has had over 200 weapons' inspectors crawling all over the country trying to find the biological weapons that America gave us during the Iran war, but Kate's system of coding the records has them foxed. Your arrival is being kept top secret. Only a handful of us know you are here: Saddam, Tariq, one or two of the Mukhabaret and myself. You will appreciate, therefore, this will be a strictly private trip; there'll be no time for sightseeing. We've booked you into *The Ishtar Sheraton* for the three nights you'll be here; you'll be comfortable there.'

'That suits me. You know I am to return to Holland on Friday with two litres of something called VX-R? Will travelling on Friday, your holy day, be a problem?'

'No, our country has become very secular under Saddam and the Ba'athists. Women have the same rights as men; ironical really, when you look at what goes on elsewhere in the Middle East such as Saudi or Kuwait. Tariq Aziz told me Kate has a research job at a world-famous garden and wants to investigate the VX-R's effectiveness as a radioactive defoliant. She asked for two lead foil containers disguised as wine presentation cases to be made. We have them ready.'

'I've only known Kate for a few weeks, but she strikes me as a highly intelligent and competent woman,' said Juan.

'She is. She won a scholarship to do her PhD at Cambridge University against some tough opposition. I'm glad she is keeping well. Incredibly, she doesn't appear to get any older; I can't believe she's over fifty. My wife, Sawsan, and I were very fond of her. Her first husband, Brigadier Amer Rashid, was a fine man too.'

'What happened to him?'

'He was killed in the Iranian war.' Azi offered no further explanation.

They drove to the hotel. Azi waited in the foyer while Juan signed the register and deposited his case in his room. They then drove to the Ministry of Defence buildings off Maidan Square, about two miles away.

Azi chaperoned Juan to a small room where entry was secured by a swipe card. There he produced several red files. 'Kate recorded everything in serial order of receipt. The details of the materials buried are at the top of each entry. Then, as you can see, the date of storage and the locations are here,' he said pointing. 'The latitude and longitudes are coded so that they are meaningless. The UN inspectors have practically worn the pages away trying to decipher them,' he laughed. 'I have to say, although I shouldn't, I admire what Kate did. Had these substances been used in anger, then I'm not sure there would be anyone left alive in the Middle East.'

Juan was examining the first entry. He was surprised at the quantities recorded: 50 litres of anthrax spores, 50 litres of botulinium toxin and 200 kilograms of something called aflaxon.

'Do you know what entry contains the VX-R?' he asked.

'Yes, number four.'

Juan turned over the sheets and carefully examined the entry:

Location No 4, Date: 18/01/82
Base. reference: lat 3.3-1105 N, **long** 43-7441 E
A.nthrax 75 litres
Tabun 100 kilograms
We.st Nile Vi.rus 15 litres
VX-R 2.0 litres

He looked at the details carefully for the dots. *It's the piece on e3 that is the key to the true location,* he thought. He turned to Azi, 'I'll need to decipher this entry tonight. What is the other site from which you wish to collect the weapons?'

'It may as well be the first one.'

'This one?' queried Juan.

'I don't see why not.'

Again, Juan carefully examined the entry:

Loca.tion No 1, Da.te: 09/10/81
Base refe.rence: lat 31-6533 N, **long** 43-9457. E
A.nthrax 50 lit.res
B.otulinium toxin 50 litres
A.flaxon 200 kil.ograms

The critical square is a7. 'Can I take these two files away?'

'Fine. Which one do you want to go to tomorrow?'

'We'll do the first one, shall we? However, until I have worked out Kate's code, and it will take me several hours, I can't tell you where we will be going. I'll need maps, preferably with a scale of one to 10,000 or better. They must cover these two lat/longs.' He showed the two base references to Azi.

'No problems, I have the maps ready. We have two 4x4 trucks and a team of soldiers ready to go from seven o'clock in the morning. The VX-R location can't be all that far away. Baghdad is roughly latitude 33.30, longitude 44.40. It must be near Fallujah, which is interesting.'

'Oh, why?'

'Because there have been reports in the papers that a high proportion of children in a village near there have been born with unusual deformities.'

'What sort?'

'I'm not sure; things like deformed hands and feet, I think.'

Juan said nothing, but was remembering Kate telling him how Stuart had come across the children born in Leicester and how this led to the investigation about VX-R. *I wonder if the radiation is somehow leaking through the sand to the village.*

'We'll pick you up from your hotel at seven; is that OK?'

'Yes; I assume someone knows how to handle a sextant and theodolite accurately?'

'Ironically, Colonel Hadir, who is in charge of the team, was taught originally by Kate. He assures me he has the necessary instruments, including a metal detector, a radio and an accurate clock.'

That evening, after dining alone, Juan went to his room and from his case removed an acetate sheet already marked with one kilometre squares. He carefully lined up the square *a7* with the lat/long from the file entry. He took out his wallet chess set and set up the position. He saw *a7* contained the black queen that had formerly occupied the square *c7*. He then calculated the exact location of the hidden weapons at *c7*. He repeated the process with the sheet containing the VX-R location.

The white knight on *e3* had formerly been on *f1*. The calculations were difficult, involving the use of sines, cosines and tangents. It took him several hours to be satisfied he had the correct new locations. *Thank goodness Kate took the time to make sure I knew what to do,* he thought. *It's as well I was taught navigation principles at Devon when MI5 were training me to pose as a master mariner; they've come in useful at last.*

CHAPTER 28

Wednesday, 15th May 2002

'Good morning, Azi. The first location is at latitude 31.6533North and longitude 43.9668East.'

'That must be somewhere near Najaf,' replied Azi.

'You seem to know your lat/longs.'

'I'd be a poor pilot if I didn't know my own country. We will take about three hours to get there as it is roughly 150 kilometres south of here.'

After checking the position of the weapons on their maps, they drove south for over two hours to Najaf. They then took a road heading southwest. After a further fifty kilometres, they stopped while Colonel Hadir took readings with the sextant. 'We are very close to being on the right latitude. He then fiddled with the radio that gave him an exact time signal from the Greenwich Observatory. After using a handheld calculator for several minutes, he declared, 'I estimate we need to head due west for about thirty-five kilometres.'

The two 4x4s left the road and slowly moved over the sandy ground that was totally barren. It reminded Juan of a mix of a moonscape and the land he had traversed with Osama bin Laden across Algeria eleven years previously. *Not even Barbary sheep or goats could live out here*, he thought as he surveyed the arid, desert scene around him.

Progress was slow and it took almost two hours to reach a point before the Colonel ordered a halt. 'The sun is almost overhead,' he said. 'It will give me an accurate reading if we wait until noon.'

They sat in the air-conditioned Mitsubishis for thirty minutes while outside on a clean, white sheet Hadir laid out his instruments meticulously, like a chef with an array of kitchen utensils. He began placing stakes in the ground and taking readings with the theodolite. He would then check his calculations, move twenty yards and pitch further markers. Occasionally he would return to the earlier posts, remove them and begin again. Finally, after five or six repetitions, he had marked out a square with four corner stakes, each about ten yards apart. He waved for two NCOs to sweep the area with their metal detectors. After searching for less than a minute and with the sun now directly overhead, he waved for the others to join him.

'This is the spot,' he said, smiling to Azi.

'There is nothing to indicate anything has ever been buried here,' replied Azi.

'It's hardly surprising after twenty years,' replied the colonel.

'OK, you know what to do, Sergeant,' said Azi to the senior NCO. A tarpaulin was quickly erected over the area for protection from the sun and the team of six men began shovelling. It was clear to Juan that they had found the right place for the ground was free of boulders and relatively easy to dig. It took only forty minutes for the team to discover the cache of stainless steel barrels and another twenty minutes to load then onto the trucks and fill the hole they had made.

The journey back to Baghdad was uneventful; there was an air of jubilation among the team. As Azi was dropping Juan off at his hotel, he asked, 'Would you like to have dinner with my wife and I this evening? There is an excellent restaurant near here on the riverbank that I know was a favourite of Kate's. You will be able to tell her you visited the *Abu Samba*.'

'That would be lovely, thank you.'

'We'll pick you up at seven o'clock. Is that OK?'

Juan invited Azi and his wife, Sawsan, into the hotel for drinks before they walked through the public gardens along the banks of the Tigris to the *Abu Samba*. Their main topic of conversation was the effect the UN sanctions were having on the ordinary people of Iraq. 'It's ironic, but it is the poorer people that are affected worse. That's generally the Kurds in the north and the Shias in the south,' said Azi. 'The Ba'athists can usually afford medicines and live in areas where the water is not cut off eighteen hours per day. Assuming we go near Fallujah tomorrow, you will see what I mean about poverty and disease when we get into the more rural areas.'

'You mentioned there had been a significant rise in birth defects in Fallujah.'

'Sawsan knows more about it than me,' said Azi gesturing for his wife to pick up the thread.

'Normally, there are very slightly more boys' births registered in Iraq than girls, about 105 to one hundred. However, around Fallujah, the ratio since the Iran war has been barely sixty to one hundred. Furthermore, twelve per cent of the boys who are born have defects, compared to just one per cent of girls.'

'Is there an explanation for it?'

'None.'

* * *

'The only way we can find whether Pearson lives on the island, or has recently bought a property, is by searching through the property sales that are announced each month by The General Registry in *The Isle of Man Examiner*,' said Ajit to Gopal. 'I told you not to get involved. You've opened a bag of worms just as I forecast. If he does live over here, then we are going to have to go through aiding and abetting another execution. We won't be as lucky with the police this time.'

'You worry too much,' replied Gopal. 'I'll go to the museum tomorrow and begin searching through back copies of the papers. However, my guess is that Pearson has only just moved back here and either has not yet found a property or has very recently bought one. In which case, there will not be an announcement in the paper for at least a month. I will reply to *The London Set-up* that we are working on locating Pearson, but that it could take several weeks.'

The three women booked into *L' Hotel Bristol* in Paris after Sajida had assured Kate that her VISA card would cover their bill. *At $400 per night,* thought Kate, *I'm glad I'm not picking up the tab.* The hotel staff arranged for them that evening to dine on *un bateau-mouche.* It was dining in style whilst sailing past the floodlit sights such as the Eifel Tower and Notre Dame Cathedral.

The following morning was spent at *Galeries Lafayette* and its sister store, *Lafayette Maison.* However, it was at *Metal Flaque* that Hala found her bridal gown. Kate gasped when she saw the price but conceded that Saddam's daughter looked beautiful in her *Valentino* dress. Mother and daughter had previously asked the hotel manager to book them that afternoon into the avant-garde coiffure, *Maachi Djelani.* They were making the most of their freedom.

On Thursday, the two Iraqi women had agreed they should see the main sights. The hotel manager helpfully organised an official Arabic speaking guide from the *Office du Tourisme de Paris* to accompany the three women for the day.

* * *

The same team of soldiers turned up at Juan's hotel on Thursday morning as the previous day. Juan gave Azi the exact coordinates of the weapon stash. They then travelled west from Baghdad to Fallujah, crossed the Euphrates, and headed southwest to Aminyat. After ten kilometres south along a minor track, Colonel Hadir called a halt.

'We need to travel eight kilometres west across country,' he declared with authority after he had made several readings from his instruments.

The terrain was largely scrub, but unlike the previous day, there appeared from time to time isolated smallholdings with a few sheep and goats. After half an hour, they stopped. Using the technique of staking the ground, the army engineer proceeded as before. He seemed satisfied his latitude was correct for he began lining his stakes in a straight line from east to west with a string. However, it appeared as if he couldn't get the longitude right. He was listening to his radio and looking puzzled at his chronometer. Each time he stopped, he would get his SNCO to sweep the area with the metal detector. Each time the Sergeant would shake his head, indicating nothing.

About one hundred metres away, Juan had noticed an old woman with a teenage girl watching them from the front of what appeared to be her small, flat-roofed farmstead. He prodded Azi and said, 'We are being watched.'

Azi looked around, saw the old woman and left the Mitsubishi. She walked towards him and they met halfway; sufficiently distant for Juan to be unable to hear their conversation. Meanwhile, Colonel Hadir had removed a Geiger counter from his truck and was scanning the area.

Azi returned and waved for Juan to join him with Hadir. 'The old girl wants to know why we are digging up her husband and son,' he began. 'Apparently, her husband witnessed the original stash being buried here nearly twenty years ago. He saw the stainless steel drums being lowered into the ground and told his wife they would fetch a fortune on the black-market.'

'So, he pinched them?' asked Hadir.

'He took the glass jars out and reburied them, keeping the steel drums to sell.'

'Well, that explains why I can't find the exact spot, but what's this about her husband being interred here?' asked Hadir.

'After he had sold the barrels, he came back from Fallujah with some whisky. Nine months later, they had a son who was born with defects.'

'Did she say what they were?' asked Juan.

'Apparently, he had six fingers on each hand and six toes on each foot.'

Remembering what Kate had told him, Juan gasped. 'Bloody hell.'

'The boy died mysteriously after six months and they buried him here where they had retrieved the drums. Her husband died some years later, after they had a daughter. That's the girl you can see with her now. She buried her husband next to their son.'

'So, what do we do now?' asked Juan.

'The Geiger is registering a strong reading just there.' Hadir pointed to a stake. 'The question is, do we carry on and disturb the corpses, or not? Furthermore, if a spade breaks one of the glass containers, then who knows what could happen?' He looked at Azi, as if saying *you're the boss*.

'How important is the VX-R to Kate's research?' Azi asked Juan.

'Can I have a word in private?' replied Juan. He looked at the Colonel and apologised, 'I'm sorry but it may be better if you don't know what I am about to tell Azi.'

Hadir shrugged his shoulders and returned to the Mitsubishis, saying, 'I'll tell the men about this being a burial site.'

'Well?' asked Azi.

'Kate believes the VX-R is the cause of the birth defects. The story the old woman has told you confirms her theory. Two boys were born in Leicester with identical abnormalities and died suddenly when they were six months old. Kate has established that the boys' fathers were in the gang that buried the VX-R here, at this very spot, all those years ago. Kate wants to smuggle the VX-R into the United States. She will then travel around the country exposing as many young men to it as possible – at baseball games, boxing matches and so on. Over an extended period of many years, maybe as many as twenty or thirty, thousands of American infants will be born with the hexadactyl defects and die. No one will ever know what caused it or who did it. It will be Iraq's retribution for what the Yanks have done since the no-fly zones were illegally created and they imposed sanctions.'

Azi's eyes had widened and his jaw dropped. He said nothing, taking in the enormity of the plan. Slowly, his face began to smile. 'It's brilliant,' he said, 'but how will she get two litres of a radioactive liquid into America?'

'She has given the problem much thought, but she hasn't finalised the details. I have committed myself to helping her.'

'I could get Tariq Aziz to carry the VX-R in the diplomatic bag when he next visits the UN,' offered Azi, full of enthusiasm.

242

'No; only you, me and Kate know of the plan. The fewer, the better. Besides, if America caught so much as a whiff that Iraq was responsible they would annihilate you.'

'Can I ask why you are going to help her?'

'I didn't tell you, but it was the CIA who executed my partner, Barbara, and the man you knew as James. It wasn't a street robbery. James was unlucky to be in the wrong place at the wrong time. Kate and I have sworn revenge. We need that VX-R.'

'Then you shall have it, but I think we should leave everything else undisturbed. It means, however, we will need to excavate another site this evening for other biological weapons.'

'We'll have to return to your Ministry to look at the files.'

'Then, we'd better get cracking,' smiled Azi, obviously approving of Kate's scheme.

Azi instructed Colonel Hadir that it was essential to retrieve the VX-R without explaining why. 'We will take great care not to disturb either the bodies or the larger containers. Once we have the two litres and transferred them into these two lead-lined cases, we will cover everything back up. Tell the men we are returning to Baghdad where they can have an hour's break while we calculate new coordinates for another dig. Then we will go to another site. It may mean we work late, but I will allow them to take a four-day furlough in lieu.'

'I am sure there will be no grumbling about that,' replied the army officer.

The farmer who had stolen the steel barrels had not reburied the glass vats as deep as originally. The accuracy of the Geiger counter enabled the two-litre container of VX-R to be found quickly.

Its contents were carefully decanted by Juan into the two one-litre containers that Kate had designed. Her specifications had been given to the London contacts when fixing the dates of Juan's visit. Two glass rectangular containers, internally measuring 17 cm x 10 cm x 6 cm had been made with 6 mm glass. Each had been embedded into a 5 mm-thick lead box. The lead screw-tops had flanges that not only prevented spillage but also stopped radioactive emissions. The containers fitted into two presentation cases made from mahogany wood and were labelled as containing *Mosul Date Wine, 1978*. Juan smiled; knowing that the only wines ever exported from Iraq came from the fruit of the date. *She's thought of everything. Surprisingly, the boxes don't feel that heavy.* He asked Hadir to sweep the boxes with his Geiger counter to check the efficacy of the lead liners. *They work.* He relaxed.

In less than an hour, the team were heading back to Baghdad. By six o'clock they were heading north to a new location near the great ziggurat at Agargouf, about twenty miles north of the city. Three hours later, in semi-darkness, the third cache had been uncovered and was on its way back to Baghdad.

'I'll pick you up in the morning at 0615 hours. We have to check in by 0710 hours for the flight to Moscow,' said Azi.

CHAPTER 29

Friday, 17th May 2002

Azi's chauffeur-driven Mercedes moved through the quiet streets of Baghdad rapidly and forty minutes after leaving *The Ishtar Sheraton,* he and Juan were walking into the departure hall at the airport.

'There's our check-in desk' said Azi, pointing to Aeroflot's baggage collection point.

Juan's hand grasped Azi's shoulder to restrain him and replied, 'I'm afraid not, Azi. That's our check-in desk over there.' He released his grip and pointed to Air India's departure desk for Geneva.

A puzzled look appeared on Azi's face. 'What are you talking about? We're going to Moscow and then on to Amsterdam.'

'No, we're not. We're booked on the 0810 hours Air India flight that is coming through here from New Delhi. Kate has been with the Husseins in Paris, not England. She is waiting for me to ring her in a few moments to confirm we're on the Geneva flight. She will meet us there with Mrs Hussein and her daughter. If I don't ring, then Saddam will not see his favourite daughter again; at least not alive.'

'You're joking?'

'I wish I was, Azi, but you know Kate better than me. When she escaped from Iraq during *Desert Storm,* she took with her several samples of the weapons she had developed in her laboratories. Do you remember Roya Talfah?'

'Of course. She drowned in a swimming pool from a heart attack.'

'Kate told me to tell you that if you try and stop me getting on the

Geneva plane with the VX-R, then what happened to Roya will happen to the Husseins. Apparently, Roya was administered with something called exciton; whatever that is – I don't know.'

'I always wondered about Roya's sudden death. She was one of the fittest women I ever knew. So,' he paused with a faint smile, 'Kate bumped her off? I don't blame her; she was a nasty piece of work.'

'As I understand it, Roya was a hermaphrodite and had raped Kate when they were in London together. Kate's motivation was revenge, pure and simple.'

'Pure, maybe. Simple, I'm not so sure. Kate is a complex woman. Don't get me wrong; I admire her greatly, but she has nerves of steel. She has lost both her husbands; life has been cruel to her. She wasn't with either of her parents when they died in Egypt because of communication problems due to the Iran war. I'd no idea Talfah had raped Kate. It explains a lot of what happened and even goes some way to explaining why Kate had to get away from Iraq.' He stopped, as if in a trance, thinking of the possible consequences of detaining Juan in Iraq. 'Let's book in with Air India and then you can make that phone call.'

The flight to Geneva took six hours, but allowing for time differences, they landed locally at midday. They moved through customs and met Kate with Saddam's wife and daughter waiting in the restaurant of the main terminal building. The five sat and chatted amicably in Arabic during their light lunch. Azi and Kate caught up on each other's news: Azi telling Kate about his and Sawsan's three children; Kate describing how she had met James after thinking he had been killed by the IRA and how they had spent ten years of happy married life together in the North-West of Scotland. Meanwhile, Juan listened to Hala enthusiastically telling him about their shopping expeditions and the wonders of Paris. Sajida admitted that her husband would be jealous when he learnt they had visited Napoleon's tomb at *Les Invalides*. 'Saddam is a great admirer of Napoleon,' she conceded.

And about as unsuccessful, thought Juan.

It was Azi who eventually asked Kate, 'How are we returning to Baghdad? We have tickets from Schiphol to Moscow.'

Even Juan didn't know Kate's final ploy.

'Here are your new tickets. You have a flight to catch at four o'clock.'

Azi took them and looked. 'To Rome?' he queried.

'Yes,' she laughed. 'I thought Sajida and Hala might like to see the Colosseum.'

'I see you have not lost your sense of humour,' said Azi with a broad grin. 'I assume from Rome we are to make our own way back to Iraq.'

Kate nodded with a broad grin on her face.

As the three Iraqis left to enter the departure lounge, 'Kate, there's just one final thing,' Azi asked quietly to avoid the Hussein's overhearing. 'Would you have done to Sajida and Hala what you did to Roya Talfah?'

Kate stared, her eyes unwavering; she replied coldly, 'Not quite. Remember President Bakr? It was October 1982; under Saddam's orders, Bakr died from my slipping enditon into his coffee. It would have been ironical if Saddam's wife and favourite daughter had gone the same way.'

Azi shuddered. He shook his head; he'd always thought President Bakr had died of natural causes. Saddened that Kate could even think of using a fatal toxin, he turned and walked away; his head to the ground as he passed through the departure gate. They would never meet again.

Kate didn't appear the least bit ruffled by Azi's reaction.

Nerves of steel, thought Juan.

'What's next?' asked Juan inquisitively, trying to change the atmosphere.

'We leave the airport through that exit over there.' She nodded towards a sign: *Sortie pour France/ Exit for France.* 'Through those doors and down the corridor is the French sector. From there, I have already hired a french-registered Avis car and we will drive back to Paris where we will pick up the Eurostar for London tomorrow morning.'

* * *

With Kate driving, it was an opportunity for the two, thrown into their relationship by fate only four weeks previously, to further their awareness of each other's background. It was Kate who opened the conversation. 'What was Molly like?' she asked out of the blue.

For a fraction or two, the question ruffled him. *Why does she want to know?*

'You would have liked Molly,' he began. 'She was not unlike you in looks except she was fair and you are dark.' *Dark in more ways than one?* 'She was warm and friendly, open and honest.' *I'm not sure about you.* 'She was intelligent but always had to work hard on her father's farm as her mother died when she was young. Consequently, she had to leave school early. She married when she was nineteen and was a widow in her mid-twenties with two boys when I met her.' He paused, reflecting on the wonderful times they had spent together.

'You must have loved her very much to adopt her family?'

'Yes, I suppose I did; I never thought about it. We had two daughters and she was a fantastic mother. You never had children?'

She turned her head from concentrating on the road and gave him a cold, piercing stare that sent an involuntary shudder from his stomach, through his groin, down his legs, to the arches of his feet. The way she shook her head before returning her concentration to the road told Juan that he had hit a raw nerve.

He knew not to press the point and continued quickly. 'We were very happy for the three years we spent together before al-Qaeda killed my family. That's when I joined MI6 and planned bin Laden's assassination.'

'Using anthrax spores?'

'Yes.'

'And you survived because you were able to take antibiotics immediately afterwards?'

'Yes, I suppose so.'

'You know bin Laden needed regular weekly dialysis because of his kidneys?'

'I'd heard that, but I saw no sign of a dialysis machine at the farmhouse where I met him.'

'Well then, he would have been on antibiotics too.'

'What are you saying?'

'I'm saying that you may not have killed him.'

It was a show-stopper as the realisation quickly sank in that possibly

Kate was right and all his efforts – seven years of planning and training – had been for nothing. Many miles passed in contemplative silence; they were bypassing Bourg-en-Bresse and would soon join the A6 for Paris when Kate began talking about herself. 'I knew Robbie before I married Amer,' she said.

'Oh?'

'Yes, his real name was James Douglas. He was a Squadron Leader in the RAF. I had just finished my PhD at Cambridge when I was seconded to help Azi oversee the development of the war game we had bought from ICL. The software was being enhanced by Dataskil at Reading and James was MoD's project officer. He called me Ava Gardner.' She stopped and smiled to herself as she remembered the good times she had spent at Reading.

That's who it was!

'Funnily enough, I saw that similarity when I first met you too...'

She turned to look at him, her eyes twinkling, clearly pleased at the compliment.

'We hit it off and we both knew there was chemistry between us. When he came to Baghdad to help with setting up the game, we had a weekend together. It was very special. Then, Emma was killed and he returned to the UK in a hurry without saying goodbye. A month or two later, he was reported as being killed by the IRA. It was, of course, a way of giving him and Stuart a new identity, but I didn't know that at the time. About a year later, I married Amer.'

'Azi said he was a good man.'

'He was.' Her eyes had glistened with his memory.

More miles passed in silence.

'Strangely, I had a brief affair with Barbara before I married Molly.'

'Really?'

'When I returned from infiltrating al-Qaeda for MI5, I had to give a written report. Barbara fronted as my secretary to do the typing. She made it obvious that she fancied me and I had hardly seen a woman in two years, let alone been with one. It was inevitable what happened and we had several magic weekends together. Afterwards, I returned to the

Isle of Man to run my father's farm and married Molly. When I decided to join MI6, after the fire destroyed my family, I discovered Barbara had become its Director. She had not been a secretary at all; she had been MI6's Head of operations in the Caucuses. The inevitable happened; we got back together again. As I got to know her better, I slowly fell in love with her. I never thought it would have been possible as Molly had meant everything to me.'

'It seems we are kindred spirits; both of us have been in love with two people and both of us had affairs with the second spouse before marrying the first.'

'I guess it really is possible to love more than once. My problem has always been that I can't tell the difference between being in love and being infatuated. When I was younger, girls always frightened me. I tended to run away; I found it difficult to talk to them about my inner feelings in case they scoffed me.'

It was becoming increasingly clear to Juan that he was becoming besotted with Kate. He had witnessed the dark side of her persona but this increased his fascination and curiosity, rather than lessen it. She was extremely attractive and unconsciously he was making secret plans despite the fact that both of them had lost their partners only weeks previously. He remembered his initial contact with Molly and how, being determined not to rush her, had been successful. *Take it easy,* he told himself. *Don't overplay your hand. Don't let her turn you down because you rushed her. For both of us, it may be a case of third time lucky.*

As they began to near Paris, Kate said, 'I informed Avis that I would return the car to their *Gare du Nord* office this evening. I hope you don't mind, but it will mean we will have to eat late in Paris.'

'Have you booked a hotel for the night?'

'Yes, but I've no idea what it will be like. It's only a short distance from the station and is only rated as one star.'

'If I remember rightly, the station is near the Sacre Coeur. There are plenty of restaurants around there.'

By nine o'clock, they had returned the car and were walking along the Boulevard de Magenta towards their hotel. Ten minutes later, they stood in the Rue Myrtle in front of a sign over a door announcing *Hotel,* and nothing else.

A hotel with no name, thought Juan. *This doesn't look too promising.*

It was a five-storey building squeezed between two shops: an *auto école* and a *mèche perruques* which Juan knew meant Afro-Caribbean wigs. However, the window was full of ladies lingerie, much of it made of black plastic. A 'heavy' with five days of growth and wearing fashionable shades, faded jeans, white trainers, leather jacket and smoking *une Gauloises* lounged uninvitingly in the doorway. Despite the hour, all the shops in the street were open. With plenty of bustling people roaming the street, there was a cosmopolitan air.

Kate looked at Juan as if asking, *Do we go in?*

She is having second thoughts too.

He gestured, *After you.*

In front of them, there was just a narrow staircase with a threadbare carpet. A shabby notice on the wall indicated: *reception* à l'*étage.* They ascended the steep stairs and met a Middle Eastern-looking woman wearing a Turkish hijab behind a desk.

'I have two rooms booked for one night,' declared Kate in Arabic.

The woman's face dropped. She was not expecting someone with Kate's relatively pale complexion to speak Arabic. She looked both of them up and down with their bags and asked politely, 'Not one room for two people?'

'No,' answered Kate affirmatively. 'We are on our way to England.'

She shrugged her shoulders, turned around and took two keys from an open wall cabinet. Handing them to Kate, she gestured to the stairs and said disinterestedly, 'Third floor; that will be fifty euros.'

Thinking, *That's cheap,* but not wondering why, Juan volunteered. 'I'll get this. *Vous acceptez VISA?*'

'*Non, payer en liquide seulement.*'

He gave her a fifty euro note. She held it to the light before accepting it.

Ascending to their rooms, they agreed to drop their bags and immediately go to find somewhere to eat. Their rooms were adjacent, shabby and smelly. A casual glance revealed how small they were. It would be necessary to walk like a crab around the four-foot bed to the so-called en suite facilities, where sitting sideways on the toilet would be *de rigueur. The last occupants had been smokers,* thought Juan, as he inspected further. At the far side, there was a solitary oblong window that looked as if it hadn't been opened in years. A faded curtain of indeterminate colour hung limply to one side. The wallpaper was red flock making the room dark and uninviting. The bare light bulb offered no more than twenty watts of light.

Kate knocked and entered. 'I think we should take the VX-R cases with us. Don't you?' she queried.

'Is your room like this?'

She nodded. 'It's only for one night.'

'We'll use my holdall; it's smaller than yours.' Juan emptied his things on the bed, noting there wasn't any suitable furniture, such as a chest of drawers.

Passing the receptionist as they descended the stairs, the woman of indeterminate age demanded that the keys be returned whilst they were out of the hotel.

'Why?' asked Kate.

'It's policy.'

'We've paid for the night and will be back soon,' retorted Kate in Arabic and carried on down the stairs.

'What was all that about?' asked Juan.

'I'm not sure, but I'm not going to be buggered about by a Turk.'

'How do you know she's Turkish?'

'I don't.'

End of conversation, thought Juan.

He had only known her for a few weeks, but he already knew when not to press her. Her slim, trim body on a fine pair of legs could not be hidden by her long sleeved dress with its ankle-length skirt. Her swaying walk accentuated her waist and hips and, as they moved along the pavement, he noticed passing men looking and admiring her. He felt like a million dollars being her escort.

They found a busy restaurant after wandering towards the Sacre Coeur. After an excellent meal, they sat outside at a roadside table enjoying a coffee and cognac in the warm evening air. The area of Montmartre was alive with people enjoying themselves: couples, both heterosexual and homosexual; transvestites and prostitutes, both male and female, plying their trade. Juan, never a prude, found it fascinating while Kate, at one point, expressed surprise at the difference between what she was witnessing and the centre of Paris that she had experienced when accompanying the Husseins earlier that week.

He held her hand as they strolled back. She didn't recoil, probably feeling safer if others saw them as a couple. Having entered the hotel and climbed the steep stairs, they passed the hotel's Turkish receptionist arguing with a couple over the price of a room. It didn't occur to Juan to ask himself why. Kate allowed him to kiss her on the cheek as they said goodnight before entering their separate rooms. He hoped their friendship was warming.

He decided he would shower in the morning. He undressed, folding his clothes over the solitary wooden stool and threw back the duvet. He looked at the sheet. It had been washed but the remains of a bad stain remained. He shrugged his shoulders, remembering the hotel in Selouane, Morocco, when he had shared a room with bin Laden and slept on a chair. He shut his eyes, but then noticed a thumping noise from the room above: 'thump, thump, thump' in a regular pattern. *Someone is having a good time.* He buried his head in the pillow and closed his eyes tighter.

He had been asleep, he didn't know for how long, but it only seemed minutes when he was woken by someone trying to come through the wall from the bedroom next door. This time the noise was: 'squeak, squeak, squeak'. Bedsprings were being exercised at a hell of a rate and a bedhead was hitting the adjoining wall. *He'll come through any minute!*

He lay there hot and sticky with sweat. He wondered why. He got out of bed. He looked under the sheet and saw that the mattress had a plastic cover. *I'll open the window,* he thought.

He drew back the curtain which hung precariously on the rail and the window reluctantly opened. He peered out. His room was at the rear of the hotel and looked over the rear of the building opposite. The flat roof of the extension that joined the two properties was one level below. In the dim light, he could make out half a dozen used condoms and several pairs of frilly knickers lying on the roof. From a window across the divide came loud moanings: 'yes, yes, yes' as yet another couple made the most of their brief time together.

This is bloody ridiculous.

Suddenly, there was a loud banging on his door.

It was Kate shouting, 'John, let me in. It's Kate.'

Fearing the worst, he rushed past his bed, stubbing his little toe in his haste. Cursing and hobbling, he opened the door while holding his foot. Kate practically fell in, a terrified look on her face. 'Someone was banging on my door, trying to open it. It was as well I'd locked it,' she gasped.

'What happened?'

'Nothing, I yelled "Bugger off" and it stopped. I don't like here; I think we should go.'

'It's two o'clock in the morning.'

She stared at him; she was clearly upset.

'Look; bring your stuff in here. I will sleep on the floor. You'll be safe. We'll leave early and get breakfast at the *Gare du Nord.*'

Shaking with shock, she returned to her room. In less than a minute, she had returned with her things stuffed into her case. He then noticed, for the first time, that she was wearing a pale green, silk nightdress. He shuddered as he glanced at her firm, athletic body. He felt embarrassed as he tried not to make it obvious that he wasn't staring. Kate appeared not to notice him admiring her well-kept figure.

'I'm afraid the bed isn't terribly comfortable and the room is awfully noisy.'

She got in the bed and whispered, 'I don't mind you getting in. I am feeling cold.'

It's probably the fright.

'Are you sure?' he asked. 'I'll be OK on the floor.'

She nodded.

He wondered if anything would happen, but her eyes were already closed. He inched nearer and gently kissed her forehead. She murmured approvingly. He studied her beautiful face. Although in her fifties, she showed no sign of aging. *She would pass for thirty-five.*

Her resemblance to Ava Gardner was uncanny.

He turned over, shut his eyes and began thinking of Molly.

Molly, forgive me.

CHAPTER 30

Saturday, 18th May 2002

Kate and Juan left the hotel before eight o'clock and were having breakfast in the *Gare du Nord* twenty minutes later.

'That was the worst hotel I've ever been in,' began Kate.

'You realise it was a knocking shop?'

'A knocking shop?' She queried the terminology.

Juan bent his left arm to form a 60⁰ V-shape. He clenched his right fist and pushed it through the V, pulled it back quickly and rapidly repeated the process several times.

She smiled; she'd got the message. 'So we spent our first night together in a knocking shop?'

'Without knocking too.'

They both began uncontrollable giggling that lasted for some time.

The Eurostar left promptly at ten o'clock for its journey to Waterloo. The three-hour trip allowed them to discuss their plans for the future. They would split in London. Juan, with the VX-R, would travel to the Isle of Man via Liverpool where he would take the Seacat fast-craft to Douglas. Kate would fly to Edinburgh, collect her car from the airport's car park and return to Badachro.

Before leaving Scotland for Schiphol, Kate had paid the full ten per cent deposit on her bungalow and agreed a completion date of Friday, 15ᵗʰ June. The week before, Stuart would drive to Scotland with a hire van and would help clear *Glenfinnan*. The pair would leave Badachro for the last time on Wednesday, 13ᵗʰ.

Kate outlined her ideas to get the VX-R into America. She thought she should buy a *Triking* three-wheeler car. She would ship it to the United States and use it for touring. The quirkiness of using an open trike had appealed to her sense of fun and she tried to justify her choice. '...the VX-R lead containers could be hidden inside the fuel tank.' Her other argument for using a three-wheeler was that its offbeat and outlandish features would diminish the possibility of the American officials asking, 'Why not hire a car to tour?'

'The immigration authorities would see me as an eccentric, laugh and allow the trike's temporary importation,' she argued.

'I don't agree. It would attract too much attention,' Juan replied. 'It would stick out like a sore thumb in America and could easily be stolen. There are several companies who organise motorcycle tours to the States; either in groups or for individuals who prefer to go alone. If we use one of them, they would ensure the bike is freighted correctly in a container and do all the paper work. A few weeks later, we would fly to the US and collect the bike in, say, New York or Boston. The best bike would be a Honda Gold Wing.'

He described how the Gold Wing had a false fuel tank located in the classical position in front of the rider that could easily hide the two one-litre vessels. '...possibly some minor mods may be necessary,' he added. 'Being a heavy bike, the increase in weight because of the VX-R in the modified chamber would go unnoticed.'

She agreed his plan was better but admitted some nervousness, as she had never ridden on the back of a bike before.

'Don't worry. The Gold Wing's passenger seat is practically an armchair – heated too. The bike will be registered in the Isle of Man and that will give us considerable credibility among American motorcycling enthusiasts.'

They agreed Juan would purchase a new 1800 cc, six-cylinder Gold Wing when he got back to the island.

On Monday, Juan arrived back in Port Erin and began organising his future. His first purchase was a Ford Focus hatchback. Next, he drew up an inventory of required furniture. He found a carpet warehouse and arranged with the estate agent to allow the carpet-layer entry to the apartment so that measurements could be made. Completion of the sale had been agreed for Wednesday, 29th May – the middle of TT practice week and the carpets would be fitted the following day. A similar arrangement was made with a furniture shop in Castletown to measure the windows for new curtains. Fortunately, little redecoration was required. He was glad he had chosen to live well away from the TT course as the island was already filling up with motorbikes. Getting around the south of the island was relatively unaffected. By Friday, he had checked the availability of crockery, white goods, a television and a telephone line. They would be installed by 3rd June. He was determined to be fully up and running by the time Kate arrived.

He had approached the island's Honda motorcycle dealer and, after studying the specification of the Gold Wing, made the order, but it would not arrive for three weeks. However, he noticed the artificial tank was not metallic; it was made of plastic. He knew the implications immediately. An X-ray would pass through and the lead containers would stick out like a sore thumb. He asked the dealer, 'Do Honda make metal tanks for this model?'

'No,' was the reply. 'It's a way of keeping the weight to a minimum.'

'Is there anyone on the island skilled enough to make an identical tank in metal?'

'You could try Barry Murton in Onchan. He's the best panel beater I know.'

From the dealer's premises, Juan drove up Victoria Road to Governor's Bridge and turned right into Onchan. Passing through the village, he turned right, went down a steep hill known locally as *The Butt*, and found Murton's small garage at the bottom.

The owner listened to Juan's requirements.

'This isn't for something illegal, is it?' he asked.

'No; if you like, I'll get Inspector George Costain to verify my bona fide,' Juan replied.

'You can't know him that well. He's recently been made the Deputy Chief Constable.'

'I didn't know. I have been away for some time. When did this happen?'

'A week or two ago.'

'I must make contact with him. He was the best man at my wedding.'

The engineer smiled as if remembering something. 'It's surprising how easy it is to lose contact with your best man when you get married,' he remarked. 'With the TT on during the next two weeks, I'm swamped with work. I can't start your job until the end of June. Will that be OK?'

'Fine; I'll have the bike by then and will bring the plastic tank for you to copy.'

That evening, having bought a Congratulations Card, he wrote a letter to George at the Douglas Police HQ explaining he was moving permanently back to the island and had decided to use the alias of John Pearson. He gave the details of his temporary location and his future new address. He finished with the lines: *I know you'll be busy in your new job, but if you can find time for a beer and a natter then give me a bell. I have much to tell you since the fire at Ballajorra.*

* * *

Two days later, Juan received a call from his old buddy. 'It was good to get your letter. How long have you been back?'

'A couple of weeks. I was delighted to hear of your promotion to Superintendent.'

'So, you've decided there is nowhere like the island? How long is it since the fire?'

'It was 5th July 1995, almost seven years ago. A day I'll never forget.'

'Me neither. After you left, what happened? Presumably, you didn't manage to assassinate bin Laden. He was hardly ever off the TV after 9/11?'

'George, there's so much to explain that I can't tell you over the phone.'

'Then why not come up to our house and have dinner with me and Joy; you remember her? She was with me as a witness when you and

Molly got married. We finally tied the knot five years ago and now have two boys, Charlie and Archie.'

'That would be great. Where do you live?'

'In Devonshire Crescent, number nine.'

'I know where you are, just up from the Quarter Bridge?'

'Yes. Tomorrow evening, say seven o'clock; we'll have got the boys to bed by then.'

* * *

George, in 1995, the Inspector of the Ramsey Division, was one of a handful of people who knew that Juan hadn't died with his family in the fire that engulfed Ballajorra farm. He had attended the meeting chaired by the Head of MI6, Barbara Renton, when the plot to assassinate bin Laden was hatched. His role subsequently had been to tie-up loose ends and cover up the trail in the Isle of Man that could have blown Juan's smokescreen. He had successfully ensured that the firemen, the local village policeman, the coroner, the hospital pathologist and, even, the local Church of England vicar had all signed the Official Secrets Act and made them aware of the consequences of their actions.

Although in the intervening years the Chief Constable, Colonel Madoc, had retired to be replaced by a former Assistant Chief Constable from Lancashire, George's cool handling of the affair had been duly noted and probably went someway to his promotion over more experienced inspectors. At forty-six, he was the youngest ever to become the Manx Deputy Chief Constable.

As he answered the door, George joked with Juan, 'Do we call you Juan Quayle, Alan Quine, or John Pearson?'

'Or Khalil,' replied Juan.

His friend's blank expression demanded an explanation to the somewhat flippant reply. 'I was briefly Khalil el Majid and had a Libyan passport to prove it. However, I am registered on the Rushen Parish electoral role as John Pearson.'

'Come in and meet Joy again.'

The evening was largely spent bringing George up-to-date with Juan's exploits: how he had prepared to become *The Daily Telegraph's* Middle East correspondent, the five years spent in Lebanon and the anthrax attack in Pakistan. 'I interviewed bin Laden days before 9/11 and was confident the execution was successful until a few weeks ago. The subsequent appearances he made on TV after 9/11 had all been pre-recorded. When I met him, he looked quite frail; I suspected he may have had jaundice. I discovered later he had to have dialysis regularly.'

'What changed your mind about the success of the mission?'

'It was something Kate said.'

'Who's Kate?'

'Ah, I'll come to her in a minute. I survived the anthrax because I had taken antibiotics – plenty of them. It was Kate who pointed out that if bin Laden was on dialysis and was suffering from jaundice then he, too, would have been taking strong antibiotics. Consequently, he possibly survived the anthrax attack like me. All the others in the room where I released the virus: his henchmen, my gofer and our minders died. It's possible that all those years of preparation were for nothing.'

'That makes sense, but who is Kate?'

'Did you ever know a Manxman called James Douglas?'

'No.'

'He was a software engineer in the RAF who designed a computer war game that was sold to Iraq. When he was installing the game in Iraq with ICL, he had an affair with Iraq's Head of Chemical and Biological Weapons Research – a woman called Kathab al Jised, or Kate. It's a long story, but James's wife and daughter were murdered – probably by the CIA, who were keen to get the secret of the war game's security system, based on a chess key.'

'Hang on,' interrupted George. 'This isn't the son of Robert James Douglas is it? He was a predecessor of mine in the 1960s. I never knew him because I didn't join the police until just after he'd retired, but some of the older members of the force still talk about him. He was Manx Chess Champion many times.'

'It could be, I don't know. After Douglas came back from Iraq, he was given a new identity by the security services to protect him and his son, Stuart. He adopted the name Robbie MacKinnon. Eventually, he and Kate got together, married and lived as Mr and Mrs MacKinnon in the North-West of Scotland.'

'So, how does Kate come into your story?'

'I had travelled to somewhere near Gilgit in northern Pakistan to interview bin Laden. My photographer had come with me. Two of bin Laden's men had picked us up in Peshawar to take us to meet him. It was a three-day journey. After the interview and having released the anthrax, the four of us started off to return to Peshawar. We got lost in a snow storm. Two days later, all three of them had died of the anthrax. I ended up walking south on my own; having no idea where I was. I was found by a nomadic shepherd who guided me across the border into India. It took months to persuade the Indian authorities that I was not a spy and was finally released in February. I decided to return to an escape hole I'd bought several years previously in the South of France – an apartment in Antibes. To my surprise, Barbara Renton was already living there. She was hiding from the Americans who had tried to assassinate her the previous November. We lived together until last month when by chance we met the MacKinnons. They were holidaying in a hotel ten minutes from our flat. They invited us to have dinner with them as Robbie had detected my Manx accent. After dinner, Barbara suggested they come back to our apartment for coffee. She and Robbie went ahead to get the coffee ready. I stayed in the hotel while Kate went upstairs to get a cardigan. On their way to my flat, Barbara and Robbie were shot in the street. The overwhelming evidence, although all circumstantial, is that the CIA had caught up with her.'

'But why would the CIA want to kill her?'

'MI6 aren't sure, but think it may have something to do with the forthcoming invasion of Iraq. Robbie MacKinnon had left instructions in his will for his ashes to be scattered at Castletown Golf Course. I went to his funeral in Scotland and volunteered to accompany Kate when she came over here three weeks ago. She stayed for a few days and saw a bungalow in Port St Mary, which she has now bought. She is coming over here permanently in a couple of weeks. You'll have to meet her. Perhaps you and Joy could come to dinner one evening.'

'I'm not sure that I want the former Head of Iraq's Weapons Research living here on the island. It sounds a bit dodgy to me. We only have three special branch officers. Maybe the CIA will want to execute her too; keeping an eye on her could be a problem.'

'She won't be a problem. I won't let her out of my sight.'

'It sounds as if you fancy her.'

'No comment.'

CHAPTER 31

Wednesday, 13th June 2002

It was India's turn to host the biannual meeting of the International Working Group on al-Qaeda; General Rao had chosen his HQ in New Delhi.

Prior to giving his opening remarks to welcome the delegates, the General had spoken privately to Phil Jay about how he had met MI6's agent, John Pearson, a few days after their previous meeting in Blois and how he had arranged his safe return to the West. He wanted to know if he should broach the subject of bin Laden's execution in his introduction or whether Phil would prefer to give a summary of the assassination himself.

'I will cover it in my report,' Phil had replied. 'However, I must thank you for what you did. When Pearson had not returned after what seemed ages, we began to believe he was dead. Indeed, it was not until very recently that we were certain he had survived the anthrax attack. Instead of returning to Britain to give us a report, he had gone to a private bolt-hole in the South of France that only he and Barbara Renton knew about.'

'Then may I suggest you give your report first, immediately after my welcome.'

It was Phil's second attendance at the committee and he began nervously. 'I am afraid I must begin with some tragic news. You all knew my predecessor, Barbara Renton.' He paused and looked around the table. They all nodded, although Phil could see that the French DCRI representative, Edouard St-Julian, knew what was coming. 'It is my sad duty to inform you that six weeks ago Barbara was murdered in an apparent street mugging in the South of France.'

There was an instantaneous outbreak of mumbling and muttering between the security chiefs.

It was a minute before the murmuring had died down.

'It saddens me even more, gentlemen, that Mrs Renton was assassinated. Although we do not have concrete proof, it would appear that she was shot by an agent from the CIA.'

The buzz around the table reached a crescendo; there were cries of 'Surely not?'

Another minute passed before the commotion had subsided.

'My colleague,' he nodded towards Edouard, 'will give you the details of what happened in Antibes presently. However, I want to formally thank him and his staff for the assistance he gave us in clearing up the mess and repatriating the bodies of Mrs Renton and her friend. I must stress, nevertheless, that although the evidence against the criminals who undertook the assassination is largely circumstantial, it is, in my opinion, overwhelming. Britain's Foreign Secretary has protested to the American Secretary of State, Colin Powell. As of yesterday, we had not received a reply other than a promise to investigate. I'd now like to move on to Barbara's legacy, the assassination of Osama bin Laden ...'

Phil Jay finished by describing to the Group, Pearson's escape through India. He thanked General Rao for his help to get Pearson back to Europe. 'It is our belief that bin Laden died from anthrax on or around the 9th September last year. The TV interviews of him bragging of the 9/11 attacks were pre-recorded.'

There followed an intense period of questioning on both Barbara's murder and the likely success of the anthrax attack. After a coffee break, it was Edouard's turn to brief the committee. He gave a full description of the events in Antibes and concluded that the French Government had also protested to the US Secretary of State. Furthermore, President Chirac intended to raise the matter with President Bush when he visited The White House next month. 'I can inform you that my government intends to use its veto in the UN Security Council against the forthcoming invasion of Iraq.'

The Mossad representative had been largely quiet in the meeting and Phil wondered if he had already been briefed by the Americans on their role in Barbara's murder. It then occurred to him that the reason the CIA had never shown any interest in joining their working group, despite at least four invitational memos from his predecessors, was because they had been getting summaries from the Israeli representative all along.

* * *

'The problem has been I had no idea when Stuart MacKinnon began his university course. I had to guess his age and work backwards. In the end I started searching as early as 1986 and coming forward. There are five different exam boards in England as well as the Welsh, Scottish and Northern Ireland ones. Then we didn't know what subjects he took for his *A* levels or Scottish Highers. It's taken some finding. However, you'll be pleased to know that he studied at Gairloch High School in Wester Ross and left there in 1988 with five Highers.'

'So, what do we do now?' asked Lee Hefferman.

'I've looked at the map. The school has a geographically huge catchment area. Kids probably get bused in from as many as thirty miles away. I will have to go up there and check out where he lived.'

'Have you tried the telephone directory?'

'No use. I've checked. MacKinnon is ex-directory. I daren't fly up to Inverness; it would leave a paper trail. I'm going to have to drive. I'll leave early this evening, drive through the night and get there tomorrow morning.'

'Don't do that. You'll need to be fresh when you start making enquiries and a day or two either way won't matter. Leave tomorrow; perhaps stop in Edinburgh on the way up.'

* * *

Juan met Kate and Stuart from the Heysham boat on Thursday, 14th June. They followed Juan to his apartment where they would stay for three nights

266

while preparing Kate's bungalow. It had been a glorious day and the sun was beginning to settle in the west when they walked along Clifton Road with Cal to look at Kate's new home. Stuart gave it the thumbs up immediately.

'I can't wait to pick up the keys tomorrow,' enthused Kate. 'I'm really excited. It's the first time I've owned my own place since I left Baghdad eleven years ago.'

They returned to the golf course clubhouse, where Juan was already a member, and sat outside on the veranda with a bottle of wine. 'From here you can see the path that goes around that headland over there.' He pointed across the first tee to a hill in front of them, two miles distant. 'The footpath goes to Spanish Head and beyond is the Calf of Man. Walks up there will make Cal a very happy dog; he'll have plenty of rabbits to chase.'

'We can't wait, can we Cal?' The dog responded with an enthusiastic wag.

'There's just one problem. When you go up there, make sure you stick to the paths,' warned Juan.

'Why?' asked Kate.

'There are chasms in the cliffs that intrude inland. They are deep fissures in the rocks, several hundreds of feet deep. They are sometimes covered by wild heather, called ling. If you fell through the heather into a chasm, it would be fatal.'

'Then I'll need to keep Cal on a leash?'

'I wouldn't have thought so. Dogs have an uncanny knack of detecting danger when we humans can't.'

The three sat relaxing in the warmth of the early evening sun, savouring the moment. Kate then asked Juan what progress he had made preparing the Gold Wing for smuggling the VX-R into America.

'I've checked the dimensions of the Gold Wing's lockable lid on the top of the artificial fuel tank. Your two containers don't quite squeeze through the opening – a matter of a couple of centimetres. However, I've discovered the tank is made of plastic. Consequently, I have found someone who will make an identical tank in metal with a slightly bigger lid. The containers will settle inside the compartment on either side of the main spar of the frame and there will still be plenty of room for the bike's tools, spare bulbs, puncture repair kit and odds and ends. If the American authorities X-ray the bike, nothing will appear amiss. However, we'll have to get new passports – Manx ones.'

'Why is that; surely, my UK one will be valid?' asked Kate.

Juan didn't immediately answer her question, but instead asked, 'When MI6 brought you back from Iraq in 1991, you told me they gave you a new identity?'

'Yes, I was called Kathryn Helena Jackson.'

'Did you keep all the documentation? The passport, driving licence, birth certificate and so on.'

'Yes. I've still got them. Why?'

'The American computers will have Kate MacKinnon marked as a wanted person. I suggest you revert to being called by your maiden name of Jackson. I'm going to have to do the same. John Pearson will, by now, be known to them as the MI6 agent who attacked bin Laden. Fortunately, when I first got into this business, I was given the identity of someone called Alan Quine. I also kept the documents. We will travel to the USA as Alan Quine and Kathryn Jackson. We'll apply for three-month tourist visas using those names on new Manx passports.'

'Are there any other problems on the horizon?' asked Stuart.

'I am going to use a company in Manchester who organise motorcycle tours worldwide. They will take care of the freighting of the bike.'

As they walked back to his apartment, Juan said, 'I've booked a table for this evening at the little bistro on the harbour. It's a two-minute walk. Tomorrow, I thought you might like to take Cal for a walk to the most southerly tip of the island. I'll show you the chasms and from the café, where we can have lunch, you will get a good view of The Calf of Man.'

Over the next few days, Juan and Stuart helped Kate move into her bungalow. They took the most of their opportunities to see the island at its best; the weather being particularly good. On Sunday, Stuart departed with an empty van to return to Leicester, promising that he and Judy would return for a break during the autumn. It would be Kate's first night alone.

Juan offered Kate a further night at his flat, but she refused. 'No, that's nice of you, but I must get used to being on my own. However, perhaps tomorrow you could help me find a small car?'

A somewhat deflated Juan agreed. *Is she playing hard to get?*

In Douglas the following day, they found a suitable car for Kate – a Ford *Ka*. Kate liked the idea of a car with the first two letters of her name on it and asked the dealer to find someone who could tastefully paint '*te*' after the model's name. Perhaps mesmerised by her beauty, he had replied, 'Certainly, I will have it done at no cost. It will be ready on Friday.' Afterwards, they visited the motorcycle dealer.

'I was going to ring you later,' he said. 'The Gold Wing arrived on this morning's boat.' He led them to his workshop at the rear of the showroom for them to see a silver-blue bike being unpacked from its wooden packing case.

'God, it's huge,' Kate gasped. 'I never thought it was going to be that big.'

'Don't worry madam, it's the most comfortable bike there is for a passenger. Your husband tells me you are planning to tour America on it.'

Kate turned and glared at Juan, then returned her gaze to the dealer and asked, 'What else has he told you?'

A somewhat sheepish trader looked at Juan and asked, 'Have I said something wrong?'

It was Juan's turn to be embarrassed. 'We're not married…yet.'

'I'll have the bike ready for collection on Wednesday, if you like.'

'That would be fine.' Juan turned to Kate and asked, 'Can you bring me into Douglas in my car that day?'

There was a broad grin on her face, 'Of course.'

Maybe I'm not going to be a widower for long after all, he thought hopefully.

* * *

'Lee Hefferman.'
'Boss? It's Ruth.'
'Where are you?'

'I'm ringing from Inverness. There are several MacKinnon families living near Gairloch, but I eventually found the right one by digging around in the local library, which is adjacent to the High School. The bad news is that MacKinnon senior was buried about a month ago and Kate MacKinnon has gone away. Apparently, Robbie MacKinnon died in France – no one knows the cause.'

'What do you mean?'

'Well, I asked whether he had had a heart attack, a stroke or something like that. However, no one seemed to know. He was cremated – not buried in the local cemetery. Mrs MacKinnon sold up soon afterwards and left last week. The house is in a nearby village called Badachro, but is empty. I asked around in the *Badachro Inn*, the local pub, but no one knows where she has gone. Her stepson was here for several days helping her to move out and load a van. She has not left a forwarding address.'

'Then we will have to assume she has gone to live near her stepson in Leicester. Writing to her at her old address in Badachro won't work as MI6 will be filtering her mail. Come back and we'll think what to do next.'

* * *

On Wednesday Juan picked up the bike. As he mounted it for the first time, he noticed the artificial tank made of plastic. He rode the bike back to Port St Mary, parked it in his garage at the rear of his apartment and had removed the tank before Kate returned in his Focus.

'I'll take it to Onchan in the morning,' he said. 'It's the beginning of our American adventure together.'

* * *

Isle of Man Examiner – Friday 22nd June 2002

PROPERTY SALES RECENTLY RECORDED AT THE GENERAL REGISTRY IN DOUGLAS INCLUDE:

The Executors of the estate of Marianne McCormick
sold No 7, The Point, Port St Mary for £245,000 to
John Pearson, c/o The Cherry Orchard, Port Erin.

Other property sales recorded were…

'Have you seen this?' asked Gobal to his colleague, Ajit.

'No, what is it?'

'The man who was calling himself Pearson, who I thought was Quayle, has bought a property in Port St Mary. I must inform London at once.'

'Hadn't you better check first to see if it's the same fellow?'

'It can't be anyone else; the timing is right.'

The following day, three letters were sent to three different addresses; one would eventually reach its intended destination in London; the other two would pass through three different addresses and take longer to reach Pakistan.

CHAPTER 32

Friday, 28th June 2002

Ashraf Khalif, the Head of the *London Set-up*, received Gopal's letter a week after it had been posted. He knew al-Qaeda's triplicate posting system was working efficiently and that the other two letters would be heading to Peshawar via different circuitous routes, but they could take up to a further three weeks to arrive. Both would reach their quarry only in the hands of a trusted courier, one travelling from Islamabad and the other from Karachi.

Khalif read the letter...

Gopal is certain he has found Pearson's whereabouts. Excellent!

He penned off two brief notes.

To Gopal, he instructed him to discreetly observe and log Pearson's movements as much as possible, especially noting his regular habits.

To Peshawar, which would travel via Istanbul and Amman, he simply asked: Is Pearson to be removed immediately with local resources or await a specialist?

Ashraf didn't expect a reply for several weeks and, so, was surprised when a coded fax, very rarely used, appeared ten days later. Translated it read: *Expect Mwt al-Swd within 96 hours. Plot and book his route to Douglas via Ireland overland. Inform Gopal he has done well and tell him when he can expect MaS.*

Ashraf had never met Mwt al-Swd, but his reputation within the organisation was legendary. The total destruction of the Ballajorra farmhouse, thought to have been a complete success until Gopal's recent

272

discovery that Pearson had survived, was one of his minor triumphs. The Bombay bomb that killed 250 Hindus and the twin attacks on the US Embassies at Nairobi and Dar es Salaam had been managed by him. Within the company, he was believed to have been a major player behind the attack on the Twin Towers. The thought of meeting him made Khalif shudder. Clearly, the execution of Pearson was considered by their leader as top priority. He had no idea how Mwt al-Swd would arrive in London, although almost certainly it wouldn't be through Heathrow or Gatwick where security was much tighter than at seaports such as Dover or Portsmouth. *He may even be crossing from Holland or Denmark. Whatever way he comes, it will be via a circuitous route.* He began researching land and sea routes to Douglas via Ireland knowing that, almost certainly, Mwt al-Swd would already have left Pakistan.

* * *

In the mid-afternoon of Tuesday, 16th July, Mwt al-Swd turned up unannounced at *The Taj Mahal*. Clearly in a foul mood as a result of a rough crossing from Dublin on the Isle of Man Steam Packet Company's ship, the *Ben-my-Chree*, he had flung his belongings on his bed, noticing the room hadn't been decorated since he left it seven years previously.

He went downstairs to confront Gopal in the kitchen. 'What have you found out about Pearson?'

Nervously, Gopal began reporting what he had discovered since receiving instructions from London. He described Pearson's apartment, his nearby girlfriend's house, their regular walks with her dog and how, recently, he had acquired a big motorbike and they went for rides together.

'What sort of a dog is it?'

'A black and white sheepdog; it's quite large – perhaps two and a half feet tall. I'd guess it must weigh at least three stone.'

'How frequently do they go walking?'

'Five or six times a week.'

'Where do they go?'

'Around the headlands towards the south of the island; I usually follow them about half a mile behind. On nice days they sometimes go all the way to the tip of the island, called The Sound, where there is a café and they have lunch. It takes them about two hours each way.'

'Are there ever many people around?'

'At the weekends things are busier, but I've followed them some days and have never seen anyone else.'

'Will it be easy to get up close to them?'

'I would have thought so. Why?'

'I don't suppose you have a sniper rifle?'

'No. We have nothing like that. All we have is a .22 Smith and Wesson revolver.'

'Is that the only weapon you have?' Mwt al-Swd gave the impression he didn't believe Gopal.

'We have no need for guns. Our main purpose here on the island is to provide funds for our cause. Ajit and I are trained accountants. From here, we control our organisation's funds in the offshore banks. There are thirty-seven Indian restaurants in the UK feeding us with their profits, that we then launder through Douglas banks to the Cayman Islands.'

'Very interesting, but can I see the revolver?' Gopal could tell al-Swd wasn't in the least bit interested in the financial workings of al-Qaeda.

Gopal stood on a stool and brought a large tin, labelled *Dried Chillies*, down from the top shelf. He levered off the lid and delved inside, removing something wrapped in polythene.

Al-Swd opened the plastic bag. The gun was in good condition. He could see it had been cleaned and oiled regularly. 'A model 351, seven rounds,' he declared. 'Ammunition?'

Gopal crossed the kitchen to another shelf. He fetched a tin marked *Anardana*, which Mwt knew were dried pomegranate seeds. A box, again wrapped in polythene, containing 25 Remington LR bullets was extracted from the tin. The al-Qaeda assassin nodded and sighed. 'This will have to do. I'll need to get close to Pearson to be certain of killing him with this. When can you take me to Port St Mary?'

'You can take our car, if you wish. Port St Mary is easy to find. It will only take half an hour to get there and if you want to scout the ground, I might be an encumbrance. I've drawn a couple of sketch maps for you.'

'It will take me three or four days to get to know the geography and the best place to make the hit. I'll come back here each evening.'

'Of course. One other thing you should know. Their walking pattern isn't consistent. Some days Pearson will drive to The Sound; they'll have lunch together and she will walk back with the dog on her own while he drives back. It can work the other way too. She'll start walking with the dog to The Sound. He'll drive there, park, walk back and meet her halfway. They'll then carry on together for lunch at the café.'

'Anything else I should know?'

'No, I don't think so.'

* * *

Kate and Juan walked to The Sound together on Saturday, 20th July. They took lunch in the café and were discussing their plans for America. 'The paperwork arrived from *Motorcycle Incorporated Tours* this morning. I rang them immediately and arranged to take the bike to Manchester on Monday. I'm booked on the 9 am sailing to Liverpool. I should be in Manchester by about three o'clock and will easily catch the evening flight back. Will you meet me at Ronaldsway in the evening?'

'Of course. I'm beginning to get excited about going; it's only three weeks away.'

Juan looked at Kate. She was the most beautiful, attractive woman he'd ever met. He'd fallen for her charms from day one, and yet...

...They'd been seeing each other daily since she had come to Port St Mary to live; they'd been shopping together; they'd been to the cinema together; they ate at restaurants together and they held hands when walking together with Cal. They talked animatedly together; they'd planned their trip to the US together, where to maximise damage and where to leave the radioactive VX-R after they returned to Britain. He'd done many odd jobs at her house, but he'd only ever hugged her socially and kissed her on the cheek.

He had begun to wonder if he'd overdone *playing it cool*. He desperately wanted to tell her how he felt, but he was scared. He didn't want to rush her and yet she'd gone along with the plan for them to share everything when they toured America, including bedrooms in hotels. It didn't make any sense. He remembered someone once telling him that *the fear of failure is greater than the joy of success. Perhaps*, he thought, *that's my problem with women.*

'We fly British Airways from Manchester to the States. We pick up the bike in New York the day after we arrive. It's going to be quite an adventure.'

Beaming, her eyes sparkled brightly. 'I think tonight is the beginning of our journey together. We should celebrate.'

'What have you in mind?'

'How about visiting that nice Indian restaurant in Douglas?'

'It could be fully booked.'

'Give them a ring.' She nodded towards the public phone box in the corner of the café.

* * *

'Guess who has just rang and booked a table for two for this evening?'

'I've no idea. Who?' replied Ajit.

'Pearson. We'll have to tell al-Swd as soon as he comes back from Port St Mary,' said Gopal.

'Well, I hope he doesn't decide to do it here.'

'Don't be daft.'

'I wouldn't put anything past him.'

* * *

Al-Swd peered through the porthole window between the restaurant and the kitchen. 'That's him all right. He'd better enjoy what will be one of his last meals. I plan to do it on Monday.'

'Can I ask where?' asked Gopal.

'About halfway between Port St Mary and The Sound; the cliffs are called Spanish Head. It's the highest point on their route and from the top you can see the path all the way down to the cafe. From there, it will be easy to dispose of their bodies over the edge of the precipice.'

'You are going to kill the woman too?'

'Of course, and her dog; if it gives me any trouble.'

Ajit swallowed hard. He had expected only Pearson to be assassinated. There was a reason why he should die, but not an innocent woman and her dog. He said nothing, but the thought of the possible repercussions and investigation by the police worried him. *If the Manx police fraud squad begin delving into our finances…*

* * *

Kate left *The Taj Mahal* in high spirits. A good meal had been enhanced by their lively discussion of plans for America. Kate had been researching likely events to target. 'On our second night in New York, the *New York Giants* have a football game against the *Philadelphia Eagles*. There will be a capacity crowd of, perhaps, 80,000; half the men there could be of childbearing age. If you take half of the VX-R to one side of the stadium and I to the other side, it should guarantee total infection.'

'Will it be necessary for us to split up? I understood the range of its effectiveness could be a hundred yards.'

She thought for a moment. 'I just want to be sure, that's all.'

After the New York match, Kate had planned that they should travel to Washington. 'There's a game between the *Washington Redskins* and *Tampa Bay Buccaneers…*' and, so, the conversation continued.

It wasn't only the schedules of the National Football League she had investigated, but baseball games, tennis matches, pop concerts and political rallies. 'I have a list as long as your arm,' she enthused.

When they arrived back at Port St Mary, she was on a high and invited Juan in, '…for something special.'

They sat in her lounge, Cal lying in front of the fire, hoping it might get lit for his benefit.

'You know, I'm really beginning to settle here,' she said as they sipped their Bailey's Cream with their coffee. 'I thought I might miss Badachro, but I don't. When I look back, it was terribly isolated and miles from anywhere. Here, we still have the same degree of freedom, but the shops are only a short distance. It's the best of both worlds. I miss Robbie, of course, but that's something different.'

The mention of Kate's former husband dampened Juan's ardour. He wanted to make a move, but couldn't. He'd never mastered how a woman's mind worked. He had only really experienced two women: Mollie and Barbara. *With Mollie I fumbled and with Barbara, she took charge. How am I ever going to tell Kate that I want to live with her for the rest of my life?*

He looked at his watch; it was almost 11.30 pm. 'I had better be going...'

'Don't go. Stay the night.'

It was out of the blue. Juan hadn't expected the invitation. He spluttered. 'Are you sure?'

'Yes, it's something I've wanted for quite a while, but I wasn't sure how to tell you.'

God I'm not ready for this.

He followed her up the stairs looking at her long, slender legs and her beautiful, curvaceous back below a slim waist. His mind was aflutter, his stomach empty, his hands cold and his heart was pounding.

She showed no abashment as she undressed, folded and laid her clothes neatly on a chair. She snuggled under the duvet. 'Come, let's explore each other,' she whispered.

* * *

The Isle of Man Steam Packet Company's regulations demand that vehicles arrive early for embarkation. Juan had left his apartment by 0745 am on the Gold Wing and arrived at Douglas Pier by 0815. The Seacat departed promptly and had disappeared over the horizon when Mwt al-Swd left Broadway for the south of the island.

On the three days that al-Swd had travelled to Port St Mary to recce, he had parked the Fiesta somewhere different on each occasion to avoid suspicion. That morning he left it on the promenade overlooking Chapel Bay and walked down the High Street towards The Point. He accepted that he had to be flexible as Pearson's walk with his girlfriend had varied and yesterday they hadn't appeared at all. Nevertheless, he had decided his plan was to follow the woman, whatever the pair did. Whether they began their walk together from her house or whether she left alone and Pearson met her later, she was the one to stalk. Consequently, he positioned himself at his concealed observation post behind some rocks on the sea-side of the road, fifty yards from her house, and waited.

True to form, he watched Kate and Cal leave the house at eleven o'clock and head up the path that ran alongside the golf course. She was dressed as usual: a warm fleece, jeans, strong, sensible shoes and a canvas bag slung diagonally across her shoulders. *Why do women always think they need a handbag whenever they go out?* he thought. *It's as if they think they're not dressed properly without one.*

He waited for a couple of minutes and then began to slowly follow Kate and her dog. As usual she carried a ball launcher – a solid rubber ball attached to a short, semi-stiff cable that allowed her to sling the toy some distance. The dog took particular delight chasing the toy, often successfully leaping to catch it mid-air and retrieve it. Al-Swd knew that once beyond the road that carried only sporadic vehicular traffic, she would exercise less control and the dog would wander over the heathland looking for rabbits and, occasionally, give chase.

He let her get a quarter of a mile ahead; there was no hurry. He knew it would be noon by the time she reached the high point of her walk and would meet up with Pearson coming the other way. His plan was simple. As she neared the brow of the path, he would begin to close up; she would be distracted by seeing Pearson. Timed right, he would catch up with them as they met. Neither would suspect him, thinking he was just another rambler.

Forty minutes passed as they plodded up the narrow, rough path, in places little wider than a rabbit run. Kate was totally unaware she was being followed. He watched the daft dog that thought it could catch rabbits running wild over the heather-covered slopes.

What mad creatures they are, he thought. *Why are they so popular as pets with the English?*

He saw no one else. He began to catch up as she disappeared over the crest of the hill. He increased his pace to a jog expecting to see Pearson hugging her fifty yards ahead. He reached the summit and to his utter astonishment, she was alone and walking towards him. She was no more than ten yards away.

What the hell? Where's Pearson? Does she know I have been following her?

She moved to her right into the heather to allow him to pass on the narrow path.

He moved to his left so that they still faced each other. She moved further to her right towards the edge of the cliff, but still ten yards from the brink, and gestured to him, *after you.*

He moved the same distance to the left.

'Where's Pearson?' he snapped.

'I'm sorry?'

'Don't play games. Where's Pearson?'

'I don't follow.'

'You were friendly enough on Saturday night.' He pulled his revolver out of his jacket pocket. She was no more than ten feet away.

My God, he's from the CIA. They've found out they didn't kill John in Antibes, she thought.

She froze on the spot, but her mind was working lightning fast. *The CIA wouldn't use a .22 revolver; he's from al-Qaeda. Bin Laden has sent him for revenge.*

She instinctively tried an old trick.

She spoke in Arabic. *'Saddam Hussein has sent you, hasn't he?'*

'Don't be bloody stupid; Saddam is shafted – finished.'

He realised he had given himself away by understanding Arabic. He raised his revolver, pointing it directly at her. In Arabic he said, *'Prepare to meet Allah.'*

Behind the stranger, no more than three yards away, she saw Cal. He had come to investigate what was going on. There was just one chance.

'GET HIM CAL,' she yelled.

There was a loud growl and the stranger swung round, twisting his foot in the heather. He was temporarily off balance for a fraction of a second. The dog was leaping through the air at chest height. He fired, but a piece of copper-coated lead weighing less than a tenth of an ounce and travelling at 680 mph does not stop the momentum of a three-stone dog travelling at forty mph. Cal had grabbed him by the throat and another bullet was fired into the dog's trunk. The force of the dog's charge pushed al-Swd diagonally backwards and he fell into the heather and bracken between himself and Kate, with Cal soon on top of him.

Kate was already desperately scrambling in her canvas bag for Cal's laucher. *I'll smash and break his nose with the ball; then grab his gun.* She knew she had no more than five seconds to use the toy weapon on her assassin before he would recover.

She needn't have bothered for as she was pulling the toy from the bag, there was a horrific, blood-curdling yell that rapidly died away. A dull thud came from below where the man had fallen. There was no sign of her assailant.

Full of curiosity, she cautiously approached the spot, her weapon at the ready. She knelt down and pulled back the covering of undergrowth. She gasped; there was a gap in the earth of two feet – a fissure, or as the locals call it, a chasm. She peered down. One hundred and fifty feet below on the rocks, swilled by the tide, lay a body with Cal lying on top of it.

She knelt, staring for what seemed an eternity, tears flooding from her eyes. Cal had died saving her. She remembered going with Robbie to buy him after their previous dog, Jed, had died aged seventeen in 1994. A big part of her life had been taken away. As she watched, the tide below was washing around them; slowly the dog floated away on the tide. She gazed in a trance as he disappeared. She was alone and felt as cold as a frozen corpse...

'YOU BASTARD,' she yelled at the unknown gunman below. 'You bastard, you bastard...'

There was no response, only the noise of the waves crashing over the rocks as the tide came in. She watched as the sea did its work. First the arms were lifted and then the legs began to float. Minutes passed; finally, the complete body floated off the rocks and it too slowly disappeared as it sank into the deep.

CHAPTER 33

Monday, 22nd July 2002

He took one look at her and knew something was wrong.

'What's the matter?' he asked, as he met her in the reception area at Ronaldsway Airport that evening.

Her eyes were red from crying and as she began to explain, she had to stop.

'Look, let's go upstairs to the coffee shop. You can take your time to tell me.'

Juan listened to Kate's story of the morning's events. When she had finished, he asked, 'Did you use your gangrennex spray gun?'

'No. Don't you believe me?'

'Yes, of course I do, but the difference is that you didn't have a hand in the assassin's death. The police will want to be sure about that.'

'Do we need to tell them?'

'I think we must. And do it at once. George Costain, the Deputy Chief Constable, is a good friend and I will give him a ring in a minute. If he asks why you didn't report it immediately, tell him you were in such a state of shock that you took several tranquilisers when you got home and fell asleep before coming to meet me off the Manchester plane.'

She nodded reluctantly.

They went downstairs and from a public phone box in the entrance, Juan rang George Costain.

'George? It's John Pearson here.'

'Hi John, to what do I owe the pleasure?'

283

'George, have you got an hour? We need to talk urgently.'

'Where are you?'

'I'm at the airport. Can I come and see you at once?'

'Yes, Joy is just about to put the boys to bed. You can have dinner with us, if you like.'

'I've got Kate with me.'

'Excellent, I would love to meet her.'

* * *

During the twenty-minute drive from the airport to Douglas, Juan quickly regaled how George, as one of the island's few Special Branch officers, had helped him make contact with bin Laden and his crew on the trawler *Dom Pedro* after al-Qaeda had purchased the atomic device from the IRA. George had been his best man when he returned from Naxcivan and married Molly. He had taken charge of Juan's estate when the plan had been hatched with MI6 for Juan to have officially died in the fire at Ballajorra.

'George is one of the few people who are aware of everything about my background and I would trust him with my life. Whatever he suggests this evening will be the right decision. He knows a little about your past too. But don't worry; this episode will sort itself out quickly. You'll see.'

The niceties of introductions over and Joy having made it clear that they were having 'nothing special', the three sat in the lounge while Joy busied herself in the kitchen.

'Dinner will take forty minutes,' she had announced.

For the second time in under an hour, Juan listened to Kate's version of the events that had occurred that morning. George listened quietly. When she had finished, he asked questions to clear up how the assailant had fallen through the heather that covered the chasm, the role played by Cal, and Kate's intention to strike the assailant with the dog's ball.

'In your description of him, you thought he could either be an Afghan or from Northern Pakistan. Why?'

'Their skin colouring is a mix of light brown and green-grey. Their facial features are chiselled with prominent cheekbones.'

'I would agree with that,' chipped in Juan. 'Indians tend to have rounder characteristics and are darker brown.'

'You said you planned to smash his nose with the dog's fetching-toy?'

'It was all I could think of at the time.'

'Why his nose?'

'I hoped the force of the hard rubber ball would break his nose and cause his eyes to water immediately; temporarily blinding him while I grabbed his revolver.'

'But you never hit him?'

'No, I didn't have to; he'd vanished through the chasm with Cal on top of him.'

George paused for a while, thinking over the events. 'There are several things that come to mind,' he remarked. 'You said he answered you in Arabic at one point?'

'Yes.'

'And he let it drop that he had seen you both at *The Taj Mahal* on Saturday night?'

'Yes.'

'And neither of you saw him at the restaurant nor have you seen him hanging around in Port St Mary?'

Both Kate and Juan shook their heads.

'But he must have done some reconnaissance to know you walk the dog regularly and that he appeared surprised when you didn't meet John at Spanish Head?'

'Unless someone else did the spying for him,' suggested Juan.

'Mmm, possible. The two guys who run *The Taj* are Pakistanis. Could they speak Arabic?'

'I wouldn't have thought so,' replied Kate. 'They probably speak Urdu.'

'I can speak some Urdu,' added Juan. 'I learned it before going to Lebanon. Why do you ask?'

'I think there's a connection. Your description of this man is similar to a man who bought several electronic devices in Back Strand Street a few days before 5th July 1995.' He stopped and looked at Juan.

'My God!' Juan's reaction was immediate. 'What are you saying?'

'I think he could be the same assassin who killed Molly and the kids. I believe he was highly skilled at reconnaissance and had probably been watching you for several days. The only explanation for the fire at Ballajorra was that someone placed the incendiary devices in the farmhouse while you and your family were at Tynwald Fair. He would have needed local help. I suspected at the time that it may have come from the two who run *The Taj*. You'll remember the Head of MI6, at the meeting the day after the fire, suggested there must be al-Qaeda sleepers on the island, possibly operating from an Indian restaurant.'

'Yes, I remember Barbara mentioning that,' nodded Juan.

'We looked carefully at the idea, but could find no evidence. The two *Taj* owners were seen at the fair, for example. However, now I am beginning to wonder. Tomorrow I will order a check through the statements made by the witnesses that day. The next question is how did he get to Port St Mary? He would hardly have taken a bus.'

'By car, obviously,' replied Kate.

'Exactly, and it must still be where he left it. First thing in the morning, I'll have the two Pakistanis checked by the Highway Board to see if either of them owns a car. We will then make a sweep for it in Port St Mary.'

George then changed tack. 'You said the pistol was a .22 revolver? How are you so sure?'

'I was in my university's military cadet force for several years. We were given extensive weapons training.'

'When he fell down the chasm, did he still have hold of the revolver?'

'I guess so. There was no sign of it where he fell through the undergrowth.'

'What finish was it?'

'A bright metal – stainless steel?'

She knows what I meant by finish, thought George.

'Not a matt black?' he asked.

'No.'

'If the weather permits tomorrow, I will get our only trained frogman out to search for the gun. The bright metal should be easy to spot with an underwater searchlight. We then might be able to check it for fingerprints and, hopefully, trace it.'

'Will the frogman be able to find the body?' asked Kate.

'No, I shouldn't think so. The currents around Spanish Head are vicious; I would think the body is miles away by now.'

Joy came in and announced dinner was ready. 'Come and get it. It's all from the freezer, I'm afraid.'

'Don't apologise, it's good that you can accommodate us at such short notice,' smiled Kate.

Conversation then centred on Kate's early thoughts about the island and how she was settling in. 'I love it,' she had replied. 'I enjoy similar freedom to what I had in the Highlands but without the isolation, and being near to John helps.'

Juan confided that they were planning to have an extended holiday in the States, travelling around on the Gold Wing that he had taken to Manchester earlier that day.

'How long will you be away?' asked Joy.

'About three months; it'll be the trip of a lifetime,' replied Kate.

'Kate has agreed to marry me when we get back,' Juan remarked.

'Congratulations,' answered George. 'Am I to be the best man again?'

Juan laughed. 'Of course, if you'll stand up for me?'

'Just say the word.'

Before leaving, it was agreed that a detective would call on Kate in the morning to take a formal statement and, afterwards, she would show him the exact place where the events took place.

'The day shift comes on at eight o'clock. I will organise a raid on *The Taj Mahal* for nine o'clock. Our fraud squad will confiscate their books and we will search the premises for evidence of guns. I have a feeling we will find evidence not only of today's events, but for those of seven years ago too.'

* * *

When by six o'clock that evening, Mwt al-Swd hadn't returned, Gopal and Ajit had become agitated. 'He should have been back hours ago,' remarked Gopal. 'Something must have happened to him.'

'What can we do? He's got our car. We can't leave here this evening; there's only you and I on duty.'

'Tomorrow morning, I'll catch an early bus to Port St Mary and look for him.'

Ajit pointed out the obvious. 'We've no idea where he could have parked the car.'

'True, but there aren't that many places in the village.'

'I don't like the feel of this. I'm wondering if we should inform *The London Set-up* of his disappearance.'

'It's too soon for that. If I can't find out what's happened to him in the morning, then we'll make contact.'

* * *

At 0900 hours the following morning, the inspector in charge of the island's small Fraud Squad, accompanied by two of his team, along with four uniformed policemen, raided *The Taj Mahal.*

Gopal, having caught the 0805 bus from Douglas, was due to arrive at Port St Mary at 0910 hours. He had decided to get off the bus at the promenade, the first stop in the port. He would then work his way down to the harbour looking for their missing car. However, a police inquiry made to the Highway Board had already revealed the make, colour and registration number of the Ford Fiesta owned by the restaurant. So it was a surprise to Gopal when, at a quarter past nine, he found his car being loaded onto a car transporter on the promenade under the supervision of the local PC.

PC Callin looked at Gopal and asked, 'Is this your car, sir?'

Gopal didn't reply and turned to walk away.

'Excuse me, sir. I asked you a question,' repeated the constable, who was now alongside Gopal. As the Pakistani began to run, he felt a hand on his shoulder, his arm being grabbed and a handcuff being fixed on his wrist.

By 0930 hours, ledgers, bank statements, receipts, delivery notes and correspondence were being removed from *The Taj Mahal.* A thorough search was revealing unexplained items of clothing belonging to a tall person who had been staying in a room above the restaurant. A Greek passport in the name of Louki Panadopollis was found inside one of the pockets. A train ticket from Cork to Dublin and a boat ticket from Dublin to Douglas that had, carelessly, not been destroyed, indicated that he had been on the island for almost a week. An opened box of twenty-five .22 bullets, with seven shells missing, was discovered in a drawer. Ajit refused to explain how the items came to be there and was taken to the police station for questioning. A scene of crime squad moved in.

By 1100 hours, Detective Inspector Bill Turnbull had taken Kate's statement and she had confirmed that the man in the passport was her assailant. By midday, she was showing the DI where the assault had taken place. To her astonishment, a small fishing boat was already waiting nearby. Over his radio, the DI was able to direct the boat to the exact spot where Kate had seen the body drift away on the tide twenty-four hours previously.

By 1300 hours, the gun had been found. Five live and two spent cartridges were found in the revolver, confirming Kate's statement. The cartridges matched the bullets found at *The Taj Mahal.*

By 1400 hours, when he had reopened his shop after lunch, Geoff Callow had confirmed that the man in the photograph was the same man that he had sold radio controlled solid state relays and a soldiering iron to seven years previously. Asked how he could be sure after such a long time, he replied, 'It's not a face you forget.'

Towards 1700 hours, the team of detectives that had been assigned to the boring task of going over 'with a fine-tooth comb' the statements of witnesses who had seen Gopal and Ajit at Tynwald Fair in 1995 reported to their boss, DI Turnbull.

'I think we've found something,' began Sergeant Swindlehurst. 'It's been made easier by recent events. The last time the two Pakis were seen at the St John's Fair that day was at twelve noon.' He stopped; wondering if he would be reprimanded for using the derogatory slang term for the two Asians.

The DI said nothing, nodding for him to continue.

'They weren't seen back in Douglas until three o'clock. It doesn't take three hours to drive seven miles. Where were they?'

'That's hardly evidence.'

'I agree, sir, but if they were to drive to the farm at Bride, what thirty minutes? Pick up the arsonist and return to Douglas – another three-quarters of an hour? There'd be plenty of time for the assassin to pick up his things and catch the afternoon boat to Liverpool.'

'It's all supposition, Jimmy, but I'll put it to the Super and see what he says.'

The Inspector went upstairs to see his boss. He regaled his Sergeant's hypothesis. George Costain listened intently. He would have liked to compliment his men for their hard work by telling them that their theory made sense and would lead to charges being made against the two Pakistanis for complicity in murder. However, the police officers thought Juan Quayle had died in the fire with his family; George was one of the very few who knew he was still alive. He had to be careful not to let the cat out of the bag. Furthermore, he was aware that the Quayle family had left the fair around noon and travelled to Port Erin for their picnic on the beach.

If the Pakis had followed the Quayles as far as Foxdale to ensure they were not going straight back to their farm, then you could add another thirty or forty minutes to their absence. I think there's enough evidence to charge them with aiding and abetting murder.

As if reading his superior's mind, Bill Turnbull asked, 'Shall we charge them with the Quayles' murders?'

'Bill, you know I'm not a ditherer, but there are political overtones to this that I am not at liberty to divulge – at least, not yet. What are the Fraud Squad's first impressions of *The Taj Mahal's* books?'

'Too early to say, except it's a centre for money laundering. It could take weeks to work through the myriad of false accounts.'

That evening, George rang Juan.

'John? It's George. We've ample evidence to charge the two Pakistanis who run *The Taj* with aiding and abetting Kate's assailant with the murder of Molly and the kids. It was definitely the same man. There's just one problem: you're not dead. If we were to proceed, it's going to have to come out about you working for MI6 and plotting to assassinate bin Laden.'

'I've thought about that, George. I think you're going to have to simply let them get away with it.'

'We won't do that. There's ample evidence of *The Taj* being a money laundering centre for al-Qaeda. They'll get at least ten years for that.'

CHAPTER 34

Monday, 12th August 2002

Three weeks after Mwt al-Swd had fallen through the heather into the chasm, a coordinated operation, organised by the Metropolitan Police, simultaneously raided thirty-seven Indian restaurants across the UK from Thurso in the North-East of Scotland to Truro in the South-West of England. Al-Qaeda's main supply of income within Britain was quashed as a result of a dog called Cal.

* * *

That same day Kate and Juan, with Manx passports showing them to be Kate Jackson and Alan Quine, found themselves flying from Manchester on a British Airways flight that arrived at JFK airport, New York in the early evening. Thanks to the organisation of *Motorcycle Incorporated Tours,* their documentation, itinerary and maps of their planned trans-American tour helped them clear customs and immigration relatively rapidly. Nevertheless, it took them an hour and a half before they emerged into the Arrivals' Hall. A representative displaying the customary placard was waiting patiently for them. 'Have you been waiting long?' asked Juan after he had introduced Kate and himself.

'No, I never leave home until I know the plane has arrived. Even though it takes me an hour to get here, I will always be ahead of our guests. Welcome to the United States. Ever since 9/11, security has become a nightmare. My name is Chuck Edwards and this is my card. If you have a problem at any time, day or night, ring me on that number.'

He pointed to the documentation he had given to Juan. 'I'm going to take you to your hotel, *Ivy Terrace,* on 58th Street near Central Park. There are plenty of restaurants nearby. I'll pick you up in the morning at ten o'clock and take you to Port Jersey where your bike has been re-assembled and is ready for you.'

'You've seen it, then?'

'Yes. I was down there yesterday to watch it being unloaded and taken out of its crate. I then supervised it being moved to a secure compound where the customs people went over it with a fine-tooth comb.'

'What did they do?'

'Oh, the usual things: check it for drugs with sniffer dogs, make sure it is taxed and mechanically fit for road. Before you can ride it away, the authorities will want to check your insurance policies for yourselves and the bike. You'll have to satisfy them you are safe riding it too.'

'How will they do that?'

'They'll watch you start it up and manoeuvre it through some cones. Nothing to worry about; I'll stay with you until you leave.'

* * *

The following morning, Chuck arrived on time. An hour later, they were in the bonded warehouse with the customs official as he checked all their documentation. He said he was a biker himself. He admitted admiring the Gold Wing. 'A better tourer than a Harley; although I shouldn't say so...' He was also envious about the idea of riding to California via the southern states. He had noted the Manx registration plate and asked questions about the TT. He wanted to know what sites they were proposing to visit and what routes they would take. Juan gained the impression that his interest was due to the camaraderie among bikers rather than officialdom.

By noon, Kate and Juan were on their way. They passed the home of the *New York Giants,* the MetLife Stadium, within minutes; it was only three miles from Port Jersey. They found the *Carlstadt Hampton Inn,* the nearest hotel to the stadium, half a mile further along Paterson Plank Road. They booked in, took a light lunch and enquired about tickets for the evening game between the *Giants* and the *Philadelphia Eagles*.

'It will be a full house. It's a big local derby. There will be 80,000 spectators. If you go down to the stadium now, you may be lucky and get some cancellation tickets. They will only sell them face to face at this late hour and not over the phone,' replied the hotel receptionist.

The ten-minute walk was productive; although they could only get two separate tickets some distance from each other. Returning to the hotel, Juan removed one of the lead containers from the bike. In their room, he poured the contents of two half-litre Coca-Cola bottles into the sink. He then replaced the liquid with the clear VX-R solution. Kate added a few drops of a cochineal-coloured brown hair dye mixture that she had concocted and experimented with before leaving the Isle of Man.

'No one would ever guess it wasn't cola,' she smiled.

'It will pass scrutiny as long as the bouncers don't have Geiger counters,' joked Juan.

'If they do, what then?' she asked with a worried look on her face.

'We're up a gum tree, but don't worry, it won't happen,' he said smiling broadly.

They spent the rest of the afternoon in bed, catching up on jet lag. They left their hotel at seven o'clock in plenty of time for the match beginning an hour later. They separated and went to their appropriate entrances. Both had agreed to purchase a hotdog and show it with their coke to any officials as they entered the stadium. In the event, they were not searched but had to pass through a metal detector. Neither Kate nor Juan understood the finer points of the game but by eleven o'clock they were back in their hotel. Juan carefully returned the VX-R to the lead container. Both had agreed the less radiation they subjected themselves to the better.

'Even though I will never have your baby...' she had joked with Juan. The poignancy of the remark was lost on Juan as he was unaware that Kate had been sterile since an operation to remove a cancerous cyst had gone wrong when she was only two years of age.

They had decided the following day would be spent on a leisurely ride to Washington DC, about 230 miles away. Kate was in charge of visits to mass events. The next game she had organised to attend was the *Washington Redskins* versus the *Tampa Bay Buccaneers*. As the game was not to be played until Saturday evening, they had three days visiting the tourist sites of the capital such as the Lincoln and Jefferson memorials; the latter Juan thought was the most impressive, particularly when lit at night. Both were disappointed with The White House – '...not a patch on Buckingham Palace,' said Kate. Visits to the Arlington Cemetery, the Vietnam Veterans' Memorial, the Smithsonian National Air and Space Museum, and Mount Vernon to see George Washington's home kept them busy.

On late Saturday afternoon, the hotel's minibus driver took them and several other residents to the FedEx Field Stadium near the Beltway. They positioned themselves at the opposite sides of the stadium as the crowds gathered for the match. The *Tampa Bay Buccaneers* won a rare away win against their neighbours in front of a packed 90,000 crowd.

That evening, back in their hotel, Kate mulled over her plan, showing Juan the tally she was keeping of her estimate of the number of men of potential childbearing age who could be infected. 'Already, 85,000 are probably contaminated and we've only been to two events.'

'How did you work that out?'

'I guess seventy per cent attending the games are male. Seventy per cent of those are under fifty. Therefore, nearly half of those present could be affected in future.'

'You do realise boys attending with their fathers as young as seven or eight could be twenty years away from having children. You and I will be long gone by then!'

'We'll never know, will we? I suspect the hexadactyl outbreak will be like the sudden spread of AIDS; the truth will be kept secret until historians in the future finally write about it.'

* * *

Kate had decided that their tour should aim at no more than 350 miles per day; thereby giving them time to see the country through which they were passing.

The day after the match in Washington, they headed further south. That evening they pulled into Greensboro, North Carolina. The following day, they stayed to watch the *Greensboro Grasshoppers* play a minor baseball league game against the *Tennessee Smokies* in front of a small, but rowdy, crowd of 4,500.

Next, they travelled over 450 miles and waited three days to see a football match at the EverBank Field Stadium between the *Jacksonville Jaguars* and *Miami Dolphins* in front of a near capacity crowd of 65,000. During their stay, they attended a pop concert and went to a crowded cinema; on each occasion with their cola bottles.

A day later they found a motel near Marlins Park in west side Miami, the home of the *Miami Marlins* Baseball team. Capable of seating 37,000 spectators, it is over 1,000 miles from Washington. Their trip had taken two weeks and Kate calculated that, by the time they had watched the local team play the *Tampa Bay Rays*, some 135,000 men could be infected.

Sunday, 25th August saw them take a leisurely day to Tampa. They lunched at the Myakka River State Park for lunch and wandered around the park marvelling at the turtles, alligators and huge spiders. They took the Sunshine Highway, Interstate 275, across Tampa Bay – a road that left both Kate and Juan gasping at the unique way its bridges and embankments cut across the bay.

An hour after leaving Tampa on Interstate 75 the following morning, Kate spotted a sign for Inverness. Over their intercom, she pleaded excitedly, 'We must go there.'

It was to be a disappointment, a small town with a population of 7,210 according to its 'Welcome to Inverness' sign. Continuing, they arrived late afternoon in Tallahassee, the state capital. They watched a basketball match in the evening between *Florida State University* and *Wake Forest* in front of a crowd of, perhaps, 4,000 people. The next day saw them press on to New Orleans. In front of a 70,000 crowd at the

Louisiana Superdome, they saw the *Saints* beat the *Carolina Panthers* at US football. Three days later, they saw a baseball game at the same venue in front of 45,000 spectators; this time the *New Orleans Zephyrs* beat the *Reno Aces* from Nevada.

Over the next two weeks they travelled to Houston, San Antonio, Austin and Dallas; on each occasion they stopped to mix with the biggest crowds possible. In Oklahoma City, they mixed with a large crowd of 100,000 commemorating the 11th of September attacks. They then decided to see as much of the 'Wild West' as they could and headed towards Albuquerque. They took their time touring through The Grand Canyon, visited Flagstaff on their way to Las Vegas, arriving on 25th September.

They had been in the US for six weeks.

Alan Quine and Kate Jackson pressed on to California, but not before riding through Death Valley.

They resumed attending large crowd events in Los Angeles. Each day they were able to go to somewhere different. Before leaving LA, however, they rode to San Diego and booked into a motel in the area known as East Village. After dinner and as dusk was drawing in, they travelled two miles down the East Harbour Drive as far as South 32nd Street, the entrance to the US Navy's base at San Diego. By a sign proclaiming, *You serve in the Navy – We serve you*, which was an advert for an insurance company, was a small car park. They dismounted.

'Ninety per cent of the traffic entering the base will pass within ten yards of here,' said Kate. 'We bury half a litre there.' She pointed to a small strip of grass near the sign. Using a trowel, bought earlier, Juan easily inserted a Coca-Cola bottle six inches under the surface.

In San Francisco the following week, the pattern of attending events continued. The two weeks spent in California's major conurbations, according to Kate's tally, suggested a further 125,000 men had been infected with exposure to the VX-R rays: plus the Navy employees who would pass the sign as they entered the San Diego base.

Two months had passed. It was time to head east for New York before winter set in. Upping their mileage to typically 500 per day, the 3,120 miles took two weeks as extra time was spent attending various gatherings in Salt Lake City, Denver, Kansas City, Indianapolis and Pittsburgh. A small diversion was also made to Dayton, Ohio where the largest air force base, Wright-Patterson, is located. There, near the boundary of the airfield on South Broad Street, they buried a half-litre bottle of VX-R.

A day after leaving San Francisco, Juan had felt as if he had a cold. He took some paracetamol that evening, but had woken in the night sweating. He ascribed the symptoms to a chill, took more aspirin and forgot about it. The effects appeared to wear off. Three days later, the same symptoms had reappeared: cold in the day, but a soaking sweat in the night. He had remarked to Kate that he thought he was catching flu. They pressed on; both wanted to get home. The novelty of sitting on a motor bike had worn thin.

They arrived in the environs of New York on an early Monday evening. They stayed in the same hotel as the night they had arrived. On their way to a restaurant, they buried a half-litre bottle in the grounds of nearby Central Park. On Tuesday, their last bottle of cola was buried in the leafy wooded lanes leading to the main entrance of the West Point Military Academy.

They returned the Gold Wing to their Port Jersey collection point at 10 am on Wednesday. Chuck greeted them and was keen to hear where they had visited and what the highlights of their tour had been. 'Riding through the Grand Canyon, of course, and crossing the Golden Gate Bridge,' had been Kate's excited response.

He drove them back to JFK Airport and assured Juan the bike would be ready for collection in Manchester within twenty-one days.

That evening, the 30th October, the BA Flight left at 1815 hours and would arrive at Manchester Airport the following morning. However, on the flight, Juan admitted to Kate that he would go and see the doctor as soon as they got home.

'Why?' she asked.

'There's a swelling under my arms.'

'Does it hurt?'

'No, but I don't feel hungry; yet we haven't had anything since breakfast.'

'Then there must be something wrong, if you've lost your appetite!'

It was meant as a jocular remark, but Juan wasn't going to admit that he'd not felt right for over a week.

Trying to change the subject, he asked Kate, 'What are your final tallies?'

'I believe there could be as many as half a million males who have been exposed to the VX-R who are of childbearing age; plus however many pass our buried bottles.'

'Don't forget that half of them may never have boys. Girls don't seem to be affected.'

'Unless, of course, the girls' problems remain dormant until they have children themselves.'

'Now, there's a thought.'

CHAPTER 35

Friday, 1st November 2002

Dr Callister sat listening to Juan's description of his symptoms.

'How often do these sweats occur and how bad are they?' he asked.

'They come and go. Last night I was awake at 3.30 am; my pyjamas were soaked.'

'Have you noticed if they're worse after drinking alcohol?'

'Yes, definitely; especially after red wine.'

'This back pain you mentioned. Have you had it long? Whereabouts is it?'

'It began about two weeks ago. I put it down to riding the motorbike around America.'

'It must have been quite a trip.'

'The trip of a lifetime, but it was extremely tiring.'

The doctor nodded, as if indicating that made sense. He then gave Juan a thorough examination. He looked at the swellings around his shoulders; poked and prodded them. He took his temperature and blood pressure.

'Can you come back on Monday? Our phlebotomist will be here. I'd like to have a sample of your blood tested.'

'OK. What do you think it is?'

'Until we get the results back from the blood test, I can't be sure.'

'Come on Doc; I'd prefer you to give it to me straight.'

'Have you been exposed to any toxic substances?'

'No, I don't think so,' he lied.

'Anything radioactive?'

'No.'

'You're in the right age group, over fifty, and the indications are you might have Hodgkin's Lymphoma.'

'What the hell is that?'

'It's a disease of the white blood cells. No one is sure how it is caused. It's best treated by chemotherapy. But let's not jump the gun. You could be simply suffering from fatigue due to your exhausting holiday in the States.'

When he returned to Kate, he lied, 'The Doc thinks I'm fatigued after our trip to the States. He's prescribed a pick-me-up, but to be sure he wants me to return on Monday for a blood test.'

* * *

Two weeks later, Juan went back to the doctor for the blood test results.

He had managed to keep it quiet from Kate that he might have a form of cancer, even though he was already sure he had. The back pain, night sweats and swellings were getting worse. He knew she would blame herself for having dragged him into the project to heap revenge on America. It was four months since he and Kate had begun living together and he had been supremely happy. Their sexual relationship was not as tempestuous as it had been with Barbara and he had noticed that his libido seemed to be lessening of late. He wondered if the suspected cancer was weakening his sexual desire. Initially, he'd had difficulty in keeping his hands off Kate; cuddling up to her at every opportunity, even when she was washing-up over the sink. The weeks before their American trip and the first month in the States had been sensually satisfying; he'd found Kate tantalisingly desirable and fulfilling. However, during the last few weeks of their trip and since returning from the States, he had become content to get into bed and fall asleep simply holding her hand. He kidded himself that Kate was satisfied with this, but deep down the dilemma worried him. The quandary of whether his impotence was psychosomatic or physical was troubling; he would lie awake fretting and losing sleep. He was certain it had a link with exposure to the VX-R.

'I don't think you should worry. Recovery rates in your age group are over eighty-five per cent. Fifteen chemotherapy treatments over three weeks should cure the problem. I know it's inconvenient having to go to Clatterbridge Hospital on the Wirral, but you'll be allowed out of the hospital at weekends.'

'So, I've definitely got cancer?'

'Yes, but as I've just said it is curable. You're fit and healthy. I wouldn't start worrying unduly. Try and see the stay on the Wirral as an extended holiday.'

* * *

'Well, what did the Doctor say?' asked Kate as soon as he had returned home.

'I have something called Hodgkin's Lymphoma,' he replied.

'What on earth is that?'

'It's a mild form of blood cancer...'

Before he could go any further, Kate had dropped everything she was doing and was staring alarmingly at her partner.

'It's all right,' he assured her. 'It's treatable with chemotherapy. Dr Callister assures me I should fully recover after a course of treatment. Unfortunately, it's got to be done at a hospital on the Wirral, between Chester and Birkenhead.'

She put her arms around his shoulders and began weeping quietly. They stood together in the hallway for some time, not saying anything. Juan felt low, but he knew he had to reassure Kate. 'It'll be OK, don't worry yourself.'

'It's my fault for getting you into all this,' she protested.

'Now, don't think like that. I'd do it all over again. America is going to get what it deserves.'

They had put Juan's apartment up for sale. As Kate had put it, 'Cohabiting couples should live under the same roof.' Juan had advertised the Gold Wing in *Motor Cycle News*. Two days later, it was sold to a dealer in Liverpool for half of what he had paid for it. Unsurprisingly, the purchaser had been happy to fly over to the island and collect it.

Three weeks later, Juan and Kate were married as Mr and Mrs John Pearson in the registry office in Castletown with George and Joy as best man and witness.

Two days later, Juan found himself registering into the largest oncology department in the North-West of England. They had chosen to travel to the mainland with Kate's car. She registered into a hotel in the nearby village of Thornton Hough. At weekends Juan could stay with Kate and they used their time together to explore North Wales.

Juan's mop of thick, mostly black hair began thinning with the radiotherapy treatment and each day he was given a thorough series of examinations by specialist oncologists; the houseman was from a Pakistani family and the registrar was an Egyptian. They tended to say little at first, but as they grew to know Juan better, they realised they had an exceptional patient who could converse in both their native tongues. Consequently, they were more honest with him than they may otherwise have been. On the Wednesday of the third and final week, Juan was seen by the senior consultant, a professor from the University of Liverpool's Medical Faculty. He was accompanied by the two more familiar junior members of his team.

'I'm going to be totally honest with you Mr Pearson, but we are disappointed with the blood test results. We would have expected by now to have seen a much better improvement in your red cell count. Do you feel any better in yourself since coming to Clatterbridge?'

'To be honest, no. If anything I seem to get tired much quicker, but I put that down to the treatment.'

'To some extent, I would have expected that. However, since I first met you nearly three weeks ago, I have a feeling your speech has deteriorated. Have you noticed that?'

'No, I can't say I have, but it's a funny thing. Last weekend, my wife, Kate, made a peculiar remark.'

'Oh, what was that?'

'She said she thought I had been "on the bottle".'

'Drinking, you mean?'

'Yes. I had only had a half of lager when she asked me.'

The professor looked at his two assistants, as if asking, *Any ideas?* Both looked back at their boss, their faces giving nothing away.

'Would you be agreeable to having a brain scan?'

'May I ask why?'

'We have discussed your case and we believe it is possible you may have a tumour on the right side of the brain that is affecting your speech. On the other hand, you could have contracted myasthenia gravis.'

'What's that?'

'It's a disease of the nerve endings. The signals from your brain are not getting to the muscles that you use when speaking. It's possible that a course of steroids could clear up the symptoms.'

The following day, the scan revealed a small tumour. An operation was hastily arranged, the growth removed and tests showed it to be malignant. Juan was given a course of steroids and warned there was a fifty per cent chance that the growth could reappear.

'What happens if it does?' he asked the registrar.

He shrugged his shoulders and replied, 'Let's hope it doesn't.'

They returned home to Port St Mary for Christmas. His apartment had been successfully sold during their time at Clatterbridge. They spent a quiet, peaceful time together in Kate's warm bungalow in front of roaring log fires.

By late-January 2003, Juan was learning to live with the cancer and the myasthenia. However, it was leaving him evermore tired and Kate found herself with a partner who was sleeping more and more during the day. Their strolls together either around the golf course or down to the harbour were becoming shorter, slower and less frequent.

'Kate,' Juan said on one occasion, 'do you remember telling me about enditon?'

'I'm not going there,' she had replied firmly. 'There's no way I am going to kill my own husband.'

'Look love, in the next few months there's going to come a time when I am going to be in considerable pain. I want you to give me some enditon so that I can slip away peacefully. It may take the Americans another year before they catch on to what we did, but when they do they won't stop with diplomatic niceties. They'll come after us come hell or high water. You must think of your future. The money from the sale of the apartment at The Point and what is in my Swiss bank account will make you a rich woman. You will be able to go wherever you want; wherever is safest for you.'

Over the next few months, Juan's condition continued to go slowly downhill. District nurses attended daily, but their body language was telling Kate there was only going to be one conclusion.

He began pleading with Kate for the enditon.

Sitting at his bedside, she would weep profusely; tears would pour down her cheeks as she realised the end was near and there would come a time when the only humane solution would be to give him the relief he craved for. 'You will forgive me, won't you?' she asked.

'Kate, darling, there's nothing to forgive. Our lives together have had a purpose. Not many couples have achieved what we have done. We have taken revenge on America for all its blatant lies about the need for sanctions against Iraq since the war in Kuwait. They are going to suffer for thirty or more years. It's time for me to pass away and for you to consider your future. Have you thought where you will go to live?'

'Not yet. But when the time comes, I'll promise to tell you.'

A week later, on the 19th March 2003, *Operation Iraqi Freedom*, the illegal invasion by joint UK and American Forces, began with cruise missiles being fired at Baghdad. It was to become known to the world's press as the *Second Gulf War*.

Kate's spirits reached an all-time low. Looking after Juan day and night was exhausting her. Watching the arrogant Western leaders, Bush and Blair, on the TV declaring that the overthrow of Saddam would create a new, vibrant, democratic Iraq made her want to scream and throw something at the television. She knew there would be years of chaos ahead as the Kurds, Sunnis and Shias would fight for supremacy.

The Iraq that had been kept under control by Saddam's iron grip since 1968 would crumble, allowing it to be raped for its oil by the West.

I've got to go back and fight the Americans. She remembered Amer, her first husband, who had been killed in the war with Iran, repeatedly warning her to 'never trust the Yanks.' The thought triggered fond memories of Amer as she realised that it was over twenty-one years since his death at the hands of the two Iranian Phantoms that had bombed the Defence HQ in Baghdad.

She began planning her route to northern Iraq. *Fly to Damascus or Amman, then travel overland, perhaps?*

CHAPTER 36

Sunday, 1st June 2003

The United States Department of Health and Human Services, HHS, is the principal agency for protecting the health of all Americans. Its headquarters, situated in Independence Avenue, Washington DC, is organised into eleven operating divisions, such as research, public health, drug safety and so on. The HHS has ten regional offices that are largely self-contained. Numbered one to ten, their headquarters in order are: Boston, New York, Washington DC, Atlanta, Chicago, Dallas, Kansas City, Denver, San Francisco and Seattle. The organisation of each region is identical to the HHS's HQ with identical operating divisions. Health statistics are forwarded from each region to the HQ on a monthly basis. Statisticians analyse the data, coordinate them and disseminate them back to the regions, as seen necessary. Consequently, the regions are kept in the dark about events elsewhere until they receive the HHS's monthly report showing national trends that are, therefore, always approximately a month out of date.

The first pure hexadactyl child was born in region number-two on Sunday, 1st June 2003, a month after the US-led invasion of Iraq had finished. The boy was born in *New York Downtown Hospital,* in William Street, Lower Manhattan. Eyebrows were raised in the large Department of Obstetrics where hundreds of children are delivered every year, but the boy was healthy and the mother and child were allowed to go home the following day. It was explained to her that the hospital would like to monitor the boy's progress monthly, in order to assess when he would be strong enough to have the extra digits removed. The statistic of the unusual birth defect would remain within the hospital's computer until the end of June when it would be automatically sent to the operating division for the *Administration for Children and Families* in the regional HQ in New York. There, it would be accumulated with returns from other hospitals in the New York region before being sent electronically the same day to the HSS HQ in Washington DC.

That week, four further boys were born with identical defects in number-two region, but at different hospitals: the *Community Memorial Hospital*, Hamilton, Madison County, NY; the *Somerset Medical Centre*, Somerville, New Jersey; the *Centra State Medical Centre*, Freehold Township, NJ and the *Virtua Memorial Hospital*, Mount Holly, NJ.

The unknown common link was that their fathers had attended the game between the *New York Giants* and the *Philadelphia Eagles*.

A week later, there were similar occurrences in HSS region number-three. At the *Shady Grove Adventist Hospital*, Rockville, Maryland a boy was born hexadactyl and six further births were recorded across Maryland and West Virginia. Unknown to the authorities, their fathers had watched the *Washington Redskins* play the *Tampa Bay Buccaneers*.

A further week passed before the first unusual birth took place in region number-four. On Wednesday 18th June at the *Presbyterian Childrens' Hospital*, Charlotte, North Carolina, the midwives attending the birth reported the abnormal defect to the senior obstetrician. She immediately contacted the senior paediatrician. They discussed the case with the parents and it was agreed that regular checks should be made on the boy with a view of assessing a suitable time for an operation. The statistic would be sent to number-four's region's *Administration for Children and Families* in Atlanta at the end of the month.

By the end of June 2003, some thirty-five boys had been born with the same defect in different hospitals across regions two, three and four. The statistics on the children were sent to regional HQs on Monday 30th June. By Tuesday 1st July, the figures would reach the HSS HQ in Washington to be analysed centrally for the first time.

On 5th July, at the *New York Downtown Hospital*, the second hexadactyl boy was born. It was the first time that a second hexadactyl had been delivered in the same hospital. The obstetrician, who had attended the birth of the first boy, was intrigued and immediately contacted her paediatrician colleague. Together, they did a search of the appropriate American literature: *The American Journal of Obstetrics and Gynaecology* and *The American Academy of Paediatrics Journal.* They drew a blank. They scoured the British paediatric journals and found nothing. Fascinated, the paediatrician contacted the two sets of parents and asked whether they were related, or whether they worked in the same environment, or whether they had they been abroad and may have contracted a tropical disease. Nothing untoward was discovered. Paradoxically she was to tell her colleague, 'The only thing that links them is that both fathers support the New York Giants.'

The dual occurrence was chalked away in the hospital's computer and would not see the light of day until it reached the HSS's statisticians on 1st August.

By then, however, the shit was hitting the fan.

The statistics from all ten regions had arrived in Washington on Tuesday 1st July. By Thursday 3rd, an initial analysis was revealing something unusual was happening in regions two, three and four.

Leadership of the HHS is provided by the Office of the Secretary.

Chief Secretary Kathleen Thompson was immediately briefed on the development.

'What's causing it?' she asked her Deputy, Jessica Sandberg. 'Why only in these three regions?'

'We don't know Kathleen. Birth defects are usually caused by exposure to chemicals, such as at Bhopal; viruses, such as Rubella; or radioactivity, such as at Chernobyl. Nothing unusual has occurred in the last year that we are aware. These children would have been conceived around August last year. Then, again, why only in the south-east? I cannot give you an answer. My suggestion is that we put together a questionnaire and insist all parents fill it in. We may then get to the bottom of the problem.'

'I doubt if we can legally enforce parents to complete such a form.'

'I suggest social workers visit each set of parents and stress its importance.'

'How long will it take to design the questionnaire?'

'Tomorrow is Independence Day, but I'll work on it over the weekend and let you see the draft first thing on Monday morning. If you give the go-ahead, then it can be faxed to the regional HQs immediately. Give them a fortnight to get the returns completed and we should be analysing them to see what's caused the defects by the end of the month.'

'OK; we'll discuss the form with the stats people on Monday morning – eleven o'clock sharp.'

* * *

On Sunday afternoon, Kathleen Thompson phoned one of the country's top epidemiologists, Professor Murray Watson from The George Washington University School of Medicine. She explained the background and asked him to meet her 'first thing' on Monday morning.

Although Chief Secretary Thompson had arrived at her office by 0800 hours, she was surprised to find the professor waiting for her. Over coffee, she handed him a copy of the proposed form that had been left on her desk the night before by her Deputy to peruse.

'We're having a meeting in two and a half hours to finalise the wording before sending it out to regions two, three and four. I would like you to cast your eye over it. We need to scrutinise it with a fine-tooth comb and make sure we don't miss anything. Then I would like you to attend the meeting with me.'

'OK; let's give it one hundred per cent.'

* * *

The meeting was held in the Board Room of the HSS HQ, situated in the Hubert Humphrey Building on Independence Avenue. 'I gave the questionnaire some thought over the weekend,' began the Chief Secretary to her Deputy and her small team of statisticians who had helped design the form. 'I have asked Professor Murray Watson from the GW University Hospital to attend. As you probably know, he's one of our top epidemiologists and he has a few ideas. Over to you, Murray.'

'The form is clinically fine and covers the main points. However, I think we should ask the parents their ethnic background, their education, and their hobbies – particularly concentrating if they ever attend mass meetings where a diverse range of people may be present; such as baseball games, football matches, cinemas and so on.'

'May I ask why?' asked Jessica Sandberg, Kathleen's Deputy.

'There is an outside possibility that a virus has been deliberately released at crowded events that either affects male sperm or female ovulation. Your draft form assumes the cause is accidental. I suspect it may not be; there could be something more sinister at work.'

Jessica nodded slowly. She could see the need to cover the possibility; although she secretly thought it was highly unlikely.

'Have you noticed anything peculiar about the boys' birth weights?' asked the professor to no one in particular.

'Their distribution is heavily skewed,' replied one of the statisticians.

'Exactly; the majority are about six pounds and six ounces. I think we need to find out which children are firstborns. I'll bet most in the bell part of the distribution curve are. When the survey is being conducted, the children should be weighed to see what increase has occurred in their first six weeks of life.'

'What will that tell us?' asked Jessica.

'A six-pound baby should increase its weight by about three pounds in its first six weeks if it is healthy. These boys have twenty per cent more digits than normal. That means they will be consuming more energy to keep warm. I have a gut feeling they may not be putting on any weight at all. The same goes for their length. They should be an inch and a half longer. The boys should be measured.'

The professor stopped to see if the team were reacting to his theories. There being none, he continued, 'We must take a blood sample; not only from the child, but from the parents too. We need to test for the existence of toxins – chemical, biological or evidence of exposure to radioactivity.'

'Are you suggesting all these parents have been exposed to either a nuclear, biological or chemical agent?' asked Jessica.

'Possibly, but it's only a hunch.'

There was a lull in discussion as all present thought through the likely consequences of a deliberate attack.

Finally, Kathleen asked her Deputy, 'How long will it take to incorporate Professor Watson's suggestions into the questionnaire?'

'No more than an hour.'

'Good. Meanwhile I'll draft a covering letter to the Regional Heads stressing this is to be given top priority and the returns are required by Friday 25th at the latest. I'm afraid the analysis will have to be done that weekend.'

* * *

Over the weekend of the 26th and 27th July, Jessica Sandberg and her team analysed the returns. As the disparate data from the three regions was analysed to become information, the Deputy prepared her report. On Monday morning, her team gathered in the Board Room. They noticed that in addition to Kathleen Thompson and Professor Watson, there were two additional strangers.

The Chief Secretary began the meeting by firstly introducing Professor Harry Atkins to the team. 'He's the Director of the Federal Government's Joint Pathological Centre in Silver Spring, Maryland. You may be wondering why I have asked him to attend our meeting; it will become clear as we proceed. Secondly, we have with us as an observer, Colonel Mike Harrington from the Pentagon. He's from the Army's Engineer Corps and a specialist in NBC weapons. Therefore, I must warn you that what is discussed here today is being formally classified as top secret. You are all government employees. I don't need to remind you of the consequences of breaking the rules on confidentiality. I'd like you, Jessica, to begin the meeting with your report.'

Perhaps overawed by the presence of the two distinguished professors, the handsome Colonel and the mention of the possibility that NBC weapons may be responsible for the irregular births, Jessica began with a nervous disclaimer. 'I must stress these are our preliminary findings only; further analysis, particularly of blood samples, may reveal other facts.'

'Yes, we understand,' replied Kathleen. 'Please continue.'

'Of the thirty-five boys on whom we have data, twenty-nine were firstborns. Despite the height and weight of their parents showing a normal distribution, at birth all the twenty-nine primogenitures weighed six pounds and six ounces plus or minus an ounce. Furthermore they were all the same length, within a tenth of an inch, at eighteen point eight inches. Their blood pressures were low: seventy-five over fifty and their heart rate, typically, one hundred beats per minute.' She paused for reactions.

'So, they were under average in all respects at birth,' remarked Kathleen.

Jessica nodded. 'Professor Watson wanted repeat measurements at six weeks. We haven't received the data for all thirty-five boys, but of those that we have, weight increase is fifty per cent less than you would expect. Growth also appears stilted. Most of the parents have observed that their sons are, and I quote, "placid."'

'Placid?' asked Kathleen, expecting amplification.

'The boys are quiet; do not get excited and seem happy to lie passively in their cots.'

'Anything else?'

'None of the parents are related; indeed the ethnic mix follows the norm. Neither do any parents work in dangerous environments nor have they been abroad to countries where they may have encountered tropical diseases. However, there is one common factor.'

'I think I know what you're going to tell me,' smiled Professor Watson.

'Preliminary analysis shows that the only common thread is that all the fathers follow either their local baseball or football teams. In region two, it's either the *New York Giants* or the *Philadelphia Eagles*. In region three, it's the *Washington Redskins* or the *Tampa Bay Buccaneers*. In region four, it looks as if it's the *Miami Marlins*, the *Atlanta Braves* or the *Mississippi Rebels*.'

'So, it's probable that some of the fathers could have been at the same match on the same day?' asked Professor Watson.

'Yes, highly likely.'

'In that case, something was released; either a spray of chemicals or germs or a radioactive substance was present.'

'I think Professor Atkins may want to say something at this point,' remarked Kathleen.

'Thank you, Kathleen. Professor Watson and I are old friends and meet socially occasionally. He told me about the hexadactyl children a week or two ago and mentioned that a literature search of all the world's paediatric journals, including British, German, French, Australian and so on, had revealed this outbreak to be unique. He was surprised when I asked him if he had searched the pathology journals. I had remembered a case being mentioned some time ago. I found it here...'

He held up a magazine.

'This is *The Journal of the Royal College of Pathologists*. In it is a case of a post-mortem that was carried out on a boy who had died a pure hexadactyl in a town called Lincoln in England. The boy had died for no apparent reason when aged six months. The PM was carried out by the local consultant pathologist. I have tried to contact him, but, so far, have had no luck. However, I will keep trying to see if he can remember anything not mentioned in the journal.'

'Do you wish to make an observation, Colonel?' asked Kathleen.

'Reluctantly I feel there is ample evidence to suggest the United States is under attack. I recommend that at your next meeting a representative from Fort Detrick attends who is a specialist in NBC weapons – my role in the Pentagon is largely administrative. Also, someone should attend from both the FBI and the CIA. If my hunch is correct, then we can expect more boys being born in the other HSS regions.'

The meeting concluded with everyone agreeing that a meeting in one month's time, on Monday, 1st September, was essential when more data would be available from other regions. Meanwhile, Kathleen agreed that the home grounds of the football and baseball clubs mentioned, where the possibility of an NBC agent could have been used, should be searched for evidence. Her teams from within her public health department would do this.

CHAPTER 37

Monday, 1st September 2003

The monthly statistical returns from the HSS Department's ten regions had been analysed over the weekend by Jessica's team. New cases of hexadactyls being born in region six, with its head office in Dallas, and region nine, San Francisco, were noted. Some twenty-nine new cases were spread across the South-West HSS regions; together with a further thirty-two new cases in the regions previously affected, there was now a total of ninety-six boys born with the anomaly in two months.

Kathleen Thompson, the Chief Secretary of the HSS, chaired the working group's third meeting. The external members included three new faces.

Brigadier Harry Holdman introduced himself as the Commanding Officer of Fort Detrick, a post he had held for almost a year. For the benefit of those who were unaware of the major function of the fort, he explained it was the centre of excellence for research into antidotes for chemical and biological weapons. He was accompanied by Colonel Harrington from the Pentagon.

The Assistant Commissioner for FBI Detectives in New York State, Bill Throttle, and Deputy Director Joe Reinfeld from the CIA HQ at Langley also made themselves known to the meeting.

Kathleen Thompson reported that the sweeps made at the seven suspected stadiums where an agent of some sort could have been released had proved negative. Nothing had been found despite painstaking searches by experienced environmental teams. Both professors asked some questions, but soon agreed that the results suggested both chemical and biological agents were probably less likely to have been used than a radioactive source. When asked why, they both thought chemical and biological substances would 'almost certainly' have left a detectable residue of some sort.

In the ensuing discussion, the FBI Agent asked, 'I would like to clear up the timescales, if I may?'

The room deferred to allow him to continue.

'The first incidence of hexadactylism was a boy born about five months ago. Is that correct?'

Kathleen nodded affirmatively.

'So the weapon was initially used a year ago, give or take?'

'That's just the problem,' replied Kathleen. 'How long is the give or take?'

'I am thinking more of when it could have come into the country, rather than when it was first flashed around the *New York Giants'* stadium. Since 9/11, our ports and airports have tightened up their security considerably. In theory, the weapons could have been lying dormant in the country for years. However, the first question a Detective is trained to ask is not "why", but "why now?" My hunch is that this radioactive device probably came into the US only about a year ago.'

'What you're saying,' amplified Joe Reinfeld, 'is that if it had been in America for ages, then they would have used it some time ago.'

'Exactly; so the date from when we must begin our search to find who smuggled a radioactive device into our country should be 1st August last year.'

'But it could have come in through a myriad of ways?' queried Jessica Sandberg.

'True, but if it had entered through a Pacific port, then surely they would have begun using it on the West Coast; similarly, if it had entered from Mexico or Canada.'

'You're making a lot of assumptions,' warned Professor Atkins.

'I agree, but we have to begin somewhere; I think this substance entered the US on my patch last year.'

'My concern is that we still haven't a clue what caused this outbreak,' commented the Brigadier. 'I will defer to your medical expertise.' He paused as he glanced around the table. 'Surely exposure to strong radioactivity would sterilise men rather than deform their sperm in some way?'

'I agree,' replied Professor Atkins. 'There is something very unusual going on and I'm beginning to wonder if we are dealing with a virus of some sort that has been engineered to target men of a childbearing age.'

'A radioactive virus? Is that possible?' asked Kathleen.

'The honest answer is: I don't know,' replied the professor. 'What I do know is that there have been plenty of rumours of research into viruses that could attack ethnic peoples. In other words, a virus that could distinguish between an Arab and a Jew is theoretically possible. Is that not so, Brigadier Holdman?'

'I am not in a position to answer that, Professor.'

Sensing a tension in his reply, Kathleen remarked to no one in particular, 'So, what you're saying is that we could be dealing with a disgruntled employee from one of our own research labs.'

'I very much doubt that,' replied Bill Throttle. 'What do you think, Joe?'

'Our labs are scrupulous with their security. I think this substance was smuggled into the US. What worries me is the number of containers that enter America each month. It must run into tens of thousands. Checking what happened to each one, where it went, etcetera, will be nigh impossible.'

'And that doesn't include new trucks and cars, such as Volvos and Jaguars. We import them in their hundreds each week.'

The two law officers looked at each other realising the mountain of work that lay ahead.

After a considerable amount of discussion that produced nothing constructive, it was Kathleen Thompson, as chairperson, who suggested that the next monthly meeting be held on Thursday, 2nd October, to monitor progress.

* * *

A month later, after the customary round table introductions, Kathleen Thompson said Joe Reinfeld had made an important discovery that could have far-reaching implications.

The Deputy Director of the CIA began, 'At the end of the last meeting, I had a chat with Professor Atkins in the lift on the way out. I asked him if there had ever been any boys born with these defects anywhere else in the world. He told me he only knew of the PM carried out on the boy with hexadactyl symptoms in England. He repeated what he had told you in the previous meeting; namely, that he was having problems contacting the pathologist who carried out the PM and I offered to help locate him. I went back to our files at Langley and discovered there had been a second boy born with the same defect in Leicester.' He paused and looked at the professor to continue.

'Yes,' remarked Professor Atkins. 'At our last meeting but one, you will remember I mentioned there had been an autopsy on a boy with these symptoms in England and I was having problems tracing the pathologist.' He stopped and looked around the table. All nodded their agreement.

'Joe's resources and contacts allowed us to trace him. He has now retired, but he told me that the boy had been born in a city called Leicester and his parents had moved to Lincoln soon after the birth. At the PM, he could find nothing wrong with the boy who had died aged six months. I then asked whether he had heard of the second case in Leicester, which Joe has just mentioned. From his reaction on the phone, I gathered the impression that he knew, but for some reason was reluctant to discuss the matter. However, when I explained that we had had over one hundred cases across America, he admitted he'd helped with a second PM in Leicester. Bearing in mind it was such a unique occurrence, I asked him why it had not been reported in the medical journals. He wouldn't elaborate and suggested I contact the Leicester pathologist.'

'And did you?' asked Kathleen.

'Yes. I introduced myself only to discover he was most reluctant to discuss the case as well; hiding behind what he called "patient confidentiality."'

'So, what did you do?'

'I asked him if he knew Professor Hawke at University College Hospital, London. He admitted he had trained under Professor Hawke's tutorage. I asked him whether he would answer a few questions if Professor Hawke vouchsafed for me. He agreed somewhat unwillingly. I rang Professor Hawke and he agreed he would contact Dr MacKinnon at once. An hour later, MacKinnon came back. He apologised and after a few questions on the background of the two boys, he told me that the local paediatrician had undertaken some research and discovered that the two fathers, one a Pakistani and the other a Bangladeshi, were not related in any way. He believed the two births were a freak of statistics. I then asked him for details about his results of the second PM.'

'And what did he say?' asked Professor Watson.

'He could find nothing that could have caused a premature death, except a very small growth on the boy's hypothalamus. I asked him why he had looked there and he replied that the boy had apparently shown signs of fatigue – he'd slept a lot, poor growth and development, and his hands and feet were always cold. He had recorded the cause of death as myasthenia gravis. I said that was impossible in a six-month-old boy. He agreed, but said, "What else could it be?"'

Joe Reinfeld, who had been listening carefully, questioned the professor, 'What was this guy's name, again?'

'Stuart MacKinnon. Why?'

'It rings a bell, but I'm not sure why. I've seen the name somewhere on the files. I'll check it out when I get back to the office.'

The discussion then moved on.

Bill Throttle announced that the typical number of sealed containers arriving at the eastern seaboard ports was 100,000 per week; ten million containers enter the United States each year. Checking the paperwork for each container that had entered the US a year previously was impossible. His staff had decided to cut down the workload by concentrating on those that had been opened in New York State. To date, nothing untoward had been found.

'Some of my team have now been moved to investigating items such as cars that do not arrive in containers,' he added. 'However, it is going to be slow work and I am not hopeful of being successful.'

The news dampened everyone's spirits. The mood deepened when Jessica reported that a further total of seventy-seven boys had been born hexadactyls; eighteen of them in regions five and seven that had not been affected previously. Only regions one and ten, in the north of the country, had not reported any hexadactyl births. 'That makes a grand total of 173 so far,' she said.

She continued, 'I have prepared a map for the meeting to show exactly where the 173 births have occurred, with dates. You will see that there is a trend.'

Using her laser pointer, she highlighted the births and moved it around the large screen in an egg-shaped ellipse. 'It's as if the viral attacks began in New York, almost certainly at the match on 13th August last year between the *New York Giants* and *The Philadelphia Eagles*.' Jessica paused to see if anyone disagreed with her hypothesis. She continued, 'The first births in each region indicate the virus moved south to Florida, then west across the southern States to California. From there they return, more or less, in a straight line to New York.'

The two detectives from the FBI and the CIA were nodding agreement.

'So, this virus, if that is what we are going to call it, entered the country in New York and left the same way,' suggested Bill Throttle.

'Unless, of course,' postulated Joe Reinfeld, 'it's still here.'

'You think they could have buried it somewhere – perhaps in a built-up area?'

The two law officers were talking to each other as if there was no one else in the room.

'It would make their exit easier. It's even possible that, if it is a radioactive material, it has been split, hidden in densely populated areas and has been affecting people for the past year.'

'Hang on,' interrupted Professor Atkins. 'Aren't we getting ahead of ourselves? We haven't a clue to the cause and don't forget the two isolated cases in Leicester. Whatever caused this could have come in to the country by a container, a car, or even in a suitcase at JFK.'

'It couldn't have come in at an airport. Security is too tight; all cases are X-rayed. It would have been spotted a mile off,' retorted Bill.

'Even if it was in a lead container?'

'Yes.'

'What if the lead cover was itself inside something metallic?'

'Such as?'

'I don't know.' The professor paused. 'Perhaps in the sump of an engine block?'

Bill Throttle was visibly stumped. His silence admitted defeat.

'People don't fly in with engine blocks,' laughed Brigadier Holdman.

'True, but visitors to the States do come with their own cars and motorbikes. Perhaps it was smuggled across the border from Canada' said the FBI man. 'Maybe, we have been looking in the wrong places.'

* * *

'Kate? It's Stuart. How's life on the Isle of Man?'

'Well, this will be our second winter, and if this one will be like the last, then it won't be too bad. The weather is very similar to Badachro's: warm, but wet.'

'And how's Juan?'

'I'm afraid he's not at all well; he may only have a few months to live. The tumour that affected his speech has reappeared and is now affecting his movement; he's paralysed from the waist downwards. The district nurses who come in daily are wonderful; I don't know what I would do without them. The doctor wants him to go back for another course of chemotherapy.'

'And is he going to go?'

'I am trying to encourage him, but he's adamant he's not going. He says he's had enough. I've told him I'll be with him the whole time. There are now family apartments in the hospital at Clatterbridge that weren't

322

there before so I could be with him 24/7. But he won't have it. I blame myself for all this.'

'You mustn't. Juan agreed to go through with the plan when he went to Iraq. He knew the potential danger of VX-R. However, that's what I want to talk about. I've had an American professor in Washington asking questions today about hexadactyl children.'

'Oh, why?'

'He wouldn't give me any details, but I got the impression that there have been several incidences across the States.'

'Did he say how many?

'No, I asked him that. He wouldn't elaborate, but when he'd hung up, I contacted Dr Edwards who had helped me with the PM on the Farooq child. He admitted Professor Atkins had rung him previously and said there were over a hundred such births.'

'What did you tell the American professor?'

'Only that we had discovered the fathers of the two hexadactyls born here in Leicester were not related.'

'Anything else?'

'Not really, I tried to put him off initially with the patient confidentiality excuse, but he got Professor Hawke, my old tutor at UCL, to vouch for him. So, I told him I had found a growth on the Farooq's boy's hypothalamus, which is true, and I had signed the death certificate accordingly.'

'You didn't tell them we had retrieved the VX-R from Iraq?'

'No, of course not.'

'I'm sorry, Stuart. I didn't mean to insult you. It's just that the less you know, the better.'

* * *

'That was Stuart on the phone. The Americans have begun to ask questions about the Leicester boys.'

'He didn't say anything about the VX-R to them, did he?'

'No, of course not.'

'It's only a matter of time before they come snooping. I have been thinking they won't hesitate to kidnap you and take you back to America.'

'You're talking of rendition?'

'Yes, I think your safest place may be back in Iraq.'

'I won't go without you.'

'Darling, you must. There's little they can do to me. Even though Iraq is crawling with Yankee troops, it's the one place where they would never think of looking for you.'

'The old theory that if you want to hide something, stick it under their noses?'

'Something like that.'

Kate sat looking at Juan, holding his hand. The man she had married had gone downhill rapidly since the discovery of his brain tumour. His mop of thick black hair had all but gone; his naturally tanned skin, inherited from his Egyptian mother, was a pasty grey; his bright eyes were dull and lifeless. He hated being confined to a wheelchair and she knew he would rather be dead than suffer the indignity that came with the debilitating disease that he could do nothing about.

'If they do come knocking at our door, George Costain will hear about it before they come to the island and give us a heads-up,' he said. 'However, by then it will be too late. You must think of going while you have a chance. Iraq's retribution will only be a success as long as you remain free.'

'I'm not sure I'd be any safer in Iraq. It's only a matter of time before someone gives Saddam away. The Americans would put a price on my head too. I like the island. We have a lovely house; I'm staying, so no more defeatist talk.'

CHAPTER 38

Tuesday, 4th November 2003

At the next meeting of the HSS working group, a new face had appeared. He introduced himself as Brigadier, retired, Keith Richardson – formerly the Officer Commanding at Fort Detrick. He was accompanied by his successor, Brigadier Harry Holdman. The representative from the Pentagon, Colonel Harrington was absent.

As usual, Kathleen Thompson was in the Chair. 'Another 106 boys have been born hexadactyl since our last meeting, making the total 279. However, in two cases, both in San Diego, the fathers have assured our investigators that they have never attended any mass meetings such as baseball matches, cinemas, and so on. Perhaps later we can discuss this new development. But first of all, I am going to let Brigadier Richardson explain his presence this morning.'

The retired Brigadier began, 'Long before I was the CO at Fort Detrick, way back in 1981, during the tenure of President Reagan, there was a war between Iraq and Iran. You may remember Ayatollah Khomeini had replaced our ally, the Shah of Iran, and set up an Islamic State with Sharia law. President Reagan stopped the supply of military spares to the Iranians, who had been extensively supplied and trained by us for over twenty-five years. He saw Saddam Hussein as the lesser of two evils and publicly declared that the US would not allow Iran to win the war. Consequently, we began shipping military hardware and advisers to Iraq in large numbers. Reagan wanted to prove to Saddam that our kit was superior to the Soviets' weapons. The Soviet Union had been

Iraq's allies for decades. On two occasions during the war, the Secretary of State for Defence, Donald Rumsfeld, visited Baghdad to pledge millions of dollars of aid: helicopters, satellite information, that sort of thing. However, we also supplied precursors for chemical and biological agents. One of the early substances given to Iraq was something that had been labelled VX-R. It was a radioactive nerve agent, a sort of gamma ray that somehow carried VX.'

'That sounds ridiculous,' interrupted Professor Watson. 'Are you saying we had invented a ray gun and gave it to Iraq?'

'Basically, yes. As far as I can find out, but, don't forget, this was way back in 1981 or 82. The boffins who made it had no idea what it might do and some idiot gave the go-ahead to give it to Iraq for testing under battlefield conditions.'

'And what happened?' asked the professor.

'Nothing.'

'Nothing?'

'The project at Fort Detrick was dropped and the records of the experiments destroyed. I have been unable to find out why. Perhaps someone feared we had opened Pandora's Box. The radiation had to be contained in lead. A lead gun and barrel is hardly a practical weapon. At that time, Iraq's Head of biological weapons research was a woman called Kathab al Jised. Unbeknown to us, she was working for the British SIS. They had persuaded her to bury all the biological weapons we were supplying. The Brits had shown her an infallible way of doctoring the records so that they could never be found. Only chemical weapons were used against Iran.'

'Why? What else did we give them beside the VX-R?'

'You've obviously never read The Riegle Report?'

'No.'

'It is a revealing condemnation of what was going on in the Reagan Administration. We supplied Iraq with biological agents such as anthrax, botulinium toxins and clostridium perfringens. Chemical weapons, such as sarin and mustard gas, were also supplied and were used against the Iranians.'

'I'm not sure what this has got to do with this committee,' observed Professor Atkins.

'I'm coming to that,' replied the retired Brigadier. 'Nothing was heard of VX-R for almost twenty years until a couple of years back. Then the Head of Britain's SIS, a woman called Barbara Renton, raised a query out of the blue to the Head of the CIA, George Tenet. She asked what we knew of a substance called VX-R. Even its name was classified and I, by this time the CO at Fort Detrick, was sent across to London to find out why the Brits had raised the query. I was told two boys had been born hexadactyl in a town called Leicester. The only connection was that both fathers had been in Iraq around the time the VX-R had been exported by our Department of Commerce. It's probable they were exposed to its rays.'

It was the turn of the professor of epidemiology, Professor Watson, to show interest. 'How did the Brits link the two boys with VX-R?'

'A good question. The only person who could have alerted MI6 to the existence of VX-R was al Jised. The Brits had brought her in from the cold during *Operation Desert Storm* in 1991.'

He paused to see if the others were aware of the code name given to the liberation of Kuwait. No one raised a query.

'I was to discover that she had married and her stepson was the pathologist at the Leicester hospital. Somehow the pair of them had made the link between VX-R and hexadactylism. They must then have contacted MI6. But, here's the rub. I was briefly the temporary Air Attaché in Baghdad in 1978 and had met both al Jised and the man she was to marry subsequently. He was there installing a war game for the Iraqis at the time. I believe al Jised is the key. Find her and you will find out how she somehow retrieved the VX-R from Iraq, even though it must have laid buried for nigh on twenty years. Only she could have smuggled it into the United States.'

There was a silence for several moments before Bill Throttle spoke. 'Brigadier Richardson has given us a description of al Jised. The problem is that he last saw her twenty-four years ago. We have a clever piece of software that can artificially age her facial composite and my men are currently showing it to all our ports of entry.'

Joe Reinfeld sighed audibly, thereby gaining everyone's attention. He looked suitably grave as his eyes went around the table. 'Until this morning I had never met Brigadier Richardson and what he has told us must remain highly confidential. The link between VX-R and al Jised has been known by us for some time. Indeed, my colleagues in London have been trying to find her for some years; ever since President Bush ordered George Tenet to retrieve the VX-R at whatever cost. We knew her stepson was the pathologist in Leicester, but in attempting to use him to find al Jised we upset MI6 and eight of our staff had their visas terminated by the British Foreign Office. I have been given carte blanche to do all we can to find how al Jised entered our country. We have lent the FBI 500 of our staff to aid the search. By the time of our next meeting, I hope to be able to report success.'

'If I can add to that,' said Bill Throttle. 'Now we are 99% sure we are looking for al Jised and, probably, an accomplice. We have, as of this morning, abandoned the searches for entry in containers. Al Jised must have entered the US some other way. It's only a matter of time before we find how she did it.'

The meeting moved on to discuss the implications of the two fathers in San Diego who claimed they had never been in large crowds. Kathleen revealed that the only link was that both worked in the Naval Dockyard. After some discussion, it was agreed that the perpetrators of the VX-R crime must have left a quantity hidden near the environs of the dockyard.

'I am confident that al Jised and her partner could not have gained entry to the navy base. I know it reasonably well,' remarked Brigadier Holdman. 'The base is guarded 24/7. The VX-R must be near the entrance. I will contact the Base Commander and tell him to make an exhaustive sweep, if you like?'

'You'd better warn him that his men must wear lead aprons and when they find it, they are to fly it to Langley immediately in a lead container,' added Joe Reinfeld.

'I think it would be better if it came straight to Fort Detrick, don't you?' asked Brigadier Richardson to his successor. Somewhat begrudgingly, the CIA man conceded, '…It would probably be safer there…'

* * *

'I have brought the meeting scheduled for December forward by two weeks at short notice and I apologise if I have inconvenienced you in any way,' began Kathleen Thompson. 'However, two major developments have occurred that are of grave significance. You will notice Deputy Director Joe Reinfeld is not here. He has sent a colleague, Harry Northfield, along. He and Bill Throttle, who you all know, will update us on the CIA and FBI's progress of finding al Jised. However, there is also some bad news. The first five boys who were born hexadactyl six months ago have all died in the last week. Professor Atkins has undertaken preliminary post-mortems on the five boys and will give us his initial conclusions first. Over to you, professor.'

'I have carried out five post-mortems in the last four days; on two occasions working with my team through the night. As you all know, the theory is that the boys' fathers have been exposed to a largely unknown nerve agent, VX-R. Somehow it has affected their sperm to create the birth defect. We, therefore, concentrated our investigations on nerve endings and those parts of the brain that are responsible for sending signals around the body. It sounds incredible, but our preliminary conclusion is the same as that of the pathologist in Leicester, namely all five boys have died of something called *myasthenia gravis in extremis.*'

'But that's an old person's disease, surely?' asked Kathleen.

'Generally, I would agree. However, in each of the five cases, we found a minute growth on the boy's hypothalamus, just as in Leicester. The warts were no bigger than a pinhead. As soon as I could, I discussed my findings with Professor Watson. Murray and I believe you must immediately prescribe beta-blockers if the other boys are to survive. It's a short-term solution while we investigate further. Murray will explain.' He nodded towards his long-time friend.

'We are dealing with a green field here. I believe the only long-term solution is to resort to surgery; firstly, we should remove the extra digits as early as practical, possibly as soon as three months. Secondly, the growth on the hypothalamus will have to be removed when the boy is strong enough to survive such major surgery.'

'That's going to present problems bearing in mind the boys are spread nationwide and are increasing in number by the day,' observed the Chairperson.

'I agree, Kathleen, but I don't see any alternative.'

'Are there enough surgeons who could carry out these operations?'

'Probably not, but if we get cracking as soon as next week then we can bring them here to Washington to learn the procedures necessary. Can your department handle that?'

'It's going to have to.'

An initial plan was drawn up and the meeting moved on to a report by Bill Throttle. 'Joe Reinfeld is today in London meeting the Head of the British MI6. We have identified Kathab al Jised, using a passport in the name of Jackson, and her partner, a guy called Alan Quine, although we suspect that may be an alias. They entered the United States last August. They toured around on a Honda motorbike that had been legally imported on a tourist visa. Somehow the VX-R must have been hidden on the bike; we don't know why it wasn't discovered by our customs security. The discovery of half a litre of the VX-R outside the Navy Base at San Diego last week suggests the rest of the VX-R was also left behind when they flew back to the UK. We have teams searching for similar quantities outside other military bases they may have passed on their journey; so far, no luck. The half-litre cola bottle that was buried a few inches under the surface of the gardens leading to the gatehouse at San Diego has been confirmed by Fort Detrick to contain the radioactive material known as VX-R.'

'So we now know for definite what we are dealing with?' queried Kathleen Thompson.

'Yes, it's the source of all our problems. We have applied to the UK Government to extradite al Jised and her partner immediately. Joe Reinfeld is hoping to bring them back to the States under arrest later this week.'

There was a spontaneous outbreak of applause around the table.

CHAPTER 39

Wednesday, 26th November 2003

The Deputy's intercom buzzed.

'George, can you come into my office for a minute?'

George Costain left his desk asking himself, *What does the boss want now?*

'Yes, sir; what's the problem?'

'I've just had a phone call from The Met. Their Head of Special Branch, Mike Watts, wants to come over to see us with a senior man from the CIA.'

'Did he say what about?'

'He didn't want to say too much over the phone, but mentioned something about a retired MI6 officer who lives on the island? Do you know who that could be?'

'Probably.' He was smiling to himself and thinking, *This meeting could be interesting.*

'You'd better put me in the picture,' said the Chief Constable.

'It was before your time, sir. Colonel Madoc was the Chief and I was a DC in our Special Branch. His name was Juan Quayle...'

George briefed his boss as best as he could. Over an hour later, the Chief Constable, who hadn't interrupted once, sighed. 'They're coming over tomorrow from London City Airport on the flight that gets into Ronaldsway at ten o'clock. I'll meet them and bring them here for you to brief them. Perhaps you had better arrange a lunch break too. I expect they'll fly back to London on the evening plane.'

'Very good, sir. How formal do you want my presentation to be?'

'Let's keep it low-key, George; there'll only be the four of us.'

'True, but they may wish to see our archives as proof of what I've told you and I'll have to get them out of storage.'

'What's in the files that make them so special?'

'Quayle's death certificates, there's two of those for a start, as well as the documents of the names given to him by MI6. Then, there's the deeds of sale of his father's farm, his will, bank statements, minutes of the meeting held here chaired by the then Head of MI6, copies of The Official Secrets Act signed by those who knew he hadn't died in the inferno at Ballajorra, and so on.'

'OK. If you think they'll want all that detail, I'll leave you to get it all arranged.'

They'll want it alright when they hear what I've got to tell them.

* * *

The following morning George was introduced to Commissioner Mike Watts and Deputy Director of the CIA, Joseph ('call me Joe') Reinfeld, who had flown over from Langley, Virginia, the previous weekend. To both the Manx policemen's surprise, they were accompanied by someone called Lee Hefferman, 'from the US Embassy in London.'

'George, I have explained to these gentlemen that you knew Juan Quayle personally, but have told them nothing more than that.'

George nodded, but remained silent waiting for someone to kick-off the proceedings.

It was Joe who began, 'I think it might help if we explain our reasons for coming to the Isle of Man. However, I want to stress that what passes between us in this room must remain within these four walls.'

'Yes,' interrupted Mike Watts. 'We are all security cleared by our respective governments and everything discussed here is top secret.' He looked at the Chief Constable to nod agreement. Both he and George acknowledged they understood the implications.

'Earlier this year, in June to be precise, something unique began to happen in the eastern United States,' began Joe Reinfeld. 'Boys began to be born with six fingers and six toes. They are what the medics call hexadactyls. Each month, as statistics began to be centralised at our Department of Health and Human Services in Washington, a pattern began to emerge. The spread of the phenomenon that had begun in New York continued south to Miami, then headed west through the southern states to California and then back again, through the mid states, to New York. Our investigations have shown that the outbreak was caused deliberately by the use of a radioactive nerve agent called VX-R. We undertook what could well be the biggest investigation ever to find out when it could have been introduced to the States and by whom. We are certain it was carried around America by a couple on an Isle of Man registered motorbike that entered the United States on Sunday, 11th August 2002, on a three-month visitors' visa. Their passports showed them as Alan Quine and Kathryn Jackson. They left America on 30th October 2002. Their bike, a Honda Gold Wing, was registered as MAN 666 X. We wish to interview Quine and Jackson.' He paused and looked at the Chief Constable.

The Chief looked at his Deputy and said, 'Your floor, George.'

'May I ask why has it taken you almost six months since the birth of the first hexadactyl to come here for Quine?'

'It has taken much hard work to detect the cause of the outbreak. Initially we thought the cause was environmental – water pollution, a leak from an atomic reactor, that sort of thing. Gradually, our scientists began to conclude that we were dealing with a deliberate, well planned, terrorist attack. We concluded their modus operandi was to congregate in large crowds where most damage could be affected by releasing an agent that was either chemical, biological or nuclear. Hundreds of sports stadiums, concert halls, cinemas and public places have been swabbed for the presence of toxins where Quine may have visited. It has taken all this time for us to gather conclusive proof that the agent was VX-R and Quine and Jackson were responsible.'

'What's so special about children being born with six fingers? Surely, it is a simple operation to have the digits removed?'

'It's baffling our best brains that it's only boys who have the defect; there doesn't seem to be any effect on girls. The worst part of all this, however, is that the boys all begin dying when they reach six months of age for no apparent reason. Post-mortems are revealing a small tumour on the hypothalamus that seems to be hindering nerve signals reaching the muscles.'

'Can you tell us the figures we're talking about?'

'So far, over 200 boys have been born this way; typically another fifty are born each month. Twenty-seven have died in the last month and all are now dying when they hit the six-month criteria.'

'There has been nothing about this in the press,' interjected the Chief Constable.

'That's because we have managed to issue what you call *D Notices,* I believe.'

'And can I ask where did Quine supposedly get this VX-R from?' asked the Manx Deputy Chief.

There was a moment of embarrassed silence. Then Lee Hefferman spoke for the first time, 'Kathryn Jackson was formerly Kathab al Jised. She had been a double agent working for MI6 in Iraq during the Iraq-Iran war. During that time she was Saddam Hussein's Director of Biological and Chemical Weapons Research. Our government's policy, under Ronald Reagan, was to issue the Iraqis with, and I quote, "whatever it takes" for them to win the war against Khomeini's Iran. Somehow, by mistake, the Iraqis received a small consignment of VX-R; just two litres to be precise.'

He paused.

It was an opportunity for George to discretely show his colours. 'I believe that, along with other biological materials supplied by America, this Kathab al Jised found a way of hiding them in the deserts of Iraq where no one could find them. Is that correct?'

'Yes. We know she was liberated from Iraq during *Operation Desert Storm* and given the ID of Kathryn Jackson.'

'She subsequently married and became Mrs MacKinnon, correct?'

'You seem to know a lot about her for a Deputy Chief Constable of a small police force,' remarked Joe Reinfeld.

'It's my job to keep my ear to the ground, sir.' An observer would have perceived Superintendent Costain was neither overawed by the seniority of those in the room nor sympathetic to the Americans' dilemma.

Lee Hefferman continued, 'We have been trying to make contact with Mrs MacKinnon since she came to Britain to find out where she hid the VX-R, but we have been unable to find her.' There was a faint hint of apology.

'I understand MI6 has warned you off looking for her on several occasions. Is that also correct?' asked the Manxman, who was enjoying having the Americans on the back foot.

Lee Hefferman looked at his CIA boss for guidance as to how to answer.

It was time for Mike Watts to defend the American diplomats. 'Superintendent,' he began. To use George's rank rather than his name was a less than subtle way of showing disapproval. 'We're not here to examine the rights or wrongs of American foreign policy of twenty years ago.'

George's rapid reply came like a bolt from the blue. 'To every action, there is an equal and opposite reaction; Newton's third law of motion, I believe.'

The blank looks on the others' faces demanded further explanation.

'Let me elucidate,' said the Manx Deputy. 'I first met Juan Quayle, that's his real name by the way, in 1991. He had been trained by MI5 to infiltrate the trade of arms between the IRA and al-Qaeda that was taking place in the Irish Sea. There was a rumour that the IRA, having acquired the infamous Gadhafi atomic bomb in the late-eighties, had decided not to use it and were about to sell it to bin Laden.'

'This was before my time here,' interrupted the Chief Constable.

The CIA Deputy nodded, 'Yes, I've researched Quayle's background; he used the pseudonym of Quine, and I know the bomb eventually ended up in the bottom of the Bay of Biscay when the RAF sank the boat that was carrying it to Ceuta. Mossad had asked us to intercept it, but you Brits got there first.'

'Then you'll know Quayle successfully wormed his way into the al-Qaeda organisation and taught in one of their madrassas for fifteen months. He returned to Britain with invaluable information on their organisation,' continued George.

'After that, our files on him are a bit vague,' admitted Joe Reinfeld.

'He retired to his father's farm in the north of the island and married. As a matter of fact, I was his best man. He had two daughters with Molly, who was a widow with two sons. However, al-Qaeda came after him and his farmhouse was burnt to the ground, killing his wife and the four youngsters. Quayle was trapped in the cellar and survived.'

'But we have copies of newspaper cuttings that say he died as well,' remarked Deputy Reinfeld.

'It was a plan devised by MI6, whose Director at the time was Barbara Renton. She flew here the following day and chaired a meeting in this very room. She masterminded Quayle to become *The Daily Telegraph's* Middle East correspondent in Lebanon.'

'With another pseudonym; this time it was Pearson – right?' asked Hefferman.

'Right. It was hoped he could get an interview with bin Laden and kill him with anthrax. It took about five years before he pulled it off, largely thanks to help from Mossad who engineered Pearson to be shot in the thigh at an anti-Israeli demonstration. That got him the sympathy of the Palestinian factions and soon afterwards al-Qaeda invited him to Pakistan.'

'But bin Laden survived; we are sure he's hiding out somewhere on the Pakistan-Afghanistan border,' asserted Reinfeld.

'MI6 were confident bin Laden had died until quite recently. They now know he had acute kidney failure, needed dialysis regularly and took antibiotics daily to resist infections. His large daily dosage of antibiotics would have saved him from the anthrax. When Quayle returned from Pakistan, he decided to lie low for a while in a bolt-hole he had bought in the South of France. To his surprise, he found Barbara Renton waiting for him. She had been given a new identity after escaping from an attempt on her life by the CIA…'

'Hang on. How do you know all this?' asked Mike Watts in an aggressive manner.

'I'm coming to that, if you'll let me finish. They lived together as man and wife in Antibes for several months until, in April 2002, the CIA caught up with Barbara Renton and successfully assassinated her and Robbie MacKinnon, who had been Kathab al Jised's husband of ten years. You can't deny this, sir? You know the murders caused political ructions in both Whitehall and the Élysée Palace.'

If looks could kill, thought George, as he stared into both the Americans' eyes.

Nothing was said for what seemed many minutes.

As if to break the frostiness that had descended on the meeting, the Chief Constable said to his Deputy, 'You haven't explained Newton's Third Law of Motion.'

'Firstly, al Jised's husband was killed by the CIA; secondly, her country was about to be invaded to find weapons of mass destruction that could not be found by the UN weapons inspectors who had been searching for them since the sanctions were imposed after the liberation of Kuwait; thirdly, MacKinnon's first wife was killed in a road accident which the Avon and Somerset Police believe was engineered by the CIA. Those are the actions. Her reaction? Retrieve the VX-R from Iraq; after all, she was the only person who knew where it was buried. Quayle helped her because your organisation had killed his partner, Barbara. I'm afraid it boils down to the CIA's actions creating al Jised's reactions.'

After another pause in the discussion, Mike Watts asked, 'How do you know all this? I don't wish to be rude, but the Isle of Man is hardly the epicentre of international espionage.'

'I told you, Quayle and I knew each other.'

No one spotted George using the past tense.

'Two wrongs don't make a right,' the Scotland Yard man asserted. 'We have come here today to interview Quayle and Mrs MacKinnon. You're not denying they live on the island, are you?'

'Yes, I am. They don't live here anymore; I'm afraid you're too late. Quayle died two months ago. I have here copies of his death certificate, the coroner's report, the crematorium entry, the Bride Parish register where his remains were interred with his former family, and his will.' George handed Reinfeld a pile of papers adding, 'You can keep them for your records.'

The Deputy Director rummaged through the loose sheets. He examined the last one carefully, and then commented, 'I see he set up an educational trust fund.'

'Yes, Bride is to have a new primary school. The current one is almost a hundred years old. Ramsey Grammar School, where he did his secondary education, is to have a purpose-built language laboratory. The remainder will be used to help pupils from the Parish of Bride to go to university.'

'Very commendable,' commented the Chief Constable to no one in particular.

'What happened to Mrs MacKinnon?' asked the Metropolitan Police Commissioner.

'I can't help you there either. After her husband's death, she sold up and left the island two weeks ago. Here is a copy of the deed of sale of her house and the closing-down statement of her account with The Isle of Man Bank.' He handed it to Reinfeld.

His eyes widened before he exclaimed. 'She took all this in cash?'

'Yes, almost a million pounds sterling.'

'That's one and a quarter million dollars.'

'Yes, she's a wealthy widow.' George could have added that Kate had confided with him that she also had numbered Swiss accounts, but his sympathies lay with Kate and the suffering being imposed on Iraqis as a result of the 2003 invasion that was now coming into the public domain.

'Did she tell you where she has gone?'

'No.' *And even if I knew, do you think I would tell you?*

'So, it seems we are unable to help you,' said the Chief Constable. 'There appears to be no doubt that Quayle and this woman, al Jised, were the culprits. I suggest we take a late lunch on the way to the airport at *The White Hart* in Ballasalla. I'll get my secretary to book your return to London on the 1600 hours flight rather than the 1915.'

'That's very kind of you,' replied Mike Watts. 'I think we have got all we can from our visit.'

By three-thirty, the five had said farewells at Ronaldsway, and the Chief's driver was driving the two senior Manx officers back to Douglas.

'An unusual day,' remarked George's boss as the car returned them to the Police HQ. 'Have you really no idea at all where al Jised went?'

'No, sir; her last words to me were, "Iraq's Retribution has barely started."'

'What did she mean by that?'

'I took it to mean that the birth defects of the boys are only just beginning and will continue for the next thirty years. Furthermore, by then, tens of thousands of girls, born in the last year, will have become women giving birth to hexadactyl boys as well.'

CHAPTER 40

6th December 2006 – Camp Cropper, near Baghdad, Iraq

'I have brought the woman claiming to be a Hero of Iraq to you, sir. I have her outside in the corridor. She tells us you awarded her the country's top honour after the Iranian war finished in 1989. If she is, as she claims, a Hero of Iraq, then only you can sanction her execution. None of us have ever seen her before. She could be anyone.'

'There is only one woman who was ever made a Hero of Iraq. You should know that,' was the grumpy reply. 'How did you pick her up?'

'As you know, we kidnapped Dave Wrigley and two others in order to get the Americans to release their female prisoners from Abu Graib jail. This one came out with the others. We interrogated her because our inside man told us that she had been a spy for the British. She has admitted, after some persuasion, that she single-handedly hid our biological weapons during the Iran war so that we couldn't use them. Just say the word and we will behead her.'

'Bring her in.'

Saddam Hussein had been tried and found guilty of crimes against humanity. He was waiting to be hanged at the end of the month, but his prison cell was comfortable, roomy, and he was allowed some callers, after they had been suitably searched for weapons, to accompany his lawyer on his daily visits. However, few came; his wife and youngest daughter had fled the country and were believed to be in Jordan; his sons had been killed in action; his eldest daughters had disappeared with their husbands, probably to Syria; most of his close advisers had been imprisoned and were either awaiting trial or execution.

He looked up at the erect, slim woman standing in front of him. He recognised her at once. 'Kathab al Jised,' he said. 'You are still a sight for sore eyes. Welcome to my humble abode. Take a seat.'

'Thank you, sir,' she replied.

'Now, what's all this about being in Abu Graib?'

'I returned to Samarra two years ago to join the fight against the damn Yankees. However, I was caught in a routine incident when shopping innocently. Some bloody Shias bombed the market; my papers weren't in order and I was arrested.'

'The Americans will use any excuse to detain a Sunni. I fear our motherland is buggered. The Shias under Maliki will take revenge on us by giving the bastard Kurds a free reign. All we had built since the 1968 revolution will have been for nothing: free schooling, free hospitals, clean water, ample electricity and a strict clampdown on corruption; the Shia shites didn't know when they were well off.'

'I know you haven't much longer, sir, but I wanted to explain my actions to you.'

'Go on.'

'During the Iran war, we were being given all sorts of biological weapons to use on the enemy by the Americans.'

'Yes, I know that. You hid them so well that we couldn't find them.'

'I had to. If we had released the 2,000 gallons of anthrax that we had accumulated and the 5,000 gallons of botulinium toxin, then there wouldn't be anyone alive on the planet.'

'You did right; it was Ali Hassan who sent an assassin after you. My wife told me you looked after her and our daughter very well in Paris. Did the VX-R your partner retrieve work?'

'Yes, but not in the way you were told.'

'What do you mean?'

'I told Tariq Aziz that it was a radioactive defoliant.'

'Yes, he told me that.'

'It was much more than that…'

Saddam sat listening for almost an hour as Kate told him the story of the hexadactyl boys, how male sperm exposed to the VX-R rays was affected and how the children died after six months. She ended by estimating that up to a hundred boys were dying every month and this could continue for the next thirty years. 'Already there could be as many as 4,000 boys dead. Furthermore, I believe girls have been affected too, but it will be twenty years before my theory is proved correct. There will be nothing the Yankees can do,' she finished triumphantly.

'Wonderful, wonderful,' he replied. 'What effect do you think this VX-R will have on girls?'

'I don't know for certain, but my guess is that their reproductive organs will also have been affected and they will in future give birth to hexadactyl children.'

'Then we will have the last laugh. Bush's father gave us the bloody stuff. He wasn't to know that we would use it to extract revenge on his son's America. How ironic is that?'

'So you have forgiven me for hiding the biological weapons?'

'Of course; I shall go to the gallows with a smile on my face knowing that the US will be unable to admit to the world that Iraq extracted retribution. For the next three decades, they will have to massage their infant mortality statistics to keep the existence of VX-R secret. I am only sorry that I cannot award you a bar to your Hero's medal. However, I want Haki, here, to make sure you are given maximum security for the future.'

Kathab al Jised has never been heard of since.

* * *

On 30th December 2006, Saddam Hussein al Tikriti was hanged. An illegal mobile phone, smuggled into the gallows chamber, recorded the event that was shown around the world. The sound was distorted, but if you listen carefully, then you will hear Saddam saying in Arabic, 'Iraq's Retribution is great, only Allah is greater.'